PRIMAL

ABOUT THE AUTHOR

Robin Baker is an international best-selling author in the field of sexual biology. His titles include the now classic text *Sperm Wars* as well as *Baby Wars; Sex In The Future* and *Fragile Science*. He is a writer, lecturer and broadcaster with over a hundred scientific papers and journalistic articles to his name. He now lives in the south of Spain.

PRIMAL

Robin Baker

Published by Virgin Books 2009

2 4 6 8 10 9 7 5 3 1

First published in Great Britain in 2009 by
Virgin Books
Random House, 20 Vauxhall Bridge Road,
London SW1V 2SA

www.virginbooks.com
www.rbooks.co.uk

Addresses for companies within The Random House Group Limited can be
found at: www.randomhouse.co.uk/offices.htm

The Random House Group Limited Reg. No. 954009

A CIP catalogue record for this book is available from the British Library

ISBN 9780753518267

The Random House Group Limited supports The Forest Stewardship Council
[FSC], the leading international forest certification organisation. All our titles
that are printed on Greenpeace-approved FSC-certified paper carry the FSC logo.
Our paper procurement policy can be found at www.rbooks.co.uk/environment

Typeset by TW Typesetting, Plymouth, Devon
Printed in the UK by CPI Bookmarque, Croydon, CR0 4TD

To Liz

For the Scott Bar moment, and everything since

ACKNOWLEDGMENTS

For inspiration

The nearly two thousand biology students from the Universities of Manchester who attended field courses with RB.

The teams of superhuman staff and other advisers who supervised them.

And the venturers and staff of the Grand Bahamas phase of Operation Raleigh, 1985–1986.

For the two halves
Ysan and Max

For rejuvenating criticism
Hannah Davis

For making Primal *so much more than* Naked
Adam Nevill

For Herculean patience and understanding
Liz and Laura

AND

For careful editing and advice
Mark Reynolds

PROLOGUE

Even after two inquests, I felt we knew little and understood less. In June 2006 nine science students and five staff from the Orwellian University of Manchester embarked on a four-week field trip to a remote unnamed island in the South Pacific. The professor leading this Pacific trip, my good friend Raúl López-Turner, was an experienced traveller and explorer. As a world-renowned expert on apes, he had spent much of his adult life in Asian and African jungles and during his distinguished career had led numerous research expeditions into the most remote and unspoilt regions of the earth. As so many hopeful students had applied for Professor López-Turner's Pacific expedition, the nine finally selected were absolutely thrilled at their inclusion and were undeterred by the exhaustive and intrusive medical examination they each had to undergo prior to the trip.

But at the end of the four-week expedition the party failed to return home. Enquiries revealed they had not even arrived back at the main island (known as 'the mainland') let alone reached its airport for the return flights to Britain. Guided by maps left behind by Professor López-Turner, the hastily assembled rescue party failed to find any survivors, or even evidence of their occupancy, on the island designated as the location of the field trip. A search of each of the surrounding atolls produced the same mystifying results. It was as if the group had never even landed on firm ground anywhere in the region. Despite no evidence of a distress call, or even of wreckage, an inquest could only conclude that their vessel sank during its voyage to the island, leaving no survivors. Health and safety arrangements were described as inadequate and the coroner declared that had the deceased Professor López-Turner been available for trial he would have been charged with criminal negligence. The grieving parents immediately sued his employer (the university) and an undisclosed out-of-court settlement was quickly agreed.

But the group had not perished at sea. A little over a year after the expedition departed from England, and six months after they had been declared dead, two of the students – Ysan Nelsen and Danny Forsyth-Blake – were found adrift in a small and barely seaworthy yacht by a passing passenger ship, one hundred kilometres from the mainland. They were naked and unconscious. Ysan was also suffering from head injuries and a broken ankle, and was airlifted to the mainland's tiny hospital. As soon as she was well enough to travel, she was transported back to England where the university hospital treated her for a blood clot on the brain and other injuries. Meanwhile Danny directed a rescue boat to pick up their remaining companions, not from the island where the original search had been focused, but, incredibly, from another island over two thousand kilometres distant. This huge discrepancy became a key issue in the second inquest into the affair. How had everybody associated with the rescue been mistaken about the destination of the field trip? And was it possible, as some suggested, that the university authorities had been deliberately misled?

It emerged from Danny's testimony that a week into the group's projected stay on the island a fire caused by a faulty generator had broken out at the expedition's base destroying all supplies and possessions, including clothing and medication. In a separate incident on the same evening, the vessel they had arrived in was lost at sea during a storm, removing their only means of both travel and communication. In a single night, their island paradise had become a hostile hell and their life a struggle that some did not survive. When a rescue was eventually made of the remaining group, three of the original expedition were missing and presumed dead. This number included Professor López-Turner, who had drowned on the night of the fire while trying to save the boat during the tropical storm. Later in their tenure on the island, Duncan 'Dingo' Hughes became the second fatality. He died courageously in a failed attempt to save the third casualty, fellow student Maisie Muir, from drowning.

One of the surviving students, Clarabel Morris, elected to stay behind on the mainland with a local man, Antonio Navarro-Diáz – the captain of the vessel that transported them to the island, before he too became marooned with the group after the storm. When rescued, Antonio was suffering from severe lacerations to his torso and limbs and was taken immediately to the mainland hospital. It was claimed he had been savaged by an ape.

Of the original fourteen people who had set off from the university in 2006 only ten returned to England, and in the summer of 2007 their homecoming was headline news. The media dealt with details of the group's story with a variety of approaches (tabloids and broadsheets giving emphasis to particular details in their own fashion), but the essential story was that young lives had been lost and the surviving complement of the expedition had been forced to fend for themselves, without clothing or supplies, on a remote island because of the irresponsible group leader, Professor López-Turner.

On their return, lecturer Salvador 'Sledge' Peterson was nominated as the group's main spokesman. TV and radio news teams from around the world were quick to offer him an opportunity to tell the story. According to Sledge, under his leadership, and with the nursing skills of PhD student Rose Stewart, and Antonio's local knowledge, they all spent their time supporting each other to manage their ordeal. Only Maisie's adventurous spirit and Dingo's bravery tragically thwarted their intention to bring every student back alive. And as a natural consequence of the group remaining in isolation for so long, couples formed and the small community passed its time working together to survive. Despite the tremendous obstacles they faced and the diminishing hope of rescue as each month passed, the group still maintained a spirit of camaraderie, companionship and conjugal harmony.

Often, Sledge was joined in news interviews by Danny, who would describe his and Ysan's attempts to sail to freedom, and by fellow student Abigail Hunt, who would give a woman's perspective on the year. Danny and Abigail, each blessed with good looks and charisma, quickly became popular figures after their appearances on breaking and leading news stories around the world. But after the initial flurry of cooperation with the news media, the survivors, in a united act, turned their back on all future publicity engagements and even rejected several lucrative offers for the film rights to their incredible story. It was a complete, unexpected, and for our times most unnatural disengagement from the media. An official statement declared the survivors just wanted to get on with their lives, not least the women who had returned to the UK either pregnant or with a newborn baby. They would allow, however, a definitive version of their story to be told in a book, with all proceeds going to the families of the lost members of the group. And to my surprise at the time, though not later, the co-authorship of that book was offered to me.

In such an acquisitive and materialistic world, obsessed with fame at any cost, the stand taken by the group did nothing but increase the esteem in which they were held. The survivors were deemed a credit to their university. And despite the exotic and erotic nature of their castaway experience, they were seen as examples of humanity at its very best – theirs was a story of bravery and resilience, and of the ordinary becoming extraordinary.

To me, and I was not alone in this feeling, the story from the survivors was conspicuously improbable. Such a tale of social and sexual propriety immediately seemed to me more suited to a Puritan enclave in North America than to a group of naked adults on a remote but eminently habitable tropical island. They were hiding something, and the carefully targeted and stage-managed appearances on the news did nothing but increase my suspicions about their story and their motivation for a sudden retreat from fame, or was it scrutiny? It was as if a different kind of survival instinct had kicked in following their rescue and return to the modern world. So what were they hiding and why?

Even as I write, eighteen months after the group's rescue, the account of their island adventure remains nauseatingly unchallenged whenever it crops up in connection to those members of the expedition who have slowly drifted back into the public eye. Because, despite their vow not to profit directly from their tragic and noble story, a few of their number have enjoyed significant compensation for being a surviving member of the group. Danny now presents a yachting show on satellite TV; Abi is well on her way to becoming a successful glamour model; and Clarabel's bark sketches of life on the island have appeared in a Sunday broadsheet's colour supplement for an undisclosed fee, and will soon tour galleries as the only permanent visual record of the year on the island.

It was a combination of my suspicion and curiosity, and eventually a regrettable emotional entanglement with one of the survivors, that led me to conduct enquiries of my own beyond the brief of the book that I was asked to write by the group. That first collaborative book was to be the official definitive version and my co-author the student closest to Professor Raúl López-Turner: Ysan Nelsen. But while writing the 'official' version of their story, my eagerness to get to the heart of what happened on that island eventually led to my writing a different kind of book for a different publisher from the one intended. Because Ysan, whatever her reasons, gave me glimpses into what I believe was the real story of that year on the island. A story the survivors had gone to great lengths to reinvent. But the only story I wished to tell.

I first met Ysan in September 2007, six weeks after her dramatic escape from the island. She contacted me initially with an e-mail via my agent. The proposition, made on behalf of the survivors, was for me to collaborate with her in writing the exclusive story of their year on the island. She explained that I was their first choice not only because of my friendship with Raúl but also because some of the members of the surviving group were familiar with my published work and considered that my scientific back-ground and understanding of field work, and the subjects related to their expedition, was sound. At all costs they wished to avoid a 'tabloid' approach, and in any case they would make all final editorial decisions on content.

Although I now live in Spain, I often need to visit the UK and I arranged to meet, first with Ysan, and then the rest of the group on my next trip. Ysan and I met at a café in Manchester just a few days after she left hospital.

She laughed as we introduced ourselves because I called her 'Why-san', having only seen her name written. 'It's pronounced Eezaan,' she said. But I struggled even to smile. She looked unkempt and seemed nervous and withdrawn. Her fair hair wasn't just short from her operation, it was also uneven, and above her left ear the scar, complete with stitch marks, was still clearly visible. Most women would have worn a wig, scarf or hat. Her clothes looked quite old and were scruffy, but perhaps with reason. A loose shirt may have made it easier to use her crutches, and baggy jeans accommodated the plaster engulfing her left ankle. She wore no earrings – her ears weren't pierced – and I could see no sign of make-up. Her eyes, though, were amazing. They were clear blue, and seemed to shine. And she had an undeniable aura, an endearing mixture of physical fragility and inner strength. I liked her immediately. But she was nervous and said little. When she did speak without a prompt, she only fed me questions about Raúl and listened intently to my answers and reminiscences. It became immediately clear to me that Raúl had made an enormous impression upon her.

As arranged, I met the others from the island the same day at what Ysan described as a 'sort of party'. It was supposed to be a reunion party, she said, but the university organised it and arranged for journalists and a *Manchester Evening News* photographer to be there, as well as their own press officer, so I wouldn't be the only outsider.

The party was held in a private room above the university refectory and, although I accompanied Ysan to the gathering, I was soon on my own. She was the last of the group to arrive and not having seen most of the others since leaving the island, she was immediately besieged by kisses and hugs. Four people were missing: two were still in the Pacific; a third was on remand for a knife-attack on his father; and the fourth had left the university, the city, his home and his marriage to start a new life. It was six weeks to the day since Ysan had arrived on home soil, but just over four for the others.

There were two tables: one laid out for a formal meal for those from the island and another with drinks and buffet food for anyone from the invited media. Ysan occasionally caught my eye and smiled, but most of the time she was deep in conversation with those around her.

It wasn't difficult to understand why the university was making so much of the group's reunion. It had been a bad year. A social science postgraduate had been gang-raped and murdered while interviewing down-and-outs. Two professors had been sacked for sexual harassment. Three students had thrown themselves off the roofs of halls of residence, and another had been savaged by a Rottweiler. The island group being found alive was the best thing to happen all year – and the press office was hoping to bleed the event for all the good publicity it could get.

I didn't get the chance to say more than a few words to any of the group. As soon as the meal and formalities finished they all rose to retreat to Sledge's house for a private reunion to which I wasn't invited. And even the few words I did have were exchanged in mutual discomfort. Sledge was positively hostile.

'"Sledge",' I said to him as an opening gambit. 'Where does that come from?'

He held up his right fist. 'From this. I used to box. Heavyweight.'

'I don't follow.'

'As in Sledgehammer.'

'I suppose that explains the scar.'

The mark across his right cheek, not far from his eye, was conspicuous. It was still discoloured and must once have been very deep.

'A word of advice,' he said deliberately. 'Write the book as Ysan tells it. *Exactly* as she tells it and we'll all be grateful to you. The university too.' He took a step closer. 'But friend of Raúl's or not . . . If you dare fabricate even one tiny thing, you'll have more than lawyers to deal with. *Comprende?*'

He must surely have had a major say in the group's decision to ask me to write their story in collaboration with Ysan, so I didn't understand his hostility and it shook me. The group had been through a lot, but was intimidation the best method of impressing your official biographer? Minutes later I watched him usher the others out of the room. Only Ysan turned to give me a tiny smile and wave.

I was unperturbed and reeling anew from the idea that I would be the writer to tell their story. Ysan's reticence, my unease about Sledge, and the editorial restrictions placed upon me, were easily suppressed because they ultimately served no purpose other than to intrigue me and reinforce my curiosity.

The prospect of writing their story would alone have been thrilling enough, but secretly I had begun to find even more in the project to excite me. To me and others who considered Professor Raúl López-Turner a first-rate scientist and now a much missed friend, the damning indictment of the media jury that he was 'incompetent' and 'guilty of manslaughter' was based on hearsay and unjust. The dead cannot speak, but now I had the chance to speak for him; writing the book would give me an opportunity to clear his name. The collaboration would also allow me to get to know the intriguing Ysan.

Much as I'd been looking forward to my first long weekend with Ysan at her family home in Manchester in mid-October 2007, it was unproductive. Ysan was still nervous, even defensive, which made progress slow and disappointing during the initial interviews. Everything she said simply matched or paraphrased the party line Sledge and the others had already fed to the media. I told her I wanted much greater detail to bring their extraordinary experience alive, and to understand the characters. I needed depth. She said there was no more depth.

When it became clear to her that I did not believe her, and insisted on her total candour, she grew uncomfortable. She became agitated by any direct questions about the days before Raúl's death, and even distressed at times by my scrutiny. Admittedly, her narrow escape from drowning and her physical injuries immediately prior to her rescue would have caused some trauma at having to recall her ordeal, but I intuitively felt it was my interest in Raúl's demise and my first questions about the apparent harmony of life on the island that were the chief causes of her reluctance.

Making matters more complicated her mother Molly clucked around us like a mother hen. I don't mean that unkindly. It's not that I took a dislike to Molly. On the contrary, in her early forties and with a young face and a brilliant figure, she was very alluring. She was slightly shorter than her daughter, but like her had striking eyes and – until Ysan lost it to surgery – long fairish hair. She had a wide-eyed expression that could pass from intelligent through vacant to confused and back again in the blink of an eye. But she did chatter. If she wasn't chattering at us, we'd often hear her elsewhere in the house talking to herself.

Ironically, if I gained anything from that weekend – apart from e-mail addresses for everybody in the group – it was from Molly. She asked if I'd like to watch the TV interviews that Sledge, Danny and Abi had given soon after their rescue; she'd recorded them, which I hadn't. Ysan reacted strangely, saying that of course I didn't want to watch them; she was going to tell me everything I wanted to know in person. When I contradicted her she left the room and went for a shower.

I settled back with Molly to watch. I wasn't particularly interested in listening again to Sledge's considered but brief statements or Abi's coy descriptions of public nudity, but I was interested in Danny's description of his and Ysan's escape. It was the only part in which Sledge gave Danny free rein. The rest of the time he would cut Danny short or rephrase something on his behalf.

According to Danny – his boyish face, cultured good-looks and cocky manner branding him a TV natural – he and Ysan had gone exploring for the day, and deep in a tall cave they'd chanced upon an ancient-looking yacht. Only about five metres long, it was designed for pottering around the coast, fishing in the bays, but not for ocean travel in strong winds and high waves.

'What the hell was an old yacht doing there?' I asked Molly.

She shrugged. 'Everybody seems to think it was abandoned by some previous field trip, but nobody really knows. And I don't care. I'm just glad it was there, otherwise Ysan might never have got off the island.'

With some sailing experience behind him, Danny decided to cast off immediately and sail the yacht to the others at Orchard Bay, but a sudden gale hurled them out towards the open sea. Ysan was thrown across the deck, breaking her ankle and hitting her head and losing consciousness, and Danny panicked. He knew he couldn't control the yacht single-handedly in such conditions and Ysan looked seriously hurt. He had to act fast so, rightly or wrongly, he decided to risk sailing for the mainland. But, after a few days, starvation and dehydration took their toll and he joined Ysan in semi-consciousness. The next thing he remembered was waking up wrapped in a sheet on the passenger ship.

Pausing the DVD, I said to Molly, 'It must have been a fantastic moment when you heard Ysan had been rescued.'

'Unbelievable! But then they mentioned her injuries, and I started worrying all over again. Broken ankle, blood clot on the brain. I was all set to fly out there, but they said they were sending her home for the operation. I couldn't believe it. I was convinced she'd die on the way.'

'Could have been risky with such a fresh injury.'

'That was the strange thing. They said that although the broken ankle was only a week old the clot was older, maybe a fortnight or more, and stable enough for the risk to be worth it for the better treatment she could receive here. But Ysan insists she only fell once, and that was on the boat. Mind you, the poor thing was pretty confused. When she came round from the operation all she could talk about was missing Maisie, and about Clarabel and her bark.'

'Mum, shut up!' said Ysan, who'd been listening from the doorway.

Then, as if embarrassed by her sharp tone, she added, 'I haven't told him about the bark sheets yet. You'll spoil the surprise.'

'How long did the confusion last?'

It was Molly who answered. 'About a week. Though I still think she's got some memory loss. But she was over the worst when Danny came to see her, and definitely by the time Sledge and Rose visited.'

Ysan turned to me. 'I *was* badly disoriented. Walls, ceilings, grey skies, pollution, the sound of traffic, sirens, the endless droning of TV. I thought I was going mad. Clothes and bedding felt suffocating, and as for the dreams ... Terrifying! And the food ... Salty, artificial; I could hardly eat. And so many people everywhere. I just wanted to be naked again, in the sun and wind, listening to the sea, the insects, the birds, everything fresh, everything blue and green and bright. The yearning still hasn't gone.'

'Probably never will,' said Molly with impatience.

When Ysan and I parted that weekend, she promised that next time I visited she'd suggest her mother went to stay with friends.

But my second session of interviews with Ysan in mid-November 2007 was no more productive than the first. Molly had scorned her suggestion that she should visit friends, and Ysan still related little of consequence. We were going nowhere. I heard the bare bones of the group's story again, up to and including the loss of clothes that had been shed for some kind of party, then listened to endless minutiae about life on the island: how Antonio made fire; the food they ate, including how they found and prepared it all; how they cleaned their teeth, combed their hair, coped with periods, maintained private toilet areas; how they never built shelters, preferring to sleep under the palms or, during storms, in the caves on the beaches. All fascinating enough, and much of which I could use, but I still suspected this was another device to avoid telling me a deeper story. Her testimony lacked spontaneity, and felt too considered, like something rehearsed. In the end, I asked her directly if she was hiding anything. Without hesitation she insisted there was nothing.

'Look, Ysan, this just isn't working,' I said as we wound up the session. 'There's no substance, no colour. No emotion here. No passion, conflict, drama. These things must have arisen. I need to get inside you all. Otherwise I'm not sure it's worth carrying on.'

'I'm sorry. I don't know what you're after.'

'I think you do.'

Judging by her expression, it was just about the worst thing I could have said. So I quickly took a different approach. 'Look, I've got a suggestion. When does term finish?'

'Eighth of December.'

'Why not fly over and stay with me on the Costa Del Sol. We could have a whole fortnight and you could still be home for Christmas.'

She seemed wary, so I improved my pitch by telling her she could relax, speed her recovery, we could talk about her postgraduate future too – I still had contacts – and at the same time I could learn a little more about my friend's last expedition. I wanted her to see the project as a chat between two friends in a therapeutic and relaxing environment. From this we would write a much better book.

To my immense relief, Ysan agreed.

During that balmy fortnight in Spain from 9 to 23 December, we became close. Foolishly close, I now realise. But although I compromised my neutrality, intimacy led to a kind of confession I don't think Ysan ever intended to make.

Surrounded by trees, no neighbours for a kilometre, mountains behind and a drop-view down a valley to the Mediterranean, the setting for my villa is beautiful and very private. But my hopes that a day or two in such tranquil surroundings might seduce Ysan into divulging the real story behind the PR – if that's what it was – were soon dashed. If anything, she seemed more defensive and anxious than she had been in Manchester.

At one point she clammed up completely, so I stalked off to prepare us a light lunch. Through the kitchen window I watched her standing stiffly in the sun, frowning. The next moment she was manically stripping, throwing her clothes in a pile on the patio as if in anger. Nakedness and a few deep breaths seemed to calm her; she began wandering around the garden, pausing to smell the scented pink roses, to finger the intricate flowers of the bird-of-paradise plant, to dip her toe in the unheated swimming pool. I stepped out with our lunch to find her framed by an arch covered with purple bougainvillea. 'Comfortable now?'

'I shouldn't be here. I should be back on the island. I've left it too long.'

Back to the island? This struck me as an odd desire. And further evidence of how much was potentially being concealed from me. But considering her vulnerability, I decided this was not the moment to interrogate her about attachment to the island.

'You're still in recovery. And what about your degree?'

'I don't care. The first opportunity. Absolutely the first opportunity, I'm going back.' She then glanced up at me. 'Is there a beach we can go to?'

There was, about thirty minutes away. In summer it is packed with families, naturists from all over Europe. In December it is almost deserted, the domain of the occasional solitary man, an illicit encounter between a boss and his secretary, a gay coupling. Although Ysan and I weren't entirely alone on any of the days we visited, each time we found a cove which gave a sense of privacy.

The effect on Ysan was immediate. In the sun, sitting on the sand, with a little food and the best part of a bottle of rum (her idea), she started to unwind. Which was a pleasure to watch, until she began to unravel.

After her breakdown by the swimming pool, I knew this was another symptom of the powerful unrest and instability buried inside Ysan and caused by more than a blow to the head. And if I wasn't mistaken there was a rage inside her too. A deep-rooted anger with someone as yet unnamed that she could not possibly resolve, even if her silence was for the benefit of the group, or the 'others' as she began to refer to them at times with an uncharacteristic sneer.

At first she only hinted that there really were a great many secrets about the island. But day by day this implication grew into a willingness to open up. She told me about their swift 'regression' to living in the most primitive conditions and her 'fascination' at seeing everybody naked following the loss of their clothes. She followed this with details of the 'confusing and terrifying' night of storm and fire, and how Raúl's drowning left her 'black in mind' and 'empty'.

On the third day she began describing the growing rivalry and hostility within the group, giving details about an escalating 'war' she had with Abi, and even let slip a story about Sledge being unfaithful to Rose and how she fell out with Danny who then attacked her.

Terrified she might suddenly stop and go into denial again, I sat tense and quiet and did nothing to break her reverie. Her words were slightly slurred by drink, but she was not insensible. And through her stories of the early days of being marooned I detected a clear ratcheting up of tension within the group and an inevitable progression towards events she could barely stand to remember, let alone describe.

'So after this fight, when did you and Danny make up again?' I asked her, hoping not to betray my own unease at her involvement with Danny. 'Because by the end of the story in circulation, you were happily going off exploring the bays and caves together.'

She patted my knee and smiled. 'I'll tell you when I get there.'

In the heat of the day on our fourth visit and with both of us pleasantly drunk, she told me the intimate details of an early relationship she had with Raúl. From this the talk of sex escalated to descriptions of the spread of sexual frustration and experimentation within the group; of things she'd seen people doing; things she had only ever thought about before the trip.

Following these more salacious disclosures, I didn't understand why she suggested we should go to the water's

edge to see who could be first to make a pebble bounce ten times on the water; but almost before I knew what was happening, on the sand just beyond the reach of the Mediterranean waves, we were having sex for the first time.

For the next two days, our work alternated with pleasure. And if those days marked the peak of our relationship, the descent arrived only too soon. And it began with her sudden confession. 'You ought to know. I should have told you ages ago. I'm pregnant. It happened on the island. Do you mind?'

I minded very much but managed to mutter that I didn't. 'Danny?'

She nodded.

'How many months? It doesn't show.'

The answer was about five; she'd conceived right at the end of her time on the island. My immediate thoughts on the matter were more depressed than analytical. They had nothing to do with the book, but everything to do with my feelings for Ysan and the hopes I'd started to nurture.

The following day she broke down while describing a meeting she had with the now deceased student Maisie, and suddenly everything was over, including the good weather. Trapped by wind and rain inside my villa for the last three days of her visit, she became morose, fractious, even hostile. But not towards me, towards Raúl.

Her hostility was a huge shock. Until then she'd always described the man and their relationship with such warmth and tenderness. Yet from no apparent motive, with December rain lashing the window panes, she was now berating him. She spoke about Raúl not really being dead. Talked almost incoherently about naked pantomimes, winking lights, testes measurements, breeding experiments. Said how much she hated Raúl. There'd been no hint of such venom before, and I grew concerned that she was having some form of serious emotional breakdown, and that if her judgment was impaired then her testimony would be flawed.

I tried to be gentle. 'I can't write any of this. You'll look stupid.'

Her blue eyes flashed with anger. 'No I won't. Why should I?'

When I pushed her gently to elaborate on some of these claims, she began to cry and shake with anger. And then made even more provocative but unspecific suggestions of there having been 'some serious trouble' among the group, and implied there had been moments of 'crisis, that you haven't got a clue about. You wouldn't believe me if I told you.' But no firm details about these events were ever forthcoming, though it was obvious that the mere mention of them was causing her considerable distress. So much so, that once her tears had dried she began to stall and I could see a visible regret taking over – even fear once she understood she had told me far more than was ever allowed.

On those three final days, there were calm spells when I thought normality and affection, even passion, were returning. But they were interspersed with further displays of her eccentricity, or something much worse: her standing and shivering in the driving rain, crying and moaning for Maisie, who had a particular significance to Ysan that I could not determine; begging me at night to whisper to the baby in her belly; calling me Raúl. And it was with some unease that I drove her to the airport at the end of her stay, my worries for her mental health mingling with concern for our book that had so recently begun to look promising. Really promising.

In the departures hall at Málaga Airport, where I kissed her goodbye, I pleaded with her to open up to me totally the next time we met. She had to. For the sake of her conscience and for the families of the deceased, and for the truth. But she would not meet my eye and her hands trembled until her flight was announced. All she would offer me was an assurance that she would think 'long and hard' about next time and 'how far' she was prepared to go.

The last thing we needed was the publication early in January of photographs of us on the beach, complete with captions that played on the titles of my past books and on her being a 'naked ape watcher'. Clearly our cove hadn't been as private as we thought.

At the time, I blamed those photographs for causing Ysan to end our collaboration, her decision arriving by e-mail in January 2008. In it, she requested that I abandon the book and never try to speak to her again. She was too busy studying for her degree. And she had nothing further of interest to say. Additional correspondence from the group's legal representation and the publisher confirmed her with-drawal and my removal from being the co-author of their story. The group had decided that in everybody's interests there would now be no book.

But feeling frustrated, thwarted and even betrayed, I couldn't stop there. The notes and tapes from our dis-cussions at Ysan's home in Manchester, and on the beach and at my villa in Spain amounted to a thorough, fascinat-ing, provocative and tantalising account through Ysan's eyes of the first three months on the island – from 1 July 2006 to the last week of September that year – and that account now forms the first part of this book: 'Ysan's Story', a dramatisation of those events, moods, and atmos-pheres that she related to me. Inevitably, I have had to fill in a few gaps and place some words in people's mouths, but I have tried to stay faithful to the story Ysan told me and not to be influenced by any of the horrendous things I discovered later.

Ysan had let slip that there was more, much more, to be unearthed about events on the island for the ten months that followed the end of her account and which she hadn't, wouldn't, or couldn't describe to me. I was determined to find other ways to dig into what really happened out in the Pacific. A desire that I was eventually able to satisfy by means of a careful and extensive examination of the remarkable physical evidence that had been created by some of the survivors during their occupation of the island. Material that came into my hands in a variety of ways. And it was this material that really compelled me to complete this book, without Ysan and without official cooperation.

'Aftershocks', in the second half of this book, is the story of my attempt to make sense of the evidence, and to piece together a faithful account of the real events that occurred during the year the group was lost to the world. My record in Aftershocks is directly contrary to the testimony of the survivors, and I make no apology for my disturbing conclusions. But it is my belief that the group was transformed on that island. Their behaviour altered in a way that was wholly alien to them – unthinkable in their lives before the expedition, and just as incongruous now they have rejoined the civilised world. But I am positive I uncovered evidence of the most animalistic, shocking and, to modern eyes, unacceptable behaviour – conduct scarcely distinguishable from that of the apes they were living alongside upon that remote island in the Pacific.

So I present here my account, from 'Ysan's Story' to the missing ten months accrued from secondary evidence and new testimony, leading to my own eventual and traumatic visit to the island. And until a time when an individual from that group steps forward to refute or endorse the claims I make, it is up to the readers of this book, and later the courts, to assess the facts and judge the characters therein.

RB
January 2009, Fiji

YSAN'S STORY

ONE

1 July 2006, morning

At midnight the half-moon slipped into the western sea leaving only the star-peppered sky to light the boat's journey – not bright enough to pick out the escorting dolphins, but just enough to show the outline of occasional distant islands. A few hours later, in the ruby glow of the not yet risen sun, scattered shapes began to emerge on deck from the darkness.

Fifteen people. Eight men, seven women ... Or nine students and six advisers ... Or one-and-a-half Spanish, twelve-and-two-halves English and maybe half an Australian (unless Dingo's accent and nickname were an affectation) ... Ysan was counting. It was the sort of thing she did – at bus stops, in lecture theatres or cinemas – for no other reason than she liked numbers, enjoyed the satisfying way they subdivided, then reassembled themselves in so many different ways. Four people had black hair, four brown, four fair, one blonde, one red – and one, none.

Unable to sleep on the cramped and fish-tainted deck, Ysan was sitting up, her lower half inside a sleeping bag. Although desperate for the loo, she couldn't face picking her way between her recumbent companions to visit the filthy seatless bowl. For a fleeting moment, she wished she were male, licensed to pee over the stern. The boat lurched, creaking the chains of the lifeboat suspended overhead and bouncing her against the wooden fixtures behind.

Five days before, bubbling with excitement, she'd climbed into a taxi, waved goodbye to her mum, and set off for the airport on the first and shortest leg of her thirteen-thousand-kilometre journey. After that, five different planes had taken her and the other participants in the university field course halfway round the world. En route, they'd landed on Fiji. Then after two long island-hopping flights to the north, they disembarked on to a short and all but deserted landing strip on an island they would come to know as 'the mainland', the main island and the only place anywhere in the locale with a town and hospital. There they'd been met by an ancient bus it was impossible to believe still worked, and transported through the heat of the tropical day along the empty concrete coastal road, zigzagging up and down mountains, in and out of valleys. Finally, while the setting sun spotlighted an eerily deserted cove, they'd climbed aboard this stinking fishing boat for the last thousand kilometres or so of their journey. Their third night on board was just coming to an end, the light rapidly brightening from ruby to rose. Many had complained of discomfort, but not Ysan. All this – excepting the boat's toilet – was the stuff of her dreams.

Turning her head from a billow of exhaust fumes, she looked towards the cabin to see who was at the helm – it would either be Raúl, the course leader, or his Spanish-speaking friend who owned the boat. She'd assumed the big guy was Spanish when he first picked them up, but didn't know for sure. He knew the seas like a native. She wondered idly if there could still be Spanish-speaking islands in the area, a distant legacy from the Spanish East Indies. In which case, perhaps he wasn't Spanish at all. The two men had been working in shifts ever since setting sail, just as they'd done earlier when driving the rickety bus. The silhouette at the helm was willowy not broad; Raúl, then. For a few moments, she watched him, wondering how she might introduce herself.

Apart from Raúl, Ysan suspected she was the only person awake. Although the other four advisers, staff from the university, had hijacked the meagre sleeping space below decks, she could see her eight fellow students. Like her, they were all around twenty years of age. Lying on the deck and clustered through lack of space, they were wrapped in sleeping bags and formless as seals. All strangers for the best part too; she only knew Danny and Clarabel well.

Raúl was working hard at the helm, vigorously turning the wheel and making the lifeboat swing and creak above her. She looked up and there was enough light now to see the underside of the beam above her head and to make out anew the carved picture of a heart with an arrow through it, *Barbie* written on one side, *apes* on the other. Reaching up, she ran her finger across Danny's handiwork. It had been a long and boring journey. She could forgive him that.

The blonde woman Abi stirred, blinked, looked around, then sank back to the deck, pulling her sleeping bag to her chin. The lumbering Dingo turned and yawned. Climbing unsteadily to her feet as the boat rolled, then picking her way between bodies and sleeping bags as it pitched, Ysan descended the steps leading below deck. When she was done with the toilet, the four advisers were awakening. Rose gave a cheery 'Good morning' as Ysan stepped over her on her way back up on to the deck.

Back on deck, the students were now creating bedlam, pinning Ysan to the top of the stairs. Three lads were trying to separate a protesting Danny – his bottom half naked – from his sleeping bag. In the struggle they knocked against Abi, who'd been putting on lipstick, making her smear her cheek. Abi's hand mirror rattled over the deck and was trodden on by Dingo. Little Maisie scurried to pick up the broken pieces. But the boat rolled, Danny was lifted from his bag, stumbled half-naked over the kneeling Maisie and fell to the deck, all the while attempting to cover his bits. Everybody was shouting or laughing, or both.

'You took your time,' smiled Clarabel, red wavy hair blowing, green eyes shining, after Ysan had picked her moment and waltzed through the mêlée to join her. 'We're nearly there.'

'How do you know?'

'Raúl just told us. There. On the horizon.'

Ysan scanned the skyline. In the distance was a cone-shaped island, little different from hundreds of others they'd passed on the way. The two looked at each other, then exchanged a jubilant hug.

'Just think, Zannie,' enthused Clarabel, 'our own Pacific island. A whole month in paradise!'

After docking in what they were told was South Bay, the group formed a human chain to unload everything from the boat and place it in the shade of palm trees. Then the boat departed, leaving them surrounded by rucksacks and box after box of dried and tinned food – and many crates of rum. After a snatched breakfast of dry biscuits and cured meats had been washed down with bottled water, the job began of moving everything from the bay to their base. The distance between the two was only a few hundred metres but it seemed a lot further in the heat of the morning: up a sandy slope, through trees, then down to a clearing and the two wooden buildings of the base.

After the first trek, four female students were instructed to leave the carrying to others and begin digging latrines. In a stand of trees just downslope from the base, Ysan and Abi dug a long, narrow trench about a metre deep for the women's toilet. Nearby, screened by bushes, Alexi and Maisie dug the same for the men, chattering as they worked.

'So where's your friend, the redhead?' Abi quizzed Ysan. 'Why isn't she wallowing in dirt like the rest of us?'

Ysan, dressed in a baggy and functional light tracksuit, had started the job with gusto. Already wringing with sweat, a magnet for flies, soil clung to her like cement. Abi, in her knotted-under-the-breasts white shirt and stylish, calf-length white jeans, leaned on a clean spade.

'Clarabel?' Ysan answered tetchily, still digging. 'Portering. Reckon she hung back 'cause she's chasing a man.'

'Who? Danny?'

'Not her type. One of the staff.'

Abi unsettled Ysan. Not her arrogant self-confidence, or even her laziness, but simply her looks, which triggered a train of unwelcome self-doubts. Abi, with her long, blonde, sleek and shiny hair, her blue eyes and perfect figure, was every shallow man's ideal, every normal woman's envy. Heads turned when Abi walked past – men to drool, women to scrutinise, looking for flaws – in a way they never did for Ysan. Should she care? The difference was only gloss. Her own scruffy-cum-comfortable wardrobe tended to hide rather than display her figure, make-up bored her and she barely bothered to brush her hair. And who needed to look good in the jungle?

The two women continued working, Ysan like a navvy, Abi like a prima donna. Then Ysan's wooden hoe stuck among roots and refused to budge. Yanking the hoe one way, then the other, she slipped and nearly fell. Cursing, she straightened up, glared, then kicked the obstinate tool while Abi watched.

Alexi and Maisie squeezed into view through the bushes, Alexi standing at the edge of their trench to look at their progress. 'Call that a trench? Ours is twice as deep. I can lie down in it already.'

'She has, too,' squeaked Maisie, beads of sweat standing on her shaven head, drips hanging from the rings and studs decorating her ears, eyebrows and nose. 'She's been imagining being dumped on by the men.'

'Oh, God . . .' Abi pulled a face. 'That's disgusting.'

Dark eyes shining, Alexi's features lit up at the accolade.

'Your soil must be softer,' insisted Abi peevishly.

'No it's not,' retorted Alexi. 'It's just that you're bone idle. Has she done *anything*, yet?' she asked Ysan.

Ysan's smile was neutral and concealed her satisfaction. She took the chance to rest, leaning on her still-wedged hoe.

Alexi turned to Abi. 'Just what do you think you're wearing?'

Ysan smiled again.

'I didn't expect to be doing this sort of thing,' protested Abi. 'Beach work . . . That's what I thought. Not digging latrines with . . . crappy bits of wood.' She slapped at the handle.

'Do you think they'll let us put up the volleyball net once we're done?' asked Maisie.

'God . . . I wish I'd gone on my photo-shoot instead of coming here,' Abi sighed.

'A weekend in Blackpool?' derided Alexi. 'Hardly glamorous, is it?'

'Nor's digging latrines.'

'Why *didn't* you go?' asked Ysan.

'Parents!' Abi said, tossing her head before mimicking their mantra: '"Degree first, Abi, my girl . . . Then, if you really insist . . ." The only upside is I won't have to see my bloody sister for a month.'

'I've met her sister,' Alexi said. 'She's prettier, sexier, brighter, and friendly to boot – and already a successful model. Abi can't handle it.'

'Total rubbish!'

'Seems a shame,' Ysan said. 'If that's what you really wanted.'

Just for a moment, Abi's features relaxed into an expression that could have been a mixture of surprise and gratitude, as if she weren't used to kindness. Ysan was beginning to see just how beautiful the girl really was, but just as quickly her features pinched back. 'It is a shame. It could have been the start of something.'

Alexi grinned like an imp. 'Yeah right. Or maybe the photographer would have just screwed you senseless and thrown away the film.'

Abi looked at Alexi, her expression a combination of loathing and inarticulate rage, before she turned her back and walked away from the trench, leaving Ysan, Alexi and Maisie to exchange smiles of solidarity before silently returning to their work.

Later on, the latrine-diggers received a visitor. Raúl drifted in so stealthily that both Ysan and Abi were startled by his sudden 'Hi'. His lanky figure seemed to merge with its surroundings, as if woodland were his natural home. Dressed only in thin and crumpled loose-fitting brown shorts and without shoes, he was tanned but unkempt. Shoulder-length, nearly-black hair hung untidily about his neck and ears and, like his beard, needed combing. With his dark complexion and greenish-blue eyes, Ysan thought him more didicoy than don, more outlaw than academic, more primitive than professor, though his accent was impeccably English.

'What do you think of the hoes?' Raúl asked. 'The real thing, eh?'

'Fantastic!' Abi said. 'Really unusual. To have something so . . . authentic.' She began caressing the implement she'd spent the last two hours cursing.

Raúl gave a lazy smile. 'Good! So, how much longer before you're finished?'

'Maybe another hour. Not long,' Abi said, and subtly changed her stance, leaning forward on the shaft of the spade to deftly push her bottom and chest out at the same time.

In contrast, Ysan's own limbs petrified, her throat closed and her tongue suddenly felt like a puffer fish, leaving no room for coherent speech. Raúl glanced in her direction. He even smiled. But after the exchange he had eyes for nobody but Abi.

Eventually, Ysan did move, drifting over to hover on the edge of his and Abi's space, but still she didn't speak. Raúl was all Abi's and she wasn't letting him go. They bantered together and only broke off when Alexi and Maisie appeared a few minutes later.

'Anyway, well done here. I'm impressed. And just in time for lunch. See you then.'

He began to move away – but Abi shouted after him.

'Raúl! Oh, sorry. Can I call you Raúl? Is that OK?'

'That's my name.'

'You wouldn't prefer Professor?'

'Raúl's fine.'

'Can I have a word later? When you're not so busy. I want to talk about my project. I've had a few ideas.'

Raúl nodded. 'It's going to be a busy day. Setting up camp, induction meeting and a quick tour of the place. Why don't you come and find me at the welcome party tonight?'

As soon as he'd gone Alexi arched her long neck backwards and stuck two fingers down her throat.

'What?' Abi said. 'I have had a few thoughts.'

'Thoughts? What, like "Fuck me, Professor"? Christ, Abi! He's old enough to be your father. He must be forty, at least.'

'Forty-two,' said Ysan with a certainty that made them all look at her. 'It's on the back of his books,' she added. 'March the thirteenth . . . What?' She blushed.

'He's written books?'

'You've read them?'

'What about?'

'Well apes, of course. You must know that. He's an expert. Travelled the world. He's written four: on gorillas, chimps, orang-utans and bonobos. He's quite famous, in his way. He's been on TV and everything. I'm surprised you haven't read his books. He'll be teaching us next year.'

There was a long pause before Alexi broke it. 'There you are! Told you. Forty-two! What are your fathers? Mine's forty-five.'

'Forty-two's not old,' retorted Ysan. 'Lots of women our age end up with men like that – including students with their lecturers.'

'And the thought appeals to you?'

Ysan felt her face go hot and hoped it didn't show. 'No . . . Not exactly. But his work does. Life in the jungle, watching and studying apes. It's been my dream for years.' What she didn't say was that ever since learning Raúl was to lead their trip, the thought of talking to him face-to-face about such matters had more than once kept her lying awake through the early hours. This trip was a big opportunity to push her future in the direction she wanted so badly.

Abi narrowed her eyes. 'You've got to admit, though, old or not, he is kind of sexy. Well . . . in an earthy sort of way. If you tousled his hair properly, trimmed the beard a bit, dressed him in a tux. He'd look great on your arm – and he must have money.'

'So you *are* planning to shag him,' Alexi said. 'You disgusting cow.'

'And you're a malicious headcase. Go and lie in your trench.'

Unsettled by Alexi's probing and Abi's advantage, Ysan turned away from the girls. If she hadn't, she would have missed the glimpse of Raúl disappearing at a run into distant woodland.

'Where the hell is he?' Sledge boomed across the clearing as the four women arrived to announce they'd finished their digging. In his early thirties with fair hair and blue eyes, the adviser was a huge bull of a man. The moment Clarabel had seen him at the airport she'd nudged Ysan and rolled her eyes.

'Anybody see where he went?' Sledge continued.

'Who?'

'Raúl.'

'There,' Ysan answered, pointing up the hill. 'He went up into that patch of trees, towards that castle thing.'

Sledge looked incredulous, then annoyed. 'Go after him, Ysan, will you? Ask him where the hell he wants us to put all this stuff.'

Throwing down her hoe, Ysan almost sprinted towards where she'd last seen Raúl, leaving before Sledge could change his mind. Here was her chance – puffer fish permitting – to introduce herself, and to talk about jungles and apes and her ambition.

TWO

Raúl wasn't in the forest and before Ysan knew what was happening she was stumbling from woodland darkness back into the full glare of tropical sun. Her eyes adjusted but still it hurt to look up, to focus on the climb. The slope was steep and the terrain unfriendly, clumps of yellow-green scrub interspersed with patches of shimmering black rock. Dark lines through the vegetation looked like tracks, but most quickly turned into dead-ends. There were a dozen open routes Raúl could have taken, all leading to the summit. Ysan chose the shortest route, the steepest, and soon wished she hadn't as snagging bushes, scorching rocks and choking midges took their toll. She went on doggedly and as she neared the brow was rewarded with easier progress.

The 'castle' towered above her. A gargantuan rocky outcrop with an aura of age and menace; a landmark as forbidding as a sprawling medieval fortress. Formed from black volcanic material it was almost bare of vegetation and pockmarked by cracks and holes.

Even from the brow Ysan saw no sign of Raúl – nor did shouting his name bring an answer. So, climbing over boulders, she skirted the castle to look down the far side – and at last saw a head slipping from sight down the slope. Again shouting his name, she began to run, becoming breathless. She was nervous too, and excited. Stay calm, she thought. Just be yourself.

She ran faster. Dust peppered her face. Her shirt billowed. Then she again saw movement – but it wasn't Raúl. Stopping in her tracks, she stared in disbelief. Ahead of her was a chimpanzee mother with a baby clinging to her back. She must be dreaming. It couldn't be possible; there are no wild chimps outside Africa. But the mother and baby weren't alone. Scattered over the hillside were another thirty or so chimps, all in a state of agitation. It wasn't a delusion. A whole troop of chimpanzees – and way too close for comfort.

Raúl's most famous book was *Chimps: The Dark Side*. She'd read it and knew in detail how murderous wild chimps were, often killing each other and strong enough to dispatch a man – or woman. Stumbling across so many so unexpectedly, Ysan felt her body go stiff and cold with fright. The largest of the males scared her, instantly. Glaring, baring great yellow canine teeth and alternately slapping the ground then standing and screaming he looked both bad tempered and unpredictable.

The cause of the chimps' agitation was Raúl himself. Ysan could see him now, his head and bare shoulders just visible as he eased himself into position among the rocks. The large male chimp was walking towards him, its gait now slow but confident; the air of an animal not used to being challenged. A few metres from the man the ape squatted. Others also began to advance, slowly circling.

Too afraid to go nearer, too in awe to disturb man or beast, and supposing Raúl knew what he was doing, Ysan eased her way back up the slope to the castle wall. She squeezed through a large crack, discovering it was a portal to a cave, big enough for her to stand upright and walk around in. The air was dank, the floor was slippery, and from above came rustling sounds. Swifts perhaps. Or bats. Finding a crude, rocky ledge on which to perch, Ysan looked out and savoured for the first time the excitement of watching wild apes. Her eyes flitted from one to another, from the quarrelsome males to the excitable smaller females, several carrying wide-eyed babies. She was absorbed.

Raúl clambered up a small pile of boulders and stood like a statue at the summit. Several of the chimps backed away from him. Others stopped in their tracks and watched him with suspicion. He'd surprised Ysan too – but for a different reason. Save for the binoculars slung round his neck, he was completely naked.

Ysan had often imagined their first proper meeting, their first proper conversation – but never like this. What should she do? Sneak away and risk him seeing her? Wait until he left? Maybe she should simply walk down and talk to him as nonchalantly as if she handled such situations every day. No way. She'd been afraid of blushing and incoherence in front of even a fully clothed Raúl.

She stayed put and watched Raúl observing each and every chimp in turn, eyeing those nearest to him one by one, then training his binoculars on those further away. She couldn't see much of Raúl in detail. He was too distant. But he was still barefoot – in *that* terrain. His groin seemed painted black almost to his navel and his buttocks were as tanned as his back. As her embarrassment and indecision subsided, she felt a mounting excitement that made her a little uncomfortable. Something primeval was playing out before her.

Raúl stood on top of the rock pile in the full heat of the sun watching the apes for ten minutes or more, then climbed down and meandered up the hill, finally veering away out of Ysan's sight. As soon as she dared, she peered out, and with Raúl nowhere to be seen, sprinted down the hill back towards the forest and base camp. But then, at the bottom of the slope a few metres from the trees, she heard her name being called and recognised Raúl's voice. She stopped instantly. A moment of surprise – she hadn't expected him to know her name – was followed by enough apprehension to prevent her from turning round. Surely he wouldn't still be . . . Her face flushed, making her even less inclined to turn round. But when she heard her name repeated, this time much nearer, she had little choice.

'Hey! Ysan! What are you doing here?' he asked. He still wasn't wearing much, just shorts.

'Oh, there you are,' she said timidly, her first ever words to him. 'I was sent to find you . . . but I'd given up. I was heading back to the base.'

'I've been with the chimps,' he said matter-of-factly. 'Renewing old acquaintances.'

There was sweat on his face and where the wind had blown his hair, strands stuck to his cheek, tangling with his beard. Sweat was glistening on his chest too, shining through the dark but very fine hairs that clothed his front.

She feigned surprise. 'Chimps! Here? How's that?'

He cleared the strands from his face. Smiling broadly, eyes dancing, he seemed to know he was unsettling her and was even enjoying the fact. 'It's a long story. I'll tell you all later. Who sent you after me?'

She told him, finding no surprise in his lack of concern. Then he seemed to dismiss her, thanking her for searching but saying he'd see her back at the base.

'I'll come back with you,' she said quickly.

'I was going to run.'

'Then I'll run with you.'

'You'd slow me down.'

'Maybe, maybe not.'

'OK.' He smiled and they set off, shoulder-to-shoulder, leisurely at first as if jogging together, then gradually faster.

It became a race. Weaving between trees, jumping over low obstacles, laughing, each was trying to get ahead of the other, to seize the best track through the vegetation. Eventually they burst into the clearing around the base, neck and neck. Everybody turned to look.

Hands on knees, they both struggled for breath.

'You're fast,' he gasped.

Ysan was elated, yet frustrated. The eighteen-year-old Ysan would have beaten him easily; at home she had medals. But after two years of study, convenience food, smoking and drinking had taken their toll and she'd needed all the effort she could muster to keep up with him. She laughed self-consciously, pleased to have broken the ice. And, for a moment, he looked into her eyes and appeared to lose himself.

'About bloody time,' Sledge shouted at Raúl from the other side of the clearing. 'Where do you want us to put all this stuff? Or shall we give it to the termites and save ourselves the bother?'

Everything had been carried from the docking point at South Bay. Perishables were safely in store, latrines and a trench for rubbish finished and Raúl had spread word of the induction meeting to be held in the shade of the trees at the edge of the base camp clearing. Without bothering to change out of her tracksuit, Ysan arrived first, perching herself on a fallen branch right next to where Raúl was sitting on a boulder. They exchanged smiles before, one by one, other group members drifted over to join them. The last of the women was Clarabel. Sketchpad in hand, she sat next to Ysan but didn't settle.

'Come on, Zannie,' she said. 'Move up! I'll burn my tits off here.'

The pair had met when they were both eighteen, at one of the reception parties that punctuated their first week at university. Feeling ill at ease and standing alone, Ysan had been sipping red wine and stuffing herself with cheap nibbles when Clarabel walked over to her, saying she looked as though she needed company. Since that day, giggling, haranguing, crying and supporting each other, they'd meandered through two years of study and minor personal crises. Ysan was scientific; Clarabel artistic. Ysan was shy and attracted to thoughtful, intelligent men;

Clarabel was brazen and went for brawn. Ysan was polite to the point of deference; Clarabel was forthright to the point of rudeness. Most of all, where Ysan invariably trod a middle road of give-and-take, Clarabel was prone to wild extremes of generosity and selfishness.

Obligingly, Ysan moved along the branch so that Clarabel could sit in the deepest shade. Unable to resist a dig, she pointed out that maybe a shirt would have helped. Unlike Ysan, Clarabel *had* changed out of her working clothes, arriving at the meeting in just a bikini and a see-through sarong, tied at the waist.

'A shirt? No chance! I'm on a mission.'

Once comfortable, Clarabel tapped her sketchpad and whispered secretively to Ysan. 'Nearly finished.'

'Nearly finished what?'

'Wait and see. You'll love it.'

Even with the women and advisers settled the meeting couldn't start. The four male students – Danny, Dingo, Ian and Pete – were playing with a Frisbee some distance away. Raúl seemed in no hurry, as if more interested in the lads' antics than in starting the meeting. Of the four, Danny was the liveliest. Shouting, running, intercepting, making trick throws between his legs and round his back, he seemed to be everywhere. Occasionally, he was throwing to Pete – 'Ugly Pete' with the strangely asymmetric face and mis-shapen nose, accentuated by a large port-wine birthmark over his left cheek – but most of the time Danny was throwing to Dingo.

Dingo, with crew-cut fair hair and piercing eyes, was the largest and most muscular of the students. His actual name was Duncan and his main features were a slight antipodean accent, persistent body odour, and an obsession with talking about sex. Whether dingoes were really sex obsessed or not, none of them knew, but the name seemed just right. Since the trip began, day and night he'd worn the same hooped rugby shirt and the same grubby shorts with a permanent damp patch at the crotch.

'Love juice, Baby! I'm on overflow,' he told a disgusted Abi.

The fourth member of the group, Ian – nicknamed 'Geeky' – was the skinniest. Evidently unable to catch or throw with any aplomb, his main role in the game seemed to be to retrieve the Frisbee whenever it landed in thorny bushes. On several occasions Dingo appeared to throw the disc into the thorns deliberately, once even shouting, 'Fetch, boy!'

In the end it was Sledge who lost patience. Striding to the centre of the clearing, he snatched the Frisbee from the air.

'Game over,' he growled. 'Everybody's waiting.'

With a smattering of excuses and apologies the Frisbee throwers trooped past him towards the meeting place. Danny, though, hung back.

'That's mine,' he said, holding out his hand.

'OK, have it,' said Sledge, 'but listen. I've got nothing against Frisbees. I throw a mean one myself. Right time and place, I'll join in. But next time you ignore us and I have to break up your game, your Frisbee's in pieces. *Comprende?*'

'Hey, lighten up, man. We didn't know you were waiting for us. We were just relaxing. After all the humping and stuff. OK?'

Watching the lads saunter over to join the meeting, Ysan sensed something was about to happen. Maybe it was the way Danny's shoulders were tensed, the way he kept glancing in her direction. When he was only a few metres away, he threw his Frisbee straight at her. Snatching to parry, she lost her balance. The Frisbee glanced off her shoulder and she fell off the branch.

Ysan had known Danny since their first day at university, meeting at a blood-donor session where they'd bantered about the 'attraction of opposites' when they discovered she was Rhesus negative and he Rhesus positive.

'Double positive, actually,' he'd said proudly, as if it had significance.

In the weeks that followed, attracted by his cheeky face and lively sense of humour rather than by his expensively tousled hair and designer clothes, she'd dated him several times. But realising that his 'look' and his humour masked an essential shallowness, she'd avoided him as much as possible since.

'Sorry, Barbie,' Danny laughed. 'You OK? You were supposed to catch it.'

Embarrassed, Ysan climbed back on to her seat. The Barbie jibes had started soon after she'd ditched him and eventually she'd discovered why he and his friends found them so funny. Her refusal to let him have sex with her had irritated him intensely and one day, on a bench in one of their lecture theatres, she and Clarabel found the graffiti *Yes, I have no vagina*. It was signed *Barbie*.

Clarabel immediately changed *vagina* to *banana* and *Barbie* to *Danny*. The jibes, though, never stopped.

'Means he still fancies you,' was Clarabel's opinion.

After asking Ysan if she was OK, Raúl publicly called Danny an idiot before beginning his introductory speech. It was the first time Ysan had seen him in lecturing mode and for a while she was more absorbed by him than what he was saying. His voice was clear, its tone conveying deep knowledge and curiosity. Yet the sleepy expression on his face and the gentle languid movements of his long arms suggested nonchalance, almost indifference. She watched him gesture up the hill towards the forest, then lazily point down the hill at the two wooden buildings. Only then did she begin to register his words.

He was telling them about the island and how privileged they were to be visiting such an off-the-beaten-track location. There weren't many left, he said, but he could absolutely guarantee that while here they wouldn't see a trace of the rest of the world: no boats, no planes, no people. None of the islands this side of the mainland was inhabited and theirs in particular was far too remote to be visited, even by drug traffickers. They were only here because his predecessor at the university, Jim Gillespie, had deliberately looked for such a place back in the sixties. Then for a few years in the eighties, Jim had brought students on field trips to help him set up a field station – and he, Raúl, had been one of them. With everything done, the trips had stopped eighteen years ago and probably the only person to have set foot on the island since had been Jim.

'Is he really that colour all over?' whispered Clarabel to Ysan.

'Shhh!'

Raúl looked at them as if to check that they were paying attention, then continued. Since he'd been working at the university, he'd run many field courses – mainly in Spain and last year in Denmark – but he'd always wanted to bring a party to this island and let them have the same experience he'd had as a student. It was a wonderful place, he told them, 'So enjoy yourselves.'

There were a few 'nasties' of course: spiders, centipedes, scorpions. Mosquitoes too, but no malaria or the like. No land snakes, either. Just lots of birds, butterflies and sea life, including coral – all fantastic. Mammals were few: only bats – plus a few feral rabbits and rats – and a surprise that could wait until later. He smiled at Ysan and she smiled back coyly.

'I saw that,' whispered Clarabel.

'Shhh!'

Next, Raúl talked about the work expected from them all: the research project they each had to do, its writing-up and the way it would be marked to count towards their degree. Of course, they'd probably all want to work on the beach, in the bays or on the coral. But they'd have to sort that out among themselves. There'd be no strictures, no timetables. Nobody saying when to get up, when to work, when to go to bed, how to behave. Everything would be entirely up to them.

'You see,' he continued, 'with no rules I get to see the real you.'

While he expounded further, Clarabel again leaned over to whisper to Ysan, saying she'd heard others talking while getting changed. Evidently on every field course Raúl ended up screwing one of the female students.

'You can just see it, can't you?'

'Shhh!'

Ysan was used to her friend's inability to concentrate. In lectures, while she assiduously took notes, Clarabel used to spend her time drawing cartoon caricatures of the lecturer and members of the audience. Her style was distinctive: she called it basic; Ysan called it pornographic.

'. . . this trip will change your lives – for the better,' Raúl concluded. 'It did mine and it will yours.'

He looked around at them all in silence, his smile enigmatic. 'Right. Back to basics. I want to show you your shower. Meet back here in five.'

While others went to latrines or simply milled around, Ysan and Clarabel stayed where they were, and to pass the time Ysan asked to see what Clarabel was sketching. Eagerly, and with a look of obvious satisfaction, Clarabel opened her sketchpad and offered it to Ysan. Ysan took one look, then groaned.

'Clarrie, you promised! You said you wouldn't.'

'I promised not to *tell* anybody. I didn't promise not to draw it. Come on, Zannie. It's a brilliant scene.'

And if Ysan's immediate fear hadn't been that Raúl would see the sketch, she might even have agreed. Caricatures they might all be, but Raúl was instantly recognisable, and the chimps had a wildness about them that captured exactly what she'd seen, felt and described to Clarabel. All this was portrayed with just a few flamboyant strokes of a pencil.

'But *that*,' said Ysan, pointing at the focal object of the picture, 'and *those*, in the background. I told you he wasn't. And neither were the chimps. Why would they be?'

Clarabel smiled condescendingly. 'That's not the point, is it? It's not meant to be a photograph. Besides, it's my trademark.'

'I know! But why? I mean . . . OK, I know why . . .

sometimes. But why *every* time must you draw your men – even your apes – with stiffies?'

Shaking her head as if Ysan was stupid, Clarabel explained: 'Realism, of course.'

'Realism?'

'Yes. Because men always have them. Maybe not in their pants but in their heads. All the time. Believe me!'

Ysan closed the pad and handed it back. 'Whatever . . . Just don't show it to anybody. If Raúl saw that, he'd know it was me. That I saw him. And he'd think . . . Oh my God! He'd think that *that* was all I was interested in. Just promise me, OK? Nobody else sees it, ever.'

'Sure, I promise.' said Clarabel, unperturbed.

'OK, so it's not the biggest waterfall in the world but as a shower – wait till you try it. It's absolutely fantastic.'

Raúl had led everyone a hundred metres or so upslope from the base and into the forest. Now they were in a clearing at the edge of a large pool fed by a four-metre-high waterfall. A fine spray filled the air and amongst the mist a fallen tree was covered with moss, as was the ground.

'The temperature's perfect, and the pool's deep enough in the middle for you to swim,' Raúl continued. 'The waterfall's our fountain, too. We collect all our drinking water from here. You'll never want to drink tap or bottled water again.'

A lad Ysan couldn't see – probably geeky Ian – commented that it looked dangerous.

'Not if you can swim!' Raúl responded. 'You can all swim, can't you? Unless something went wrong with your selection, you should all be fit, healthy, disease-free – and able to swim. It's essential on a venture like this.'

'Disease-free?' Clarabel asked Ysan in a whisper.

'Probably what all those blood samples and swabs were for. Remember? Those weird medicals . . .'

'Of course I remember.' Clarabel waved her hand in the air to attract Raúl's attention. 'When you say disease-free . . .'

He smiled and said they'd checked for all the 'nasties', including STDs if they were interested.

The revelation was so unexpected, so matter-of-fact, that Ysan wondered if she'd heard correctly. Clarabel was smiling broadly, and Ysan smiled with her, knowing how often Clarabel had lain awake, worrying, yet had still refused to have herself checked.

'But what if somebody has an accident?' asked Ian, staring down at the pool.

'What kind of person is more interested in safety than sex?' whispered Clarabel.

Ysan thought Ian a caricature of the archetypal 'serious' student. Bespectacled and weasel-faced, slight and round-shouldered, during the flights and boat journey he'd worn old-fashioned, mother-ironed, long-sleeved shirts, and flannel trousers complete with turn-ups. Even now he was wearing flannels, not shorts. There was nothing timid about him, though. Hitching his glasses on to his nose in a hawkish manner, he commented that the whole place looked dangerous, not just the waterfall. 'What happens if any of us is ill?'

Acknowledging Ian's concern, Raúl insisted he had everything organised. Rose could handle simple first aid, he said, gesturing towards the black adviser. After graduating Rose had been a nurse for a few years, before giving it up to start a PhD in marine biology. Anything more serious that she couldn't handle, they'd go straight to the mainland or call for help. There was a radio on the boat.

But Ian refused to be mollified. 'If we need the boat for the radio, why has it gone?'

'It hasn't gone. Antonio – that's the guy who owns it, the Spanish guy ... He's taken it up the coast a short way to Safe Harbour – that's all. It'll be moored about an hour's walk away, just through the forest. We get sudden gales here. The boat wouldn't last five minutes in South Bay. Don't worry. Antonio knows what he's doing.'

But Ian wouldn't let it go. The trip had been so cheap for them, he said. Just a couple of hundred each. And with the university always saying it had no funds for anything he didn't see how Raúl could possibly have the money for all the safety backup a trip like this would need.

Raúl's usual nonchalance appeared to be fraying. Shaking his head, he described to them how he'd actually been on the island five years running with Jim. The arrangement was just the same, except then it was Antonio's father who'd had the boat. Nobody had died. They'd never needed any emergency services.

'Just behave sensibly,' he told them. 'Don't throw yourselves off the cliffs. Don't go swimming alone. Don't eat anything you don't recognise in the forest. You'll be fine, trust me. Just enjoy yourselves. It's a wonderful place.' He paused, then looked around at them all. 'And as for the money ... The reason it was so cheap for you all was because I managed to get us a sponsor.'

'Who?' Ian asked.

'Never mind. It doesn't matter. Nobody you'd know.'

'And another thing. Why weren't we allowed to bring cameras?'

It was one question too many and Raúl's demeanour crumbled. 'Lots of reasons. More than I can go into right now.' An edge sharpened his voice for the first time since Ysan heard him speak. 'So let's get back to the base. It's been a long day and we still have a party to organise before it gets dark.'

Giving Ian no chance to question him further, he moved away to begin the walk down the hill.

When Ysan and the others from the mossy log stood to follow, Danny, Ian and the other two young men on top of the bank immediately began to laugh and point at the damp patches spreading across the girls' shorts and skirts.

Clarabel turned on them. 'Oh grow up, Danny!'

Raúl paused on his descent and turned to watch.

'Yeah, grow up Danny,' said Sledge, turning on the young man and pushing him with just enough force to make him slip then stumble into the water.

45

The other three lads were so taken aback that they scarcely flinched when, one by one, Sledge pushed them into the water too. Finally, as if to prove that he'd been acting in fun rather than malice, the muscle-bound adviser threw himself into the pool to join them. Before long the five men were all pushing and dunking each other in the water.

Clarabel whipped off her wrap-around and handed both it and her sketchpad to Ysan. 'Wish me luck,' she said, before running over the moss to jump into the water as near to Sledge as she could.

It was the start of a procession, one person after another jumping into the water, until Ysan realised she was the only woman who'd lacked the foresight to wear a bikini under her clothes.

Last to undress was Abi, taking off her shirt, then draping it over her shoulder as on a catwalk and stepping over to Raúl. 'Aren't you coming in?' she asked him, ignoring Ysan by his side.

'No. Things to do.'

'Shame,' said Abi, pouting.

She unzipped her trousers and shimmied out of them, receiving wolf whistles from those behind. Without looking, asking or explaining she handed her shirt and trousers to Ysan.

'Sure?' she asked Raúl again, unnecessarily adjusting both her top and bottoms.

'Sure,' he said, his eyes dilating.

Abi pouted one more time, then sauntered to the pool to slip smoothly into the water, leaving Raúl and Ysan the only two on land.

'Beautiful, isn't she,' said Ysan, the words masquerading as a compliment but really a probe, noting that Raúl's eyes had followed the blonde every step of her way.

'Just gloss.' He shrugged. 'The woman beneath the clothes – that's what interests me.'

Taken aback, Ysan searched his face. Was that innuendo?

Did he mean skin? Or beneath the skin? Confusion made her smile as their eyes met.

'Clothes demean,' he said as if explaining. 'Ask a chimp.'

She looked even more confused, finding his answer bigger than her question.

He laughed quietly. 'Time to go, I think. Are you coming or staying?'

Intrigued by his words, wanting to talk more, but nervous of seeming forward, she hesitated. In her hand was Clarabel's sketchpad. It would be dynamite if she left it unattended, so she had little choice. 'Coming with you . . . if that's OK.'

She moved to walk beside him. After a few steps – behind her back, where Raúl couldn't see – she opened her hand and dropped Abi's white clothes into the dirt.

When the base camp came into view, Raúl gestured for her to stop, and pointed to the far side of the clearing. A small group of chimps was investigating the storeroom. At their approach, the apes quickly slipped away into the forest.

'Surprise, eh?' said Raúl.

'Fantastic,' said Ysan. 'But how did they get here?'

Before Raúl could answer, there was a commotion on the far side of the clearing. The chimps reappeared, running after each other. Last to reach the clearing, screaming as a large stone struck her, was a mother carrying a baby. Ahead of her, the other chimps turned, preparing to fight. Defiant screams from the apes merged with the shouts of a man. Amidst the uproar, the only male chimp in the group began to move forwards until the stone thrower ran from the forest, hurling yet more missiles. The apes scattered, screeching and defecating as they ran.

Seeing Raúl and Ysan across the clearing, the swarthy bearded man stopped running. Laughing, he waved his arms at the disappearing apes. '*Se cagan!*' he bellowed to Raúl.

Raúl spread his arms in distant embrace. 'Antonio . . .

hombre! ... mi amigo,' he shouted. '*Eres un puñetero cabrón muy brutal. Lo sabes?*'

'Doesn't he understand any English?' asked Ysan, completely fazed by the man's behaviour.

'Understands a bit. But he only speaks Spanish and the local lingo.'

'So what was all that about?'

Raúl chuckled. 'He said "they shit themselves." He really doesn't like the chimps.'

'So I see,' she said, surprised that Raúl could view his friend's behaviour so lightly. 'And you said?'

'That he was a cruel bloody bastard.'

THREE

'Tell Sledge that I've gone with Antonio for fruit and stuff,' Raúl told Ysan. 'And to start getting the party organised. Oh, and to have another go at fixing the generator.' And with that, he and the boatman strode away down the hill.

A bedraggled Sledge returned soon after with Rose and Clarabel. They were soaked to the skin but invigorated. After changing into dry clothes, Sledge set about organising everybody. Some were sent to collect firewood, others water, and Ysan and Clarabel were detailed to help Henry and Jill with the cooking.

To Ysan, this thirty-something couple were a complete mismatch, both physically and temperamentally. Henry reminded Ysan of a mournful crescent moon. With a receding chin and protruding forehead, when he stood with feet and legs together his head tilted forwards. His face wore an expression ranging from doleful to irritated. Jill, on the other hand, exuded tolerance and cheerfulness and was pure farmer's wife: curvaceous rather than fat, but rounded just about everywhere from face to bum.

As she watched the couple make preparations it struck Ysan that six staff to look after nine students was an odd top-heavy arrangement, but she assumed the strange ratio must be something to do with safety or field skills.

'We need more pasta,' Ysan told Henry. 'Where's it kept?'

Henry was too busy swearing at the pot he was stirring and Jill answered for him. 'Through the common room, on the left. Bags of the stuff. Next to the rice. Bring some of that too. Replace what Henry just burned.'

When Ysan and Clarabel returned, Henry was still complaining. 'How the hell are we supposed to cook for fifteen people like this? What was Raúl thinking? Crappy pans on crappy fires. I can't spend a month doing this.' Several small wood-fires had been lit and above each, perched precariously on stones, was a pan with something boiling inside. Other fires were simple stone barbecues.

'We'll manage,' Jill said, through a tight smile.

'I can't believe this is still the first day,' a tired Ysan said to Clarabel. 'Feels like we've been here forever.'

'But with the best to come, the party!'

When Raúl and Antonio returned to the clearing they were carrying a whole range of freshly picked fruit and vegetables, plus a couple of large fish.

'Where did all that come from?' said Henry.

'Just a question of knowing where to look and how to catch,' replied Raúl. 'So, where's the rum? And where's Sledge?'

Henry passed Raúl a bottle.

'Sledge? Storeroom. Last time I saw him he was kicking hell out of the generator.'

The speed at which the tropical twilight fell surprised the new arrivals. One moment they could see easily, the next there was only firelight and moonlight. A throbbing noise suddenly erupted from the storeroom. The engine gathered momentum, then died away. Moments later, it throbbed again, and this time didn't stop. The dozen light bulbs strung around the clearing and another inside the common room glowed dimly, then burst into life. Everybody cheered.

A few minutes later, Raúl, Sledge and Antonio came out of the storeroom to another ovation, then slipped away again.

After a short search, Ysan found Raúl and Sledge inside the larger of the huts, the so-called common room, relaxing in two large rocking chairs. The room was made almost entirely of wood – from the walls, floor and ceiling to the assorted furniture. The only exceptions were the four multi-paned windows made of yellow-tinted plastic. Now it was night, the lighting was subdued and glowed from the single flickering light bulb suspended from the middle of the ceiling. Sledge was swigging rum straight from the bottle and chuckling. 'It was a bugger, I grant you. How long since it last worked?'

The two men seemed scarcely to have registered that Ysan had walked into the room. Waiting for their attention, she looked around for somewhere to perch. Her initial awe of Raúl had waned a little, but standing while he and Sledge were seated made her feel acutely uncomfortable. Sledge offered his bottle. 'Here, Ysan. Have some rum. You look in need.'

'Thanks . . . but I've got some outside.'

'Have some of mine anyway.'

Ysan took a token sip from his bottle then handed it back. As Sledge rocked – first to give her the bottle, then to take it back – his chair creaked ominously, as if only just managing to support his muscular bulk. Dressed in a grubby white singlet and scruffy brief blue shorts, he looked like a cross between hammer thrower and heavyweight boxer.

Ysan looked from one man to the other, unease blanking her mind and flushing her face. All she could think was to deliver her message and escape. 'Henry asked me to find you,' she said. 'To tell you the food's ready.' She turned to go.

'Ysan!' shouted Raúl as she reached the door. 'If you're really interested, I'll tell you about the chimps later. Come and find me once the party's going.'

Avoiding turning round in case her face was red, Ysan said she would, then left. But once outside the open door she stopped. In her fluster she'd forgotten something. Taking a few deep breaths, she steeled herself to go back through the doorway, but didn't get a chance. Clarabel came round the corner carrying food on two plastic plates. 'Henry said to take it to them before it got cold,' the redhead explained, hair falling untidily over her freckled face, her loose cotton blouse scarcely buttoned.

Ysan shook her head. 'The Moll Flanders look already?' she said. 'You may as well be topless.' She began to button up Clarabel's blouse. 'What would you do without me around to look after you, eh?'

Holding the two plates, Clarabel could do little to resist. 'Probably have a lot more fun,' she protested.

'There,' said Ysan as she fastened the last button. 'Ever heard of demure?'

'Demure? What's that, French for "wallflower"? Anyway, I'm having a Moll Flanders sort of day.'

'So I saw. At the pool. I take it you made an impression.'

'Lots of lovely frottage,' Clarabel grinned. 'You should feel those muscles.'

'OK, so you've made a start. Now how about waiting a day or two before you jump on him? Try and work up a bit of respect. Just a suggestion.'

'Are you kidding? And let somebody else jump on him first! That Rose has been clinging to him like a limpet all day. Besides, what do I want with respect? Here . . .'

She handed Ysan one of the plates, and undid some of her buttons. 'Now how much can you see?' she asked, leaning forwards a little.

'Just about everything!'

'Great! Let's go.'

But Ysan's uncertain expression held her back.

'What's the matter?'

Ysan shook her head. 'Nothing,' she muttered, wishing that sometimes she could actually be more like her friend.

Clarabel pulled a skittish face. 'Hey! Come on. I'm not telling you how to land Mister Ape Man, am I? You deal with Raúl your way and leave me to deal with Mister Universe my way. Who knows, maybe we'll both get what we want.'

'Clarrie, I'm not trying to *land* anybody. I want to talk with him, that's all. Impress him. Maybe work with him one day.'

'Sure! Come on, Zannie. You've scarcely stopped talking about him since you knew he was leading this trip. And I saw that smile during the meeting. You can't fool me. The signs may be subtle but I know when you've got the hots for someone.'

'I haven't got the hots for anybody. I want to talk to him . . . about apes and a career. That's all.'

It wasn't the whole truth. Over the years, since first seeing Raúl's picture on his books, since imagining the man and his life then watching him on television, her erotic fantasies had occasionally included him. And doubtless, after that morning's tableau, nonsexual as it was, he would pop up again fairly soon. But she wasn't about to admit this to anybody, not even Clarabel. Partly because she didn't consider she had a chance of 'landing' him anyway and didn't like being seen to fail, but also because if forced to choose, she'd opt for the life and the career rather than the man. To have both would be great but seemed greedy.

Ysan gestured for Clarabel to lead the way to the common room. 'Come on. The food's getting cold.'

Once through the door, Clarabel repeated the message from Henry and, leaning forwards, offered Sledge her bowl. Whether he saw her carefully prepared display or not, he sprang from his rocking chair. 'Thanks, but I'll eat it outside. Coming?' he asked Raúl as he reached the door.

Raúl declined and Sledge left the room, Clarabel trotting closely behind. Ysan hung back.

'Later,' said Raúl. 'The chimps, yes? I'll talk to you later, if that's OK? I'd just like a few moments on my own.

Collect my thoughts. It's been a busy day. A busy five days
... a busy year.'

'Of course. I wasn't ... It's just that ...' A little girl
again, blushing and frustrated at her inarticulateness as she
struggled to give herself some sort of presence. 'I wondered
if you knew. There's not enough pasta – or rice. We used
four bags of each today. At this rate we've got nowhere near
enough for a month. I counted. In the store.'

'Really?' Raúl seemed amused at her concern, enough to
lift his mood a little. 'We'll have to tell Henry not to burn
so much, won't we? Don't worry about it, Ysan. Thanks for
pointing it out but it won't be a problem. I promise. Now
please. Just give me a few moments.'

Bright red for about the fifth time that day, Ysan left the
room, despairing of ever being able to project herself as
serious and capable enough in front of him. But despite her
anxiety she was certain she was right about the food
supplies.

After the meal, Raúl asked Antonio to turn off the generator.
Fuel was precious, he told everyone. They hadn't been able
to bring much. As a rule, the generator would be switched
off every night at nine. 'Plenty of time to back up your field
notes; I know it's a pain, but do it. You'll regret it if you
don't. Plan the next day's work too. If you need the latrines
once the generator's off, you'll have to use torches. Besides,
the lights kill the atmosphere round here. Wait and see.'

'Generator!' Danny said. 'Have you seen it? It's tiny. I
could carry it.'

'I've smelt it,' Maisie added, standing with them. 'A really
brilliant idea, storing our rucksacks and clothes in the same
room as a stinking machine.'

'It's diesel,' added Danny. 'The machine's straight out of
the ark. It spews more than it uses. It'll never last a month.'

'You know about generators do you, Danny?' said Ysan.
'That's news to me. I thought all you knew was how to sail
Daddy's yacht.'

The lights went off, but nobody cared. Raúl was right. The firelight and moonlight, not to mention the rum and dope, intoxicated them all. Henry and Jill were in charge of the rum, which entailed no more than handing out a bottle to anybody who asked, and at the centre of the clearing Antonio sat cross-legged working away with a seemingly endless supply of cannabis, handing out joints to anybody who asked and gabbling away at his grateful clientele in Spanish. By eleven, the group was sprawled untidily around the moonlit clearing, the advisers chatting together at the hub. The still night air reeked of fire smoke, alcohol and marijuana. Fireflies danced against the dark backdrop of the surrounding forest. Mellow conversations mingled with a cacophony of cicada and cricket song. Cheerful tranquillity reigned.

Clarabel attacked the rum and dope with zeal, determined, she told Ysan, to be very drunk and cuddly when she eventually moved in on Sledge. Ysan tried to be more careful, taking only small amounts, enough to give her the nerve to talk to Raúl, but not enough to stop her being coherent. It wasn't working. Her courage was ebbing, not flowing.

'You don't need courage,' said Clarabel. 'He invited you.'

'I do! In the common room he told me to go away.'

'Just bad timing ... Oh! And again,' Clarabel said, pointing. 'Abi's got there first.'

Ysan took one look at the firelit tête-à-tête that was unfolding, and dropped her head. When she spoke it annoyed her to hear a tremble in her voice. 'OK, that's it. He won't want to talk to me now. I'm too tired anyway. Some other time. Good luck with Sledge. I'll see you tomorrow.' She knelt up on the grass and swatted straw from her thighs.

Clarabel reached for her wrist. 'Oh no you don't. You promised. Together, you said. We just wait, OK? He won't talk to Abi for long. She's got nothing to say. If it's more courage you need, drink more. Drink faster. Who needs coherence? If you get into trouble just flash those eyes of yours. Touch his knees. Worth millions of words.'

Ysan slumped back down with a sigh. And patiently, the pair sat, drank, watched and waited.

Clarabel was wrong about Abi. Half an hour later the blonde, her white clothes almost luminous, was still smiling, posturing – and touching Raúl's knees – with no sign of her audience ending. Noting that Rose had started touching Sledge as well, Clarabel eventually made a decision. 'It's no good. We've got to move in. Take over.'

'I can't!'

''Course you can.'

'Maybe after one more drink,' Ysan said, her words slurred.

But Clarabel claimed the bottle for herself. 'I think you're drunk enough. Can you still stand?'

Ysan leaped to her feet, almost steady.

'Good! Then help me up. Not sure I can.'

She could, but staying up was touch and go. So was walking and it was with great concentration that the pair of them tottered off to muscle in on the advisers' conversation group.

'Hi,' said Ysan, breaking out in a nervous sweat while a grinning Clarabel stood unhelpfully and unsteadily by her side. 'Can we join you?' She turned to Raúl. 'And can you and I have that talk?'

'Excuse me, *we* were talking,' complained Abi, glaring at Ysan with such force, Ysan's instinct was to apologise, capitulate and leave. But Raúl motioned for her to stay. Glowering at her as she sat, Abi carried on as if Ysan wasn't there.

Clarabel employed a less deferential approach. Sledge had been sitting next to Rose so closely they were almost shoulder to shoulder, but Clarabel got between them by simply stumbling, falling and landing accurately in a sprawl across Sledge's lap. 'Oops!' she apologised. 'Sorry. Bit drunk. You OK? Sorry.'

Sledge lifted Clarabel bodily, his broad hands circling her waist and Rose shifted sideways to make room, her movements slowed by reluctance.

Patiently, Ysan waited to be included in Abi and Raúl's conversation, but Abi made sure it never strayed far from her own ambitions, her training school, her bits and pieces of work so far. Raúl said little, but watched Abi intently. In turn, Ysan watched him. Watched to see which bits of the 'woman beneath the clothes' he appeared to be enthralled by. Then her concentration was broken.

'You don't want to talk to him,' Henry was saying to her. 'Talk to me . . . us. Hey! Where's your bottle? Here, have another.'

'Henry!' Jill scolded, who until then had seemed asleep, her head resting on her husband's lap. 'Slow down. You're slurring. You sound drunk.'

'Drunk! Of course I'm drunk. Been working at it all night.'

Ysan smiled self-consciously as she declined Henry's offer, then shifted position to try to get Raúl's attention. Her initial nervousness had given way to a feeling of awkwardness at being ignored. Awkwardness spiralled into irritation, and finally into action.

'Maybe I will have another,' she told Henry, reaching across Abi to take the offered bottle, before deliberately spilling rum over Abi's white trousers. Loudly, Ysan apologised, made a fuss over what she'd done and even gave Abi a hankie to attend to the stain. Then, after a long swig for courage, she addressed Raúl. 'I saw you this morning, you know? At the castle.'

Raúl just stared at her, while Abi huffed as she rubbed at the rum spots. 'What do you mean?' he eventually said.

Ysan smiled, raised her shoulders and in her nervy drunkenness almost giggled. 'I . . . saw you.'

More eye contact. More silence. Abi looked from one to the other, puzzled, until Raúl turned to her to say that perhaps he should talk to Ysan now, that he'd enjoyed their chat, that they'd talk more soon. It took Abi a few moments to realise she'd been dismissed – even longer to accept the fact and leave, helping herself up by placing a hand on Raúl's bare hairy shoulder. 'So I'll catch up with you later, then?' she said.

'Tomorrow. I'm beat. I'll just talk to Ysan, then I'm going to bed. See me tomorrow, after breakfast.'

With a final glare at Ysan, Abi stalked off to join the other students, now playing cards. Ysan took a tiny swig from her new bottle and watched her go, feeling good, then in mild panic: now what?

'Have you told anybody?' asked Raúl.

'No, of course not.' The lie brought her further anxiety and a sudden desire to change the subject. 'So, the chimps,' she said quickly. 'I really want to know. How did they get here?'

Despite her drunken fluster, her brain had put together all the right words in the right order. Raúl was still staring into her eyes, his face unreadable. She assumed he was wondering what she was thinking about him, in relation to what she had witnessed that morning.

'OK,' he started slowly. 'The chimps. Right . . . Well, it was Jim, my professor. He wasn't *my* professor then, of course. Not in the sixties. I'd only just been born . . .'

The rum was catching up with him. Smiling patiently as he struggled, she concentrated hard, striving to unravel his rambling. The story she slowly gleaned was that forty years earlier, Jim had released thirteen chimps – six males, seven females, mainly young adults but four of them older, more experienced. It was partly a liberation, through pity. The apes had been in a private zoo Jim visited; in tiny cages which were never cleaned. Mainly, though, it was an experiment to see how they'd cope after a lifetime of captivity. Which male and which female would cope best, produce most descendants. A breeding experiment.

'Really exciting stuff,' said Raúl, his brain at last connecting to his tongue. 'Discovering what chimps are really made of.'

'But isn't it better to watch *wild* chimps? In their natural habitat, rather than . . .'

'You might think so, but not necessarily. You see, in their natural habitat, animals carry an awful lot of baggage: family, territory, history, culture. Stuff like that. Clouds everything. Can't see a thing. But strip it all away, take them back to the beginning, give them a blank page, then you can see them properly, for what they are . . . You know what?' He leaned towards her, as if exchanging a confidence, near enough for her to smell the rum on his breath. 'I'd say, without question, we learned more about the true nature of chimps from Jim's tiny experiment than from thousands of hours of watching natural groups. It ought to be done with all the great apes.'

He leaned back. An opening? Drunkenly flustered or not, Ysan coiled to snatch the moment, then spoke carefully, controlling her excitement, and asked him if Jim's experiment had been so important, why Raúl hadn't mentioned it in any of his books.

'You've read some of my books?' he asked, clearly surprised. 'Which ones?'

'All of them. From when I was a teenager . . . Everything you described, all those questions and ideas. I found it all really exciting. I still do.'

He said he was flattered, and she gave a tiny laugh.

'Can I?' she asked tentatively, indicating the joint that was just burning out in his hand. He passed it to her but after a tiny draw it was dead.

'I'd give anything to do what you've done,' she said, encouraged by what she felt was a new-found intimacy. 'I've dreamed about little else since I was fourteen. How does somebody like me set about it? Make a start?'

'The usual. Get a good degree, get somebody to take you on for a doctorate. As for me, I started right here on the island, with a tiny piece of research on Jim's chimps. Curiosity, hard work and luck, that's what you need. A bit of nepotism doesn't hurt either.'

The sudden thought that she could actually make a start while on the island was so unexpected, she could scarcely contain herself. 'Can I do that?' she asked excitedly. 'Here. Instead of working at the beach with everyone else, can I do some research on these chimps? Could that get me started?'

He smiled indulgently. 'I guess so. I suppose there's no harm, if that's what you want.'

FOUR

Y san lay in her sleeping bag and watched the advancing dawn snuff out the stars one by one until only the morning star remained. A small party of fruit bats flapped overhead making for the inland forest and, in the glow of the morning, all her dreams seemed possible. Time and again she went over the conversation with Raúl from the night before, reliving snippets and snapshots, revelling in him knowing her now, scarcely believing they had shared a joint, a bottle, while he listened to her fantasy and agreed to her watching apes. She couldn't wait to get started. Another group of fruit bats flapped into view, thirty or fifty this time.

Sleep under the stars, Raúl's first circular had offered.

'What if it rains?' Ian had asked at the airport.

'It won't,' he'd replied. 'We're arriving just after the rainy season. It'll be hot and dry. I promise.'

And he was right. Too hot to sleep indoors, it would have been almost too hot to sleep anywhere if people hadn't been so tired. The welcome party had been brief but heavy – too much alcohol and dope and not enough food. Most people, exhausted even before the party began, were in bed soon after midnight. One by one they'd dragged themselves up the rickety external staircases onto the flat wooden roofs of the two buildings. Everyone except Raúl and Antonio – in the two positions to her right – had crawled into rather than on to their beds. Even now, as Ysan looked around, theirs were the only two bodies to be seen on her roof – the rest were merely humps in sleeping bags. Many, though, could be heard, the women to her left snoring quietly and almost in synchrony. In contrast, Antonio's rasping snorts were loud, erratic and out of time with everybody. King of the snorers was Sledge. Even from deep inside his sleeping bag on the far side of the roof from her, his rhythmic booming drowned all other sounds. Raúl, so near, was silent.

It was coincidence that Ysan had ended up sleeping next to Raúl, just a metre or so apart. She and Clarabel had been the first to put their sleeping bags side by side on one of the empty roofs, not knowing it was really meant for the staff. Raúl and Antonio had been the last to arrive and put theirs in the only places they could. Raúl would have had no idea – nor cared – whose bag was next to his. Ysan cared, though. Once she'd seen him arrive in the moonlight and watched him lie down, his nearness hindered her sleeping. Now, seeing him slumbering through the peace of dawn, it pleased her to have him so close, half-buried in the folds of his sleeping bag. Idly she wondered if, when he woke, she'd be the first thing he'd see.

Across the roof, Sledge's snoring faltered and stopped. In its wake, Ysan heard shuffling and the sound of a sleeping bag being quietly unzipped. A pale female arm emerged from Sledge's bed and, with the dexterity of an elephant's trunk, collected garments that littered the nearby roof boards. Next a tousled head appeared. Finally, like a moth from a cocoon, Clarabel crawled into the open. Clutching her clothes to her naked voluptuous body, she glanced nervously around then ran barefoot across the rooftop. Within seconds, she slithered into her own sleeping bag next to Ysan's. Only a short distance apart, with sleeping bags pulled up under their chins, the two faced each other. Grinning, Clarabel held up four fingers. Ysan shook her head and mouthed, 'I don't believe you.' Clarabel shrugged, smiled again and closed her eyes, but not for long. Sweat flies began buzzing around, seeking titbits from nose and lips. Simultaneously, the two women pulled their bags over their heads, Clarabel to doze, Ysan, safely hidden from the world, to fantasise further – about her future, about Raúl – until the heat of the sun drove everybody out of bed and off the roof.

Sitting in shade near the common room, Ysan waited patiently for Raúl to finish his breakfast and join her. They'd arranged that while others went to the beach, he'd spend an hour or so getting her started with the chimps, showing her the best place to find them and discussing what she should record. From where she was sitting, she could see him clearly. He was standing, eating, laughing, talking to Sledge and Antonio. Barefoot – as always. Dishevelled – as always. Just wearing shorts, drooping at the front – as always. She felt like pulling them up and tying the draw-string; felt like pulling her comb from her rucksack and taking him in hand. She tried to imagine him in a tuxedo, but failed. Somehow clothes didn't suit him. They hung badly and looked untidy. Something to do with the shape of his shoulders, the slimness of his waist and hips, his primeval aura.

Abi joined him and took him to one side, immediately flirtatious, showing him pieces of paper, rubbing shoulders with him as they scrutinised them together. Bare skin gleaming with freshly applied sun lotion, she was wearing white again: a halter-neck bikini top, brief but tailored shorts. She looked as poised and polished as Ysan felt scruffy and dull.

Ysan sprang to her feet and walked quickly over to them. After a cursory 'Hi!' to Abi she looked up at Raúl and widened her eyes. 'Whenever you're ready.'

Abi's face darkened. 'Aren't you coming to South Bay, to the beach? To get me started?'

'Of course,' Raúl answered. 'Just as soon as Ysan is set up with her project. I'll join you around midday.'

Ysan resisted a triumphant glance at Abi's mortification and followed Raúl downslope from the base, past the latrines and through a small stand of trees until they arrived at impenetrable scrub. There, side by side, they walked along its edge.

'Where are we going?'

'The orchard.'

'What sort of orchard?'

'Wait and see.'

As defence against biting flies and thorns, Ysan was wearing a long-sleeved shirt, denim jeans and trainers; underneath was a bikini, in case she had a chance to sunbathe. 'Do you never wear shoes?' she asked him.

'Not if I can help it.' He paused. 'So you saw me naked yesterday?'

She smiled. 'I did. But you were a long way away.'

Raúl shook his head and laughed. 'Now it's your turn.'

Ysan blushed. Raúl laughed even more. 'Tell me what got *you* started on apes. What first fired you up? Can you remember?'

Ysan smiled. 'Yes I can. It was before I got to know your books.'

'OK.'

'It was Mister One.'

'Mister One?'

She laughed, embarrassed, and told him that she was ten, maybe eleven, when her mother's boyfriend bought her Mister One as a birthday present – a cuddly toy, really cuddly, a really big chimp, with enormous balls . . .

'Anatomically correct, then,' Raúl interrupted.

'And when you squeezed them, he gave this funny hoot . . . and this long pink willy poked out . . .'

She'd thought he was hilarious, and so did her mother.

Of course, he soon broke. But that was the start of her ape-toy collection. Then, when she was about thirteen, she started trying to find out what apes were really like. 'And that's when you came on the scene. Your gorilla book. I thought it was amazing.'

They came to a standstill. Raúl suddenly seemed awkward, as if something were bothering him. She felt awkward too, worrying her story was too childish, wishing he'd say something. In the end he just smiled, hung his head, and started walking again. 'It's around about here,' he said, rummaging in the bushes. 'A passageway. The only way through. The chimps keep it open by all their coming and going.'

Dropping on to all fours, he led the way through what was effectively a tunnel perhaps twenty metres long. Then the vegetation thinned and they were able to stand, albeit with a stoop. Seconds later they were in the open.

Ahead was a lush plantation. Mature and overgrown trees, shrubs and creepers created a majestic, tangled backdrop of light- and dark-green foliage. Everywhere were splashes of bright colour. Pendulous branches, weighed down by orange, yellow and green fruits, intertwined with other branches bearing white, yellow, pink and red flowers that held promise of yet more fruit in the months to come. Butterflies flitted between the blossoms and brightly coloured birds chased each other among the trees. The sounds of insects – buzzing flies, droning bees and strident grasshoppers – were everywhere; nearby, a pair of birds sang a ding-dong duet. Every so often a swirl of air carried a sweet heavy scent – and occasionally something less pleasant.

'When you said an orchard, I thought . . . but it's so big! What a fantastic place. How come? It can't be natural.'

Raúl told her it had been Jim's idea, but that he and Antonio had done most of the work. Cleared the place. Planted it. Over a thousand young trees, bananas, oranges, all sorts. They hadn't known what would survive, so they tried everything. Gourds, sweet potatoes. Loads of seeds too. Bags of them. Just scattered them around. It took five summers to get it established.

'Now look at it. Antonio and I couldn't believe it when we came back last October. First time we'd seen it in nearly twenty years.'

'I don't know what to say. It's beautiful. But why? Why do it?'

Chuckling softly, Raúl said it was for the chimps. Because the forest was so unproductive much of the year, Jim had worried that chimps couldn't live there any better than people – and for a while they really had struggled. The orchard was meant to be a supplement, a lifeline, and it had succeeded. Jim had been thrilled the way things worked out.

'Where is he now? Does he still come here?'

'No. He's dead,' he said, and explained that Gillespie retired about ten years ago but still returned for a further five summers to check on the chimps. 'Until Antonio and I came back last October to look the place over, rebuild everything, prepare for this visit, no human's been here since.'

The pair of them looked around in silence, Ysan absorbed by the thought of the man and his dream. Of the satisfaction derived from liberating a group of apes from captivity and planting an orchard so they could survive. Then, as a powerful odour invaded her nose, her thoughts returned to the present. 'What's that smell?'

'It's that tree over there, the one covered with bees. Heavy, isn't it? Can't say I like it. Reminds me of semen.'

Ysan flushed. Sex never seemed far away in his conversation. 'I quite like it . . . I think. But I don't mean *that* smell. The other one.'

'Oh, that! Surely you recognise that.' But instead of telling her what it was, he changed the subject and pointed out the grass between them and the orchard's edge, drawing attention to how short it was. 'Rabbits,' he said. 'They were Jim's idea too. To keep the cleared areas open, producing short grass all around the perimeter of the orchard. From the air it must look just like an oval racetrack.'

Ysan suddenly pointed with excitement. 'Look, chimps! On the ... well, the racetrack. Just coming out of the orchard. About a hundred metres away.'

'Now can you guess what the other smell is? Best watch where you tread. Anyway ... they're all yours. But one thing, though, don't tell anybody else about the orchard. Not even Sledge. Not yet. If everyone starts visiting, they'll scare off the chimps. So just you, me and Antonio, for the moment.'

'I won't,' she said, flushed with pleasure at being one of the privileged few. 'Of course I won't.'

She hoped he'd stay a while, so she could watch the apes with her icon. But it didn't happen. Having brought her to the orchard, Raúl told her he needed to get the other students started at South Bay. 'Get a feel for the place and the work,' he told her. 'Make a few sketches of the chimps you see. Write down distinguishing features so you'll recognise them again. Get to know them as individuals. Give them names – or numbers, if you prefer. Perhaps you'll spot your perfect Mister One. But only stay a couple of hours until you've acclimatised. We don't want you passing out with heatstroke or dehydration. Promise?'

She nodded, but was reminded how people always underestimated her. She supposed it was her looks, and her anxiety before authority. But she was tougher than that. Tougher than she seemed. Reminding herself of this, she settled down in the shade to watch the chimps.

She needed to be high up, and found the ideal place about eight metres up in a majestic redwood. Where multiple branches forked, there was a naturally fashioned seat – big enough, flat enough, just about comfortable enough, and hidden from view.

From there she made her sketches and notes and gave the chimps numbers. The first male she saw she called, not Mister One, but M1 – it sounded more scientific. The first female she called F1, and so on. Babies were B and those she couldn't sex were U, for unknown. She'd reached M2, F6, B2 and U4, and was just getting into her stride, when all the chimps disappeared into thick cover. She waited and waited. Just one more, she kept telling herself. A new male. Then she'd leave.

Rabbits spread across the racetrack. Ysan checked her watch – three hours since Raúl had left. She was hot; tomorrow she would wear less. But she had plenty of water, she wasn't hungry, and she was enjoying herself. Just a bit longer. Raúl would probably still be on the beach with Abi anyway. He'd never know. She stretched her stiff limbs, exercised her neck, raised and lowered her shoulders.

A male chimpanzee appeared, followed by two females. Studying them through her binoculars, she then checked her sketches and notes: M1 with F4 and F5. M1 was the huge male that had approached Raúl so confidently at the castle the first day. The same male that Antonio had pelted with stones. The living embodiment of Mister One.

Sighting the chimps, the rabbits stopped feeding. A youngster ran nervously in a circle before returning to its mother. Suddenly M1 let out a scream and charged. The rabbits turned and ran straight into an ambush. Five chimps – Ysan had no chance to identify them – burst from the bushes and tried to cut off their prey's retreat. Most of the rabbits were fast enough to zigzag their way to safety but a few – including a doe and her kitten – were surrounded. In the mêlée that followed, chimps collided with chimps and rabbits with rabbits as predator and prey careered across the grass. The baby rabbit escaped down a hole, but its mother was caught. Moments later the apes were wrestling each other for the screaming doe's body.

M1 snatched the prize and ran to the racetrack's edge, the other chimps following. Biting open the screaming rabbit, M1 pulled out her guts and offered them to F4. Next he wrenched off the rabbit's head, removing it with a single twist and yank. Then, holding the detached head in his hand, he skipped over to a rock where, with a dexterity that suggested he'd done the same many times before, he bashed and split open the doe's head like a coconut. Finally, he picked out and ate the brains.

Ysan lowered her binoculars. From the moment the ambush had been sprung, she'd resigned herself to seeing a rabbit die – but the screaming, the live dismembering, the eating of the brains; she hadn't been prepared for anything so carnal. Pushing herself back into the safety of one of the forks, she took a few deep breaths and set about composing herself. In the distance, the chimps settled down and began to groom each other.

Calmer, Ysan checked her watch: three and a half hours since Raúl had left her. Suddenly the chimps all stood and began to move away, sloping off deep into the orchard, looking over their shoulders. Now she could hear voices, Raúl and Antonio, chattering away in Spanish, striding on to the racetrack. Feeling guilty, Ysan couldn't decide what to do. Dithering, she watched and waited, assuming the men had come to collect food for the evening meal.

The professor and the boatman looked incongruous together. Raúl was taller but Antonio was heavier, with the bulk and physique of a man who lived by his strength. Swarthy, rough, rugged, but friendly and charismatic, not at all intimidating, he intrigued her. How had he come to be in the Pacific? And what bound him to Raúl?

Suddenly both men dropped their shorts and leaned forwards like long-distance runners at the start of a race. Raúl counted to three and then they burst into a sprint, downhill, along the right-hand part of the racetrack. From there, they ran on, stumbling and jumping headlong down the steep, grassy slope that led to the sea, their destination the black sand, black rocks and swaying palms of the bay beneath the orchard, its two slender headlands reaching like long dark open legs into the sea.

Through her binoculars, Ysan saw Antonio win the race by metres, then attack the sea in boisterous celebration,

69

splashing through the shallows before diving cleanly and expertly into the depths. After swimming underwater for a distance, he hauled himself on to rocks jutting out from the knee of the northern headland, then waved back at Raúl who'd waited at the water's edge. The latter checked his watch, then shouted across the calm water between them. Antonio dived back into the sea, but instead of returning to shore turned on to his back and simply floated.

Ysan focused on Raúl, who was pacing the water's edge, occasionally glancing at his watch while the boatman continued to float. Then he swam out to Antonio's side and a few moments later the pair returned leisurely to shore. After talking briefly on the sand, they ran the hundred metres or so up the beach, not stopping until they reached the first vegetation. Raúl appeared to count for a long time, maybe to a hundred.

Ysan was bemused. What were they doing? It seemed more rehearsal than recreation, but for what? And why were they both naked? There was no sign of anything sexual in their behaviour; not the slightest hint of interest in each other's bodies. They seemed to be naked for the sake of nakedness.

Next each man picked up a large rock, staggering off with it up the hill towards her. They drew close, coming to a halt no more than twenty metres from her tree, where they discarded the rocks and chattered breathlessly in Spanish. They pointed down the hill, then to the sides, as if discussing distance. Raúl tapped his watch, then they laughed and slapped each other on the back. Finally, still naked, they walked jauntily down the hill, gesticulating as they went.

Ysan waited until the two men were masked by palm fronds, scrambled down from her tree and headed back to the base.

FIVE

2 July 2006, evening

That evening Raúl was in great demand, but while the other students clustered around him, each waiting to talk about their work, Ysan stayed apart. Restless with excitement about the hunting chimps, eager to share everything with him, she could hardly contain her impatience, but stoically waited her turn. Seated on a rock at the clearing's edge, she had only fireflies, a notebook, a torch and now a different kind of observation – how much time Raúl was spending with Abi – for company.

In between making a back-up copy of her notes about the chimps' attack on the rabbits and catching glimpses of Raúl with Abi, she thought also of the pantomime of two naked men playing private games in the orchard. Absurd, but also erotic with their distant bouncing swinging genitals, their working muscles and taut sinews, all gleaming with sweat and sea water. Sinister too, in a way. All that effort for what? What the hell were those ritualistic manoeuvres?

Finally, Raúl came over, offering a swig of rum from his bottle by way of apology for keeping her waiting. Ysan accepted and let it burn a path into her stomach. She handed it back and Raúl asked about her afternoon.

All the time expecting him to cut her short or dismiss what she'd seen as nothing new, she described the ambush and carnage on the racetrack. Instead, with mounting enthusiasm, he only interrupted her account to ask questions and check details. He'd never seen apes hunt rabbits. 'And the hunting party included females? Really unusual,' he enthused. 'And how did M1 crack open the skull?'

She really had witnessed something new. As the implications of what she'd seen shuttled between them so too did the bottle. It was, she told herself in the midst of rum-stoked euphoria, the most exciting conversation of her life.

To Ysan's surprise, instead of leaving when they'd explored every last detail of her account, Raúl stayed and wouldn't be swayed when Ian and Abi tried to sequester him.

'Nice name, Ysan,' said Raúl. 'Unusual. Sounds Asian. What does it mean?'

'I shouldn't tell you,' Ysan sighed. 'It spoils it.'

'How come?'

'It doesn't mean anything. It's an acronym. My grandparents' initials. "YS" my mother's mother, "AN" her father.'

'So it might just as easily have been Anys?'

'Actually, I never asked.'

Small talk wasn't Ysan's forte, but the rum began to help. 'And Raúl?' she said. 'Spanish, isn't it?'

He smiled self-consciously. 'It means "wise wolf".'

Silence followed. Ysan took a draw on the joint then passed it back. She noticed his fingernails, unbitten and clean for a man; his fingers slender like hers. Rolling on to her front, she looked up at him sitting erect – almost yogic – by her side, back straight, legs half-lotus. Backlit by the moon, the fine dark hairs on his bare shoulders and arms, just like those on his chest, were shining silver. The image of him running up the racetrack carrying a rock flashed into her mind, nearly making her laugh.

'Your Spanish is pretty fluent,' she remarked at last.

'Just lucky,' he replied. 'Mother Spanish, father English, ergo bilingual. Effort: zero.' He paused. 'Sorry, bad habit. My father used to talk like that.'

Through the mellow fug of pot and alcohol, he reminisced about his relaxed and informal childhood. His parents' summer parties in Spain were an absolute riot – nudity, pot smoking, public sex – he'd seen it all, long before he had hair on his chest. Pausing, he took his turn with the joint. Then came university, he said, and suddenly life became serious. 'The place was overrun by prudes and God-fearers. If I hadn't met Jim and become so caught up in his apes and his crazy projects, I'd probably have dropped out long before graduation.'

'Are your parents still in Spain?'

'No. Well, yes. At least, that's where their ashes are. They died. Everyone's dead. There's nobody. Not any more.'

'Nobody?'

He apologised. For some reason he thought she'd know – but why should she? Not long after his parents, he'd also lost his daughter and her mother. A car accident, nearly a year ago. He was away, running the field course in Denmark. 'Then it came,' he said impassively. 'Completely out of the blue. One phone call and my life ended.'

Ysan rolled on to her back and picked out the few stars bright enough to shine through the moon-silvered sky. Only two days ago the man by her side had been an uncomplicated icon, a beacon for her ambitions, a magnet for her fantasies, an utter stranger. Now she knew of his spirit and the tragedy in his past. Suddenly, she felt overwhelmed – and hopelessly young and inexperienced.

'Ysan,' Raúl said quietly.

He received no answer. She'd heard him, but flat on her back and with eyes closed, joint between her fingers, her mind was floating.

'Ysan,' Raúl said again, louder than before. Still she

didn't respond, until she felt him take the joint from between her fingers. Opening her eyes, she saw him take a last draw before stubbing the butt out in the grass. 'It's finished. It nearly burned you.'

'Sorry. I drifted off. I ought to go to bed.'

'You can't go to bed yet. The evening's hardly started.'

He turned to shout to Antonio, who was playing cards with the lads. The boatman grinned, took a package from his pocket and threw it. The missile pierced the air like a knife, the cellophane wrapper catching the moonlight like a dagger's blade. Raúl caught it deftly and set about making another spliff, his hands shaking slightly. Eventually, he lit his untidy creation and handed it to Ysan. Then, while she smoked, he slowly sipped from his bottle. Both were silent, lost in their separate worlds. She imagined them in a jungle, searching for gorillas. She wondered whether for Raúl the end of one life might mean the beginning of another.

Just then, Clarabel stalked into the clearing and threw herself to the ground. Snatching the joint from Ysan's hand, she drew deeply.

'Did you find him?' said Ysan.

'No, he's not here. And guess what? Neither's Rose. Any rum?'

Raúl offered her his bottle; Clarabel thanked him and drank at length, her disappointment transparent.

Antonio loomed over the trio, blocking out the moon, his appearance so sudden Ysan wondered if he'd actually been waiting for Clarabel to reappear. He and Raúl exchanged a few words.

'He's bored,' explained Raúl. 'He wants us to go to the beach, the four of us. How about it?'

'Won't all the others want to come?' said Ysan. 'Abi's watching us like a hawk.'

Raúl barely faltered, proposing that if he and Antonio disappeared into the bushes and the two women made as if visiting the latrines, they could circle round out of everyone's sight and meet up just inside the forest. Nobody could follow and nobody would even know they'd gone.

Meeting up in the forest as arranged, Ysan and Clarabel discovered both men still shoeless – and torchless.

'More fun this way,' said Raúl, telling them to leave their torches too.

As they crossed the wooded ridge between base and beach they were bathed in pools of darkness. The moon rarely lit the ground but shone strobe-like in their eyes as trees marched across its face. Speaking little, concentrating on their steps, the quartet's few words competed with an orchestra of insects: some shrill, others coarse; some continuous, others staccato. More than once, an owl flapped noisily through the trees.

Despite their bare feet, Raúl and Antonio ploughed unconcerned through the vegetation, crushing leaves underfoot, which filled the night air with scents, some aromatic, others acrid. On one short stretch, the waft was putrid – as from a dead animal. Then first the trees and later the vegetation thinned, heralding the distant sound of surf, the smell of salt water.

The main beach at South Bay was large and, like Orchard Bay, isolated by two headlands, extensions of tall, unscalable cliffs that seemed to grow out of the beach. Black boulders – some huge, others small – littered the sand beneath the rock faces, forming a variety of coves and smaller bays. In the moonlight, rocks and shadows merged to form fantastic shapes. Even on the open beach, there were shapes near the sea. Shapes that could also have been rocks – until they moved. Or perhaps sea turtles – until one human shape rolled over to arch over the other.

'Sledge,' Raúl said with a chuckle to Antonio.

'And Rose,' added Clarabel, without humour. 'So this is where they were.'

Leaving the distant pair in peace, the four skirted the main beach to settle in a small and private cove. The walk had sobered them all a little but Raúl and Antonio had brought the necessary provisions, and for a while the group indulged themselves, speaking little while absorbing the tranquillity of the moonlit sea.

'See that bright, reddish star up there,' Raúl said quietly to Ysan while pointing almost overhead.

'You mean Antares,' she whispered back, 'the one in Scorpio?'

Raúl smiled, then hung his head.

'Sorry,' said Ysan. 'I didn't mean to show off. They're beautiful, aren't they, the stars? So bright, even with the moon.'

So why had they come here? Ysan wondered. Surely not just to look at the stars.

The air was hot and humid, the surf soothing and soporific. Ysan could feel herself drifting away, until roused by Raúl and Antonio conversing loudly in Spanish. After a jocular exchange, they jumped to their feet, dropped their shorts and kicked them off.

'What are you doing?' asked Clarabel, amused, taking a good look at both men.

'Time for a swim,' replied Raúl. 'Wake ourselves up. And Antonio's feeling mischievous. He wants to go to the main beach to freak Sledge and Rose. Coming?'

Clarabel raised her hands for the two men to help her to her feet. Then, without any hint of embarrassment, she also undressed.

'Come on, Zannie,' she urged as Ysan stayed seated.

Ysan shook her head. 'Can't,' she explained. 'If I stand up, I'll fall down. Sorry. You all go. I'll be fine.'

'Sober you up,' Raúl told her.

'It'll be fun,' added Clarabel.

'Best not,' Ysan said.

'See you in a bit then,' called Clarabel as the trio stumbled off towards the main beach.

Ysan watched them go, smiling at how luminous Clarabel's pale buttocks were in the moonlight compared with those of the deeply tanned men.

In part, she'd been telling the truth. She'd seen the warning signs: stars that danced the occasional jig; dizziness if she turned her head too sharply. But drunkenness wasn't the real reason she'd opted out of the midnight swim. She could have stood, run and swum if she'd wanted. The real reason was deeper rooted, less ephemeral. She was shy, never once having been naked in public. Even at school they'd had cubicles. Envious that the others could strip so naturally, she sought consolation in more rum, each swig a show of disaffection, each glance between gulps a search for distraction.

Eyeing the moon – more than half, less than round – she challenged herself to guess how many days until it would be full. Four? Five? Then she counted the seconds between the hisses of the surf: one elephant, two elephant . . . About ten. Six waves a minute. Three hundred and sixty an hour. How many a day? But no, it wouldn't always be this calm. A tiny gust of air swirled round her, bringing the smell of the ocean. Does the sea smell of fish, or do fish smell of the sea? She kept almost drifting off, but each time her eyes began to close she took another tiny swig of rum.

Suddenly she was wide awake. A lone figure appeared, weaving between rocks as it re-entered the cove: Raúl, meandering as if not entirely sure where he'd left her. She tried to stand to attract his attention, but without strength in her legs stayed seated. She waved and shouted instead.

'Where are the others?' she asked as he arrived.

Raúl picked up his shorts and used them as a towel, drying between his buttocks and round his genitals and the thick pelt of black pubic hair. Then, as if it never even crossed his mind to put the shorts back on, he cast them aside, kneeling on the sand in front of her. 'Messing about in the sea. All four of them. I've come back to fetch you. And the drink and the clothes.'

'Sledge and Rose?'

He laughed, eyes and teeth reflecting moonlight. 'Caught them *in flagrante*. You should have heard Sledge curse when he realised we were watching.'

Ysan didn't share his amusement. 'Are they all naked?'

'It's a tropical beach. It's midnight. What do you expect?'

'I don't know what to expect. I've never been on a beach at midnight before. Any beach, never mind tropical. Am I . . . so unusual?'

'Unusual?'

'Being shy. About being naked in company. I've never done it. It's a big deal.'

Raúl apologised, but said she should come anyway, no need to undress. 'It's not obligatory. Nobody would care.'

'Of course they'll care. They'll laugh at me. Tease me. No. If I'm coming . . .'

She made to stand but couldn't, settling for kneeling instead, even then swaying, momentarily putting a hand to the sand to steady herself. Then, crossing her arms and reaching to her waist, she began to lift her thin long-sleeved T-shirt.

No sooner had she dragged her top over her face than everything went wrong. The smallish neck of the garment caught under her nose, her elbows hooked in the sleeves, and with a wave of dizziness she fell forwards, flat on her face. She couldn't right herself, she couldn't take off the top, and the more she tried the more impossible everything seemed. Raúl laughed as she struggled prostrate and entangled before him.

He lifted her to her knees, her head still shrouded in the shirt. He brushed the sand off her tummy and breasts, before disentangling her arms and head and pulling her shirt back down to her waist. Ysan wasn't laughing.

'I was trying to take it off, not put it back on. This is a big deal for me. Who said you could touch me, by the way?'

'Why not wait until it's not such a big deal, eh?' Raúl chuckled. 'Maybe you've drunk too much rum to swim tonight anyway.'

'Rubbish,' snorted Ysan, taking another long swig to prove her point, fixing him in the eye, daring him to avoid the eye contact. He didn't, his steady gaze and almost pitying smile both embarrassing and irritating her.

'So,' she continued aggressively, 'is this how you do it every year? The drink, the draw ... maybe a bit of moonlight.'

Raúl didn't ask her what she was talking about, so she assumed he knew.

'You have a reputation, you know. Abi hasn't stopped telling everyone. Ever since we arrived. Says it's going to be her this year.'

This wasn't the gentle, nervous, sober Ysan speaking – nor the slightly drunk Ysan, with her ripples of doubt and self-consciousness smoothed over. It was Ysan under the influence, over the top, out of control: irrational, irascible, competitive and outspoken. 'Well? Say something. Is it true? Do you screw a student every year? Is that why I'm here tonight? Rose for Sledge, Clarabel for Antonio, and me for you? Get us drunk. Get us naked, then ... Three copulating couples by the second night. Is that a record?'

Shut up, Ysan, she told herself. Just, shut up.

Raúl stayed calm. 'I really do think you've had too much rum,' he said gently, reaching to take the bottle from her as he spoke.

Clutching the rum to her chest, keeping it just out of his reach, she said, 'No!' then faltered. 'Well, maybe I have.' Still she wouldn't let him take the bottle. 'I shouldn't be talking to you like this, should I? I'm forgetting ... I mean ... I'm sorry. You don't need to answer. Of course you don't need to answer.'

He gave a quiet laugh. 'Which means that I do, otherwise you'll just think the worst of me. I'll be honest with you. Not every year by any means – and I'd be bragging if I said as often as Sledge – but, yes, more often than not, I suppose I do. It does happen. Sometimes even when I don't mean it to. And three copulating couples in one night would be some way off the record ...'

'And your wife?' she said, eyeing him. 'She was OK with this? You didn't feel guilty or anything?'

He bristled and began to stand. Now she'd gone too far,

she thought. He was going to stalk away, ignore her for the rest of the trip. Maybe forever. But he didn't leave. Instead, he stood over her.

'No, I didn't feel guilty . . . or anything. Why should I?' His tone was one of muted anger. 'Don't judge, Ysan. Never judge. Just observe. OK? You've no idea what worked for us – what made our relationship tick – so don't presume. We had a child together who we both adored. And when I was home we slept together. Beyond that we lived separate lives. Just think how often I was away, working – Africa, Borneo, wherever. I could be gone months at a time. Over a year sometimes. We were apart far more than we were together. How could we possibly have had a normal relationship?'

The more animated he became, the less Ysan could focus on what he was saying. She registered that they hadn't actually been married; that they'd both agreed to their 'open' relationship. She registered too his opinion that the biological bond between them was stronger than any piece of paper. But most of all, she registered, as he stepped this way and that to emphasise a point, his cock and balls swinging from side to side right in her eyeline. Eventually she broke into uncontrollable laughter.

'I'm sorry. I was listening, honestly. But . . . I've never had a lecturer waving his willy in my face before.'

The laughter brought tears to her eyes. For a few moments Raúl was on edge, but the sight of her cracking up mellowed him. His shadowy features broke into a smile. As he sat back down on the sand he laughed.

'I guess pomposity and nudity don't mix, eh? Serves me right. But you hit a nerve, you know. Nobody knows this, except Sledge and the girl. But last year, when the phone call came to tell me about the accident, Sledge had to come and find me. I had a private room. And that's where I was . . .'

He didn't need to complete the sentence. Ysan knew well enough what he was saying, and suddenly nothing was funny any more.

'So,' he continued, 'all those years, all those women . . . No, I didn't feel guilty. Not really. But since that phone call. Since the thought that while they were dying, I was . . . Well, I vowed to them. I vowed never again. So if Abi really thinks . . . Well, you can tell her. It's just not going to happen. Not on this trip.'

Ysan's mind wrestled with his message. Never mind Abi, she wanted to say to him. What about me? In a flash all her erotic fantasies about him became wishes. Her dreams for the future could involve more than just working with him.

'I'd better go,' he said. 'They'll be wondering where I've got to with the rum. Are you coming?'

'Don't think I can. I really am legless now.'

He tried to help her to her feet, but halfway up her knees buckled and she twirled round on to her back, nearly dragging him down with her.

'God, how embarrassing,' she giggled up at him.

Laughing in sympathy, he helped her struggle back on to her knees. 'Don't worry. We've all been there. Stay here. I'll take the others some rum and their clothes, then I'll come back and sit with you.'

Ysan's torpor was rapidly turning into heavy-lidded sleepiness. A trivial thought gained inflated importance. 'Tell Clarrie to be careful for me, will you? Please. I'm supposed to be looking after her.'

'If you want, but somehow I don't think she needs much looking after. Besides, she's safe enough with Antonio. He'll take care of her.'

'That's what I'm afraid of.'

'And he's been snipped.'

For a second, she couldn't process what he'd said. Snipped? What had they been talking about? When she remembered and understood, she let slip a secret in return. 'They'll be doubly safe then,' she said.

A moment later, she was alarmed by a wave of vertigo.

'Raúl . . . I think I'm going to faint.'

Stooping, he held her by the arms and tried to steady her, but when she began to keel sideways he gently lowered her to the sand. Turning on to her side, she curled up and closed her eyes. The vertigo increased, threatening retching, then faded.

'I'll stay here a few minutes,' she muttered. 'Just lie here for a bit. You go. I'll be fine.'

He didn't leave. She could sense him kneeling over her. Felt him move hair from her face. Lift her head to give her a pillow of some sort. Cloth. Damp cloth, with the smell of a man.

'What do you mean "doubly safe"? You mean the pill? Is Clarabel on the pill?'

Dimly, distantly, she could just about hear him. And just as dimly, she was aware of muttering an explanation. 'It's her tubes . . . her womb. Just give me a few moments. I'll be fine. You go . . .'

SIX

It was dawn before Ysan opened her eyes, her cheek half buried in a pillow of sand, a large fiddler crab with its oversized red claw only centimetres from her nose. A wave rolled up the beach and lapped over her feet. She sat upright and the crab scuttled away to safety. The sound of laughter carried from the sea.

'I've been waiting for the tide to reach you,' shouted Clarabel. 'Come in. Cure your hangover. This is fantastic.'

Shakily, Ysan took off her jeans, staggered to the water's edge, then swam out to join her friend, to tread water by her side, to submerge occasionally, trying to clear her head.

'Where are Raúl and Antonio?' she spluttered.

'They left around three.'

'Oh, Clarrie. I made such a fool of myself last night.'

Clarabel, swimming naked, spat out a stream of sea water. 'Don't think about it. You looked very sweet, all curled up on the sand.'

'I didn't want to look sweet. I wanted to look serious, capable, reliable. Not a cute pisshead.'

Ysan dipped her head under the water again, surfaced, spat and shook her head. Then a few waves, larger than the rest, set her bobbing, and a rush of nausea made her swim toward dry land and shade.

Back on the beach, while Clarabel stayed naked, Ysan kept on her now sodden T-shirt and briefs, letting them clam to her wet skin and dry in situ. Ysan was used to the sight of her friend's body with its pale freckled skin, pendulous breasts and rampant mahogany-coloured pubic hair. For the past year, they'd been sharing a flat along with two other women, and Clarabel would often wander or lounge about naked. In contrast, Ysan covered up.

As Ysan struggled with her nausea, Clarabel chattered incessantly about how Dingo kept slapping Ian and calling him names; how Abi and Alexi, flatmates back home, had bickered endlessly, seeming to love to hate each other – 'We won't end up like that, will we?' – and about how Maisie went topless, showing off her nipple rings. She'd shown off the rings down below too, just to the girls, behind rocks, giggling like little kids. Alexi had asked to wiggle one. Abi called her a pervert . . .

'Clarrie . . . Shut up! Just for a minute or two. Please.'

'OK, OK.'

Clarabel threw on a light dress, and sat in silence for a few moments. Ysan, pulling on her jeans, resumed the conversation. 'How about you and Antonio? Is that two men in two days?'

'No, as a matter of fact,' said Clarabel. 'Well, almost. But I said no.'

'You said no!'

'I do sometimes, you cheeky bitch. He was fun . . . and nice. But we didn't do it.' She winked. 'Maybe tonight.'

'Oh, Clarrie. Please be careful. You don't know the first thing about him.'

'That's where you're wrong. I did some digging while you were comatose.'

Raúl had told her that Antonio's father had been a schoolteacher in Spain, escaping during the civil war a week before Franco had rounded up all the 'intellectuals' in his town. For some reason – a long story involving Raúl's professor, Jim – the father ended up in the Pacific, on the mainland where he married a local girl. She died when Antonio was only eleven. Then a year ago, his father died too. Now Antonio was on his own. 'No brothers or sisters, no wife, no special girlfriend – one hundred per cent available!'

'Please, Clarrie?'

'What? You're such a killjoy. What's to worry about? You know the hand Sod dealt me. I've no chance of getting pregnant and Raúl's tests made sure we're all free of the clap. What can he possibly do to me, except give me a good rodding occasionally?'

'He can hurt you. That's what he can do – and in more ways than one.'

'No he can't. I'm immune.'

'OK, have it your way.' Ysan watched Clarabel shake sand out of her hair and pull her fingers through the tangles and knots. The simple action made her feel sad but touched by the huge affection she felt for Clarabel, a girl who had spent her childhood in a succession of foster homes and never known her biological parents. Pregnant at sixteen to her fourth foster father, she had a fall six months in and went through an emergency Caesarean and hysterectomy. The tiny baby wasn't even taken to intensive care. Clarabel held her in her arms until she died. For half an hour she had been a mother; it could never happen again.

While Clarabel was always bolder, more independent, Ysan often felt she was fulfilling the roles of both the stable mother and the inexperienced daughter her friend would never have. But for the most part, they just looked out for each other like sisters. 'So what *did* the pair of you do all night?' Ysan smiled. 'You couldn't talk to each other.'

'Never mind me. What about you? Did you and Raúl make like the apes before we all came back?'

'Clarrie, you know nothing about apes. But whatever you

mean, we didn't. We just talked until . . . I passed out. God, how embarrassing.'

Back at the base, Ysan and Clarabel breakfasted on crispbread and canned meat from the store and fruit left over from the night before. Then they made their way to the women's latrines, just as the boys were leaving theirs.

'You look shit, Barbie,' said Danny. 'Screwed your way to an alpha plus yet?'

'How many times?' added Dingo, swaggering by Danny's side.

Clarabel glared at them and steered Ysan inside. 'Piss off.'

Ysan gathered her sleeping bag, some biscuits and a bottle of water, and strode away to her tree, where she settled in the branches overlooking the racetrack. The chimps appeared and sat about, picking at fruit. Several of them curled up to sleep in the sun. Ysan, her head still pounding, was on the point of dozing herself when she heard Raúl shouting her name. Calling out, she guided him to the bushes directly beneath her.

'I still can't see you,' he said. 'Where are you?'

She had to shake and part the branches before he could see her. Then he climbed adeptly to her perch. 'Nice spot. So how's it going?'

'Fine. Quiet.'

An awkward silence followed. Ysan pretended to watch the chimps while wondering whether to apologise for the night before. But Raúl stepped in first. He shouldn't have left her there in that condition, even with Clarabel at hand. Before they could take the conversation further, a fight broke out among the chimps.

One of the females tried to grab another's baby, triggering a cascade of chasing and screeching. Raúl leaned into Ysan's shoulder, one arm behind her back to support himself so that he could point with the other. 'I think those two are sisters,' he said. 'The one doing the grabbing had a baby last October but seems to have lost it, so she's trying to steal another to take its place. Look at the other females . . . and how disinterested the male is . . .'

And so he went on, fired up by everything he saw, only calming when the chimps also calmed. Even then, he remarked on how the group rearranged itself after the skirmish.

'Shall I draw a map? Show who's sitting where?' she asked eagerly, easing back to rest against his arm.

'Up to you,' he shrugged, moving his arm away. 'It's your project.'

She began the sketch. Raúl watched her for a while. 'Are you making backups of your field notes? Keeping them in different places? Just in case?'

'All of them. Of course.'

'I thought *you* would be. I know Abi's not.' And then, he asked, 'Do you mind if I take off my shorts?'

Surprised but faking indifference, she made light of the suggestion. 'I guess that's up to you. If it really makes you more comfortable . . .' Her hands went clammy; her skin prickled. Was this some kind of clumsy pass, despite his vow of abstinence?

He shifted his position until his back was against a trunk, slipped off his shorts and held them in his hand as if intending to use them as a fly swat. 'Not embarrassing you, am I?' he asked. 'You must be getting used to me by now.'

He was partly right – she was getting used to him – but his nudity was still an uncomfortable distraction.

Raúl talked, seemingly trying to justify himself. He'd not only grown up amidst nudity, but also spent much of his working life amongst naked tribes. He was happy naked and miserable clothed – simple as that. Nothing to do with sex then? she wanted to ask, her mind spinning.

'You know that Attenborough film?' he continued. 'With the wild gorillas, where he's sitting with a group of them. One huge silverback male. Several females. Couple of babies too.'

Ysan nodded.

'I've done that. Sat with them. Shared their space. But naked. Can you imagine? Feeling so much part of their world.'

'The naked ape-watcher, eh? Sounds risky. What about nettles, thistles, mosquitoes?'

'All bearable for the most part. In order to keep a sense of, I don't know, anthropoid propriety.'

She smiled indulgently, then asked mischievously, 'Is that what works for Antonio too?'

'What do you mean?'

She was thinking of the naked pantomime, of course, but said, 'Last night's swim. With Clarabel.'

'Don't mock,' he said. 'Antonio might come across as crude, uncouth even. But there's a side to him you don't yet know.'

When young, Antonio had worked the islands near the mainland with his father, the pair of them diving naked from their boat for shells to sell in the mainland markets. Antonio had never lost that sense of naturalness he'd acquired as a child. It was one of the first things Raúl and he had discovered they shared, all those years ago, when they'd first met on the island – he one of Jim's students, Antonio there with his father. Almost misty-eyed at the memory he stared into the middle distance. So she sneaked a look at his penis.

Like the rest of him, its skin was tanned, and there was a dark blemish on the shaft, near the base. Hanging limp, with the foreskin pulled back, it looked bigger than her earlier, hazier, glimpses had suggested. In fact, it looked bigger than it should for one so flaccid – but what did she know? This was her first sustained close-up view of a man's genitals in bright light. Her half-dozen sexual encounters so far had been fast, furtive and under cover of darkness: the cramped back seat of a car; a coat-strewn room at a party; in her mother's lounge while her mother showered. On every occasion – before, during or after – she'd seen little and felt less, with any groping more to do with condoms than foreplay. But what she did know, even with her limited experience, was that at that moment Raúl certainly wasn't thinking about sex. There was no sign of it. Not a hint. Which was a pity because she was and had been ever since he'd stripped. Since hearing his vow, having sex with him had become an instant unquenchable obsession. She just needed him to give her a sign . . .

'Don't move,' he suddenly commanded.

'Why?'

'Just don't move,' he repeated, leaning precariously forwards, nearly falling on to her. He swished his shorts at the tree trunk above her head, grabbing on to her shoulder to keep his balance, then swished again and again.

She shrieked, pushed herself frantically back into the fork and in the process nearly kicked Raúl out of the tree as a large spider – the size of a saucer – parachuted past her, all the way down to the ground. She convulsed for several seconds after it had gone. Then, when blind panic subsided, she burst into tears, drawing her knees to her chin and hugging them tight.

'Hey. Hey,' said Raúl with a tiny laugh. 'It's OK. It's gone.' Moving as close as he could, he took hold of her hand. 'Not too keen on spiders, eh?'

She struggled to stem the tears and to rid herself of the image of the spider floating past. Raúl squeezed her hand and spoke soothing words. Slowly, she calmed.

'How long had it been there?'

'A while. That's why I took my shorts off. Just in case . . . I didn't fancy using my hand. Even I don't like them that big. I was hoping it would just go away without your seeing it.'

'Was it poisonous?'

'Only a little.'

'Only a little?'

'It wouldn't have killed you. You OK now?'

'Absolutely brilliant.'

* * *

In the days following the spider incident he spent more time with her than even she felt was fair. Each day, he'd join her in the tree for about five hours, and only then leave to visit South Bay to see how the others were getting on. One hour a day would have been nearer her share. The other students – with Abi predictably the most vociferous – saw his behaviour as favouritism and complained that they weren't getting the attention they expected from the man in charge. He told Ysan that he knew no better way of passing the time than being with her, in the orchard, watching and talking about apes. It was nearly a compliment, though she suspected a reverse order to the attractions was nearer the truth.

His phrase 'passing the time,' seemed particularly apposite, his manner comparable to that of a man whiling away his days at a pavement bar. A man, though, who was waiting for something – and with growing impatience. As Ysan grew to know his ways she began to notice when his normal insouciance gave way to an underlying restiveness.

A major reason Raúl preferred to pass his time at the orchard was of course his 'anthropoid propriety'. In the orchard with her he evidently felt he could be naked; with the others on the beach he evidently didn't. From the moment he'd removed his shorts to protect her from the spider, Ysan never again saw him wear clothes in the orchard. Arriving barefoot and naked, he would leave five hours later the same way. She just knew that if she'd ever claimed offence or embarrassment, her share of his time would drop.

Once she'd understood that his nakedness wasn't a prelude to sex, and excitement had passed through disappointment to resignation, she scarcely even noticed. Having seen every mole around his groin, every vein on his penis shaft, every crease of his foreskin – none of it meant anything any more. Of course, if she ever saw the thing erect and pointing in her direction it would be a different matter. But until then it was just one more part of his body.

Late in the afternoon four days after the spider incident, the chimps failed to appear even briefly and Raúl was restless, twitching, sighing, eyes studying the sky. 'There's a storm heading our way. A week ago, when we left the mainland, they were forecasting it for tonight but there's been no sign yet.'

'Rain?'

'Not in July. Just a gale and heavy seas.'

The storm was preying on his mind, though he wouldn't say why. When the time to visit South Bay had long passed, when the racetrack and orchard were darkened by late-afternoon shade, Ysan asked, 'Shouldn't you be going?'

'Not today,' he said. 'I'd rather stay with you. Do something interesting for once. Let's give up on the chimps and go look for rabbit skulls. Let's start where you saw the male cracking open the skull.'

Relocating the rock where M1 had cracked open the rabbit's skull took a while but, once found, the site didn't disappoint. Scattered amongst the mixture of grazed and tufted grass they found abundant signs that such events were by no means rare. There were several skull fragments of different ages, and when the pair of them knelt to examine the rock more closely, they saw a few fresh traces of blood and plenty of old bloodied stones.

'You were right,' he said.

'You mean you doubted me?' she smiled.

They stood and he returned her smile. 'OK, let's see what else we can find. I'll take the top half of the slope, you take the bottom. Back here in an hour.'

Ysan watched him walk off to make a start, his stringy gluteal muscles contracting and relaxing at each stride, a jauntiness in his gait. She was buzzing with excitement. They were going to do some research – *together*. Maybe he hadn't given up on her completely. Maybe everything was still possible. Maybe all she had to do was hang in there and be patient. Maybe, after everything, all she really had to do . . .

She sat down to take off her shoes. Stood and removed her jeans. He was watching her from across the racetrack, standing, smiling, gazing on while she unbuttoned her shirt then dropped it to the ground. She untied her bikini top – never once used for sunbathing – removed it, held it in the air and waved it at him, aware of her breasts swaying. He waved back. She dropped it and for a while she just stood there, thumbs on bikini bottoms, waiting as if teasing him, but in truth undecided, the last step seeming so huge.

'Is that all?' he shouted playfully from across the racetrack.

'Promise you won't laugh,' she shouted back, beginning to push down, feeling the garment falling, reaching her ankles.

She stepped out, naked alfresco for the very first time.

'About time too,' he called. 'See you later.'

He turned and carried on with his search. He would too, she told herself. Up close. She checked herself over, ruffling her fair pubic hair, flattened by clothing, to make it stand. Then, armed with nothing but a notepad and pencil, she set off across the soft grass to begin her part of the hunt.

As she walked, gusts of wind ruffled her tiny body hairs, cooled her sun-soaked skin, made her nipples stand erect and dried those parts that for two clothed decades had seemed continually clammy. Naked, her limbs seemed longer, her gait more fluid. She felt elegant, energised. Felt like running, for no other reason than to savour her newly discovered sense of freedom and grace. She felt strange. She felt good. And as each liberated step tugged at something intimate inside, she felt an erotic excitement that she dearly wished she could satisfy.

SEVEN

7–10 July 2006

A fternoons spent with Raúl carried a price for Ysan: hostility – jibes from Danny, obscenities from Dingo, the cold shoulder from Abi and ambivalence at best from the others. Ysan wasn't alone. Clarabel was paying much the same price for spending her afternoons with Antonio.

'I wouldn't mind if we really were having sex, like you two,' Ysan complained.

They discussed on and off whether a vow such as Raúl's could be broken – whether it *should* be broken. Or if it could be a cover for his not fancying her or for being impotent, psychologically scarred by the fact he'd been screwing around while his daughter was dying.

'Actually,' commented Ysan, 'I never have seen him up. Not properly.'

'Well there you go: erectile dysfunction. It's the only explanation with you going naked all the time with him.'

Although the pair were spending their afternoons with 'their' men, they weren't together in the evenings. From the second night onwards Raúl and Antonio vanished from the base soon after the evening meal. Nobody – neither Sledge nor the two women – was privy to where they went.

'Just old haunts,' was Raúl's stock answer, though once he disclosed to Ysan, 'Last night? Safe Harbour – to use the boat radio. Check on the storm.'

'In the dark?'

'In the moonlight,' he corrected. 'It's not a problem.'

There were bonuses to his absence: less drinking, less smoking, earlier nights, more sleep, even though that sleep was frequently interrupted by others coming late to bed. Henry, always drunk, was incapable of being quiet as Jill helped him up the awkward wooden steps, out of his clothes and into their sleeping bag. Sledge and Rose were quieter but prone to stifled laughter. Then, in the early hours, when Raúl and Antonio returned, mouse-quiet though they were, Ysan always woke and, as Raúl lay down just a metre away, she would gaze over to him, or sigh softly hoping to attract his attention. But he never spoke.

And there was another type of nocturnal disturbance too. Before this trip, Ysan had never heard other people having sex at such proximity. Yet now, rhythmic sounds and muffled giggles and groans could be heard at least once every night. All the advisers, married or not, had brought double sleeping bags, three of which were now cloaking couples. Couples who, as far as Ysan could tell, rarely missed a night. To Ysan's surprise, Henry and Jill were the noisiest. Henry managed to perform even when so drunk he could barely walk. Sledge and Rose were considerably quiet but not silent, and Clarabel and Antonio were only just the other side of Raúl, so she heard everything.

'Try and be quieter tonight,' Ysan urged Clarabel.

'Can't, sorry. And if you take my advice you'll stop pussyfooting, crawl into his bed and test his reflexes. And if we're wrong and he passes, for Christ's sake start making some noise of your own.'

The sexual restraint between Ysan and Raúl somehow led to its own intimacy. All the while they were up the tree together or in the orchard, they touched each other freely.

When they sat facing each other, feet played with feet. When they sat side by side, shoulder supported shoulder, arms draped waists and hands rested on thighs. Ysan's arousal never faded, as if her body expected an invitation at any moment. And once or twice Raúl's penis betrayed that it was intention not dysfunction preventing that invitation. Nevertheless Ysan felt they were lovers in all but deed. And that meant she felt free to ask questions that previously she would have censored. Some were frivolous: 'Raúl, when you were with the gorillas, did they take any notice of your bits?'

'My God, did they ... Couldn't leave them alone. Sniffing, poking. Even the silverback.'

'Weren't you scared?'

'What do you think? One yank from emasculation. One bite from being a eunuch. Of course I was scared.'

'And turned on?' she asked, more from genuine interest than a wish to tease.

'Not exactly,' he said with a muted grin.

Some questions were simple curiosity: 'Why did Antonio get himself snipped?'

'Pure stupidity!' At just twenty, Antonio had been obsessed with a woman twice his age who already had a family – four daughters – and wouldn't let him move in unless he was done. Then after just one year she went back to her husband. But that wasn't the worst of it, because a couple of years ago he'd paid a fortune to have the operation reversed, and the crooks had told him he was fertile again.

'But he's not? And *you* know and he doesn't?'

'I ran the test myself. Took a sample back to the lab after our last trip. Not a sperm in sight.'

'But you didn't tell him?'

'No. And neither must you.'

And one question was serious, concerned with her future: 'What are you going to do when the field trip is over?'

Raúl's mood immediately changed and at first he hedged. So she came right out with the real question that had been bothering her. 'How come you've never offered to supervise my doctoral studies?'

'You may as well know. I've had enough. Finished. Handed in my notice a month before we left. This trip is my last obligation.'

'Finished? With apes? I can't believe it.'

'Not with apes, of course not. They're all that's left. Finished with universities. Everything that goes with them. Cities, people. It's just one gigantic prison – no, a zoo. It's time I escaped.'

'Where to?'

'Don't know for sure. Somewhere without roads, without any bloody cars. Who knows? Maybe I'll live here. In the past I'd have loved to supervise you. Would have been proud to. I just don't want to be part of the system any more.'

'But . . . couldn't you supervise me here?'

She stopped in mid-plea, perplexed by the sight of him. He was shaking his head, a single tear trickling down his cheek. Seeing she'd noticed, he twisted to her and kissed her hard on the lips. So hard that it never became sensual.

'What's the matter?' she asked when they separated for air and balance. 'What did I say?'

He insisted it was nothing and seeing what a struggle he was having to regain his composure, she gave up. After an awkward interlude, he suggested they climb down the tree to search for stones and skulls again. To her relief, it wasn't the end of their intimacy. At the foot of the tree, they stopped to hug, front pressed against front, her nipples taut. Walking along the racetrack, they held hands, sometimes with fingers intertwined. And more than once they exchanged a gentle kiss. But other than that they simply worked, Raúl with total concentration, Ysan badly, her mind cluttered with images of carnal acts and the echoes of his whispers. She couldn't understand how he could resist. What strength of will, what clarity of purpose, what resolve was stopping him from sinking with her to the ground and giving their bodies free rein? She wanted him and to be his.

'Just one thing,' she said as Raúl prepared to leave for South Bay. 'Tonight . . . I want to sleep with you. Is that OK?'

When he raised his eyebrows, she lifted her palms and promised, 'Just sleep.'

Raúl left the base with Antonio after supper and returned later than on previous nights. But on his return, instead of settling down on his bag with his shorts on as usual, he slipped inside with them off. At which point, Ysan crawled across the moonlit roof and wriggled in beside him.

This would be her first full night with any man; the first time fully naked together; the first night stretching until dawn. And although the inside of his sleeping bag was hot like a sauna, the greater ambience – the brilliant moon, the ceiling of stars, even the hiss of a meteor – made the moment magical as she turned on to her side, pressed her breasts against his back and nuzzled his ear. He did little in return, but she still found herself dizzy with arousal.

She tried for a while to keep her hands to herself and let them rest where they fell. But hands being hands and sleeping bags being sleeping bags, at one point she wrapped her hand round something hard and froze. Raúl's reflexive groan of pleasure was followed quickly by the single word, 'Sleep.'

It took a while for her disappointment to settle, her self-esteem to mend and her hopes to rebuild, but eventually she did manage to doze. So did he. But neither of them would sleep for long.

Ysan woke around three in the morning, first to a sound she didn't recognise, then to Antonio speaking to Raúl.

'What's that noise? What did he say?' she whispered.

'He said, "Hear the lion? Hear it roar?"'

'Which means . . . ?'

'The storm's coming. About ten minutes away. Are you ready?'

The distant chaos drew nearer until it sounded like a train thundering down the mountain. Then a few light deliciously drying movements of warm air were followed by the first real gust, so strong it took Ysan's breath away.

Every loose object on the roof came to life. Sheets of paper swirled around. Water bottles fell over and rattled across the floor. An empty sleeping bag and lilo lifted into the air to fly across the roof like magic carpets. Springing from Rose's bed to stumble across the roof, Sledge was just too late to stop his bed gliding over the balustrade. Cursing, he fumbled for his shorts and plimsolls among the swirling debris then ran off in desperate pursuit. Reluctantly, Ysan left Raúl's bed to crawl back into her own, to weigh it down with her body, to prevent it taking wing as well. Sleeping with him until dawn would have to wait.

As Raúl had promised, the storm was dry – no rain or cloud, just a gale-force wind that howled over the roof. People zipped themselves into their sleeping bags and spent what was left of the night deafened and buffeted.

Raúl and Antonio left the base before daybreak and when Raúl returned alone in the late afternoon he was met by a tetchy inquisition from the other staff. But in high spirits, he didn't apologise. He and Antonio had been to Safe Harbour to make sure the boat was unharmed by the storm. But on the way back Antonio had suffered with his guts and elected to be ill in the forest rather than the camp, saying he'd meet them all when he felt better.

'I told him we'd be at South Bay,' Raúl continued. 'The waves should be fantastic with this wind. Good night for a beach party, don't you think?'

His gaze sought out Ysan and he winked.

EIGHT

The sun was setting as everyone trekked to the party, Ysan hanging back to leave with Raúl, helping him secure the base against the gale. He tore off half a dozen bin liners from a large roll and stuffed them in his pocket, throwing the rest of the roll for Ysan to carry.

'For rubbish?' she asked.

'And other uses,' he smiled. 'You'll see. A beach party's a beach party.'

Antonio was on the beach when they arrived, not at his best but with no intention of missing out. Barking orders in Spanish while Sledge did the same in English, he organised a bonfire in the centre of the beach, directing the lads to collect larger pieces of firewood. Once the flames had settled, he improvised a barbecue using stones. Then the alcohol was unleashed: cartons of something fruity and spirit-based, the labels indecipherable and slightly faded.

With the fire and the moonlight, the gale and the surf – and the unidentifiable drink – the group was soon animated. Despite the heat, people were drawn to the fire. Danny's group had water pistols and they ran shooting at each other and occasionally stalked the women. Conversations and laughter were punctuated by the crackling of the fire, the scream of wind in the palm trees, and the thundering of the distant waves.

The higher the others' spirits, the more keenly Ysan and Clarabel felt estranged from them. They sat apart, away from the fire, under the tree line at the back of the beach, waiting on the promise that Raúl and Antonio would join them. The two men talked earnestly, not drinking, and stood apart from the rest.

Eventually, Raúl and Antonio made their way up the beach towards the girls. En route, Antonio heaved a large branch on to the fire, releasing thousands of red sparks that were whisked away by the wind and doused by the sea. For a while, comfortable in each other's company, the four sat and scarcely spoke. Back by the fire, Jill instigated a drinking game, a 'boat race' – men against women. She shouted for them to join in, and when Raúl translated, Antonio grabbed Clarabel by the hand and dragged her down the beach to take part.

'What about his stomach?' asked Ysan.

Raúl shrugged.

Left alone, the pair sat shoulder to shoulder without speaking. On the sand they were sheltered, but the gale's fury still whipped the tops of the palms overhead, twigs and leaves intermittently raining to the ground. Looking at the distant fire and the laughing drunken silhouettes about it, Ysan placed her hand on Raúl's knee. He didn't respond.

'What is it?'

No answer.

'Come on, something's wrong. What is it?'

When he turned his head to face her, his eyes were wet, glistening in the moonlight. 'It's today,' he said, his voice almost a whisper. 'The anniversary.'

It took her a moment to realise what he was telling her.

'A year ago today.' Teardrops collected in the corners of his eyes. He looked away.

'I'm sorry. I didn't . . . How old was she? Your daughter?'

'A bit younger than you. Couple of years, maybe.'

An excited shout came from the fire. The first contest had finished. Plastic beakers were refilled for a second. A gust of wind howled through the treetops.

'Was she like you? Did she look like you?'

Raúl smiled, 'Not a bit,' then swallowed hard, the profile of his Adam's apple beneath his beard rising then falling. 'Her hair was fair . . . As fair as yours. Blue eyes too . . .' He swallowed again. 'The brakes failed. On a cliff road. They went over the edge, on to rocks and into the sea.' He took a deep breath. 'They found Carina's body about a kilometre along the coast. Clothes gone. Flesh completely cooked. Never found our daughter . . .'

A tear moved down his cheek and disappeared into his beard. Another gathered on the end of his nose.

Ysan pulled him to her, let his face nuzzle into her neck, the tears trickle inside her shirt and down the valley between her breasts. She kissed his hair and forehead, his eyebrows, his eyes. She inhaled the acetone smell of tears and distress, the heavy scent of male underarm. She could think of nothing to say. She'd never been in this position before, with a man, a man she cared about. With Clarabel, yes. With girlfriends during her schooldays, lamenting a lost boyfriend or a failed exam. But nothing like this.

'I still dream,' Raúl mumbled at one point, 'still fantasise that one day somebody will tell me it was all a mistake. That she isn't dead. Can you imagine how that would feel? She should have lived here. Somewhere like this.'

Around the fire, the drinking game ended. People milled about still laughing. Then on a swirl of wind, between the roar of waves, Ysan heard the phrase 'skinny dipping'. Jill was excitedly trying to recruit all around her. And she and Abi were soon both beckoning Raúl. Ysan held him closer, but Raúl raised his head from her shoulder, wiped his eyes and nose with the back of his hand and shouted over with a cracked voice that he was on his way. Rising, he helped Ysan to her feet.

'You don't have to go,' she said.

'A swim might do me good.'

Pulling her to him, he delivered a gentle kiss made wet by tears, followed by a simple 'Thank you.'

By the time Ysan and Raúl reached the fire, the others were out of sight in the water. A towel on the sand caught the wind and began to move, flapping and jumping like a bird with a broken wing.

Raúl took the bin liners from his pocket and asked Ysan to help him collect all the towels, clothes and shoes that were scattered around, to prevent them being blown away or buried. When the task was complete, Ysan went back to the fire and found Raúl staring blankly into the flames. 'Shall we join the others?'

He made to push down his shorts but she told him to stop. 'Let me.' She knelt on the sand to pull them down and help him step out. While kneeling she lightly kissed the shaft of his penis. Just butterfly kisses at first, but enough to make him grow, inviting further kisses. When at last she stood, her thoughts scrambling and body surging, he responded in kind by undressing her, first top then bottom, and when on his knees he gently buried his face between her thighs. After a few moments, Ysan dropped to her knees again so they could embrace and kiss, until she said urgently, 'Please! Here on the sand . . . in the firelight.'

Toppling Raúl to the ground, she straddled him and eased him inside her. But he climaxed quickly and at the last moment withdrew, groaning more in anguish than pleasure.

She was disappointed but ached with guilt. She wanted to soothe him, even apologise, but as she hesitated, and before the riot within her body had a chance to subside, he was on his feet. For a moment she thought he might stride off and leave her, but he paused before the snap and rush of the flames, as if mesmerised by the fire.

As remorse, disappointment and frustration all twisted

about inside her, Ysan distracted herself by collecting her clothes from where Raúl had thrown them and the wind had scattered them. Separating out her bikini, she shoved the rest into one of the bags, then turned to Raúl. Screwed-up shorts in hand, he continued to stare at the blazing branches. Suddenly he threw the shorts into the flames. They both watched them burn.

'What did you do that for?'

'I'll manage. Come on, let's go.'

Near the cliffs, Ysan bent to step into her bikini bottoms.

'What are you doing?' Raúl's voice was quiet and his tone almost nonchalant again. 'It's a midnight swim.'

'I don't care. With you I'll be naked. Whenever. Wherever. But not in front of Danny or Dingo.'

Before Raúl could answer, before Ysan could dress, somebody staggered into the cove. A woman, silhouetted, in the act of unlacing the top of her bikini. She stumbled and nearly fell. 'Raúl. Where are you?' It was Abi. She was drunk. 'Raúl, it's me. Where *are* you?'

He stepped from the shadows.

Abi's laugh was so hard it broke into a shriek. 'Raúl, are you alone? Have you got rid of her?'

Weaving towards him, she tried to push her bikini bottoms down but tripped and sprawled in the sand. Raúl walked over and reached down to help her. But rather than be lifted, she climbed up his body to wrap her arms round his neck. She kissed him. Gently, Raúl tried to push her away and told her to stop, but she ignored him and swung about his neck, trying to bring their lips together.

Naked, Ysan walked into the moonlight. Pretending she didn't know Abi was there, she talked loudly to Raúl and made a show of using her bikini to wipe between her legs. 'I can't believe I'm still leaking.' Then she said, 'Oh . . . Hi, Abi. Trouble standing?' Ysan walked to Raúl's side. He was now holding an unsteady Abi by her elbows at arm's length. Ysan leaned against his shoulder to support herself while stepping into her bikini bottoms.

Abi's face twisted into something horrible. 'Bitch! Fucking whore!' She stepped back and looked at Raúl in astonishment before her face crumpled. She turned quickly and stumbled away, only pausing to snatch up her bikini from the sand.

Ysan reached behind herself to secure her bikini top. 'Sorry. Couldn't resist.'

Raúl shook his head. 'Doesn't matter. Nothing matters. Not any more.'

Although the group had stripped on the main beach, Antonio had led them to swim in a more sheltered bay further away, taking the remaining alcohol too. And when Raúl and Ysan arrived, most of the others were now sitting on the sand, drinking. Only Clarabel and Antonio were still in the water, Clarabel on Antonio's shoulders, legs wrapped round his neck. Choosing the moment, Antonio dived forwards, catapulting Clarabel screaming into a huge breaking wave. As Antonio surfaced, Raúl waved, and the boatman abandoned Clarabel and struck out for shore as if having something urgent to say. Back on land, he ran past them all, only turning his powerful head to mutter a few words to Raúl, who immediately followed him up the beach.

'What's wrong?' asked Ysan, feeling a jolt of déjà vu.

'It's his guts again. Stay here. Have a drink before it's all gone. I'll make sure he's OK, then leave him to it.'

Fifteen minutes later Raúl was back and breathless.

'How is he?' asked Ysan, offering him the plastic cup full of punch she'd been saving.

Raúl downed it in a gulp. 'He'll live. He's gone for another swim. To wash it off.' Raúl seemed restless, excited. He glanced with short sharp turns of the head from sea to beach and at the people scattered about. Ysan offered to get him another drink and when she returned asked if they could go somewhere else to drink it. Somewhere quiet. But Raúl demurred, saying he was worried about Antonio.

'I don't understand,' said Ysan.

'Don't understand what?'

'I don't understand you.'

'Who understands anybody?'

'I want to finish what we started. I thought you'd want to as well. Now that . . .'

'It's still complicated.'

'Is it? Are you sure? We go somewhere quiet. We have sex. We both feel good. How complicated is that? You made your gesture. Far more than most men could manage.'

Raúl downed his drink, gave a quick look out to sea, scrunched his plastic cup, threw it away, then looked at her. 'I'm not treating you very well, am I?'

The next time it lasted longer and brought another first for Ysan – she came during intercourse. And long after she finished, Raúl kept going. 'I want to remember,' he said, while kissing every part of her face.

'Me too,' she said, savouring his heightened pleasure. When the end came it was sudden, but he still found time to withdraw.

'You know I'm on the pill.'

He didn't respond and she didn't push him. Instead, she lay on the sand, wrapped in his arms and knew she was falling further with every kiss and caress. But soon he became restless. 'Antonio?' she asked.

Raúl nodded, then hauled himself to his feet. 'I can see the beach. He's not come ashore. He's been out there for at least an hour now. I'd better go and check.'

Ysan put her bikini back on and wandered out of their dark cove. Raúl ran across the beach and dived into the sea. She could see Antonio too. Raúl reached him and the two men trod water side by side before leisurely swimming ashore, like a scene she'd watched before. As the two men left the water, Raúl shouted across to Henry and Jill. 'See that? The glow in the sky?'

'It's the lights at the base,' said Jill.

'But nobody's there.'

'Maybe someone's gone back. Sledge and Rose . . .' But on hearing their names the pair stood up.

'I'd better go back and have a look,' said Raúl. 'I'll take Antonio. You'd better come too, Sledge. Have you seen it?'

'It's just the lights, isn't it?'

'They weren't on. I was last to leave.'

'Why do you need me?'

Raúl was adamant. 'Sledge, I want you to come with us. Now.'

'Bloody hell. Let me get dressed. I need shoes.'

In the cove, Sledge paced about in the sand, frantic. 'Where the hell are our clothes?'

Raúl raised his hands. 'They were here when Antonio and I came back from the woods.'

'Well they're not here now?' Rising in anger, Sledge's voice echoed off the wet rocks.

As the two men fell to arguing – Raúl claiming the bags must have been washed away and Sledge accusing Danny and his mates of playing a practical joke – Rose ran to the smaller bay to see if anyone had a torch, only to return with no torch but more people. Soon all fifteen, and all of them but Ysan, Abi and Alexi still naked from skinny-dipping, were milling in the moonlight and shadows, searching and getting in each other's way. Sledge quizzed Danny so aggressively that his frightened denial was too convincing for even a practiced liar and Dingo began to bristle, telling Sledge to 'Lay off him.'

Eventually, Raúl called out to them all. 'Our clothes are not here. With the tops tied, the bags must have been blown into the sea. There's nowhere else they could be.'

Sledge grimaced. 'This wind's off-shore. They'll already be miles out there.'

As a group they hurried down the beach and tramped the tide-line looking for bags, clothes, shoes – anything. From time to time someone would shout a warning and they'd all scurry up the beach with an extra-large wave snapping at their heels. Agitated, some began complaining about the loss of a favourite top or sandals. Clarabel saw humour in the sight of so many naked people searching for their clothes. But Sledge, wading through the shallows, was apoplectic. He'd had a brand-new army knife and an expensive watch in his shorts pockets. When a wave knocked him off his feet, and he crashed to his hands and knees bellowing in frustration and anger, Clarabel had to turn away and stifle a giggle.

Firing staccato Spanish at each other, Raúl and Antonio began pointing out to sea. Then Antonio ran into the water and swam to a rock sticking out from the surface. When he returned, he was holding Rose's white bikini top in one hand and a shredded black bin bag in the other. Taking charge, declaring that all the clothes discarded were lost, Raúl announced that he, Antonio and Sledge would go back to the base and bring people what they could.

Sledge threw his arms into the air. 'We can't bloody go like this.'

'We've no choice.'

'But we've got nothing on our feet.'

'I'll go with you,' said Ysan. 'I've got shoes. I left them under the palms.'

'Four of us, then,' said Raúl. 'That's more to help carry.'

Raúl and Antonio set off at pace, and wearing trainers Ysan managed to stay close behind them, but Sledge lagged, cursing at every step. Pummelled by the gale and deafened by the wind crashing into the palms, they crossed the wooded ridge between the beach and base, but as they neared camp the glow in the sky grew brighter. Nobody spoke, but long before they arrived they knew what they would find.

'Fucking hell,' said Sledge when he at last caught up with the others to see the fire. The storage room had already collapsed. Somehow, the blackened skeleton of the main building was still standing until most of that crashed to the ground too, catapulting sparks and burning wood across the clearing. Ysan, Raúl and Antonio stood still, speechless. Secondary fires began but in the lush vegetation they slowly died.

Sledge was first to speak. 'God, Raúl. Everything was in there. Clothes, bedding . . .'

'And food,' added Raúl. 'And medicine. Absolutely everything. We've lost everything.'

'How the hell?'

'The generator maybe. A cigarette. What does it matter now?'

'What the fuck are we going to do?'

'I don't know.'

Raúl looked first at Ysan, then exchanged looks with Antonio before announcing that he and Antonio would fetch the boat from Safe Harbour and pick everybody up from South Bay in the morning. Then they'd all sail to the mainland. Antonio had clothes on the boat so he could go ashore and buy clothes for everybody. Get them ashore too.

'Then what?' said Sledge.

Raúl shrugged. 'What do you think? No shelter, no food. We go home. Game over.'

Ysan's thoughts were frantic. Nothing logical or tangible in them, just a terrible instinctive feeling that if she let Raúl and Antonio out of her sight she would never see them again. Her voice shaking, she told Raúl she was going to Safe Harbour with them.

'No. You'll slow us down.'

'I won't! You know I won't.'

'No!' His tone was final. 'This time you really would. It's black in there. You don't know the path. You'd be cut to ribbons.'

'Then you may as well all wait till morning,' Sledge said. 'No point you trekking across the island in the dark.'

'It's no big deal,' said Raúl, already moving away with Antonio. 'We're used to it. We know the tracks. The sooner we get the boat to South Bay the better.'

Ysan watched them leaving and shuddered. She felt abandoned. In desperation, she ran after them and grabbed Raúl by the shoulders. 'Please take me with you. Don't leave me here.'

Raúl glanced at Antonio and with a gesture of his head indicated that he should move on.

'You can't come. Trust me. You'll thank me, you'll see.' He was cupping the back of her head, vigorously stroking her hair, but in a hurry to be gone. 'See you in the morning.' He kissed her hard, then turned and ran, leaving Ysan trembling with panic as the bright bodies of the two naked men were sucked into the impenetrable dark of the forest.

NINE

S ledge's feet were a painful mess. With her shoulder under his sweaty armpit, Ysan did her best to be a crutch for the big man, but struggled to support his weight. At each step he yelped, and after only a few metres had to stop.

'Let me go back to South Bay for help.'

'One more try,' he begged. But again his feet failed.

As Sledge lowered himself abjectly to the ground, Antonio came towards them, also limping. Rarely had Ysan been so pleased to see anybody. Her feelings of abandonment lifted. The Spaniard slumped beside Ysan and began massaging his right ankle.

'Can you speak Spanish?' Ysan asked Sledge, her own half-dozen words not enough to ask Antonio what had happened.

'I can order a beer,' Sledge said through gritted teeth.

Bypassing words, Ysan pointed to Antonio's foot. His gestures in reply confirmed he'd tripped and turned his ankle. Then she spoke Raúl's name and pointed towards Safe Harbour. Antonio replied by also speaking Raúl's name, pointing towards Safe Harbour and adding, '*Mañana*. South Bay.' *Mañana* they all understood.

Leaving the men to nurse their injuries, Ysan returned alone to South Bay, picking her way in the moonlight between trees and bushes. The moment she appeared, she was bombarded with questions.

'Where are the others?'

'Was it a fire?'

'Did you bring clothes?'

'Shut up and listen,' yelled Rose, taking charge. 'Go ahead, Ysan. Tell us what's happened.'

Ysan told her story to an increasingly dismayed and horrified audience, before turning to Rose and saying that Sledge and Antonio needed her urgently and she'd take her to them.

Once with the men, the ex-nurse could do little. Neither the light from the burning base nor the brightest moonlight was enough to see clearly. Only the men's reactions as she carefully poked, prodded and bent their feet could tell her how bad their injuries were. The best she could do until daylight, she said, was protect Sledge's feet from infection and strap Antonio's ankle – but both needed bandages. Ysan offered her bikini which Rose accepted gratefully. 'Now go back to the others. We'll need Abi and Alexi's bikinis too. And see if you can find my white top. I still had it earlier.'

For the fourth time that night, Ysan picked her way between base and beach. Hung over, dehydrated, and in pain front and back from scratches, she also felt energised by a sense of purpose, the challenge and the exertion. Clear of the trees she ran down the slope and through the palms, so intent on her errand she'd all but forgotten her nakedness – until she was greeted by a chorus of wolf whistles and comments.

Clarabel jumped to her feet and sidled over to Ysan.

'What a crowd,' she said. 'Danny and Dingo are being total assholes, the girls are whining and Henry's being sick. Listening to Abi, you'd think all this happened just to spite her.'

Ysan walked over to Abi and passed on Rose's request.

'Good one,' she said. 'Nearly fooled me.'

'I'm serious. There's nothing else for a bandage. Alexi, you too.'

'Sure. As soon as the moaning cow gives you hers.'

Maisie scuttled to Ysan's side with Rose's white bikini top, then joined Alexi and Ysan in haranguing Abi, telling her not to be so stupid and selfish.

'No. Sod off, all of you.'

Finally, Ysan lost her temper and yelled: 'Danny, Dingo, get those damn clothes off her!'

Danny whooped with delight and the four lads all moved eagerly in Abi's direction. The threat worked.

'Don't you fucking dare.' Abi unclipped her top. Still spoiling for a fight, she added a condition. 'It's yours in exchange for those trainers. It's your fault everyone else's were lost.'

'Don't be ridiculous. I've got to get back to Rose before the moon sets. I've got to run.'

'OK, run,' said Abi. 'But as soon as it's light, as soon as you've finished pretending to be such a hero, the shoes are mine. Deal?'

Short of time, Ysan agreed. Abi peeled off her bikini and threw it to the ground for Ysan to pick up, then Alexi elegantly donated hers in her turn.

Ysan sprinted from the palm trees back up the hill to Rose.

As the sun rose, the quartet slowly made their way from the ruins of the base to the waterfall. Antonio led the way, hobbling to relieve his strapped-up ankle; the two women followed, helping Sledge. Once there, Rose sat him near the water and removed thorns and spikes from his feet one by one with her nails. His soles were completely swollen. After washing him gently, Rose re-bandaged as best she could, stroked his thigh and gave him a sympathetic smile.

Driven by thirst, the rest of the group arrived from South Bay. The sight of them was a shock to Ysan. The night before in the moonlight, bodies had been seen but not seen, as if wearing body stockings. Now, in the clearing in daylight, bodies shone in sharp relief. Ysan was so absorbed in the novel pageant she forgot her own bright nakedness for a while. It was the sheer variety that intrigued her most: Rose's dark skin and Alexi's pale brown amongst the many shades of pink; Clarabel's and Jill's curvaceousness alongside Alexi's and Maisie's boyishness; Dingo's muscularity against Ian's feebleness; Clarabel's sprawling mahogany carpet compared with Alexi's neat little black triangle and Maisie's shaved furrow; Ian's tiny penis against Pete's heavy genitalia. Ysan had genuinely never known the male organ could be so big when floppy. What did he do with it when wearing clothes? She was totally fascinated.

'Shoes!' demanded Abi, holding out a hand. 'I'm not putting my feet through that again.'

Abi's face was blotched by the remains of yesterday's make-up; the long blonde hair was now tangled, not sleek; her figure was shapely, but her nipples were so pale, her breasts looked malformed, like a face without eyes – and, an extra surprise, her narrow streak of pubic hair, trimmed for a thong, wasn't fair but jet black.

'Are you handing them over or what?'

Ysan dropped her trainers at Abi's feet.

Everybody was staring and comparing, bingeing on sights previously censored. But nothing was said. Not even Danny and Dingo made bawdy mileage from the group's misfortune; everyone's body language betrayed thirst and heat more than shame and discomfort. Ysan found herself neither embarrassed nor particularly self-conscious. Everybody she could see had some feature to be proud of; everybody also had imperfections. Which of her parts were which, she'd wait for others to proclaim, but she saw little to fear from comparison, not even with Abi. In fact, as she watched the blonde strutting around with her nippleless breasts and uncoordinated landing strip, she felt a glow of self-satisfaction.

Rose, skin glistening in the dappled sunlight, stood on the bank by the poolside and clapped her hands to attract attention. Raúl could arrive at South Bay at any moment, she said, and would probably expect them to be there ready for an early start back to the mainland. But it was important they didn't rush this visit to the pool. 'Drink plenty of water,' she said, 'especially if you've got a hangover. It might be a while before you can drink again.'

They needed to eat too, and collect food for the journey. Rose asked Clarabel to try to find out from Antonio where he and Raúl used to collect the fruit.

'I know where it is,' Ysan said.

As soon as they had all slaked their thirst, Ysan led the assembly downhill to the orchard, taking them through the tunnel 'nose to bum', in Clarabel's words. 'I wish I'd brought my sketchpad,' she joked, clambering on all fours behind Pete.

'I wish I'd got my glasses,' mumbled Ian, just behind her.

The orchard vista amazed them all. Ysan was struck by how possessive she'd become, dismayed at the sight of 'her' fruit trees being ransacked, and the chimps and rabbits scampering away from the invasion. Eventually Rose insisted they all return to South Bay. They should make baskets out of large leaves, she instructed, to carry as much food as they could for the journey – but they shouldn't dawdle as it was almost midday. Raúl could have been waiting for an hour or more, wondering what had happened to them. Maybe worrying.

But when they arrived at South Bay, Raúl was not there.

With nothing to do but wait for Raúl to arrive with the boat, everybody settled to doze in the shade of the palms. They'd been active all morning after a long night with little sleep. Ysan dropped off like the rest, but worrying about Raúl and their predicament she couldn't help waking every few minutes to scan the sea. Each time she hoped to see the fishing boat rounding the eastern headland or chugging across the bay, but it never came. She was finally woken by flying sand as Antonio lurched past on his way to the sea. Watching him, she was reassured by his presence, until a sudden thought drove her to join Sledge and Rose, who were just waking.

'Sledge,' she said, giving him a chance to focus on her. 'Which ankle had Antonio injured when he arrived at the base last night?'

'Didn't notice. I had enough problems of my own.'

Ysan turned to Rose. 'I'd have sworn it was his right. But you've strapped his left.'

'That's the one he said. To be honest, neither of them looked particularly swollen to me, and he's hardly limping now.'

Ysan left them, following Antonio's tracks to the open beach until sun-baked sand burned her feet, making her skirt round the cliff-shaded perimeter instead. By the time she reached the water's edge, Antonio had swum the bay and hauled himself on to rocks at the far end of the eastern headland, from where he scanned the sea in the direction of the castle. Staying in the shade, Ysan waited for him to return.

'No Raúl?' she asked as he reached her. He shook his head and reeled off a few sentences which seemed to be saying he was worried.

'I worry, too,' she said. 'I want to go . . . Safe Harbour.' She pointed at herself and in the direction she thought was correct. 'You take me.' She pointed again. 'Now. We go. Yes? *Si*?'

He pointed at her bare feet.

'No problem. I manage,' she said and in return pointed at his ankle.

'*Mucho mejor. No problema*,' he said, stamping his strapped foot on the damp sand and he started back across the beach with an easy stride.

'Why not just let Antonio go?' said Rose with concern when Ysan explained her plan.

'I need to know Raúl is safe. He might be lying injured in the forest. I can't just sit here waiting for news.'

'Raúl will be fine,' said Sledge, his fair eyebrows knitted with frustration and anger. 'It'll be the bloody boat. It was all but fucked on the way over. Probably hasn't started. Raúl will be radioing for help – if the radio's still working. We could be here for days. Maybe I should go. I'd soon fix it.'

'Not on those feet,' said Rose. 'And Ysan, I'm not sure you should go either, but I can see nothing's going to stop you.'

Antonio walked briskly, leaving Ysan to follow as best she could without hurting her feet. From the moment they entered the forest, flies swarmed around their faces and groins, feeding off Ysan's weeping scratches from the night before and seeding thoughts of infection. Just after the waterfall, Antonio gave a hoot of delight, sprinted over to a particular tree and returned with a few sprigs. Stripping off a handful of leaves, he crushed them in his nicotine-stained, hairy-backed hands, then rubbed the juice all over his forehead, genitals and thighs.

'*Las moscas ... No les gusta. El olor,*' he explained, waving at the flies then holding his nose.

Ysan took some leaves and crushed them. Smelling the result, she agreed with the flies. The juice was acrid. She rubbed some on her forehead then hesitated.

'Is it OK?' she asked, indicating the scratches on her front.

'*Si! Si!*' he said, gesturing her to turn round, leaving her to rub juice on her breasts and tummy while he did the same on her back.

'*Gracias,*' she said. Turning round she was amused to see that touching her had aroused him.

'*De nada,*' he replied perkily, before setting off at pace up the hill.

Antonio's herbal treatment was far more effective than Ysan had believed possible. Otherwise she would not have heard the muffled distant buzzing of flies that attracted her to investigate a clump of bushes beyond the trail. Parting the branches, she was engulfed by noisy insects until waving them away she saw – between leaves and in shadow – part of a bearded face. Gasping, she clapped her hands to her face and closed her eyes. 'Antonio!'

She looked again, unable to breathe, and was sure her heart had stopped beating. But this time she realised the tortured statement of a body in the undergrowth was actually a male chimpanzee. And one so recently dead the blood oozing from its mouth was still shiny-wet. It was M3.

Antonio ran over. She pointed at the body and then mimed an attack. 'What killed him?'

He shrugged. '*Los otros chimpancés.*'

Ysan looked at the bloody face one last time. 'Don't suppose you know of a plant that keeps away killer chimpanzees, do you?' But she was too frightened to even smile at her own joke.

From the waterfall onwards, the forest floor was carpeted with soft leaves, allowing Ysan to travel easily and keep up with Antonio. But the open areas they had to skirt because of the shrubbier vegetation and its sticks, spines and thorns. On one such stretch, for the sake of speed and Ysan's feet, Antonio gave her a piggyback. She felt weak but grateful too. Arms round his sweating neck, breasts against his hairy shoulders, groin against his backbone, her whole body bouncing and rubbing against him, she couldn't stop herself feeling aroused. But when he set her down on soft ground she also couldn't stop marvelling at the speed with which his ankle had healed.

Further on, they crossed two drying streams. At the second, Antonio removed the grubby strapping that had once been Abi's bikini, and offered it to Ysan. Pulling a face, she threw the material to the ground and trod it into the mud. Antonio grinned his approval. When they finally descended to Safe Harbour through a last stretch of softly carpeted woodland, Ysan guessed the entire trek had taken about an hour and a half, and to her immense relief, thanks to Antonio's attentiveness, her feet had coped.

The spectacular vista at Safe Harbour was similar to that at South Bay and Orchard Bay: black sand, palm trees and tall cliffs leading out to sea as rocky headlands. But here the bay was more enclosed, almost circular, and the cliffs were higher. At sea level were a number of rocky overhangs guarding deep caves. Ysan could see immediately why this was a safer place to moor a boat than South Bay.

'No boat?' she asked Antonio.

He shook his head, pointed towards one of the overhangs and spoke quickly with what she understood to be relief. Whatever else had happened, Raúl had at least arrived here fit enough to get to the boat and set sail.

'So . . . Raúl . . . South Bay?' she asked.

Antonio crossed his fingers. '*Si! Vamos!* South Bay.' They turned and set off back the way they'd come.

Ysan didn't follow immediately, arrested by the sudden realisation that she'd been looking at the back of the castle. The top of the southern headland of Safe Harbour was unmistakeably the same landmark she'd noticed from South Bay and elsewhere. Suddenly, she had her bearings. Antonio had taken her in a large semi-circle round to the far side of the ridge that she'd once climbed in search of Raúl. The journey would have been much shorter had they taken the path she'd taken that day. But maybe, without the fierce sun and vicious plants, Antonio's was a better route.

'*Vamos!*' Antonio shouted from up the slope.

'I'm coming,' she shouted back.

The thought that spurred Ysan on during their trek back to South Bay was that by now Raúl would be there – and waiting, probably fretting to get under way before dark. If he wasn't . . . she couldn't allow herself to consider such a thing.

As she and Antonio neared the waterfall clearing they were half an hour away from sunset, but the forest was darkening. Although glades were still brightened by shafts of orange sunlight, spotlights for dancing flies, large areas were already grey and colourless, as shapes and shadows merged. Ysan gestured that she needed a drink and a shower. Antonio agreed. But approaching the fall, its waters still silver in the gloom, its sound more a gurgle than a thundering, they saw black shapes move in the mist: a group of chimpanzees. Ysan counted ten. And the air was suddenly thick with the smell of their shit.

Antonio shouted to scare the apes away, but they stood their ground. He shouted again, then picked up sticks and threw them, but the chimps were unperturbed. So he ran at them, bellowing as he drew near. The line parted, giving him passage to the water, but then closed ranks behind him. Suddenly Ysan found herself cut off from Antonio and the pool with two images jostling in her mind: Raúl and his lack of concern among thirty chimps and the bloody face of M3 in the undergrowth.

So when several chimps moved towards her, she panicked. Walking backwards, she tripped. Scrabbling back to her feet, she slipped. Darting away from the nearest chimp, she encountered another. They were surrounding her.

'Antonio!' she screamed at the figure now treading water in the centre of the pool.

'*Venga!*' he called back, beckoning her with both hands.

Ysan dithered, her nerve failing as the chimps drew nearer. Scenes of carnage jumped into her mind: rabbits beheaded in the orchard; monkeys disembowelled by chimps in Raúl's book. She froze, her instinct to flee wrestling with the conscious thought that attack would be better than the horror of being pursued. She took a deep breath, counted to three and, eyeballing the chimp nearest to her, sprinted forwards, flapping her arms ludicrously and shouting wildly.

The chimp hesitated, moved a little, then turned and ran. So did the others, leaving Ysan a free path to the bank and the water. Antonio laughed and applauded as she leaped in.

TEN

11–12 July 2006

On the slope down to South Bay, Ysan overtook Antonio in her desire to see Raúl. She was greeted by Rose, shouting from the semidarkness. 'Did you find him? Please say you found him.'

'He isn't here? But the boat's gone. He should be here.'

Rose buried her face in her hands. After a deep breath, she looked up and led Ysan by the hand towards Sledge. 'He must have stepped on something poisonous in the dark. Or got ape shit in the wounds or something. But he needs antibiotics. If this infection goes systemic, if he gets septicaemia here . . . He's a strong man but . . .'

Sledge was lying under the palm trees propped on one elbow, face drawn with pain. Even in the meagre light from the rising moon, Ysan could see how his feet, ankles and legs were swollen to the knee.

'So where is he?' Clarabel sounded more mystified than concerned. 'If he's not at Safe Harbour and he's not here . . .'

Maybe she and Antonio had only just missed him, Ysan suggested, trying to keep the note of desperation from her voice. But maybe the boat had broken down when he was just out of sight? Or he was injured and couldn't get back? There was nothing anybody could do in the dark, but if he wasn't back by morning, they'd need to check the coastline and see if he was stuck somewhere.

'Might he have gone straight to the mainland?' asked Clarabel. 'Called in here while we were all at the waterfall, couldn't see us, so just set off?'

'Not without Antonio.'

Raúl had once told her that the islands were surrounded by tricky reefs, rocks and currents. There were no reliable charts. A light boat could go in a straight line, but not the fishing boat. Raúl knew the waters pretty well, but Ysan was sure he wouldn't leave without Antonio unless there was no alternative.

'Talk to me,' she said, peeling a banana. 'Stop me falling asleep while I eat. I'm starving. What did you all get up to today?'

'Not much,' shrugged Clarabel. 'Just sat in the shade and waited for the boat. Really boring. Oh ... except for the Oscars.'

For entertainment, the lads had decided they were going to award Oscars for different parts of the female body. Immediately, Abi had proclaimed it degrading and stalked away, but Alexi, Maisie and she had joined in, even voted.

'It was fun,' Clarabel said, chuckling. 'They started on nipples, then breasts, then bushes ...'

Ysan listened, nibbling sleepily, idly wondering if she'd been mentioned. Abi's nipples had won 'weirdest', Rose's 'most suckable'. Clarabel's breasts won 'best earmuffs' and her pubic hair 'best rug' ...

The list became more pornographic, Rose's mouth winning the *Deep Throat* award, and Alexi 'best supporting actress' to Abi in an imagined threesome. Ysan nearly drifted off, not concentrating again until Clarabel piqued her curiosity. 'You got one or two as well, but I'm not telling in case they go to your head.'

It took Ysan several minutes of cajoling before she'd let on.

'OK, promise you won't crow . . . Pertest tits, sexiest bum and . . . you also got the Grand Prix – the Golden Hole. Yep, your cunt. They voted mine most fucked and yours most fuckable. Cheeky buggers.'

'But when would they . . .'

'When it comes to seeing women's bits, the lads' eyes are like lasers. All afternoon they've been staring, eyes glued to our groins, riveted, waiting for the next glimpse. You can bet they got an eyeful before you went off on your excursion. Guess what Alexi thinks? She reckons this wasn't an accident. That it's all deliberate: the lost clothes, the base burning down. She reckons the lads did it, so they could flash and gawp at us.'

'So that was your afternoon? All tits and cunts.'

'More or less. We all got thirsty but nobody could be bothered to go to the waterfall. So we managed on coconut milk instead. Rose kept telling us it was a laxative but . . . well, what the hell. But have you any idea how difficult it is to open a coconut with just a rock? Anyway, eventually the lads decided they'd go to the orchard for fruit. For all of us, not just themselves. Probably went for a wank too, the state they were in. We talked about that a bit. And of course we wondered how you were getting on.'

'Were you worried?'

'Not really. You had Antonio with you. How was he, by the way? I hope you kept your hands off each other.'

'Of course!'

'Really? He didn't try anything on. Even alone and starkers with this year's pertest, sexiest and most fuckable.'

Ysan buried her banana skin and curled up on the warm sand. 'He was the perfect gentleman.'

Waking to daylight, Ysan was beckoned down to the beach by Clarabel.

'Look,' she said when Ysan arrived, 'it's Antonio. He left

at first light.' She was pointing at the castle, just visible between the tops of palms. 'Near that shiny rock. Amazing, isn't he?'

Ysan scanned the landscape for the shiny rock, but the instant she saw it, it stopped shining. Then she picked out Antonio, an ant-sized figure far away; a tiny, moving silhouette on a ledge a little way down from the top of the castle.

'How on earth did he get up there?'

She didn't ask what he was doing. It was obvious. If the boat had broken down and was floating anywhere between Safe Harbour and South Bay, if Raúl was marooned on the shore somewhere, Antonio would be able to see him.

Hearing shouts, the two set off for the palm trees where the advisers were summoning everybody to meet. Rose announced that they were moving base to the orchard – nearer to food and fresh water. Dingo offered to piggyback Sledge for the move.

Sledge added that somebody would need to stay at South Bay in case Raúl arrived. He would draw up a rota. But the main thing, Rose added, was that they all made sure they drank plenty of fresh water and avoided the sun as much as possible. They had no protection now and she had no medication if they burned or dehydrated.

Sledge was manoeuvred on to Dingo's back as the latter crouched. It looked impossible for the student to stand upright under Sledge's weight, but with the strength and determination of a weightlifter, and a little assistance from those at his elbows, Dingo managed not only to straighten – to applause and cheers – but also to walk. And slowly, the naked entourage trudged up the hill, through the woods and past the still smouldering base, those at the front doing their best to clear a path and warn of pitfalls. Several times Dingo stumbled and twice he fell, causing Sledge to curse with pain. Through the tunnel, Sledge had no choice but to drag himself along on his backside until he could be carried again. Eventually, he was lowered to the sand under palms at Orchard Bay, where he was attended with water from the fall and fruit from the orchard. The food, though, stayed untouched; he only wanted to sleep.

As Sledge slept, Rose sat by his side and kept checking his brow, looking for signs of fever. From time to time she'd feel his pulse or kiss his hand. Once she kissed his forehead and several times, gently, his lips. Each time he stirred, but never woke.

After breakfasting in the orchard, the nine students took Rose's advice and trekked to the waterfall, where they bathed in the pool and drank from the fall.

'Ysan,' said Maisie, her squeaky voice as always making Ysan feel that she wanted to clear her throat for her. 'Come with me, please. I want a pee.'

The pair were sitting on the fallen trunk, its cover of moss soft and cool against their buttocks, watching the others messing around. Maisie's hand was between her legs, shielding her hairless groin from flies. Ysan was feeling tetchy, totally preoccupied by thoughts of Antonio at the castle and the news he might bring about Raúl. 'Didn't you go while you were in the water?'

'Couldn't manage it, not with everybody around me.' Grudgingly, Ysan followed Maisie and stood guard by a stand of bushes while Maisie peed. 'Christ, these bloody flies! They're driving me mad. They stick their noses everywhere.'

'I think it's their mouths,' Ysan said tersely.

Only on the beaches had Maisie been able to relax since becoming naked. Elsewhere, she was continuously tormented. She'd tried a leaf tied with vines to cover herself, but rapidly developed a rash that bothered her even more than the flies.

Ysan couldn't feel much sympathy. Since seeing everybody naked she'd discovered she had a bias. Where it came from, she didn't know. Some deep sense of aesthetics perhaps. An innate variant of Raúl's sense of naturalness.

Whatever it was, she'd decided she was a hair person. Just as she'd always liked to see men with long hair, beards and hairy chests – and loved Raúl's carpeted groin – she now found that she liked to see women with hair down there too. To her eyes Clarabel's untidy mass looked wonderful; her own and most others' smaller and tidier triangles looked good too. But Abi's and Maisie's unnaturally prepubescent crotches made her uneasy and the discomfort they invited from flies felt like some sort of Gaian justice.

'Why did you do it?' Ysan asked. 'What have you got against hair?'

Maisie dropped her head. 'Nothing. I shaved off all my hair when my brother died. Cystic fibrosis. He made it to twenty-five and died just before I started university.'

'Sorry, I didn't know . . . but why the hair?'

'Honestly?' piped Maisie. 'I don't know. Grief? Guilt? Penance? Self-loathing? You tell me. But as soon as he died I did this sponsored shave for the Cystic Fibrosis Foundation, all the hair on my body, except the eyebrows – I couldn't lose those. I raised five hundred pounds, and made a deal that for every year I stayed shaved there'd be another five hundred. The rings came later,' she added as if it were linked, 'to go with the image. Add a bit of interest.'

'Do you ever regret it?'

'Of course! Every time I look in the mirror. Every time I shave. And now,' she laughed, 'every time I walk in the forest. But I'm determined to stay shaved for at least a few years, to raise as much money as I can.'

'Come with me,' said Ysan, seeing a way to make amends for her earlier attitude. 'Antonio showed me something yesterday. Let me show you.'

After clambering up the hill, they halted at Antonio's fly-repellent tree and there, looking unconvinced, Maisie followed instructions, rubbing the liquid over her hairless mound and thighs. Watching, Ysan began musing aloud about bodies. About how neatly women were designed 'down there'. She'd never thought about it when clothed.

Everything was in exactly the right place for naked, outdoor life. 'All nicely covered, tucked away and hidden. Not yours, of course, but . . .'

Maisie paused in mid-rub, looked up, then gave Ysan a coy smile. 'Have all these naked bodies made you feel horny?'

'Not really. Only for Raúl.'

'Christ, they have me,' Maisie said, resuming her rubbing. 'Can't stop thinking about sex. It's terrible.'

Rubbing away absently at her groin, she smiled at Ysan again, this time so disarmingly that Ysan felt guilty about her earlier tetchiness. She still felt peculiar at the sight of Maisie's bald, multi-ringed genitals, but saw the girl in a new light.

Apart from Henry and Jill waiting for Raúl at South Bay, everybody clustered around Sledge to discuss their situation. From Antonio it wasn't difficult to work out he'd seen nothing from the castle. When someone suggested and mimed that Raúl might have gone straight to the mainland Antonio shook his head. '*Demasiado complicado. Solo yo. Raúl, no! No posible.*'

Ysan swallowed at the terrible lump in her throat but it kept coming back. Clarabel placed her hand on Ysan's shoulder and squeezed. The men were stony-faced, the women looked frightened.

Sledge sat up to grab a pebble and throw it in anger. 'He's not at Safe Harbour, he's not here, and he's nowhere in between. So if Antonio's right that he wouldn't go straight to the mainland, there's no fucking alternative, is there? The bloody boat's gone down and he's gone down with it.' He looked around as if daring anybody to disagree. Maisie suddenly let out a sob and Clarabel's grip on Ysan's shoulder tightened.

Ysan exploded. 'Don't say that! Why must he be dead? Even if the boat sank, he could have made it to the shore. He could be lying somewhere, injured. We have to keep looking.'

'Antonio's already looked.'

'From the top of the castle. Maybe Antonio would have seen the boat from there, but he could easily have missed Raúl. We've got to look harder. Closer. Search the coastline. Safe Harbour to South Bay. Every centimetre.'

'Talk sense, Ysan. How the hell can we search the coastline?'

'Swim! Walk! Climb over rocks!'

'Stupid! Sheer bloody suicide. The coral's lethal. So are the rocks.'

Ysan stalked away.

Clarabel took two steps after her. 'Where are you going?'

'Where do you think?' She had to know, had to make sure Raúl wasn't injured or in pain. And she desperately needed to put her thoughts in order. It couldn't wait and she couldn't explain.

Worry and anger drove Ysan into the water to strike out from shore. But caution made her stop and tread water. She looked back at the figures watching her. In the end it was pride that motivated her to continue. She'd seen Antonio swim beyond the coral and learned quickly which route was best. White water marked the reef's position, its absence where the crossing was easiest.

She swam short distances underwater, blinking furiously as the salt water stung her eyes, looking for the widest and deepest gap in the coral. On her third dive down she found a route and swam through and then carried on beyond the northern headland, the water cooling instantly as the sea bottom plummeted out of sight. She then turned and headed into the next bay, over more coral and back into warm water. To her surprise the surface current was with her again, taking her into shore as if within each bay the surface currents circulated clockwise. This new bay fronted another typical beach, and by her reckoning there would be one more such bay and maybe a smaller third between Orchard Bay and Safe Harbour, and all needed to be searched.

Every few minutes while swimming towards the distant shore she trod water, scanning each overhanging rock, each cave, and shouting Raúl's name whenever she saw potential cover for an injured man. Nothing. Then on shore, after crossing the beach, she explored the palms and the slope into the jungle.

But there was no sign of Raúl or his fate: no meaningful flotsam, no slumped or sleeping body, no footprints in the sand. Nothing. This was only one bay of three but already she felt dispirited, tired, helpless and useless. Beside a palm she sank to the ground and looked out to sea. Maybe the others were right. Maybe Raúl had drowned.

ELEVEN

12–13 July 2006

Ysan woke with scarcely two hours left until sunset, one of which she would need to swim back to Orchard Bay. But rising to her feet she was unable to move at the sight of the footprints, aligned side by side with her own. She immediately thought of Raúl. But her surge of excitement rapidly turned to fear. Whoever they belonged to hadn't woken her.

'Who's there?' she shouted. 'Come on, I know you're there.'

No answer.

Was somebody watching her? The tracks wandered in and around the palm trees – but as a figure of eight with no exit – as if the person were teasing her, playing games. Standing still, she looked and listened, then ghosted round the tree trunks, hoping to surprise a skulking figure. When she came to a large fallen branch, she was grabbed by the ankles, and a second later she was on the ground, face in the sand, her scream muffled, the intruder astride her back.

She raised her head enough to speak. 'Very funny, Danny,' she said, spitting out sand. 'Now let me go.'

'Hey, Barbie. How'd you know it was me?'

'That wart on your right knee.'

Struggling to free herself, she managed to squirm on to her back. Danny stayed astride her, pinning her body with his weight and holding her wrists above her head with his hands. Leaning forwards, his face moved so close to hers his tousled hair hung down and tickled her cheeks. She could smell oranges on his breath.

'Oh, God!' she despaired, feeling the state of him pressed against her belly. 'Forget it, Danny. Let me go. You've had your thrill.'

He didn't move.

'Raúl's gone missing, he may even be dead. Do you really think I'd be up for sex?'

His hazel eyes brimmed with mischief and excitement. 'You're naked, I'm naked. Nobody's watching. Just a quickie. Make up for two years ago.'

'That was your one and only chance.'

'I was paralytic.'

'So was I, otherwise you wouldn't have had that chance.'

She wasn't afraid of him. Everything was a game to Danny. 'Stop now. I haven't got time for this.'

He stared at her lips and licked his own. 'A kiss. Then I'll let you go.'

Ysan struggled again and failed to get loose. She groaned with exasperation, before obliging him with a peck on the lips. Smiling, he dismounted.

They sat side by side, waiting for him to calm down. 'Why me anyway?' said Ysan. 'We've had our time, you and me. We know it doesn't work. Plenty of the others fancy you. Why not Abi?'

'Abi! Love the body, hate the soul. Or at least, I thought I loved the body. Not so sure now. Those nipples are seriously weird.' He gazed into her eyes, the way he always used to when about to compliment or plead with her. 'She really hasn't undressed as well as you, you know. Nowhere near. Nobody has. Your body. That walk. It's you I'm lusting after all over again. You or nobody.'

Ysan smiled, but raised an eyebrow. From experience she knew this kind of flattery and charm came easily to Danny, but it was hollow. In small doses she enjoyed it just the same.

'So is that why you followed me here? To get me on my own? See if I would?'

'Naagh. I knew you wouldn't. Fun trying, though. I came because I was worried about you. We all were. But it was me who volunteered. So, how can I help?'

Ysan gave him another quick kiss, this time in thanks and helped him to his feet. 'Just keep your eyes open.'

They scoured the beach together until the light began to fade, but found nothing and headed back.

The sun was on the horizon as they entered Orchard Bay. Danny grazed his leg on something floating in the water and was bleeding. Even so, once clear of the coral they began to race, Ysan taking the longer route down the side of the southern headland to take advantage of the clockwise current, Danny heading directly for the fire now burning on the beach. Later, Danny blamed his defeat not on currents but on his injured leg and the fact that he'd kept looking back to check for sharks.

Wet from her swim, still fretting about Raúl but relishing her victory, Ysan reported on her search to Sledge, then joined Clarabel at the fire. Clarabel dragged a charred palm leaf package from the ash and opened it to reveal a thick fillet of steaming fish. 'Saved you some,' she said. 'Antonio caught them with a trident he made from flakes of stone tied to a stick. Resourceful, aye?'

Ysan devoured it.

'Cut it fine, didn't you? I was getting worried.' Then seeing how anxious Ysan was, she put her hand on her friend's thigh and said gently, 'You're doing all you can. Maybe you'll find him tomorrow.'

The next day Ysan and Antonio swam out to search the other bays. The wind was stronger and the waves bigger than before. Several times she lost control and panicked about rocks or coral, but each scare passed and by midafternoon, they had covered the whole shoreline, finding neither Raúl nor the boat.

'Aren't you worried?' she asked him. 'Upset?' She mimed tears.

Face impassive, Antonio clenched his fist and put it over his heart. Ysan wasn't sure what he meant, but took it to be a 'yes'.

They returned by the safer route, over land, through the forest. Ysan was too sad to speak and barely noticed what she was walking through. Either Raúl really was dead or . . . what else? Old conversations were replaying in her mind, resurrecting the traitorous visions she'd had on the night of the fire. Was Antonio's stoicism genuine? Or were he and Raúl playing a game with the whole group, setting some sort of test?

As they reached the beach, they were intercepted by Abi. 'Did you see Geeky?' she snapped.

'We were looking for Raúl,' Ysan replied curtly, in no mood for chitchat.

'I know. But did you see Geeky?'

'No. Why?'

'That long streak of piss has run off with my shoes.'

'*My* shoes, actually. Good for Ian. I hope he tossed them in the sea.'

Ysan found Sledge and Rose and reported on their failed search. 'That's it then,' Sledge said. 'Raúl's dead and we're fucked. With no radio and no transport, all we can do is sit here and wait to be rescued.'

'He can't be dead,' said Ysan, close to tears. 'Not in a stupid boat. He just can't.'

'We don't know anything. It's only been two days,' soothed Rose.

'Sorry Ysan,' said Sledge. 'That was out of turn. There's nowhere else to look for him. But Raúl knows this place better than anyone, so there's got to be a chance he'll show up. What I've been thinking about is this: it's three more weeks until our plane arrives home without us; then it's got to take at least another couple of weeks for people to realise we didn't just miss the plane and to organise a rescue to pick us up. Five weeks, minimum. With no clothes, no proper medical facilities, nothing. Look at my feet. Anything could happen – gangrene, septicaemia – the same kind of thing could happen to any of you. What I'm saying is, before any of us can be rescued, we've got to survive first.'

At that point, Maisie came by. 'Any of you guys seen Ian yet?'

'Why in hell is everyone suddenly obsessed with Ian?' asked Ysan.

'He went to the waterfall,' said Rose. 'Looking for the source of the water. Said there had to be some nearer than the waterfall. All the stuff in the pool had to go somewhere. So he got it into his head to follow the outlet stream from the waterfall down to the sea. That was early this morning. We haven't seen him since.'

Ysan shook her head and walked away. With Raúl missing, she didn't give a damn about Ian. She went in search of Clarabel, the only person she knew she could open up to.

Clarabel held Ysan close. Ysan cried hard on her shoulder – for Raúl, for her dreams, for her future. Once Ysan's eyes began to dry she blurted out the thought that would not fade. 'I keep thinking he's not dead, but set the whole thing up. And Antonio's in on it.'

'Then you're crazier than Alexi. If he'd wanted to get us all naked, wouldn't he be here with us now, enjoying what he'd created?'

'It's not just about being naked. It's something he said about the chimps. About stripping them of everything . . . Taking them back to the beginning . . . A blank page . . . He reckoned it should be done with all the great apes. What are we to him if not great apes?'

'But what for?' said Clarabel. 'What would be the point?'

'To see how people coped with liberation. How we behave, compared with the chimps. Write a book on us.'

'He could never publish it,' Clarabel argued. 'He'd go straight to jail.'

'Not if everyone thought the whole thing was an accident.'

'Come on, Zannie. Be sensible. If he wanted to study naked humans, he'd go and watch some tribe somewhere, not use us.'

'No, that's the point. He wouldn't. He said there was too much baggage in an established society. Family, culture, stuff like that. This is better. Starting from scratch in an unknown territory. Same as the chimps.'

'But he'd ask for volunteers, not force us. There are plenty of nutters who'd jump at the chance.'

'Nutters. Precisely! Nutters who knew they were being watched. Part of an experiment. They'd be useless. They wouldn't be comparable to the chimps.'

Clarabel laughed sarcastically. 'And we are? Ridiculous! The chimps have been here – what – forty-odd years? We'll be here forty-odd days at the outside. There's nothing Raúl could learn from us in that time that would be worth the risk – to him, to his reputation, to all of us. And Antonio in on it, too? That's even crazier. He's already making spears and lighting fires for us. How's that seeing how we coped? And you've forgotten something else, too, Raúl isn't even around to record what's happening.'

'Maybe he's watching us. Maybe he's in the orchard.'

'We'd see him. Bound to. Then what would he do? Anyway, I thought you were meant to be in love with him. How can you even begin to think he'd do something like this?'

'So you'd rather I believed him dead?'

Clarabel pulled Ysan's head to her breast, rocked her gently and stroked her hair. Ysan closed her eyes. 'Thanks. I'm OK now.'

She walked off to the orchard alone. If Raúl was alive, how could he treat her like that? Treat them all like that? It was inhuman, barbaric, obscene. What sort of man could do that?

Ian returned to Orchard Bay that evening and walked straight past a still simmering Ysan without a word or glance. Normally she would happily have ignored him in turn. But seeing his arms and legs covered with dried blood and his back raw with sunburn, she called out to him, asking if he was all right.

'Fine. Never better.'

'Did you find out where the water went?'

'Sort of,' he said, avoiding eye contact, coyly shielding his unimpressive groin with one hand. 'It disappears underground. Probably comes out at the back of one of the big caves further along. Don't know which, but it doesn't really matter. The whole hillside seems to act like a sponge, water oozing out of the rocks in all sorts of places. There are dozens of trickles at South Bay and there's bound to be some round the orchard too. I'll look tomorrow.'

Clarabel interrupted. 'No need. Antonio already marked out the best spots. My God, Ian, what happened to you? You look as though you just wrestled a chimp.'

'I'm fine. Just a few stumbles. So how come Antonio didn't show us the water before? Why wait till now?'

'Between searching for Raúl, making tools and catching food? He showed us as soon as he could. Shouldn't you have Rose check you over?'

'I'm OK.'

'Geeky!' roared Abi, storming on to the scene. 'Where are my shoes?'

Ian glanced down at his bare feet. 'Sorry, Abi. They came off while I was wading through the stream. Without my glasses . . .'

'Pillock,' Abi yelled, and Ian squealed with pain as she slapped his red-raw back.

With Sledge's makeshift bandages long since discarded, the shoes had been the group's last vestige of clothing. Now everybody was completely naked. If this was all part of a plan, thought Ysan, if Raúl's aim really had been to strip everybody of everything, he'd succeeded. And now five long weeks of survival stretched ahead of them, the experiment would begin.

TWELVE

14–27 July 2006

Ysan slept poorly, her restless mind continually jarring her awake with thoughts of Raúl as her belief that he was still alive wavered and her anger at him subsided. By first light, she found herself trying to will him back to life, to share with him still.

With Sledge's permission, but without it if necessary, she would ignore all that was happening around her and carry on with the chimp project, work at it for as long as it took for them to be rescued. It would keep her closer to Raúl and give her a sense of purpose before she went mad from anxiety and speculation. So at dawn she refreshed herself with an early morning swim and rehearsed her arguments for convincing Sledge that her intention to continue with her project was both safe and sensible.

Sledge's response was pragmatic: 'We all have to do what we can to get through each day.'

Her first day back on ape watch was difficult and uncomfortable. She missed her notebook and her sleeping bag cushion. She missed her binoculars too. But more than anything she missed Raúl. Which was why, en route to her tree, she collected a swish stick to place on his seat, to look at when she felt low, to imagine him there, still on spider watch. To picture his Svengali eyes, his lean body, the pair of them playing, talking, touching, his feet stroking hers.

Around midday, when she couldn't cry any more, the chimps settled down and a breeze developed, which drew her attention to something blue flapping amongst the bushes further up the hill. It was Sledge's sleeping bag, having taken flight the night of the storm. Entangled by branches and badly torn it was still perfect for her needs. Wedging the bag firmly on her tree seat she had a moment's guilt at not taking it straight back to its owner – but only a moment's. As her bare buttocks sank into the soft material she needed little convincing that her needs were greater than his.

The group's reaction to Raúl's disappearance and presumed death upset Ysan. As far as she could see, she was the only one to believe he might still be alive, the only one who, even in doubting him, seemed to care. Maybe his death was too intangible: no body, no shipwreck. Nothing to grab people by the throats and choke them with grief. Ysan had seen tears; mainly Maisie merging Raúl with her brother, crying about death's cruelty rather than for Raúl. Clarabel too, remembering the brief times the four of them had spent together, had wept in memory a little. But not the rest, not even his friends from the past – Sledge, Henry, Jill and Antonio. They seemed to accept his death, push any sorrow to the back of their minds and immediately get on with the task of survival.

The group resigned itself to a few weeks of back-to-nature living they knew they must endure before rescue. Case after case of dehydration, swollen insect bites and injured feet emphasised Sledge's mantra: before they could be rescued, they had to survive. Rose was kept busy. But even with her care and advice, there seemed to be no end of new and immediate problems. Not least, the legacy of a sudden fruit-rich and vegetable-light diet: diarrhoea and stomach cramps were ever present, frequently raising the fear of food poisoning. And nobody would dare to eat anything unusual unless it was first examined by Antonio.

As they struggled to manage without even the most basic trappings of modern life, Antonio was kept busier than Rose. After a new medical problem was announced, he would run off and come back with a piece of plant for Rose to use in treatment. Sticky leaves were plasters for fingers and toes, juices from plants soothed a multitude of ailments from sunburn to mosquito bites. He even knew which juices would calm stomachs. There was one problem though, which affected all of them at some level: withdrawal.

Ysan was never a smoker of nicotine and only occasionally drank alcohol to excess, so withdrawal for her meant no more than a few days of a mild craving. The real smokers though, Clarabel and Danny, and the real drinkers, Henry, Dingo and Alexi, were often unstable and inconsolable. Antonio could help the smokers a little, providing twigs that when stripped of bark and chewed had mildly nicotinic properties. 'Fairly pathetic,' according to Clarabel, 'but better than nothing.' He couldn't help the drinkers.

For a few days, Alexi became snappy and humourless, even developing the bizarre habit of crawling into bushes and sitting for hours, just staring. Dingo was perpetually irritable – even unapproachable – and made Ian's life a misery, pushing him so hard into thorny bushes that it set back his recovery from sunburn by several days. Henry made Jill's life hell too – until he collapsed. Shaking and hallucinating, he began to see snakes on the trees, in the bushes, on the beach, crawling over his body. Curled up on the sand, sweating and groaning from his cramps, and sometimes screaming in his sleep, he even sank so low as to verbally abuse Jill without regard to who was near, as she nursed him.

'DTs,' said Rose. 'Nothing we can do. Just wait and hope it passes.'

His episodes and delirium made him unrecognisable for three days. From then he slowly recovered in silence, but the episode had frightened them all.

'How come Antonio's not suffering like the rest?' Ysan asked Clarabel one morning as the pair were cleaning their teeth, each rubbing a broken twig around the gums. Another of Antonio's repertoire of plants, the stick oozed a pleasant-tasting sap as it was pressed against the teeth.

'Just made of tougher stuff, I guess.'

At first, apart from Ysan and Antonio, the group was reluctant to leave Orchard Bay. Waiting for rescue throughout the first week the fear of sunburn and injury corralled them all together for much of each day. They slept on the beach and stayed in the shade of the palms, cliffs, rocky overhangs and caves around its perimeter for most of the morning and afternoon. Swims in the sea were hurried to avoid burning; any walks to drink from the freshwater trickles were taken by the shadiest routes, not the most direct. Necessity drove them twice daily to the orchard for food, and irritation from the ever invasive sand and salt occasionally drove them to the waterfall for a shower. But wherever they went, they returned quickly to the comfort and security of the beach, to while away the hottest part of each day.

Thanks to the mountain at the centre of the island, Orchard Bay, along with much of the south-eastern quarter of the island, was shaded for a couple of hours each afternoon – from about three until five. If it hadn't been, tedium and withdrawal might have had worse repercussions. Instead, this was the only time of day when people could venture out into the open, swim without fear of burning, explore the coves, caves and bays further along the beach, and if they wished play improvised ball games – usually with a coconut or an orange. It was the best time for trekking to the orchard and waterfall, and the best time too for preparing the main meal of their day.

Antonio fished for himself and the other four advisers, but let Clarabel and Ysan share his catch. Ysan suspected he was doing it to pressure the younger men and women to make an effort and share the responsibility for the group, but didn't doubt he would fish for the others as well if their health began to suffer through their diet. Henry and Jill did the cooking for the seven of them, and Ysan always collected something from the orchard on her way back from watching the apes. In response to Antonio's pressure, most of the students gave fishing a try at least once but only a few persevered and even fewer became proficient. Maisie was the exception. She fished conscientiously each afternoon and shared what she caught. But when Danny made a rare catch, he'd sidle off and cook it for himself. The rest of the students were hopeless at fishing. The women concentrated on collecting fruit from the orchard and shellfish from the bays, but the lads more or less messed about and ate what they picked, or occasionally just helped themselves to the girl's food.

The reluctance of the others to wander far from the beach during the first week suited Ysan. Only Antonio ever intruded upon her vigil. Like the ever present ants he was forever running from place to place on errands. Even so, she managed enough uninterrupted observation to see several hunts and witness two more brutal slayings of rabbits – their heads split open on rocks with a terrible wet thump.

When chimps weren't around she still thought about Raúl, and the fantasy and hope that he was alive and observing them was better than accepting the alternative like the others. Nor would she let the notion die unless he failed to appear when the rescue came. Until then, all she needed was to banish those thoughts of a terrible finality from her wayward mind by a conscious act of will. She even began to feel enthusiastic about what she was achieving. Having suffered nothing worse than three days of sunburned nipples, she also grew more confident about her prospects of survival.

Often she amused herself by imagining the details of Raúl's coexistence on the island. He had to live apart from the group to avoid influencing their behaviour; he couldn't skulk nearby because he'd be seen. So Antonio had to function as their observer and minder, protecting them. And as their trainer too, taking them 'back to the beginning', helping them shrug off the burden of civilisation and to develop their natural but neglected resilience as a species.

What would their equivalent be – naked, in possession of fire and a modicum of hunting tools and skills? Early Stone Age? How long would Raúl allow Antonio to prepare them? One week? Two? Leaving three or four weeks for the experiment proper. Was that long enough? Would Antonio then disappear too, as the experiment worked itself through? And at the end of it all, would they both simply turn up and reveal all?

The more Ysan developed her theories, the more they appealed. Small scale the experiment might be, but it was absolutely unique with the smack of ingenuity she recognised as Raúl's hallmark. Curiously, it all started to make perfect sense, and her fantasy verging on the hope, verging on the belief, that it was true sustained her for most of each day and part of each night. The few times her fantasies and theories faltered, her doubts affected her deeply. When alone in the orchard she would still cry. At night, she'd wake with a start, her stomach churning from nightmarish images of wild seas, sinking boats or the stifling sensation of drowning. Then she'd lie alert, staring at the stars, her eyes wet. But the sight of them would transport her back to the sauna of Raúl's sleeping bag, and to rue the sad fact that they had never stayed together until dawn.

'Ysan! Over here!' shouted Maisie from a distance. 'You must have a go. See how many you can get. I got all seven.'

It was late afternoon and Ysan was returning from her day's work, carrying a basket of fruit and dragging a large branch, a contribution to the permanent pile of firewood in the centre of the beach. Near the water's edge the female students were clustered around Clarabel and something was amusing them.

'Have a go at what?'

Clarabel handed Ysan a letter-sized sheet of bark, paper thin but tough with a smooth inside surface that was jet black. Where it was etched though the colour revealed was a pale yellow-brown. There was an untidy pile of them beside Clarabel.

'Clarrie, this is brilliant. Where did they come from?'

'I drew them.'

'Not the drawings, the bark. Is there more? It's just what I need. It's driving me crazy not having a notebook. Where did you get them?'

Clarabel explained that Antonio had found them for her, from trees upslope from the waterfall. The bark peeled off naturally and just lay around on the ground. 'It needs a fairly sharp stone to make the scratches, but once you get the hang of it . . . Anyway, never mind the bark. Look at the drawings. We want names. Let's see how much notice you've been taking.'

Ysan looked at the drawings in more detail, then laughed. Etched into the bark were sketches of seven disembodied male genitals: not drawn in Clarabel's usual distorted style but crafted precisely, in full medical detail.

'Well . . . the pencil stub is Ian's, the egg-in-a-nest is Sledge and the elephant's trunk is Pete . . .'

'Everyone got those three,' said Clarabel. 'What about the others?'

'I'll get there . . . The longish foreskin is Danny. The one with a sort of waist behind the knob . . . is . . . Antonio, the snake is Henry and the stinkhorn with the dribble is Dingo.'

'Stinkhorn?' asked Clarabel.

'It's a kind of toadstool.'

'And they look like Dingo's prick?'

Ysan giggled. 'Not precisely.'

Handing the sheet back to Clarabel, she said quietly, 'You didn't draw Raúl?'

'I rattled them off today. I didn't mean anything . . .'

'Of course not, sorry. So who didn't get them all?'

'I didn't,' Alexi said, blushing. 'I've got better things to do all day than stare at men's pricks. They're all bloody ugly.'

'Give me the sheet,' said Maisie. 'Let's go and try them on the lads.'

The men quickly resigned themselves to the fact that they'd be growing beards, Crusoe-style. Most of the women resigned themselves to the prospect of sprouting hair in unfashionable places. Few found the idea appealing and for Maisie the thought was distressing. 'How much *does* hair grow in five weeks?' she asked, rubbing her hand over her already stubbly head. At home, she shaved every week. Once a fortnight at the outside.

The consensus was that it would grow about a centimetre; too much for Maisie who said that in all conscience she couldn't claim to have stayed shaved for the year and would therefore lose all future pledges. She panicked and experimented with stone razors, even sand abrasives, in a bid to stay hairless. Until Rose, seeing her rashes and cuts and still growing hair, told her she must stop, the risk of infection was too great. Hardly an hour went by though that she didn't examine her various parts and bemoan how vigorous her hair had always been.

For lesser reasons, the other women inspected themselves with dismay as dark shadows appeared under their arms, on their legs and, in Abi's case, on her groin. Abi kept asking if her roots were showing. Only Ysan was unconcerned, never having shaved or plucked in her life. All part of her innate lack of interest in appearance and glamour. The small fair tufts under her arms, the fine almost invisible down over her legs and the dozen or so long almost blonde hairs that somehow always escaped the crotch of her bikini had never seemed cause for attention or embarrassment. And they certainly weren't now.

All the women wondered how they'd cope with menstruation. Alexi was the first to find out and put her own unique stamp on the occasion. In the afternoon shade, a group had been idly throwing around an orange. The game should have been nonphysical, but as always Dingo found a way of ending on the sand grappling with a woman, his muscular hulk looking as though it might break Alexi's almost unhealthily slim frame. Stealing the orange she'd been clutching, he left her sprawled on the sand – which was when Ian pointed out that her leg seemed to be bleeding. Then they all saw the red smears colouring her light-brown thighs.

'Shit,' said Alexi, black hair falling over her face as she bent to examine herself before looking up, her dark eyes questioning the women. 'I've started.'

'Gross,' said Ian, with a grimace.

'Nothing gross about it.'

Alexi ran her hand between her legs, then licked one of her fingers, drawing groans from the men. When Ian said he was going to be sick, Alexi sprang to her feet to advance on him, holding up her hand to show that it was still loaded, threatening to rub it over his face. Ian, still sunburn-red, turned and ran with Alexi in hot pursuit, both so thin they looked like a pair of animated matchstick people. When she gave up the chase, Alexi went straight into the sea, washed herself, then came back out.

'Brilliant,' she said, her eyes now bright, almost proud. 'No tampons, no bloody pads and no stains. I could get used to this nudity business.'

Unable to imagine being quite as blatant as Alexi when her time came, Ysan could nevertheless see that she had a point.

Ysan was never entirely alone in her tree. Every branch around her was home to something – and all were walkways for marching columns of tree ants. All day long they trudged from canopy to ground and back again carrying bits of leaves, seeds, dead insects and – the ants were on her side, she decided – dead spiders. Another constant companion was the lizard, living there since day one, for which she'd developed great affection. Naming it Raúl, she imagined that it also protected her from those spiders too large for the ants to kill.

On the racetrack below her tree was a large crow-like bird with glossy black plumage that reflected the sun. It probably had young, because it would arrive, collect a beakful of small lizards or insects, then fly off in the direction of the ominous black façade of the castle, visible between branches and leaves. Ysan couldn't watch the bird all the way to the landmark, but she knew where it went, where it nested, because from time to time she saw the sun flashing there on its plumage, in a cave mouth just down from the castle top, the 'shiny rock' Clarabel had once pointed out.

Her ape-watch project aroused scant curiosity among her fellow students, even Clarabel took no more than a courteous interest. A few asked where she went each day.

'On the high side of the racetrack,' was all she said, lying that she chose a new location each day. 'But I'm always well hidden,' she stressed, wanting neither company nor to relinquish Sledge's sleeping bag.

Such meagre information seemed enough to satisfy them; nobody asked to come with her and nobody followed her. Ysan, for her part, made a point of never climbing or descending her tree, or even appearing near it, unless she was certain she couldn't be seen.

And back on the beach the early anarchy lasted only until Sledge's feet healed. Then, as he'd threatened, he sought out the slackers and imposed order. First and foremost he decreed that the evening meal should be both totally communal and totally cooperative. Soon there was nowhere for the lazy to hide. By the time the second week of waiting for rescue was drawing to a close, the preparation of the evening meal was running like a military exercise. From the moment the mountain's shade spread across the orchard, nobody was allowed to be idle unless they had a sanctioned medical excuse. Maisie was given the job of helping Antonio fish for everyone, with Rose helping whenever she could. Clarabel and Ian foraged for shellfish. Alexi and Abi collected fruit and vegetables from the orchard. The least popular job, collecting firewood, fell to Danny and Dingo, and Pete was appointed under-chef to Henry and Jill. Ysan was simply told to contribute as and when she could once she'd finished her work for the day. Sledge supervised and everything clicked into place.

Ysan's thirteenth day up her tree was quiet for watching chimps but the crow was back again. Curious about the location of the bird's nest, and ignoring the danger of falling, she changed her position, shuffling along a creaking branch until she could see the bird in flight with the castle as a backdrop. As if winking at her, the rock briefly flashed then went dark again before the crow was anywhere near it. It must be its mate, or maybe its young were ready to fledge and were venturing out. Not for the first time, she longed for binoculars.

Binoculars! What had happened to Raúl's binoculars? The first time she'd seen him naked, surrounded by chimps near the castle, they had been around his neck. When she'd raced him back to the base shortly afterwards, he no longer had them. Maybe they were still there. Maybe she could find them and use them. Or maybe . . . The shining rock wasn't a bird, it was glass: the lenses. How stupid she had been. Raúl hadn't disappeared to wait for his little experiment to unfold. Antonio wasn't the observer, there to report to Raúl at the end. Raúl had never needed to stalk them. With binoculars, the pair he'd stashed on day one, he could watch them from the castle at a safe distance. Not perfectly – not all of their haunts would be in range – but much of both beaches, the racetrack, her tree, even the waterfall would be visible. He'd see most of what they got up to, and Antonio would fill him in on the rest.

As her heartbeat slowed and her breathing settled, she wondered if she were crazy or if she could actually allow herself to believe Raúl was still alive and watching over them?

She glanced back at the castle. The distant rock winked again.

THIRTEEN

Ysan's belief that Raúl could be watching from the castle made her mischievous. Early the next morning on the beach with Antonio she pointed at the castle and said, 'Raúl.' Then mimed looking through binoculars. The Spaniard stared at her for an age before grinning, laughing, then shaking his head. She picked up a flat wet pebble from the water's edge, angled the stone backwards and forwards to catch the light, then again pointed at the castle. Antonio laughed even more than before. Smiling, Ysan said, 'Yes! Raúl . . . At the castle. We go, *Si? Vamos!* We climb castle. You, me.'

She mimed climbing the rocks. Antonio's amusement switched to purpose. 'OK,' he said. 'OK. *Vamos. Ahora.*'

'*Ahora?*'

'*Si! Ahora!*'

Grabbing her hand, he pulled her across the beach towards the orchard tunnel, watched in confusion by others, not least Clarabel who was just waking. Pausing only to collect some forest food – a juicy radish-flavoured root and a celery-like shoot – for them to eat as they went, they reached the foot of the castle. He asked by gesture which way she wanted to climb; she indicated the same route as when he scanned for Raúl and the boat, a climb which she recalled took him right past the shiny rock. He chose a spot and began to scale.

Staying with him for a full five metres, Ysan thought she was doing well. Then he began a short traverse using only fingertips and toe holds. She couldn't follow. Tree climber she might be, rock climber she wasn't, not to that standard. Suspecting that he might deliberately have chosen a difficult stretch that even he couldn't climb, she urged him on while she timidly returned to the ground. To see him again, even intermittently, she had to retreat along the hill brow to the forest edge. When eventually he rejoined her there, it was almost with a sense of triumph.

'*Mira! No hay Raúl.*'

Frustrated by her impotence to prove anything, and irritated by his obvious belief she was misguided, Ysan tried another tack. 'The boat, then. Where's the boat?'

She gestured at the harbour, made rowing and steering motions and engine noises. Antonio took her arm forcefully. '*Ysan, mira! No hay Raúl,*' he said, pointing at the castle, and '*y no hay barca,*' pointing at the harbour.

He turned her about and pushed her in the direction of the forest. '*Ahora. Vamos volver.*'

'OK, OK. I get the message. You won't show me. But they are here somewhere. I know they are.'

'So what was all that about?' Clarabel asked once Ysan was back at the camp.

Ysan kept her voice down. 'I thought I saw Raúl up at the castle.'

Clarabel smiled.

'He was watching us,' Ysan insisted. Clarabel's mouth widened to a grin. 'Through binoculars. We went to check it out.'

'That's all right then,' the redhead replied. 'And there was me worrying you'd run off with my man for an early morning shag.'

Ysan had expected disbelief and wasn't particularly aggrieved to hear it. With only a couple of weeks to go until rescue, she'd soon be proved right. In the meantime, she resolved to point out the winking rock to Clarabel and the others at the first chance she had but it never winked again.

By the third week Raúl was rarely mentioned by the others. Ysan struggled to understand their detachment. If they thought he was dead, they should surely show something. But it was almost as if he'd never existed, their situation now so divorced from the academic enterprise he'd brought them on that he seemed unreal, of a different time and place.

Tans had deepened, feet had hardened, stomachs had become more robust and their ability to cope with heat and dehydration had improved. No longer did the majority spend their time feeling introspective, ill and vulnerable; none seriously doubted they'd survive to be rescued. Reluctant though many were to admit it at first, Sledge's organisation had led to greater efficiency, freeing much of the day for guiltless leisure. Combined with a new confidence to move around in the sun even during the heat of the day, everyone became more active and more adventurous. Groups began leaving Orchard Bay in the early morning – trekking to South Bay and beyond for a change of scenery or to the waterfall to splash around in fresh water – returning home in time for the afternoon's chores.

'Gets more like a naturists' holiday every day,' observed Clarabel one evening.

'More like a scene from the early Stone Age,' suggested Ysan.

'What are you doing?' Ysan asked Abi, Maisie and Jill who were sitting under the palms, weaving leaves.

'Making clothes,' chirped Maisie.

'Like it?' said Jill, standing up to show off a miniskirt of shredded banana leaves.

She paced up and down, swinging her ample hips like a model, and the skirt fell to the ground.

'Whoops! Still a few design problems,' she said, pulling it back up. 'Not sure I'd want to sit down on these hard leaves for long, either.'

Abi and Maisie were knotting grassy leaves to vine waistbands – the Hawaiian look.

'Thought it might keep off the flies,' said Maisie.

'Flies?' snorted Abi. 'Men, more like. You can have a bunch of foreign sailors gawping at you, but I'm not.'

They'd all begun to feel that rescue was drawing near. This was the day –1 August 2006 – when they would have left the island on the first leg of their journey back home. They'd been on the island for the whole of July. It would be another five days or so before their plane arrived in Manchester without them. How many days after that before rescue arrived was pure speculation. But it *felt* close, even closer for Ysan who'd harboured the hope that before the rescue Raúl would appear with Antonio's fishing boat. This was the latest he could reappear without them missing the plane, leaving him with little to explain except a chapter of accidents.

'You don't need to make clothes,' laughed Ysan. 'They'll have blankets. Or spare clothes. They won't make us travel naked.'

'It's not only for the rescue,' said Abi. 'I'm sick to death of the lads staring at me and fiddling with themselves. Always having to think about how I'm sitting. Maybe you don't care, Miss Golden Hole, but I do.'

'If only we could catch the rabbits,' said Maisie. 'We could use their skins.'

'Or chimp skins,' ventured Jill.

'I could take you to one,' said Ysan with a grin, 'but it's probably fairly manky by now.'

The three women wore their creations that afternoon, but not for long. The vines kept breaking; and the temptation to yank at passing skirts proved too much for the lads, and

Henry too. Maisie ended up running in and out of the palm trees, holding up her skirt and screaming with breathless laughter, while Danny and Dingo ran after her in excited pursuit.

'It was bloody uncomfortable, anyway,' Maisie told Ysan after she'd been caught and stripped bare. 'And didn't really keep off the flies. It scratched and gave me a rash too.' Sweat from the chase coalesced on the bristles on her scalp. Beneath the rings in each black eyebrow, her brown eyes were shining with excitement.

In the third week, Antonio began to irritate Ysan. Invariably he'd appear in the late morning, jog alone along the racetrack and disappear in the direction of the tunnel. Two or three hours later, he would return. At both times of day the chimps were awake and likely to take an interest in the rabbits. 'Where does he go?' she asked Clarabel once, though she was fairly certain she knew: to report to Raúl, where else?

'Don't know. Probably nowhere in particular. Just goes for a run.'

To Ysan's embarrassment, on a day that Antonio didn't go running, he brought Clarabel up onto the racetrack for sex. After looking around, presumably for her, they chose a banana grove at the orchard's edge; well hidden from all directions except her tree.

Although she'd heard plenty of night-time activity since being on the island, Ysan had never seen other people having sex before – not real people having real sex, not people she knew – and politeness and discomfort at first made her look away. But every few seconds her eyes flicked back to see what was happening and in the end she gave in and simply ogled. Be objective, she told herself, pretend they're chimps. But novelty and curiosity created wave after wave of guilt and erotic excitement. Feelings that surged, merged and faded, then swelled all over again, until she gave in and did something about them. She was very quick, much quicker than the couple she was watching. Their road to climax was long and energetic with several stops, changes of position and restarts, leading eventually to an aftermath that was more collapse than relaxation. Ysan felt as spent as they were and when they'd gone all she could sense was voyeuristic guilt. Shortly afterwards, two chimps started humping, and she was glad to be distracted back into her dispassionate scientific observation.

Antonio and Clarabel were the only people that Ysan saw having full intercourse. Sledge and Rose did everything but penetration, and Henry and Jill did nothing but argue about it. 'Not without condoms!' Jill shouted above Henry's animated and plaintive attempts at persuasion. 'How can you even ask me?'

It wasn't only couples Ysan found herself watching. One by one, each of the lads – and Henry – crept into the orchard to indulge in solitary masturbation. A furtive face could often be seen peering out from within the tree-line of the orchard, glancing down, glancing out, glancing down, the movement in the shoulders saying it all. If any one of them arrived alone, she could almost guarantee he wouldn't leave until he'd relieved himself. Of the five, the most frequent was Dingo, and watching him was an education. Always suspecting his never-ending obscenities and innuendoes to be cover for a *low* sex drive, she could see from her tree she was wrong. Whereas others would relieve themselves once then quickly go, Dingo would stay and leisurely masturbate two or three times in an hour.

To her surprise and satisfaction Ysan found she could watch the lads dealing with themselves without a flicker of either arousal or revulsion. They may as well have been chimps. So just as she did with the chimps and for fun, she made a note of who, when and where, suspecting that Raúl would very much approve of her record keeping.

'Walls and a ceiling. Floorboards and carpets instead of sand and crabs scuttling everywhere. My God, I can't wait.'

With only one more day until their plane landed without them, conversation turned more and more towards their rescue and return. Nobody could sleep, kept awake by the wind, the rustling palms and thoughts of home. Ysan lay in the darkness, listening in.

'On a yacht. Just gliding over the waves.' It had to be Danny.

'Fuck that, mate. Indoors, in bed, with my woman. Jesus Christ, I'm going to fuck her bloody brains out.' Unmistakeably Dingo.

'My own bed,' whined Abi. 'I'm fantasising all the time. My lovely comfy mattress and sheets.'

'Well I like it here. Space and freedom. Sleeping under the stars, living off the orchard. You can stick rescue as far as I'm concerned. It wouldn't bother me if I was here all summer.'

Murmurs of 'Shut up, Alexi' rippled around.

'I mean it. I even love being naked. I didn't think I would, but it's fantastic.'

'If naked's so great, how come you're always slagging us off?'

'Because you're male and vile.'

'Lesbo!'

As insults were traded, Ysan tuned in to Jill. 'I had the stupidest dream,' she was saying. 'I found a mail-order catalogue on the beach, full of the most gorgeous clothes. Pages and pages. I tore out the order form, put it in a bottle, and threw it into the sea. A few minutes later, a plane dropped off my order. A big red parachute. The clothes were fantastic. Long flowing dresses, sexy tops. But do you know what I forgot to order? Knickers. I didn't get any knickers. So there I was, posing around on the beach in all these fantastic clothes, but feeling embarrassed because I wasn't wearing knickers under them.'

'Know what I dream about?' said Henry. 'A decent bottle of claret. A huge steak – on a plate – swimming in Béarnaise sauce. Not a fish or bloody coconut in sight. All cooked specially for me. Served by flirty waitresses . . .'

'Waiters,' interjected Alexi. 'Toadying waiters. Totally servile and fully dressed. Not a willy in sight.'

'Serving hot crusty bread, freshly baked,' said Abi. 'Butter melting as it spreads. Oh God! Have I had that dream.'

'And cakes,' Jill continued, 'and ice cream, and after-dinner chocolates. With coffee and brandy.'

'And cigarettes,' chimed in Clarabel. 'Or a joint. What I'd give for a smoke.'

'Stop it,' laughed Ysan. 'All of you. You're driving me crazy. And you're making me feel sick.'

The day their plane was due to land in Manchester without them, they planned a special meal: they'd build an extra large fire and make a special effort to catch lobsters, robber crabs and the best fish. Preparations began early in the day. Teams were sent into the orchard looking for the vegetables – the sweet potatoes, yams, palm hearts and other things they couldn't name. Food they knew was there but took time to find. Maisie and the lads even tried to make bows to kill a couple of rabbits, but gave up because no vine proved strong enough to fire arrows at force without breaking.

Ysan took the day off from her tree and volunteered with Clarabel to dig for medium-sized clams that they all considered a delicacy. Early in the afternoon, arriving at a small and shady cove, they came across a pole standing upright in the sand and festooned with spitted fish. Ysan counted twelve, all large. 'Antonio's been busy,' she said, looking around to see where he was.

He emerged from the water like a kraken and waded towards them carrying a large flatfish. He impaled his still wriggling catch on the pole then pulled Clarabel to his wet body and kissed her. For a moment, Ysan thought he was going to do the same with her, but instead he simply grinned then jogged back to the sea.

* * *

'Have you noticed Jill won't let Henry near her?' Ysan asked Clarabel during a break, eager to relax and catch up on gossip.

Kneeling by Clarabel's side she was feeling good, the picture of health and womanhood. The sun, diet and exercise had turned her skin honey-brown and her hair almost blonde, taken a little weight off her waist and firmed her hips and thighs. In some mysterious way her breasts felt bigger, tighter, perter. Abi's Oscar for best figure was under threat. She knew it would mostly disappear when she returned home, but for the moment . . . she just hoped Raúl's binoculars were powerful enough to appreciate the new improved Ysan while he had the chance.

'She was talking about it the other day, as it happens,' said Clarabel, lying supine, staring at the overhead sky, red hair spread out on the sand, breasts falling to either side, pure tropical Pre-Raphaelite. 'We were all talking . . . all the women. That's what we do all day while you're watching your chimps. We talk. Endlessly. The same things over and over again. I'd be going crazy if I didn't have my sketching. God, I'll be glad to get home.' She hesitated and glanced towards Ysan. 'I'll miss Antonio though. I wish I could take him with me.'

'You really like him, don't you?' It would have been a naff thing to say to most people. But not to Clarabel, who once boasted she'd had sex with one guy within ten minutes of meeting him. 'Come on then,' said Ysan. 'Tell me! What is it about him? Do you know?'

'You mean apart from being able to bitch at him without him understanding a word I say?' she joked. 'How long have you got? He's a friend. He's kind. He cares for me. He makes me laugh. He's a hunk. He's passionate. And if you really want to know, and it's obvious that you do, he's also the best fuck I ever had.'

'Now that is saying something. Mr Perfect, eh? But back to Jill and Henry. What did she say?'

'It's simple enough. She's petrified of getting pregnant.'

'Aren't we all?' Ysan said quickly, before realising what she'd said. 'Sorry Clarrie, I didn't . . .'

'I know. Ridiculous though, isn't it? I'd give anything to get pregnant again, but can't, and devote my life to ultimately pointless sex. Jill can have a baby whenever she wants and decides to give up sex altogether.'

At the plane-landing banquet that night Ysan had no appetite. While the others ate, swam, sang and played charades, she picked at her food and scarcely spoke. Rose asked what was wrong and when Ysan told her about a sour coconut she had sipped that afternoon Rose assured her she wouldn't stay unwell for long.

'Might make you sick for half a day or just give you the trots.'

At that moment, Ysan felt both were likely. So when Jill began recruiting teams for a 'boat race' using coconut milk and shells in place of alcohol and cups, Ysan gave in for the night and used the distraction to walk away from them all, away from the brightness of the fire, to lie down in the darkness of the palms. Feeling tired and uncomfortable in her own skin, she might have gone straight to sleep if she hadn't been disturbed.

'Barbie. You OK? I saw you leave.'

'Fine, Danny. Thanks, but go away. I need to sleep.'

Against the backdrop of firelight, Danny's silhouette withdrew down the beach to become lost amongst the others. Ysan watched him go, but then couldn't still the spin cycle of insomniac thoughts: Raúl – his experiment, her fantasy, his return; her mother – the shock in store that same day when their plane arrived without them, hoping her worry would be brief; Mister One – tucked in her bed, waiting; her stomach – the lingering taste of coconut; then back to Raúl.

Down the beach the staccato chatter, eruptions of laughter and droning of songs continued long into the night, not subsiding until the mighty stack of firewood was exhausted.

Then, one by one, people came to lie around her under the trees. Even then they talked endlessly and excitedly about rescue and home. It was almost daybreak before they'd all fallen asleep, Ysan, the last, lulled eventually by a gentle mixture of snoring, surf and rustling leaves. She slept badly and almost as soon as she awoke, she was sick. The sour coconut taste lingered all morning.

FOURTEEN

W hile others filled the days that followed by watching and waiting, scanning the horizon for a helicopter or boat, Ysan pushed herself to work, to collect as much data on her rabbit-eating chimps as she could in the time she had left. But concentrating proved difficult. Not only did the ever present thought that rescue was imminent seduce her into watching the horizon as much as she watched the chimps but also, although she'd only been sick once, two days later Abi and Ian followed suit. If serious sickness gripped the whole group, might rescue be snatched from them? On day five of waiting, secretly panicking over fresh twinges in her guts, Ysan even neglected her work and spent the day with Clarabel, lazing under the palms and swimming gently in the shade of the cliffs, as the others had been doing all along.

Midafternoon under the palms Ysan was lying on the sand, nearly asleep. By her side Clarabel was kneeling, staring vigilantly at the horizon, as were others dotted around the shaded parts of the beach. 'I so hope it's today,' said Clarabel. She paused. 'Just think, Zannie. Everything that's happened. Everything we've seen.' She stretched out her hands and quivered them in frustration. 'My God! I can't wait to get my hands on pens and paper. Record everything before I forget it all.'

'What better record than the bark sketches?' Ysan smiled lazily.

She actually preferred Clarabel's sketches on bark. She thought the colours were just right, stronger than pen and paper, suiting her style. Clarabel wrinkled her nose with pleasure and generally agreed, but she was worried about getting them home safely. The same went for Ysan's notes. For the moment, Clarabel's sketches were stored on a ledge under one of the cliff face overhangs, while Ysan's original data sheets were in a hollow high up in her tree and the backups were in a fallen hollow trunk a few metres from her tree's base.

The next day, day six, Ysan was back in her tree and feeling relieved: Antonio had identified the cause of the sickness that by then afflicted over half the group. He'd spotted some red-brown clouds in the sea at Orchard Bay and, drawing in the sand, explained it was plankton, ingested by shellfish and poisonous to humans. They should avoid eating clams until the plankton had gone.

Ysan was also feeling pleased with herself. Overnight, she'd had more thoughts, more insights into Raúl's experiment. Six males, seven females. What a coincidence. Four of them older than the rest – a bigger coincidence. Excluding Raúl and Antonio, the liberators, the age and sex make-up of Raúl's group of people and Jim's group of chimps were all but identical. Raúl had made his 'liberation' as similar to Jim's as possible.

'You clever bugger,' she said aloud, more than once, towards the castle.

'Morning, Barbie. Want to swim out to the headland? Keep a lookout with me for a while?'

Danny looked every centimetre a beach bum: cocky

stance; bronzed body; gleaming, hairless pectorals. He just lacked the surfboard.

'I'm working today. Could be my last chance.'

He looked so crestfallen she compromised: 'We can get breakfast before I go, if you like.'

They went into the orchard and gathered bananas, oranges, monkey nuts. Danny even found a couple of small melons – a rare treat, as the season was ending, and Ysan's favourite. In the morning shade, they sat cross-legged on the racetrack and ate together. As Danny struggled to peel a stubborn orange, she scrutinised him, scarcely recognising him now as the lad she'd once dated. He'd grown up a lot, inside as well as out, his decent beard and now genuinely tousled hair veneering an even deeper change, signs of caring for others. Her, for one, but others too. She'd seen him defend Ian several times, verbally at least, in the face of Dingo's vindictiveness. And he was always trying to cheer Alexi through her recent frequent downers, caused, she claimed unconvincingly, by not wanting to leave the island. Danny's laddishness often bubbled through, but the island had revealed a side to him she hadn't previously known existed. All she said though was, 'You look better with a beard.'

'Itches like hell,' he retorted, scratching furiously with orange-stained fingers. 'You're looking good too. Living here suits you. I swear your tits are bigger and your waist is slimmer. The sun's turned you blonde. Come to think of it, you're Barbier than ever.'

She pulled apart a melon and buried her mouth in its flesh. It tasted delicious. Just what she wanted. Juice ran down her chin and dripped on to her tummy. More ran down her arms and dripped off her elbows on to her thighs.

'Aagh!' exclaimed Danny suddenly, throwing away his orange. 'Not worth the bloody effort.' As he picked up a banana instead, Ysan became aware of his rising erection.

'The chimps do that, you know. The males. Just like that.'

'Do what? Peel a banana? Boy, your research is going well.' He grinned cheekily, making his beard look almost false, incongruous, as if stuck with glue to a boy's face.

'No, they sit like that. Showing off their stiffy.'

'I thought you'd never notice. Impressive, eh? So does it work?'

'Work?'

'For the chimps. Does it turn the females on?'

'Not really. And before you ask . . .'

'Why not? Don't you ever get horny? Don't I stand any chance? I thought maybe . . . Now Raúl's gone . . .'

'Sure I get horny. Maybe as often as you. But I've got plans, lots of plans. And getting pregnant from a quickie with you isn't one of them.'

She remained good-humoured, genuinely not wanting to hurt him. But after Raúl – a man who'd explored jungles, romped with gorillas and who'd dared such an audacious experiment – Danny seemed colourless. They hadn't gelled before and there was no chance of it happening now.

'Blow job, then. Reward for finding you melons.'

Ysan laughed. And in the next instant retched and coughed.

'You OK?' he asked when she'd eventually composed herself.

She nodded. 'Went down the wrong way.'

'How about a hand job?'

'Shut up, Danny. You're putting me off my food. Just finish your breakfast and go and watch for our boat. I've got work to do.'

Almost as soon as she was up her tree, Ysan saw the chimps lay down an ambush for the rabbits out for a morning feed. Carefully parting a few leaves, she looked up at the castle. 'Morning, Raúl,' she whispered. 'You OK today?'

The racetrack fell quiet. The rabbits continued feeding and Ysan's eyes began to water. An image floated into her mind: Raúl's skeleton on the seabed, in dark water, picked clean by fish. Then another image followed, he was there with her, in the tree, their feet touching. Then the pair of them naked, among gorillas, in the future. And her last sight of him, disappearing into the black forest. All swirled together, no longer images, more like feelings. Wiping her eyes, she sighed and took a deep breath. 'Please don't be dead,' she said aloud.

M1 screamed. The hunt had begun.

The hunt unfolded as it always did. This was the eleventh she'd seen, and every one had followed exactly the same pattern as the first. In fact, the sequence was so predictable, Ysan was surprised the rabbits hadn't learned that seeing M1 with a couple of others spelt danger.

She'd gradually taken a dislike to M1. Not so much the way the big chimp dispatched the rabbits when the hunt was successful. He was a predator and they were his prey and although his brutality had been a shock that first time, now she could handle it. It was more the way he treated the other chimps. Unlike the others he seemed to enjoy inflicting pain just as much as he enjoyed getting his own way.

Raúl had once told her that M1's likely father had been 'a real psycho'. One of the original thirteen released on the island, this male, bigger even than M1, had set about attacking and maiming, even killing, as many of the other released males as he could. Maybe it was the stress of being taken from captivity and dumped on the island. Or maybe it was in his genes. Either way, M1's father was one of the few apes that had ever made Raúl nervous.

Today the hunt was successful, the sixth success against five failures. After watching carefully where M1 discarded the skull, Ysan waited until the chimps had gone then climbed down from her tree and made her way to the spot. Prodding the head with her bare foot, she saw that the skull had been picked clean, save for traces of blood. No fur, no brains, no eyes in the sockets. She retched.

She'd examined rabbit remains many times before with no hint of nausea. But today, the sight and smell of the empty blood-stained head penetrated her senses and went straight to her stomach. Moving into the shade to recuperate, she curled up and went to sleep.

She was woken by the sound of rustling bushes to her left. Chimps? Or people? Clear-headed now, she wandered on to the racetrack to investigate. It was deserted. The boat had arrived then. That's why nobody was here. They were all getting on the boat. Panic that she might be left behind was halted by a glimpse of movement, this time to her right and in the direction of the rustling. Three chimps came into view: M1 and a couple of females. The sight looked very different at ground level, but she recognised at once what was happening. It was the beginning of another ambush.

It won't work, she said to M1 in her head. Not with me here. What are you doing, setting up another hunt so soon? Usually the ambushes were spread a day or two apart to give the rabbits time to calm down. Backing slowly towards the trees, Ysan looked for cover, hoping to watch the next hunt at close quarters, but despite her stealth, M1 had seen her. He was looking straight at her, walking hesitantly in her direction, the females in close attendance. Her back now against a trunk, she watched the three chimps slowly, cautiously, drawing nearer while, to her left, the rustling grew louder. The deployment was classic, but where was the target? The only flesh between attackers and ambushers was . . . her.

Staring at M1's cold expressionless eyes, she panicked. Run! But where? Across the racetrack to her tree? Chimps were faster than her and they could climb. Into the orchard then? But bushes wouldn't stop them. Nowhere was safe. Fright drained her brain, making her light-headed, faint, triggering an image: M1 trying to wrench her head from her shoulders. Her heart stood still. What to do? Think! Avoid the big male. Charge the females, like once before. Frighten them.

Seeing no alternative, she ran. But so did M1, immediately screeching his signal to attack. The ambushers were three small females, who burst from the bushes to her left. Terrified now, convinced she was about to die, Ysan stopped moving, fear paralysing her legs until her instinct screamed. Screamed a warning. Told her indecision was fatal, and she ran again, straight at the ambushing apes, waving her arms, screaming loudly, sending three rabbits into flight from cover, startling the three apes, who moved aside to let her pass – and surprising Antonio and Clarabel, who appeared on the racetrack from the direction of the waterfall. They called over to her. No longer screaming, Ysan ran towards them, only once looking over her shoulder to see M1 and his gang stop, then begin to retreat.

'You OK?' asked Clarabel, bemused. 'Why were you running? I thought you were supposed to watch them, not scare the crap out of them.'

Breathless, trembling, embarrassed, Ysan laughed. After all her panic, there had been rabbits there. 'I must have looked really stupid,' was all she could think to say.

As the day wore on, Ysan's sickness returned. By the evening she felt so bad, she simply retreated to the palm trees and tried to sleep, and when that didn't work, she went to find Rose. 'Please tell me I'm not ... I can't be pregnant,' she begged.

Rose prodded and poked and quizzed her. 'Feeling sick? No period? Breasts tender, bigger, tighter?'

At each question Ysan's heart sank a little. 'But I can't be.'

'Oh yes you can.'

'But I was on the pill.'

'You stopped, suddenly.'

'And he withdrew ...'

'Men's timing only needs to be a fraction off ...'

'Is it definite?'

'Not absolutely. But ...' Rose paused for a second. 'Something else. It doesn't happen to everyone. Maybe you didn't even notice, but about a fortnight ago did your nipples tingle for a few days? Maybe too tender to touch?'

Ysan's heart reached the floor. 'I thought it was sunburn.' Her brain went into overload and all she could do was stare blankly at Rose's sympathetic face. Rose placed her hand on Ysan's shoulder and gently squeezed.

'Try not to worry. We'll be home soon. Plenty of help and support. Plenty of time to think about things.'

'You mean whether to have it or not?'

'Whatever. No need to rush anything. There's plenty of time. Don't worry. I'm here for you.'

Ysan floated on her back, staring at the stars while gently rising and falling with the waves. It was past midnight and the evening had swirled past her. While everyone around her talked of rescue, or the lack of it, she'd eaten little and spoken less. All she could contemplate was the tiny life that might be inside her and what it meant she should do next.

Consumed by dread and loneliness, her mind floundering, she rolled on to her front and swam hard until she was breathless. Then she floated towards the shore and again looked up at the stars. Pregnant to Raúl. What would she have thought during her teenage years – lying on her bed, reading his words or watching his videos – if anyone had foretold such a future? Would that girl have dreamed about raising his child? Of taking it with her – with him or without him – through the jungles of the world? Would she have scorned the difficulties? Of course she would. It would have seemed like nothing to her then. Hadn't her mother raised her single-handedly? Other women managed to carve out a career studying apes with a baby in tow. If they could manage, so could she.

But the father of her child might be dead or mad. Teenage dreams had suddenly become adult reality, demanding adult decisions. Plenty of time to decide, Rose had said. Plenty of time. So why did she feel she had so little? Dragging herself to the shore, she slumped like flotsam on to the wet sand, placed her hands on her stomach, and squeezed her insides until they hurt.[1]

---

[1] Unlikely though it might seem, this pregnancy and its outcome were to become a pivotal conundrum of the group's story. Of course, as soon as Ysan told me that she had conceived to Raúl so soon after arriving on the island, I asked what had happened because when she returned to England it was without a baby but pregnant again, this time to Danny. She hesitated for a moment then said, in a matter-of-fact way, 'I lost it. A miscarriage. First trimester. Not surprising, really.' And once I'd learned more of what had happened to her I had to agree. Only later did I realise that I didn't know much at all.

FIFTEEN

14 August–4 September 2006

While the others watched and waited for a rescue with varying degrees of impatience and agitation, Ysan stayed hidden up her tree, sometimes working, sometimes fretting, sometimes crying as formless feelings, disjointed thoughts and ever stronger bouts of nausea overcame her. She felt alone even in company, because that was what she'd chosen. Having sworn Rose to secrecy, she'd told nobody about her pregnancy, not even Clarabel. In fact, she'd lied outright to Clarabel, deflecting suspicion by first inventing a period, then claiming that her sickness had totally gone. No deep logic drove her deception, no strategy. Just a gut response to her situation, plus an instinct for self-protection: not yet knowing her feelings herself, she had no space for another person's emotion. In the end the charade proved futile. It took Clarabel just two weeks to see through her pretence.

'You're pregnant, aren't you?'

Stretched out on the mossy carpet at the waterfall after a swim, staying cool in the spray, Ysan blushed violently beneath her tan. She and Clarabel were side by side, staring up through the mist at the leafy canopy, watching bright-red dragonflies hawk after insects in the treetops. Ysan tried further bluff. 'Of course not. I just had a period. I told you.'

Clarabel turned her head. Even if secretly she'd had doubts she was right, the sight of Ysan's flush would have dismissed them.

'Come on, Zannie. I'm your best friend. You haven't had a period, I know you haven't. You're still feeling sick. You're off your food. You keep having little chats with Rose. And look at you! Your ribs are showing, you've got a real waist and suddenly you've got tits to die for. I've been there. You're pregnant. Share this with me, please. Let me help.'

Ysan's resistance folded. 'Oh, Clarrie. I didn't know how to tell you. I'm not even sure what to think. Rose says all's well, there's nothing to worry about. But don't congratulate me either. Not yet. And please, please, don't be jealous. I couldn't cope.'

Clarabel smiled. 'You spoil all my fun.' Ysan laughed, then cried tears of relief.

'I think you need a hug,' Clarabel added, holding out her arms, making Ysan weep harder, wishing she'd told her earlier.

'This is becoming a habit,' said Ysan as she shuffled across the moss into Clarabel's embrace. 'What happened to my looking after you?'

Lying together, they stayed wordless for a while, though not silent. Clarabel made soothing sounds, stroking Ysan's fair tangled hair, wet from their swim, occasionally wiping her cheeks. Ysan snuffled back tears, relieved to have shared her secret at last, relieved to have found comfort.

'Is it hell?' Clarabel asked at last.

Ysan sighed, not knowing how to explain. The sickness, the confusion, the fear, the abandonment ... It should be utter hell, but somehow it wasn't. All her emotion seemed on hold, as if behind a dam wall, waiting to burst through. But when? Back at home with a better perspective after talking to people, unravelling her options, testing her support, or the lack of it?

'You don't need to handle it alone,' said Clarabel, as if reading Ysan's mind. 'I can help.'

Ysan held Clarabel tighter like a child would its mother, tuning into her heartbeats.

'Do you think you'll have it?'

It was the question Ysan had been dreading. 'I need to see Raúl,' she replied, knowing how it would sound.

Clarabel stiffened, stopped stroking. Then releasing Ysan she sat up, concerned. 'Oh, Zannie . . . I thought you'd accepted . . .'

Ysan shook her head, not wanting to speak. Clarabel's brow furrowed, her eyes squinting into the distance. Ysan found herself distracted, pondering how beautiful Clarabel's red hair looked against the dark-green canopy, sunspots sparkling behind.

Clarabel sighed. 'I'm not jealous, by the way. But I am sad. Sad for myself . . . Sad for you, because of Raúl . . . Sad for the baby . . .'

'The baby?'

Clarabel searched Ysan's eyes. 'Because I don't think you're going to have it . . . Are you?'

'I don't know,' she said. 'Nothing's definite. I need to get home. I can't think straight here. Everything's so unreal.'

In the days since learning she was pregnant, Ysan thought of her mother often. Pictured her talking to herself, coping with the days of waiting for news and rescue. Pictured too the joy of their eventual reunion; the moment she told her she was pregnant; the discussions that would follow, the talking over options; introducing her to Raúl when he eventually showed. Then talking all over again. She couldn't wait for it to start, for the decisions to be made. Couldn't wait for her emotions, her life and her future to be put back in order, to regain some sort of shape. Until then, as day followed day and rescue still failed to appear, she was grateful she at least had Clarabel for sympathy and Rose for reassurance whenever things seemed bleak.

'I'm so scared, Rose. I'm sure something's going to happen to me. Something awful. Before we're rescued.'

'What's wrong?'

'I don't know. I just don't feel right. I'm Rhesus negative, you know. So if the baby's blood mixes with mine . . .'

Rose smiled, holding Ysan's hand as they knelt facing each other. 'You should have said something before. You're sure it's Raúl's, right?'

'Of course.'

'Then there's no danger. He's Rhesus negative too, and so's the baby.'

Ysan hunched her shoulders, smiled coyly at Rose and apologised for being so pathetic and knowing so little. 'I'm so glad you're here,' she said.

'Now don't fret,' said Rose. 'You have a healthy baby in a healthy body. The circumstances aren't what you'd wish for, but you couldn't be in better shape. In these conditions, if there'd been anything the slightest bit wrong with you – or the baby – you'd have lost it by now. Your body knows when it's being stretched too far. It's got a final defence. Trust it.'

But Ysan couldn't trust her body – nor her mind, yet what she needed most of all was to think. And the best place to think was up her tree, away from everything. Away from Clarabel's subtle pressure, Rose's knowing looks, every-body's earnest talk of boats and rescue.

University would begin in October, the baby was due in April, her degree exams were in May and June. Even the most careful planning couldn't have timed a conception more likely to make her fail everything. Then what? By the time she should be trotting off to some distant jungle to begin her doctoral research, she'd have a five-month-old baby to look after. How competitive would that make her? How many university committees would invest their precious grant money in an average sort of girl with a poor degree, a spider phobia and a young baby? So was that it? The end?

There was one thing on her side. It wasn't just any baby
... It was Raúl's. Might that make a difference? He had
never told her his plans for after the island. Not really.
Would a baby matter? Wherever he was going, would he
want a baby and its mother with him? He'd tried so hard
not to have sex with her, then not to get her pregnant.
Surely the last thing he wanted now was another child. Or
maybe it was just her he didn't want. Maybe he'd run a
mile. Maybe this, maybe that. Thinking was going nowhere.
She needed to talk to Raúl. She needed to know. *He* needed
to know. How could she clamber aboard a rescue boat, his
baby in her belly, without his knowing? Wait days, weeks,
months for him to deign to reappear? She couldn't. She had
to try to tell him *before* they were rescued.

Alone, she trekked to the castle and, standing at its foot,
shouted into the air.

'Raúl! It's Ysan. I'm pregnant. It's your baby. I need to
talk.'

Over and over, she repeated the message. No answer. No
bearded face appearing over a high ridge. She went into one
of the dark, disgusting caves and shouted again, listening to
her message echoing around the unseen walls and tunnels.
Nothing.

On another day, she stood alone on the racetrack and
waved her arms at the castle to attract his attention. Then
she made the universal gesture of pregnancy, tracing out a
swollen stomach with her hand, before peering at the castle
for a response: a winking light, an ant-like figure in the cave
entrance, anything. Over and over, she repeated her gestures
and signs. Over and over she looked for a response. Nothing.

She trekked alone to South Bay, found a private cove
visible from Raúl's cave, and wrote a huge message in the
sand with her foot. 'YSAN. PREGNANT. YOURS. TALK.'
Sitting in shade above the Y of her name, she watched and
waited. A sand devil – a mini-twister – raked the beach and
wiped out her words, so she wrote them again. Again she
watched. Nothing.

If he was any sort of observer, he must have seen her signs – so all she could think was that he wasn't interested, or didn't care. Or worse: he was dead after all. Forlornly she looked up at the castle for signs one more time and, as she did so, she felt the dam inside her break and every drop of emotion gush forth to flood body and mind. She began to cry. *Now* it was hell.

She couldn't tell Clarabel. It had to be Rose. 'I'm not sure I want it.'

Rose immediately looked puzzled, worried, mildly disapproving.

'You mean you've decided to have an abortion. When we get back.'

Put so starkly, it made Ysan dither. 'Well, yes. I mean, no. I don't know. I just don't see how I can cope with a baby. I mean ... If I was you ... With a career already. With a man I could rely on. With money. But I've got nothing, except my plans and dreams. A baby could spoil everything.'

A gale was blowing. Ysan's long hair was tangling, whipping across her face, stinging her eyes.

'Don't panic,' Rose said softly. 'You have time to think about this.'

As was her habit, she reached out to hold Ysan's hands while they talked.

Ysan wouldn't let her, wanting action, not comfort, saying an abortion could be weeks away. She was running out of time. When she got back she had to write up her project while it was still fresh in her mind. It had to be good, her passport to a career. Then she had essays to write, reading to do. University started again in only a few weeks. 'I need to lose it now, Rose. While it's still small. Too small to notice. Too small to hurt me. While I can still pretend it was never there.'

The same height, the two women stared at each other, eyes on a level. 'I'm sorry,' said Rose. 'There's nothing I can do. And if you take my advice, you won't try to do anything either.'

'I don't want to do anything. I just want it to happen. I mean . . . Don't you have to be careful? During the first three months . . . in case you have a miscarriage? Can't I just *not* be careful?'

Rose warned that miscarriages couldn't be taken lightly, even that early, especially in a place like the island. Besides, as she'd told Ysan before: a healthy baby in a healthy body and almost nothing will shift it. Nothing natural, that is, except perhaps an overdose of stress. 'And if you're stupid enough to try anything unnatural, you're on your own. I wash my hands of you.'

When three weeks had passed since their plane landed, desperation began to take hold. No matter what was attempted in the name of distraction, heads kept turning towards the horizon. Increasingly, expressions betrayed concern more than anticipation, tension more than excitement. Three weeks was a long time for the people back home to take to organise their rescue, whatever the complications.

Emergency services on the mainland might be disorganised, even unconcerned about a bunch of foreigners who'd gone missing. Surely, though, one or more of their parents, someone from the university, or a journalist sniffing out a good news story, would jet out to the mainland to speed up the rescue. From there, all they'd need was a boat and map of the islands. How difficult was that? Sooner or later, they agreed, a rescue party would reach them. There was no need to panic. Not yet.

To a degree, 'sooner or later' placated everyone, except Ysan. Gripped by the feeling she was running out of time, she was falling apart. An irrational sense of having been abandoned – by Rose, by Raúl, by the university, even by her mother – was creeping over her. Only in her tree did she find any sort of peace, and even that was fragile. Sitting on

Sledge's sleeping bag, she would rest her chin on her knees, rock gently backwards and forwards and try to face what lay in store for her.

One blustery afternoon, after a fourth week had passed – making her eight weeks pregnant – Ysan climbed down from her tree to head back to the beach. Standing on the high side of the racetrack she had the sudden urge to run. When she reached the grove of banana trees, she rested a while, looking back at the path she'd just taken. As soon as she regained her breath, she ran back up the slope, then down again, her swollen breasts bouncing painfully, her chest wheezing for oxygen in the hot air.

Clarabel and Antonio appeared at the edge of the orchard, and Clarabel called out to her. 'What are you doing? You look totally demented. You'll have tits down to your waist if you bounce them around like that.'

Ysan came to a halt a few yards from them. 'Like yours, you mean.'

'Mine are supposed to be like this. Yours aren't. Why are you running?'

'Why do you think? I'm exercising. Keeping fit.'

'Keeping fit? Pregnant people don't keep fit, they take it easy.'

Clarabel gestured for Antonio to walk ahead. 'Go, Babes. *Hasta luego*,' she said. '*Cinco minutos*.'

Antonio reacted badly. He rattled off his distaste and trudged away in the direction of the tunnel. 'Talk about a bear with a sore head. He's been really grumpy the last couple of days.'

'What are you doing here at this time of day anyway? Shouldn't Antonio be fishing? Shouldn't you be gathering clams?'

'We're escaping. They're all arguing again.'

'What about?'

'The usual: beacons, boats, behaviour. Sledge slags off the lads. They slag off the girls. But what about you? Why all the running? I hope you're not trying to do any damage.'

The accusation hurt, but Ysan genuinely didn't know if it was true. Something inside was driving her to run, despite the fact that running – or the danger of a fall – might harm the baby. Did that mean she was running to harm the baby? She hadn't rationalised it. She was just following an instinct. 'I just feel like running.'

'Well you shouldn't. Think of the baby.'

'Perhaps it would be better if I lost it. Raúl doesn't want it.'

'Don't say that.'

'It's true. I told him, but he just wasn't interested.'

'Zannie, please don't talk like this. You're scaring me. You haven't spoken to Raúl. How could you?' Clarabel was on the verge of tears. 'Have you any idea what I'd give to be in your position? You've got a baby inside you, Ysan. A tiny person. Please take care of it.'

'Stop it, Clarrie, please. Don't you think I've thought all this? But I've got to think of myself as well. Why is the rescue taking so fucking long?' She began to cry in frustration, and Clarabel cried with her. They hated what they were doing to each other. Both poised themselves for another hug, to soothe and to reassure, but neither could make the move. To Ysan it felt, for the first time, that she couldn't trust Clarabel to have her interests truly at heart. And from what she could see, Clarabel felt exactly the same.

'Don't pressure me,' Ysan added. 'Only I can decide.'

Clarabel's expression raced from anger through fear to panic. 'At least stop this running nonsense. Swim if you must, but don't run, don't fall, don't harm it. Please? I'm begging you. Don't lose it. You could regret it all your life.'

Ysan tried to smile reassuringly through her tears. 'I really don't think there'd be any shifting it. It's like Rose told me: a healthy baby in a healthy body. It's after it's born, that's the problem.'

'Oh, Zannie . . . Look, if you really, really don't want it. If it's going to mess up your plans, your career . . . Give it to me. I'll look after it. All you've got to do is keep it healthy and have it. Please! Just have it. I'll do the rest. I promise.'

Stunned, Ysan stared at her. 'Is that all what I'm going through means to you? A chance to get your hands on a baby?'

She turned away, stumbling a little before getting into her stride, then walking quickly round the corner and out of Clarabel's sight. Then she ran downhill, daring herself to leap every obstacle. She ran all the way down the slope, through the palms, over the sand, then she threw herself into the sea and swam hard over the coral to the toe of the northern headland. There, chin on her knees, she scanned the horizon. Watched for a boat. Her life was crumbling. She had to get home. And soon.

SIXTEEN

5–10 September 2006

Nearly five tense weeks had passed since their plane landed without them in the world beyond the island. Despite continuing assurances from Sledge and Rose that they would be rescued, more people, more often, were voicing fears. Something had gone wrong. Nobody was looking for them any more. Assumed dead, drowned at sea, interred in a sunken wreck, they might have to live out their days on the island. Everybody was suffering, but some still tried to keep hope alive, including Clarabel and Ysan.

In one way, the rift between them hadn't lasted long. Within a day, they'd apologised to each other, hugged, and gone back to spending their fairly meagre spare time together; those few spells when Ysan wasn't up her tree and Clarabel wasn't with Antonio. But in another much deeper way, the rift hadn't healed at all. They both sensed the trust was gone, the sure knowledge that they would support each other without question. So many subjects were suddenly taboo – Raúl, the baby, Clarabel's infertility – and their conversations became cautious and stilted.

Ysan ran often, though she made sure Clarabel never saw her. And she swam, racing anybody who cared to join her

– usually Antonio – to the headland and back. She pushed herself to the limit with abandon, the better to stop familiar thoughts from haunting her.

Up her tree, working, she occasionally found peace, but it was becoming elusive. Most often her mind was a clutter. Where was Raúl? What had happened to the old, carefree Ysan? Where was rescue? Why wasn't her mother leading the search? Sometimes such stupid, baseless, melodramatic thoughts so overcame her that she genuinely believed she was going mad: Raúl would beat her to death for becoming pregnant; Clarabel would poison her and take the baby. In every scenario, she was going to die, never to be rescued. Spontaneously, she'd burst into tears, cry for an hour or more, then just as suddenly think clearly again, record fine details of the chimps' behaviour. She'd find pleasure in the smell of blossom, the feel of wind on her body, the sound of insects and birds, the sight of naked people going about their business. Then all too soon her brain would turn on itself, fill with indecision, fear and despair and darken again with irrational thoughts. It was little consolation to observe that she wasn't alone in her mental suffering.

Maisie had for a while become inconsolable. As her hair grew, she became obsessed by the thought that her bond with her dead brother was breaking. The lost money for the foundation was also tearing at her conscience. She went back to stone razors, sand abrasives and, in final desperation, pulling out hairs by the root one by one. It became a manic malaise more than a considered campaign, an orgy of self-harm, distressing to everyone. In the end, Rose stepped in. 'From now on, why not do the opposite. Make *hair* your bond to your brother. Grow it long, grow it thick, make it beautiful. For him.'

To back up her words, she persuaded Sledge, who could afford it better than her, to pledge money to the CF foundation for the next five years. To pay by the centimetre for the longest hair on Maisie's head.

'And I'll sponsor your pubes,' piped up Danny, 'if you'll let me do the measuring.'

It was Alexi's mental state, not Ysan's or Maisie's, that caused the most concern. Millimetre by millimetre her body had begun crossing the line from attractively slim to unhealthily thin. She'd stopped eating and her mood rarely lifted beyond depression and paranoia. She'd even stopped sparring with Abi. 'It's so peaceful here. So beautiful,' she said to Ysan late one afternoon. 'A good place to die.'

They were sitting by one of the barbecue fires where Ysan was keeping an eye on spitted fish. Alexi joined her, slumping down by her side to stare away from the flames.

'We're not going to die,' Ysan said.

'Sure we are. One by one. And I'll be the first. Bury me at the waterfall, will you? I love that place.'

The first release of the growing tension within the group came one night before dinner. Henry, Jill and Pete were preparing vegetables when suddenly Henry began to shout. 'Take your fucking eyes off my wife, donkey dick. Don't even think about it.'

He was squaring up to Pete, pushing at his chest and shoulders, making the younger but taller man stagger backwards. But the effect was ridiculous because Henry was sporting an erection.

'I wasn't.'

'You were.'

'I wasn't. This is crazy. I'm out of here. You can finish the bloody dinner yourself.'

Pete began to walk away, then turned angrily back. 'One of these days, fish breath, your worst nightmare will come true. And it'll be your fault.'

'Try it, you ugly bastard. Just fucking try it.'

Pete stalked away but let 'Don't tempt me' hang in the smoky air.

Henry watched him go, but caught Ysan looking at him.

'What are you staring at? Of course I've got a stiffy. If you sit like that, I can see fucking everything.'

'Then don't look.'

Jill arrived at Henry's side and swung him round to push him away. No sooner had she begun to apologise to Ysan for her husband's behaviour than there were sounds of another commotion further down the beach.

Ysan scrambled to her feet and ran towards the fracas. Near the sea, Dingo was bent double, bellowing with shock and pain. In front of him, her face almost pressed against his, Alexi poured out obscenities. When Dingo straightened his back he began to throw punches at the stick-thin girl. Alexi dodged two wild swings, but the third connected with a horrible slap and knocked her sideways and down to the sand. Dingo threw himself on to her and continued punching her about the ribs and head. With her so fragile and Dingo out of control it looked like he'd kill her.

People arrived from all directions. It took three of the other men to haul Dingo to his feet. When Henry went to hold Alexi back, she turned on him, manically slashing at his body with a clenched hand. Jill and Abi finally restrained her, holding her arms while Maisie prised a sharpened shell from her grasp and threw it into the sea. Looking and behaving like a starving street urchin caught picking pockets, Alexi struggled to break free but had neither the strength nor the energy.

'Fucking half-caste bitch,' Dingo shouted. 'She cut me!'

Blood ran freely from a diagonal slash across his abdomen, only centimetres from his genitals.

'Serves you right, you bastard. Don't you dare do anything like that to me again.'

'It was only my fucking finger,' shouted Dingo as Sledge and Rose reached the scene. 'Next time it'll be my prick.'

Muscles bulging, eyes glaring, finger pointing and stabbing at Alexi, blood was now dripping from his penis.

'Then next time I'll cut the bloody thing off.'

'And if she doesn't, I will.' Abi stepped to Alexi's side. 'He did the same to me this morning, the perve.'

'What the hell's going on?' demanded Sledge, only to be answered by a babble of angry voices.

He told everybody to shut up and listen, eyeballing them one by one, looking fierce with his Viking beard of sun-bleached gold and red. 'I never want to see anything like this again. You lot –' he pointed at the lads '– are going to keep your hands, pricks, fists and racist remarks to yourselves, and you ... Christ, Alexi, what the hell were you thinking?'

'I'll tell you what I was thinking. We're never going to get off this island. And this fucking animal was bound to try something despicable. And I thought I'd do us all a favour if I sliced off that bag of worms between his legs right now. And I damn near did too.' Without waiting for a further reprimand, she stumbled up the beach towards the orchard, her heels kicking up sand and her frail figure belying the weight of the words she'd left behind.

Henry turned on Sledge. 'It's no good trying to lay down the law, Sledge. You can bellow all you want, but nobody's going to take any fucking notice. If we don't get off this island soon – and I mean very soon – something's going to give. It's got to. If Dingo doesn't explode, I fucking will. Everywhere I look there are cunts. It's more than flesh and blood can stand.'

That Henry ogled and lusted was beyond doubt. All the women had caught him staring brazenly, often several times a day. Even so, as he stood on the beach, his gaunt body next to the bullish Sledge and Dingo, his outpouring of carnal frustration seemed incongruous.

'Well you're going to have to stand it, aren't you?' replied Sledge. 'Christ, Henry, you're a bloody member of staff. You're supposed to be setting an example here. If I can cope, you can.'

'It's all right for you. You're shagging Rose every chance you get.'

Ysan turned away, leaving the two men to bicker.

'Where are you going?' Rose asked sheepishly.

'To find Alexi.' She wanted to talk to someone in as much mental pain as herself.

'She could be anywhere. It'll be dark soon.'

'I know where she is.'

Under the trees at the waterfall everything had lost its colour, but even from a distance Ysan could see Alexi's frail silhouette. She was sitting on the fallen tree, knees under her chin, rocking slowly backwards and forwards.

'Go away!' she ordered, making herself even smaller by pushing her head between her knees.

Ysan sat by her side, listening to her breathing – short and sharp but noisy, almost asthmatic.

'You're not the only one who wants to escape,' Ysan said.

'I want to be alone. Go away!'

'Calm down. Breathe slower. I thought we could talk.'

After a long silence, Alexi slowly raised her head. 'See the fireflies? They're dancing. Near the fall. See them? Like fairies.'

Ysan placed her hand gently onto Alexi's back, but it was shrugged away.

'Do you think the vines are strong enough?' said Alexi.

'For what?'

'A noose.'

'Nowhere near.'

Alexi straightened a little. 'Men like Dingo, I hate them. Been dumping on me all my life.' She took a few deeper breaths, struggling to get her lungs under control. 'Do you know why Abi calls me a headcase, or loony?'

Ysan struggled to find a thread in Alexi's words. 'Because you hate men?'

A firefly danced by and Alexi tried to snatch it from the air, but missed. 'I have phases. Highs and lows, each lasting weeks, sometimes months. Abi reckons I'm a manic depressive, but I'm not. The malicious bitch even said I should be on medication; blamed it all on mixed-up genes. Four continents. One grandfather English, his wife Punjabi. The other Native American, his wife ethnic African. How mixed-up is that?'

'I'd be proud of that. I don't even know my father's name, never mind his nationality. Wouldn't know where to start looking for my roots.'

'Scandinavia?' Alexi said, with almost a smile. 'Not even your father? How come?'

'I was conceived on holiday. On a French beach. Mum drunk and stoned. Could have been any one of six total strangers.'

'Good for her. Cut the bastards down to size. Sperm is all they're good for. I hate them. Most of them. Perhaps one in a thousand, or a million. Right time, right place, right phase. Otherwise . . .'

'Bad experiences?'

Alexi shrugged. 'Nothing major. My dad was a bit free with his slaps. I had an uncle who used to fondle my bum. And my brother went through a stage when he wanted me to catch him wanking. Perfect training for this place.' She stretched her legs in front of her, arms propping her torso upright, a long thin shadow among shadows. 'What did you want to talk about?'

Ysan had almost forgotten she'd said it. 'I don't know. Pain. Hell. Inside-the-head stuff, inside the heart. I thought we could help each other.'

'You? Ysan the ape watcher, working away on your project while the rest of us crumble? *You* need help? *You're* in pain? Are you sure we're talking about the same thing here?' The words were said kindly and in surprise, not sarcasm.

'Don't tell anybody else,' Ysan began. 'Rose and Clarabel know, but don't even talk to them about it. I'm pregnant. Just over two months. I don't know what to do, or where to turn. It's driving me crazy as in mad. I'm the headcase.'

'Raúl?'

Ysan nodded.

'Christ! Then you've been dumped on too. A dead man's kid. I didn't realise. You poor cow. What are you going to do?'

'I don't know. What would you do?'

Alexi stifled a chuckle. 'Same as I did when I was fourteen, I guess. My biology teacher gave me the ultimate practical. And no, it wasn't rape. I adored him. One in a million you see. But I couldn't have his baby.'

'You were young. So you went for an abortion?'

'Knitting needle first. Then hospital. But that was me, the real loony. What are *you* going to do?'

'I don't know.'

'Look . . . let's not go back. It's too dark. Let's spend the night here, just the two of us. We'll bitch about bastards, swim in the dark, sleep on the moss, wet ourselves for fear of scorpions and spiders, then breakfast in the orchard. Two screwed-up women making a stand for insanity. What do you say? How about it?'

The night was fun but the next day, up her tree, Ysan's thoughts coiled tightly again. Alexi's crazed outburst on the beach had seeded a realisation that Ysan couldn't quell. It was illogical, scary, impossible: but suppose somehow Raúl had engineered for his experiment to run not for weeks, but months? So many months that she had to give birth on the island. Under a bush. With buckets of blood. She'd surely die.

Her fear for the future pushed her closer to losing control in the present. She wasn't deliberately trying to work out ways to rid herself of the baby before it killed her, but her thoughts constantly moved in that direction. In the morning, she contemplated jumping from her tree, to see if the jolt might do what running and swimming had not. But she couldn't. At midday, she took the leaf-stripped handle of her swish stick and, with Alexi's words banging through her brain, pushed it inside herself, daring her hands to push it further and further, but they wouldn't. Then in the afternoon, triggered by the distant sight of Sledge humping Rose, she wondered about sex. Not sex the satisfier of lust, the bringer of pleasure, but sex the destroyer. An old wives' tale? Maybe. But what about rough sex with someone new? Surely rape could cause a miscarriage? She imagined an anonymous man slamming against her belly, his penis a piston inside her, its tip hammering away at a fragile, formless lump in her womb, and her body wanted to make it happen. At least, in its way, it was 'natural'.

But which of the men could she dare, or bear, to seduce into angry unrestrained intercourse? Not Antonio, Sledge or Henry – they had partners, and Henry was weird. Not Ian – too feeble, too small. Not Danny – too much baggage. Not Dingo – way too obnoxious. It would have to be Pete, ugly Pete, huge Pete, his battering ram more than enough to reach, pound and squash deep inside.

As if ordained, Pete arrived midafternoon to sit alone in the banana grove.

Ysan ghosted down her tree and crossed the racetrack. 'Hi! What's up, Pete?' she asked with forced perkiness.

'Trying to make a bow.'

Unsmiling, he looked up at her. She'd not noticed it before but something had blunted or hardened his steel-grey eyes. 'To kill rabbits. I've bet Maisie I can shoot one before she can spear or snare one. But the vines are useless.'

They didn't know each other well. Even after several weeks on the island together they'd hardly spoken. And never one to one. But Ysan had heard things. Mainly from Danny. Like Ian, Pete was still a virgin.

While Pete struggled with his bow and vine, Ysan inspected him closely. The island had been good for his physique. He'd grown a beard too. All the men now had one, matching their ever longer unkempt hair, but some were more impressive than others. Sledge's sun-bleached Viking was the winner, but Pete's came a close second. It was fair and nearly as full. With it, his facial asymmetry was evened out and his disfiguring blemishes almost hidden.

Pete looked up at her again. 'Do you know you're the only one that calls me by my name?' he said. 'The others just call me Ugly.'

'I wouldn't do that.'

Then he smiled, displaying his teeth in all their crooked, grey-black glory. 'I believe you, and thanks. But you may as well, you know. I've got used to it.'

Ysan averted her eyes. The teeth were a major turn-off. As she stood over him, his penis was beginning to swell. As it grew, it fell sideways under the weight, and nestled like an anaconda along the line of his groin. 'Sorry,' he said, 'it doesn't mean anything.'

Plan crumbling, destroyed by those awful teeth, Ysan floundered. 'No, I'm flattered . . . it's, um, impressive . . .'

The terrible smile reappeared. 'Thanks,' he said. 'Was there something you wanted?'

'No. Just wondered what you were doing, that's all. We don't seem to have talked much before, do we? Anyway . . . see you later.'

She made a quick exit, walking at first, then jogging towards the bay; all the while thinking there had to be another way.

'How do you say "I want" in Spanish?' Ysan asked Clarabel that evening as they sat and watched Antonio swim, phosphorescence tracing his path.

Clarabel shrugged. '*Quisiera*, I think. Why, what do you want?'

'Just wondered.'

'The least you can do is tell me why.'

'You won't like it.'

'Try me.'

'I want to ask Antonio to tell Raúl I'm pregnant. He visits him most days, you know, when he goes for his run.'

Clarabel groaned and held her head in her hands. When

she looked at Ysan again, her eyes were glistening. 'I thought you said you'd told him.'

'I tried. Maybe he didn't hear or see. But he'll listen to Antonio.'

Antonio beckoned from the sea for Ysan to join him in their usual race.

'How do I say "Tell Raúl I'm pregnant"?'

'Beats me.'

The cove was deserted. Ysan stood by Antonio's side, her stomach churning. She picked up a flat stone and skimmed it into the sea. The stone skipped twice before sinking, each brief bounce splashing phosphorescent green, then tracing purple as it sank. Antonio copied her and a competition developed.

'Antonio . . . *Quisiera . . . tu . . .*' Running out of Spanish, she continued, 'to tell him –' pointing at the castle '– that I'm pregnant and that it's his.' She ran her hand over an imaginary swollen belly, then pointed again at the castle.

Antonio looked confused, then a strange smile crept over his face. He pointed at himself, then at her stomach, then – confusion again – vaguely towards the castle.

'*Si! Si! Mañana,*' she said.

'*Mañana? Allí?*' he asked, again pointing vaguely towards the castle, then at her, then himself. Looking confused again, he glanced around at the cove. '*Por qué no lo hacemos ahora?*'

Ysan recognised *ahora*. '*Si! Ahora!* Even better. *Mejor.*'

Once again Antonio pointed at her stomach, then himself. '*Quieres decir que . . . Quieres follar, Si?*'

'*Si!*' she repeated on a reflex, without understanding. 'You go tell him – and tell him it's his. *Ahora! Ahora* is good.'

'*Ahora!*'

'*Si!* Well . . . After the game. Give me a chance to win.' She picked up a likely looking stone. 'First to ten,' and she mimicked a stone bouncing off the water ten times.

'*Diez.*' Antonio held up ten fingers. '*Primero a diez. Pues follamos, si?*'

'*Si!*' she confirmed, feeling quite proud of herself.

After one mighty throw, Ysan lost her balance and fell to the sand. Antonio helped her to her feet. But pulling her towards him he tried to kiss her. Wriggling her mouth free, she placed her hand over his lips. 'Antonio!'

He tried again.

'No! Stop it! Clarabel – my *amigo.*'

'*Si! Amigos.*' He held her firmly. There was no anger in his face, no violence in his eyes, his manner was always playful, never aggressive. But he wouldn't let her go. She struggled to break free, repeating, 'Antonio! Stop it! Let me go!'

She broke free and they both laughed nervously when he caught her again and they fell on the sand, where he pinned her down by the wrists. And they laughed even more when he parted her legs and manoeuvred until all he had to do, to turn their game into rape, was push. It was then she stopped laughing. 'No!'

He looked hurt, even confused, but lifted his weight from her body and sat on his heels between her calves, his penis bolt upright. '*Querías quedarse embarazada? Si? De yo? Querías decir que quieres follar, si?*'

Breathless, she smiled up at him. 'A bit embarrassed, *si,*' she said, 'but it's OK. Just don't do anything we might both regret. OK?'

After lying still for a few moments and smiling sweetly, she rolled onto her side and scampered away on all fours. But he was too quick, catching her before she could stand, and too strong with his hands gripping her hips to hold her firmly. For a second time all that was needed was a push. Laughing again, he said, '*Quieres follar. Ahora! Si?*'

'That's not fair,' she complained, but could not stop her own laughter. 'You've at least got to give me a head start.'

But he didn't let go. And she couldn't say whether it was he who pushed gently forwards into her or she who sank gently back onto him to take the final step in betraying

Clarabel. And once he was inside her, Ysan did nothing to make him withdraw. Every agonising guilt-ridden thought over how she was cheating Clarabel was countered by another, that here was the chance to end her mental torment.

Shifting her position, she even widened her legs and lowered her back a little, so that he could thrust more easily and it was getting faster and deeper and harder. She had no thought of sexual pleasure, nor did she experience much. All that filled her mind was a womb, an amorphous embryo, and a deadly penis thrusting ever nearer.

Antonio was giving his first gasp of climax when Ysan saw two pairs of feet in the moonlight and tried to pull free, but Antonio was oblivious and wouldn't be ousted. They were still joined when, spraying sand and screaming obscenities, Danny launched himself to wrench Antonio from her back.

For a moment, the two men wrestled on the sand. Then Antonio disengaged, stood and pulled Danny up by the hair before striking him with one massive punch at the water's edge.

A small wave lapped around Danny's unresponsive face, washing away the blood that had begun to dribble from his nose. The next wave covered his face completely, swirling into his open mouth. He came to, spluttering.

Ysan knelt by his side, made him sit up, slapped his back. 'You OK?' she asked, splashing his face with water. His nose streamed blood and looked broken. Dazed though he was, Danny still glared at her. 'Why him?' He pushed her away so roughly she fell backwards into the water. Back on his feet, he faced Antonio before brushing past the bigger man and, hand over his nose, stumbling out of the cove.

Now it was Clarabel's turn to confront Antonio. Cursing him she triggered a tirade of Spanish in reply, aimed first at her, then at Ysan. He pointed wildly after Danny, at Ysan, then jabbed his finger at Clarabel. Still yelling, he turned his back on them both and began to walk away, before stopping and taking a few paces back towards Clarabel.

Speaking loudly but more slowly, he jabbed his finger at her again, pointed one last time at Ysan, then stalked away up the beach and out of their sight.

Ysan was still sitting distraught in the water, waves lapping her legs, when Clarabel stormed over to her. Ysan put her hands over her face, repeating, 'I'm sorry! I'm sorry!' Then she fell forwards onto the wet sand and sobbed.

'Sorry!' Clarabel waved her hands about her head. 'I don't want sorry, I want an explanation. Do you hate me that much? You just can't bear to see me happy now your own man's gone? You bitch! How could you?' She sank to her knees by Ysan's head. 'Why? Just tell me why.'

Raising herself slowly to her knees, Ysan couldn't look at Clarabel. With matted hair stuck to her face, wet sand caking her breasts, belly and hands, her eyes streaming tears and nose running, Ysan tried to explain. 'Not planned . . . Just happened . . . Couldn't stop . . .' Wiping her nose, she clogged it with sand from her hands. Wiping her eyes, she filled them with salt, making them stream even more.

Clarabel slapped her across her sandy, hair-plastered face. 'Stay away from him, do you hear? No more games. No more races. No more jaunts to the castle. Just stay completely away until we're rescued. And stay away from me too.'

Snivelling, hating herself, still wondering how it had happened, Ysan felt sick to her stomach and watched Clarabel walk out of sight. She then stared blankly at the lapping waves, stupidly counting time: one elephant . . . two elephant . . . three . . . What would she do now? What *could* she do?

As she looked out to sea she was tortured by another thought that made her turn to face the castle, its distant façade a mosaic of silver and black in the angled moonlight. Raúl's cave was plain to see, a large black shadow where once a rock had winked. Could Raúl have made them out from that distance in that pale light? Slumping back to the beach, she curled onto her side, then started counting time again.

SEVENTEEN

11–15 September 2006

Ysan spent the night in the cove. Huddled between rocks, sheltered beneath an overhang, she had only mosquitoes, fiddler crabs and raw memories for company. Still not really understanding what had happened, she at least understood she had no defence. Everybody she could have hurt, she had hurt, every friendship she could have destroyed, she had destroyed.

In advance of daylight, she skirted the main beach, had breakfast in the orchard and a long shower in the waterfall. Still gripped by the misery of guilt, she ensconced herself up her tree well before any of the others appeared on the racetrack.

On and off as the morning limped along, Ysan silently cried. Guilt over betraying Clarabel, revulsion at what she'd been trying to do to her baby, worry that she might have upset or angered Raúl, sadness over the pain she must have caused Danny and embarrassment at facing Antonio, all mingled to increase her sense of wretchedness.

The only thing to distract her was the appearance of Maisie on the racetrack, armed with a stone-tipped wooden spear. She crept along the orchard edge, taking advantage

of every piece of cover. Crouching, she held the spear like a javelin. There were chimps in the distance and rabbits much nearer, so near they'd soon be in range. The competition to be first to kill a rabbit was still alive. Whereas many had talked, only two had acted – Maisie to add rabbit to their diet, Pete to add purpose to perfecting a bow. So far, both had failed.

It embarrassed Ysan to remember that her first impression of Maisie was as a mouse: small, shrill, hairless, white. How much that image had changed. Small in body still, but no longer in stature, she had befriended everyone in the camp and worked for others with heart, conviction and energy. Her present mission failed, the spear landing lamely, and the rabbits disappeared safely into cover or burrows, leaving her standing despondent on the racetrack. In the distance a party of chimps, M1 at their head, trotted inquisitively nearer. They'd seen Maisie hunt rabbits several times. But this time, they moved closer to Maisie than Ysan had ever seen them with any of the others from the group in the orchard. Closer even than the day Ysan had lost her nerve. Their movements were slow and determined but tense around Maisie and their faces watchful. It was hard to determine their motivation: was it merely curiosity or were the chimps going into a stalk?

Maisie eventually left and the chimps melted away soon after. But it was late afternoon before Ysan felt robust enough to face everybody. Should she crawl in, apologise to everybody? Or stride in, head high, claiming she'd done nothing wrong? Her instincts wouldn't let her do either, but then neither could she think of an alternative.

As a gesture, she collected a basket of fruit and a branch for firewood, but when she arrived on the beach, the evening meal was in disarray. Antonio hadn't returned, and the day's fishing catch was meagre. She was greeted with hostility. Even Sledge spoke to her frostily when asking if she knew where Antonio had gone.

'No idea. Sorry.'

'You OK?' asked Rose tersely, as she arrived at Sledge's side.

'I suppose.'

'I don't think you're the most popular person at the moment.'

'So I see.' She walked on and was intercepted by Maisie.

'Glad you're back,' she said warmly. 'I was getting worried.'

'You're probably the only one.'

'Take no notice. They'll get over it. If you want to talk, come and find me, OK?'

'Thanks. Maybe a swim first.'

She swam for half an hour. When she emerged from the sea, Abi was on her way down the beach to go in. Hips swinging, arms hanging loosely by her sides, each foot landing precisely in front of the other, catwalk style, Abi was looking more self-assured than ever, and perhaps with reason. Although initially – with her apparently nippleless breasts and massacred pubes – she had, in Danny's words, 'undressed' less well than Ysan, time and nature had redressed the balance. Abi's body had tanned deeply, her nipples now shell-pink on brown. And now her pubic hair was full, its black mat was a feature not an anomaly, an attractive contrast with her blonde hair. Blonde again because, although close examination could still discern two tones where darker roots met dyed blonde, the sun had done a good job of bleaching both into a more even whole. And as for the walk . . . Ysan had no idea what it was about her own walk that other people found sexy – it was unconscious, natural – but it couldn't possibly rival Abi's practised sashay.

'Once a thieving tart, always a thieving tart. Raúl from me, Antonio from Clarabel. Who's next I wonder?'

Ysan walked past her. 'I didn't steal Raúl from you. He never wanted you.'

'Who's next up for Zannie?' Abi yelled after her. 'Sledge? Henry? Pete? Come and have your fill!'

As Ysan approached the barbecue fire, the others were obviously still talking about her and Antonio. Danny glared. And from that angry stare she knew he would look for a chance to make her pay, to hurt her as she'd hurt him.

Ysan joined Maisie in a quiet corner. She commented on how striking Maisie looked now her hair was growing.

'Still feel more hedgehog than woman, but thanks.' Her only complaint was about her 'bush' because her favourite ring was now hidden. 'No point having one if you don't flash it occasionally. I mean my ring, not my cunt.'

Alexi arrived on the beach and made her way over to them. 'He raped you, didn't he?' she said to Ysan. 'They're all saying you threw yourself at him but I told them, no way. You wouldn't do that. It was him, wasn't it?'

'It wasn't rape. But you're right, I didn't throw myself at him, either. I can't explain it. It just sort of happened. I'd never set out to hurt Clarabel.'

Alexi snorted. 'I still think he raped you. You're too nice, Ysan. Just tell it how it is and sod their feelings.'

Sniggers drifted their way as Abi joined the lads.

'Look at that whining waste of space,' Alexi went on. 'She's been dying for a chance to dig her knife into you, ever since Raúl made it obvious he preferred you. I'm going over to cut her down to size. Tell her she's got shit on her arse or something. Take that snooty smile off her face.'

Ysan and Maisie watched her go and pick a new fight with Abi. It was good to see her back on form.

Ysan woke to a blood-red sunrise and a new sensation. At first she thought it was just a tiny muscle, contracting occasionally in her abdomen wall. Then suddenly she realised.

'Maisie! Alexi! Wake up! Quick – hands!' The trio had spent the night together in a cove away from the rest.

Gently, she placed their hands palm down on her stomach.

'Feel it? Can you feel that?'

'What?'

'Wait . . . That! That twitch! It must be the baby. My God! Can you believe it?'

'My God! You're pregnant?' said Maisie, eyes wide.

'Nine weeks,' said Ysan. 'Today's the thirteenth of September.'

Early next morning on the main beach, Clarabel approached Ysan. 'New friends?'

Ysan couldn't meet her eye and didn't answer.

'More fool them. And Antonio's not back yet, you know. You've driven him away. Anyway . . . that's not why I'm here. I want to show you something.'

In silence Ysan followed Clarabel to a cove just off the main beach. There, tucked away, protected from the wind, Clarabel pointed out a drawing furrowed in the sand depicting Ysan and Antonio having sex. Moving on to other coves, Clarabel pointed out more. All were poor imitations of Clarabel's own cartoons. Childish captions gave away the authors: *Barbie fucks Kentonio, Roll up for the Golden Hole, Chimp or bitch?*

'Why show them to me?'

'So you know what's going on. Mad as I am at you, for some crazy reason I don't like to see them laughing at you behind your back.'

Clarabel wasn't looking at her. Throughout the encounter, the women's eyes had met only twice, and then only briefly.

'You could have rubbed them out,' Ysan said.

'That's for you to do.'

'You won't stop us drawing more,' said Abi as they all sat round that evening's fire.

'Good. But perhaps you could extend your range. Depict the night you tried to get off with Raúl.'

Abi laughed and denied it all, but the lads wanted more information so Ysan addressed everybody, explaining with relish and in detail how Abi had made her embarrassing drunken attempt at seduction. Soon all the lads were laughing at Abi.

The tiny victory was short lived. The next day the taunting of Ysan from Abi and the lads continued un-diminished, but Ysan no longer felt hopeless or alone. With one magic twitch, her foetus had metamorphosed from a parasite threatening death to a passenger offering compan-ionship. So far, it hadn't twitched again, but she knew it was thriving. 'We don't care, do we, Baby?' she said into her tummy in the tree the next day as she watched people come and go, imagining the terrible things they were thinking or saying about her.

As Ysan came down from her tree to add that day's bark sheet of data to her cache in the hollow trunk, she began to feel fortified by how her new bond with her baby made her ready to meet whatever the group cared to throw at her. She'd been as cautious as ever in making sure she wasn't seen leaving her tree. But as she threaded through the bushes that shielded her movements, she was suddenly and violent-ly grabbed from behind. An arm went round her stomach, a hand went over her mouth and she was yanked back against a man's body.

'Bend down, bitch. It's my turn now.'

They were the first words Danny had spoken to her in four days. 'No excuses this time. If you can do it with him you can do it with me.'

Ysan bit his hand and drove her elbow into his stomach. His grip weakened and she managed to swing round to face him, but he still held her by the wrist. She tried to prise open his hand, but he was too strong. 'Let me go. You're crazy.'

'Too right! Crazy for caring about you. Crazy for not just fucking you when I had the chance, like he did.'

There was no boyishness in his face now. No good humour, no cheek; his expression a fusion of anger, loathing and lust.

'It's called rape, Danny. It's against the law.'

She still found it difficult to be frightened of him. Still felt that 'No!' would eventually work.

'Law of the jungle now, Barbie doll. Your word against mine, who's going to believe you now?'

Ysan tried to yank her arm free, but Danny twisted her wrist, turned her round and bent her arm up behind her back. He was behind her again with his free arm across her throat.

'Let go! You're hurting me. I can't breathe.'

'Good! Now shut up.'

He tried to force her to her knees. The pair staggered forwards into a bush. 'Fucking get off. I'm pregnant.'

He laughed bitterly. 'Fuck me, you really do think I'm crazy. Last time we couldn't do it in case you got pregnant. This time we can't because you are. Didn't stop you letting him though, did it? Give up, Ysan. It's going to happen, one way or another.'

He tried to force her to her knees again. They staggered around crashing into bush after bush as Ysan refused to go to ground. 'Get down on your fucking knees and bend over. I don't want to hurt you, but I will if that's what it takes. You owe me this.'

'I don't owe you a damn thing,' she shouted, reaching blindly behind with her free hand for his genitals, intent on maiming him. She couldn't grasp them.

With one leg he tripped her and they hit the ground. Struggling and rolling, they slipped under a row of bushes and emerged on the racetrack at the top of a steep slope. Once on the ground Ysan's struggle became more desperate than ever. Kicking out with her legs and wrenching her body from side to side, she forced them downhill until they came to a stop against a pair of legs.

'Having fun?' It was Sledge.

Danny released her immediately. Ysan rose to her knees and Sledge helped her to her feet. Danny sat up behind her. When he turned on to his knees, Ysan broke from Sledge, lurched at him and kicked him hard between the legs. Her aim wasn't perfect, but it was good enough to make him fall on to his side, curled around his groin. His face blanched with pain.

'Ask Danny,' she said and strode away.

Sledge caught up with her. 'You OK?'

'He tried to rape me.'

'Seriously?'

'It seemed pretty serious to me.'

'So are you OK?'

'I'm fine.'

Sledge looked back at Danny as if trying to decide whether to stay with Ysan or go back and mete out punishment. 'I'll deal with him later.'

They walked in silence. Ysan couldn't stop herself shaking. Eventually, as they neared the palms she spoke. 'Sledge. Without thinking, where should we be? West or east of the mainland?'

'I don't need to think. We're east. Didn't you see the map?'

But all she'd seen was the crappy photocopy that had been part of the original circular asking who was interested in coming on the trip.

'That's the one,' he said. 'The island had a nature reserve symbol on it and a field station. It was east of the mainland, about a thousand kilometres.'

'Are you sure?' she asked.

They were under the palm trees now and the few people scattered around were watching them, listening to them.

'No question. I checked in the atlas. I found the mainland – forget what it was called though, too many vowels – and the one with the field station was definitely east. Why?'

'Because if you're sure. Absolutely sure. Then, well ... we're not on that island. This one's west of the mainland.'

Sledge smiled. 'Sorry, Ysan, I don't follow.'

'We travelled west from the moment we left the mainland. When the sun set the evening we boarded the boat, it was over the sea and opposite the mainland. When it rose the next morning, it was behind us, and then ahead of us when it set that evening. Remember? When it rose just before we arrived, it was cradled by that saddle-shaped island, due east from here.'

An audience gathered around them.

Henry's face purpled with rage. 'What are you saying? They've been looking for us in the wrong place? A thousand kilometres east instead of a thousand kilometres west?'

And then there was a moment of silence, before every single voice suddenly made itself heard, drowning out the crackle of fire and the slap of surf. From the tree-line three parakeets burst into flight.

Turning her back on everybody, Ysan walked away. She had no interest in anything they had to say. Only in the terrible understanding of how Raúl had thwarted their rescue. Not with a fictitious map that could send him to jail, but with a bad one. One that could be blamed on secretaries or photocopying machines.

Behind her, Sledge became the focus of everyone's accusations and desperate questions. 'Of course the original map, with our island clearly marked on it, will be at the university somewhere. In fact, I know where it will be – Raúl's office.'

'Raúl's bloody office!' Henry's voice was almost a scream. 'It was bloody cleared before we left!'

Ysan stopped in a cove, out of sight of the others. At the water's edge, she sank to her knees and looked up at the distant castle. 'You clever bugger. You clever, sick, sadistic bugger.'

But she wasn't alone for long; Abi had followed her. 'I should think you would crawl away and hide. I can't believe you're having his baby. Danny's just told me. You're disgusting. It's obscene.'

Ysan didn't turn around. 'Fuck off!'

'How did you do it? What filthy little tricks did you play to get him so besotted with you?'

Ysan shook her head. 'Just go away, Abi. I didn't need to play tricks.'

'He was *always* with you. If I'd spent half the time with him you did, you wouldn't have stood a chance.'

Ysan looked up at her and thought her mad.

'We've worked it out, you know. What your whoring has done. The night of the fire, you and Raúl were the last at the base. Leave a candle burning, did you? Or was it a postcoital fag? Too shagged out to check? And later, you were last to see him. Why didn't you stop him from going to Safe Harbour? I'd have stopped him. If I'd spent that evening with him he'd be alive now. And we'd all be home.'

Ysan stood up fast and turned so quickly, Abi flinched. 'Pathetic. You can draw your stupid pictures and call me all the names you want. Poison the lads against me, blame me for anything and everything. Who cares? I don't! Who cares why Raúl preferred me to you? He just did. And now I'm carrying his baby. So who gives a shit who is prettier or sexier? Get over yourself and grow up, you silly bitch. What does beauty matter when your personality is so ugly and your brain is such a fucking mess?'

Abi was too shocked and angry to retaliate straight away. She seemed to be hyperventilating and looked so stricken by what Ysan had said, the finger she raised and pointed at Ysan's face was shaking. 'You're poison. You're finished here. I swear on my life. It's over for you.'

Ysan only rejoined the group briefly that night to listen to their reactions to her revelation. They'd all had their doubts about rescue as each week passed, but the realisation their rescuers might be two thousand kilometres away on the opposite side of the mainland was the end of hope.

She heard Sledge doing his best. 'We mustn't give up. Nowhere is completely isolated these days. OK, so we haven't seen a boat or plane – even a high-flying plane – since we've been here. But that doesn't mean we won't. Maybe even tomorrow, or the day after, or next week, or next month.'

'But if they're searching in totally the wrong place . . .' said Henry.

'I accept that. We have to forget about being found by a systematic search, but eventually somebody will just stumble across us. They have to. And probably fairly soon. We've just got to stay calm. Keep a grip.'

But nobody was keeping a grip. Least of all Abi, who in the dark hours after midnight began to whine out loud they'd never be rescued, that her life was in ruins.

'Shut it, you stupid cow,' bellowed Dingo. 'One more whine and I'll beat the shit out of you.'

Sledge rounded on him in the darkness. 'No, you shut it, Dingo. If there's any beating to be done, it's my job – and it won't be on a girl.'

Henry screamed as if in agony. 'Will you all fucking shut up and let me sleep.'

To escape them all, Ysan walked off down the beach in the light of the fading fire. With so many wild thoughts of her own to restrain, she saw little hope of sleep anyway.

How long would it be, she wondered, with tension in the group spiralling, before she overdosed on stress? But she mustn't. Now her baby was precious, the thought of its loss was horrific. Yet miscarriage – once desired, now to be avoided at all costs – was according to Rose still a real risk for another month. All Ysan could think of for protection was to avoid others as much as possible and make a superhuman effort to stay calm.

She walked in the direction of the cove where she and Antonio had betrayed Clarabel. Be calm, she urged herself, watching the crescent moon rise from the indigo sea. Breathing deeply but gently, she scanned the beach until she saw the spot where she'd knelt for Antonio. Calm. How long ago was that now? Just four nights? Really so few? And still he stayed away. But where? With Raúl? In the castle? Or else . . . they'd gone. Both men, taking the boat. Antonio had finished his job; the new stone-agers had been given just enough training to cope. Now they were liberated, set free like the chimps. But to do what? Breed? Raúl didn't need to watch them any more. He could come back in, what, five years? ten years? to see how his experiment concluded.

'Don't panic, Baby,' she said aloud, hands on her stomach. She thought of Raúl's books, their conversations, the essays she'd written at university. Breeding experiments – what was needed? Blood samples and swabs – for DNA analysis. Behaviour profiles. Physical measurements: height, weight, everything. Raúl had all of those. And testis size – the experimenter's window into testosterone, sperm counts, maleness. Researchers always measured testis size, whether for chimp, lion, or any other animal. Also humans? Had Raúl really found an excuse to have the men's testes measured before the trip? Long ago, Danny had made an outlandish claim that each of the lads had their balls and penis measured and photographed. All the lads had maintained that this had happened, but the girls assumed this was a conspiratorial wind-up, a laddish fantasy. But suddenly it made some sense.

Unable to wait until sunrise, she ran up the beach in the moonlight. 'Sledge!' She shook his shoulder to wake him. 'Sledge! We need to talk. It's urgent.'

EIGHTEEN

15–22 September 2006

'Now you can ask me.' Sledge, fresh from a wake-up swim, sat with Ysan at the water's edge.

Ysan looked towards the horizon. Dawn was beginning to glow. 'Did all the men have their testes measured?'

'That's your burning question? Yes they did.'

Ysan closed her eyes. She was right, but it didn't bring her any pleasure. 'Why, Sledge? Did you never ask yourself, or Raúl, that question?'

'Why? Did you wake me just for this? I thought it was urgent.'

'It is. You can't just say "why?" You must have thought it bloody strange. I mean, testis size? What could that possibly have to do with this trip?'

'Nothing at all. But Herbert, the doctor in charge of the medicals, was a friend of Raúl's. Mine too. They were helping each other out. Raúl needed everybody checked for fitness and health, Herbert needed as many measurements of people's bodies as he could get for his own research. You must have heard of him. He's looking for long-term links between cancer risk and the size, shape and symmetry of different organs. Mainly breasts, but testes, penis and clitoris too. It's important stuff but not easy to get people to take part. So in exchange for free medicals, Raúl volunteered us. It's happening all the time. Everyone was supposed to sign a form agreeing to their measurements being used for research. Didn't you?'

'Probably. I was so desperate to come on this trip I just signed everything. So that's why they stretched something over my breasts and did things down below. They were measuring.' She hesitated, confidence dipping. 'No! Sod it! It still doesn't feel right. Raúl wanted those measurements to use himself. I'm sure he did.'

Sledge shrugged, then looked her up and down. 'You look fantastic in this light. Like you're on fire.'

The eastern sky shimmered with fiery apricot and pitch, like lava, painting their bodies orange-red.

'You too.'

For a few moments they feasted on the sight of each other, two splendid naked people bathing in the flames of a spectacular primeval dawn.

'Anyway,' she began. 'Never mind the sunrise . . . This will sound crazy, but . . .' And she told him of her suspicions that Raúl set the whole thing up as a breeding experiment. And if she was right, a man as scientifically rigorous as Raúl wouldn't return until they'd produced enough babies for some sort of conclusion. 'Maybe about twenty babies, or three or four each. How long would that take? Five years? Ten? Nearer ten, probably. That's how long we'd be looking at.'

When she finished, Sledge smiled, shook his head and reached out to rest his huge hand on her leg. It was the first time, as far as she could remember, he'd actually touched her. With fingers like carrots, the nails bitten and grimy, he squeezed her knee. Then patted her leg, higher on her thigh, and said how he admired her and the way she'd coped with pregnancy, and Raúl's death, and with Abi and Danny's attacks. He was impressed with how she'd worked too, and was even impressed with how tenaciously she'd stuck to her crazy story about Raúl.

With each compliment, each pat, each squeeze, his hand moved slightly further up her thigh. She'd been waiting for the migration to stop, but it hadn't, not yet, and was nearly . . . 'But a breeding experiment. He'd never have dreamed he could get away with it. And where would he go for ten years?' His fingers brushed her pubic hair. She flinched. He apologised and moved his hand away. Said he had no idea he'd been doing it. The movement between his legs suggested otherwise.

'It's . . . OK,' she said, wanting to save his embarrassment.

'Take it easy, Ysan. Let me do the worrying. The group needs a new focus: we should build a raft. To keep up morale. Plan a way off the island. We could be waiting a long time for someone to just find us by chance. But don't say that to the others, not yet. Just you and me for the moment, eh? Just you and me.'

For a brief, furtive moment, his hand went back to her thigh.

'Of course. Just you and me,' said Ysan.

She jumped up, thanked him for listening and left him on the shoreline. For her, whatever he thought, measured testes meant one thing – a breeding experiment. Which in turn meant being abandoned for years without a boat. And Sledge was right: a raft would be the only means of escape.

For her baby's sake as much as her own, Ysan had every intention of following Sledge's advice and taking it easy, as easy as her new view of their situation would allow. That didn't mean doing nothing. But it meant avoiding people – and it meant working, using the chimps and her project for distraction and to rein in the anxieties that could become suffocating when they caught her off guard in moments of inactivity.

Trusting that Danny hadn't located her tree the day he'd attacked her, she climbed each day to her seat and stayed there as long and as late as she could. Danny did revisit the bushes beneath her occasionally, but never once looked up.

It not only made her feel safe, but superior too, as she looked down on him and the others.

'Stay calm, Baby,' she would say whenever it kicked or she began to panic, trying to suppress the idea of years on the island, of being part of an insane breeding experiment, and giving birth under a bush. She was smart, she was healthy, she could cope.

She worked on hating Raúl. He was mad – she could see it now. Cruel too. And not just to them, but to their parents. How was her mother coping? And Maisie's parents, her father already struggling with alcoholism, her mother suffering from depression, legacies of the stressful life and death of their only son, now having to cope with the disappearance of their only daughter? Had they given up hope of ever seeing their children again? 'Talk to yourself, Mum. Keep on talking,' Ysan found herself saying aloud.

Hate him, Ysan would tell herself. Despise him. Think of nothing but revenge. And most of the time she succeeded. But most of the time was not all of the time. Raúl was an icon, her lover, the father of her baby. And she occasionally caught herself suffering the same wild fascinations that must have spurred him into madness. What would happen to them if they never left the island? Would they form faithful, traditional couples? Who'd pair off with whom? Would they build huts, live in boxes? How quickly would early Stone Age turn into suburbia? Would all the women have babies, except Clarabel? Would all the men father children, except Antonio? Who would have the most? Who would attract the most female interest? Sledge the alpha? Vicious, oversexed Dingo? The good-looking, but shallow Danny? The feckless Henry? The weak and socially challenged Ian? 'Ugly' Pete with his unnatural endowment? And with how many different women would their offspring be carried?

And then she'd call herself a hypocrite and work again on the hate.

A week passed. They reached the equinox, 22 September, and still Antonio had not returned. Ysan asked Sledge how long the boatman would have to be gone before Sledge took her theory seriously, and asked Clarabel how long it would be before she'd start talking to her again. 'Longer than this' was the short answer.

Nobody in the group spoke out loud of being a castaway for years, but Ysan could detect the change in attitude. There was now more talk of surviving on the island than of rescue. Laughter was rarely heard on the beach. The camaraderie was turning into something else. Clarabel was uncharacteristically sullen and solitary. Henry and Jill rarely spoke to each other. Dingo was more volatile than ever. Abi and Alexi were shouting at each other daily, and often about Ysan. And even the raised voices of Sledge and Rose could be heard at any time. By merely setting foot on the beach, the change in atmosphere, the tightening of tension, was now palpable.

Nursing nausea and sitting alone under the palm trees as night began to fall, Ysan watched Ian approach up the beach from the fire. Head down and slouching, he seemed more miserable and diffident than ever. He avoided eye contact with her and shifted from foot to foot. Even in the fading light, Ysan could see his arms and back were covered in bruises.

'Abi sent me. She wants you to come to the fire. She wants you to see something. Sorry.'

'What on earth happened to you?'

'Oh, you know. I keep bumping into things. No glasses, you see. But really . . . I think you should come to the fire.'

Ysan shook her head. 'No way.'

Since war had been declared at the water's edge, the two women had either glared at or ignored each other, and Ysan had no intention of being the first to give in. 'Go and tell her to come and ask me herself.'

Ian looked back in Abi's direction, then nervously at Ysan's feet. 'You should come. Really. She's got your notes. She's going to burn them.'

NINETEEN

22 September, evening

'Look who's here.' Abi sat by the fire with Ian, Dingo, Danny and Pete around her. 'Could be your lucky night, boys. She's probably ready for another shag.' She fanned her face with one of Ysan's data sheets. A pile of them lay beside her on the sand.

'Where did you get those?'

'Danny found them in a hollow tree. They burn really well. Look.' Abi threw one onto the fire.

'You spiteful bitch,' said Ysan, moving towards her tormentor.

Danny barred her way, then Dingo moved to hold her, first by her arms then, sliding behind her, by wrapping one arm round her chest and another round her stomach. Blatantly he cupped and squeezed one of her breasts and pulled her back so hard against him that his groin pushed between her buttocks.

Abi threw another sheet and watched it burn. Then held a third in the fire and raised it in the air to watch the flames catch before discarding it when they singed her fingers. 'What did you say these were, when you first told us about your project? Passport to the future, was it? Your career launcher? What career's that? Castaway mum?'

Beaming with excitement and satisfaction, Abi looked up at her audience, glancing from one lad to another. They were enjoying themselves too, but in a different way. They were aroused by Ysan's helplessness and the sight of Dingo groping her breasts and groin. Ysan struggled again to free herself, but Dingo's rough grip was too tight and determined. 'Let me burn one,' she demanded. 'They're mine. If anybody's going to destroy my work, it should be me.'

Dingo freed up a hand. Abi selected a sheet and passed it to Danny. 'Be my guest.'

Ysan took the sheet from Danny and glanced at the bark in the firelight. 'Three weeks ago,' she said. 'Only two females joined in the ambush. They failed miserably.' She threw the sheet theatrically into the fire.

'Another!' she demanded and read it aloud. 'Two weeks ago, on the Thursday. Four hours watching and I didn't see a thing – except Danny tossing himself off under a banana tree. Took about four minutes?' To a nervous ripple of laughter, Ysan threw that sheet onto the fire too.

'Another!'

Abi obliged, but now reluctantly.

'Ah, yes ...' said Ysan. 'Early this afternoon. A real shock. I saw an alpha male buggering an underling. It looked exactly like homosexual rape. I bet you didn't know animals did things like that, did you?'

As another sheet burned, Abi rose belligerently, all the remaining sheets of bark in her hands. 'I'm bored, and this is all rubbish.' She threw the entire collection into the fire. 'Shall we go for a swim, boys?'

'Stop right there,' Sledge bellowed, stomping towards them. 'Dingo, let her go. Now what's going on?' He walked into the circle of firelight, Rose and Clarabel behind him.

'Just a bit of fun,' said Abi.

Ysan exploded. 'Fun?' After slapping Dingo away from her, she turned and told Sledge what Abi had done.

Abi denied it. 'It was a joke. We were just burning blank sheets.'

Henry, Jill, Alexi and Maisie joined the group and everyone watched as Ysan poked a stick into the fire, raking the burning bark until she hooked out a smouldering fragment. She doused it in sand, then took it over to Sledge. 'Does that look like a bloody joke to you?' she said as he angled it in the firelight and moonlight. 'She's destroyed my work.'

'Let me see!' said Abi, as if aghast, moving so close to Sledge's side that her breasts nuzzled his biceps; close enough to hold the bark with him. 'Oh my God!' she said. 'Danny, they weren't all blank. Honestly, we thought they were, didn't we boys? I'm so sorry, Ysan. All your work. What can I say?'

It was a fine performance spoilt only by a knowing smile between Ysan and Clarabel, both on the brink of laughter. 'The complete set,' Ysan said. 'The malicious cow burned the whole lot.' Biting her lip, she paused for effect. 'So it's a good job I took Raúl's advice and always made a backup. I had hours to kill while watching those chimps.'

'Can we talk?' Ysan asked and caught hold of Clarabel's arm, not letting her walk away. It had been a fortnight since they had fallen out.

Clarabel agreed though not with any enthusiasm or warmth. In the weak light of the half-moon they walked along the water's edge. They weren't smiling now. Nor linking arms as they once might have done. 'How are you, Clarrie?'

'Fairly miserable. Fairly lonely. Missing Antonio. Missing you . . . the old you, I mean. But Christ! I don't know what I'd do if Abi did that to my sketches. Probably kill her.'

'I think I would have done too if I hadn't made that backup. She'll never find the originals. Don't suppose you've made copies. Have you?'

'Talk sense!'

'Is it all because of me and Antonio? You being mad I can understand and Abi being pissed off about Raúl. But why should all the lads hate me?'

'Isn't that obvious? You were their Golden Hole, the unattainable prize. Shagging Raúl was one thing. He was top dog. They could understand that. But Antonio? Why him, not them? You made them feel inferior. Not good enough in the hierarchy of men. Especially Danny, who now totally loathes you. To them, you're well and truly soiled. From goddess to the nympho-whore of the big boys in just one night.'

'Thanks for that.'

'It's how their minds work. So, yes, they all hate you: Abi, the lads. And I can't say I blame them. *I* hate you as well.'

If Ysan hadn't seen the flicker of a smile on Clarabel's mouth, she would not have held back the tears that were already burning her eyes. She swallowed. 'We couldn't really hate each other ... could we?' Ysan tentatively reached out a hand, placed it gently in Clarabel's. Clarabel didn't look at her, but she didn't take her hand away either. And for a while they stood together, watching the moon set behind the mountain.

'I am so sorry, I really am. Please forgive me, Clarrie. Please let's be friends again. Surely you of all people know how these things can happen without meaning anything.'

Clarabel turned and looked into her eyes, her face inscrutable.

Ysan squeezed Clarabel's hand. 'You and Sledge ... I heard you had sex the other day. In the banana grove. Somebody saw you.' It was just one of the many things Ysan had seen for herself from her tree. 'I'm not condemning. I know Antonio's gone, and I know Sledge's hands are beginning to wander – but what about Rose?'

'But Rose isn't my best friend, is she? You could even say she stole Sledge from me in the first place.'

Ysan looked up at the sky and shook her head. 'Clarrie, that's such crap. That's Abi logic.'

And within a moment they were laughing together until Ysan gasped. 'It's kicking. Would you like to feel?'

Ysan guided Clarabel's hand to the spot.

'I heard you'd had a change of heart. I was really pleased, honestly. Oh . . . Mighty little bugger, isn't it? Ysan, you're so lucky.'

They sat, then lay so that Clarabel could press her cheek to Ysan's stomach. Clarabel made noises of rapture as the baby squirmed. Ysan stared at the bright stars while stroking Clarabel's hair until her friend fell asleep. But sleep was a long way off for Ysan. She wondered how many more battles she would have to fight with Abi and her petty but increasingly aggressive allies. And for how long? Thanks to Raúl, the war could rage for years. But at least she had Clarabel back. Or did she?

This wasn't their old friendship reborn, unscarred. It couldn't be. Both had suffered, both had changed, and their needs were different. And it was the baby that had finally softened Clarabel. Not Ysan at all.

TWENTY

The next evening Antonio returned to Orchard Bay as nonchalantly as if he'd been away for an hour instead of a fortnight. Clarabel threw her arms around him and, before the others could greet or question him, the couple took off for a secluded cove. Ysan slipped away in another direction.

As a half-moon slowly appeared in the bay, Ysan sat hidden among rocks, absent-mindedly heaping sand over her feet and trying to figure out what Antonio's return could mean. How did this fit in with Raúl's breeding experiment? Had he stayed through choice, or because Raúl made him? And did Antonio's continuing presence mean that Raúl was also still on the island? Because if he was, then so was the boat; they wouldn't need to bother about a raft.

Voices rose through the sound of surf as people approached. Ysan, wary of leaving footprints, clambered over rocks to hide in the inky moon-shadow of an overhang.

It was the four lads with Abi. 'She's got to be in one of these coves.'

'Could be any of them, we'll never find her.'

'This is the right time. She's always out here on her own.'

'Let's follow her tomorrow.'

The quintet moved on, their voices sinking back into the sound of surf. Ysan moved deeper into the shadows. An hour later, from the back of her cave, she watched them head back to the main beach in silence.

Ysan rose early and made for her daytime hideaway to watch the chimps. When she returned to the camp in the afternoon, Sledge called her over. 'Guess what? You were right about the island. We are west of the mainland. Antonio confirmed it.'

'Did he say where he'd been?'

'*Explorando!* That's all he's said to anybody.'

'Exploring?'

'That's what he said. He also said, when I got it across to him that I wanted help with building a raft, that I was "*tonto*". Evidently the local winds and currents would take a raft straight into the open Pacific. "*Suicidio*," he said.'

'So what are you going to do?'

'What do you think? Build a raft, of course.'

With Antonio back on fishing duty, they all anticipated eating better that night. Before dinner, as Antonio returned with his catch, Clarabel dealt with a moment of potentially excruciating embarrassment in typical style. Bringing Antonio and Ysan together again for the first time, forcing a platonic handshake, she pointed at his genitals, then at Ysan's groin. 'Never again,' she declared. 'That way we stay friends.'

To drive home her point she lifted Antonio's penis with one hand and made a chopping gesture with the other.

Laughing coarsely, Antonio responded by putting an arm round each of them, giving them a simultaneous and vigorous hug. '*Mis dos mujeres. Que guapas*,' he said with a broad grin, then strode away, chuckling, to deliver the fish to Jill and Henry.

'I'm not entirely sure what that means, but I think he got the message,' said Clarabel.

Ysan linked arms with her as they watched him go. 'You

needn't worry, you know,' said Ysan. 'It won't happen again.'

'Too right it won't.'

Unnerved by the conversation she'd overheard the night before, Ysan begged Clarabel and Antonio to spend that night with her on the main beach. And with their protection, she slept soundly.

Early next morning, Ysan departed to collect more bark from above the waterfall, so she could begin a second copy of her data to replace the set Abi had burned. She had arranged to meet Clarabel at the waterfall afterwards, because loath though she was to admit it to herself, she was still feeling nervous about being alone.

Maisie caught up and walked with Ysan for a while. The rings in her eyebrows glinted as her eyes darted from Ysan to the orchard, to the racetrack, to the distant chimps, and back to Ysan again. Her whole body was animated with excitement. She'd found a new stronger vine and had set snares the night before. 'There'll be rabbit for dinner tonight,' she said. 'Pete stands no chance now.'

The pair paused on the racetrack, ready to go their separate ways. 'Come with me?' said Ysan, unable to stifle a note of pleading. She told Maisie about the conversation she'd overheard.

Maisie looked at Ysan as if she were a frightened but foolish child. 'They won't do anything. They wouldn't dare. They're all talk.'

Ysan smiled in embarrassment. 'I'm just being silly, aren't I?'

Suddenly, a cacophony of screams filled the air. On the racetrack, about thirty metres down from where they were standing, a group of chimps clashed. Three small dark shapes immediately fled squealing from the maelstrom of dust clouds and the suggestions of sudden violent motion within it. But at the centre of the commotion, a knot of sinewy and hunched figures still wheeled about each other, leaping, striking out and baring their hideous yellow teeth.

As the discordant shrieks rose to a crescendo, Ysan gave a tiny shiver. 'Sounds like we're surrounded by banshees.'

But her comment only made Maisie laugh. 'That'll be us lot in a few more weeks. Just you wait and see.'

One pair of chimps rolled about the ground. Another smaller chimp rose slowly from where it had fallen. M1 broke through the dust clutching the remains of a dead rabbit, and those apes still able to run followed after him. Soon all the chimps had dispersed into the orchard and the racetrack was empty and quiet again.

The two women hugged before parting. 'Be careful,' Ysan said.

Maisie winked at her. 'No problem. They're all scared of me.' And ran off towards the rabbit warren.

AUTHOR'S NOTE

And that was it. Suddenly it was over. Without warning. There was not even a hint that the notes I was scribbling were to be the last. One minute, as Ysan spoke about Clarabel and Antonio, she had sat by my side on the beach in Spain, relaxed and close, occasionally touching my knee or arm as was her way. But when relating her meeting with Maisie, she began pacing backwards and forwards, leaving furrows in the sand. Her voice faltered and she began to cry. I asked why she was upset but she turned away, her head bowing and her hand over her mouth. Sobbing, all she would do was shake her head. I stood to comfort her but she squirmed away, crying that she couldn't do this any more.

I was perplexed, wondering if I'd said or done something to prompt her anguish. And I wondered if what was to follow – because we were nearing the time in her story when she must lose her baby – was too painful for her to relate.

Ysan returned home for Christmas, leaving me wondering how I might ease her through the agony that this part of the story would clearly cause her the next time we met. Little did I realise I would never have the chance.

AFTERSHOCKS

TEN MISSING MONTHS

Ysan's meeting with Maisie on the racetrack was on 25 September 2006. The yacht on which she and Danny sailed from the island was plucked from the ocean by a passenger ship on 4 August 2007. What happened during those missing ten months, Ysan never revealed to me, leaving only the spin and PR the group had provided for the news media. But with old friendships fragile, egos inflated, jealousy rife, tempers inflamed, and libidos at bursting point, the ten months remaining to be described could not possibly have been as harmonious as the group wanted everybody to believe.

Why had Ysan broken down? How had she miscarried her baby after everything her pregnancy had survived so far? When and why did she make up with Danny so completely that she eventually conceived to him? What exactly were the circumstances surrounding Maisie's and Dingo's deaths? I wanted to know the answers, and I also wanted to know the secrets behind all of those other undisclosed events that Ysan's eyes and manner suggested to me but which she either couldn't, or wasn't being allowed, to relate.

CAUSES OF DEATH

January–February, 2008

The official inquest into the fates of Raúl, Dingo and Maisie took place on 14 January 2008 and had little hesitation in concluding 'accidental death through drowning' for all three. Sledge's assertion that Raúl made an error of judgment trying to sail in impossible seas was accepted without question. So too were the accounts by several members of the group that Dingo and Maisie had died while swimming near the coral reef of Orchard Bay. They heard Maisie shouting, saw her struggling, then saw Dingo swim to her aid. Then both disappeared, and by the time Sledge and Antonio swam out to them there was no trace of either. No indication of whether they'd been the victims of sharks, currents, coral, or all three.

I decided not to go to that inquest. In Ysan's e-mail (dated 7 January), she had not only ended our collaboration but had also asked me not to try to see or contact her again. Devastated though I was, I didn't abandon all hope immediately. If her decision had been a knee-jerk response to the tabloid photos of us, maybe with time she would see that she had been too hasty. I judged that a change of heart on her part would be more likely in the long-term if I didn't flout her wishes so blatantly in the short-term. So I stayed in Spain, shut away in my villa, putting the finishing touches to 'Ysan's Story', and growing steadily more fascinated by thoughts of what might happen next. But Ysan didn't change her mind and, as I read the various reports from the inquest, I chided myself for not being there.

The newspapers fell into two camps: those with more interest in what they thought the group was hiding, and those who saw more mileage in apportioning blame. The first camp had, like me, seen the television interviews and noticed the way that Sledge's forceful media persona kept Danny and Abi in the background. 'Like a headmaster afraid his pupils might blab about what he keeps in his cupboard' according to one source. These same papers, reporting on the inquest, all remarked on how uncomfortable Danny had looked when being questioned on oath. The coroner had given the others a fairly easy ride but Danny had obviously riled him. According to another source:

Danny Forsyth-Blake paid a price for his cockiness. Suddenly the coroner turned on him. 'I have a warning for you, Mr Forsyth-Blake. I know that you and your group haven't done so yet, which is admirable, but if you think you are going to profit financially from hiding things from this inquest, I'd urge you to think again. You have been under oath and the law takes a dim view of people giving false evidence, even if it isn't germane to the cause of death. So if I hear the slightest whisper that you, or any of your friends, have tried to cash in on information you've withheld from me today, you will live to regret it because I shall have no hesitation in referring you all for perjury. Are you sure there's nothing you want to tell me?' And for a moment, Mr Forsyth-Blake looked as though he was going to crack.

I phoned Tom Sykes, a friend of Raúl's and mine from our student days, who I'd heard had been present at the inquest as an observer, and quizzed him for his opinion of the people and their evidence.

A linguistic psychologist, Tom claims that by studying spoken language, body language and eye movements he can tell 'scientifically' (unlike the rest of us who do it by gut reaction) whether somebody is hiding something or not. According to him, everybody in the group when questioned had been 'constructing' their memories, not recounting something they'd actually seen. Their sentences contained far more 'hedging' phrases than average.

'So they were lying?'

'Well, not lying exactly. More like not quite telling the whole truth.'

Such reports and comments on a cover-up tickled my interest, but initially it was the reports in the newspapers in the second camp that stirred me most. The inquest's fairly straightforward deliberations on causes of death hadn't been the end of the matter. Driven on by Dingo's police-sergeant father who seemed determined that somebody should take full blame for his son's heroic death, there followed a heated debate over the extent and nature of Raúl's negligence, even whether the case should be handed to the Crown Prosecution Service for further investigation. In the end, the coroner decided against such an action.

I searched the reports for any mention that Ysan had put forward her conspiracy theory about Raúl and Antonio, but found none. In fact, I found no mention that she – or Alexi for that matter – had even given evidence. So either Ysan hadn't been called or, once placed under oath, she had come to her senses.

Two main questions concerning Raúl were explored. The first was why a man of his experience would make the mistake of trying to sail in such bad conditions instead of waiting for the storm to pass. The second was why his contingency plans had been so badly conceived that the group wasn't rescued for over a year.

The answer to the first question was fairly obvious. Raúl had tried to sail the boat the night he died because by the time he'd arrived at where it was moored the vessel had already broken free from its moorings and if left would have smashed to pieces. The inquest acknowledged as much. But even that act of bravery was turned against him by Dingo's father, who insisted that Raúl had panicked because he knew that, if the boat went down, the criminal negligence of his ill-conceived contingency plans would be exposed.

I should have been there to defend my friend's reputation. Nobody at the inquest really knew the man. Raúl would never have left England without making sure that if anything went wrong all the young people in his charge would be safe. Whatever the reason for his swimming out to the boat, it could not have been due to panic at being found guilty of negligence. But, knowing all the others were safe, he might have acted rashly to save that particular boat. It had once belonged to Antonio's late father and was probably the only tangible link Antonio still had with the man he adored. Raúl, who greatly valued friendship, would have known how important that boat was to Antonio and how devastated he would be if it were destroyed. If anything, it was bravery and friendship that drove him, not fear of discovery.

The debate about negligence centred on the desperately crude third- or fourth-generation photocopy of a map that Raúl left behind at the university. Sledge and Ysan had worked out what happened exactly. The rescue party was attracted to the only place on the map of note, about a thousand kilometres east of the mainland, whereas the group were on a totally insignificant island the same distance west, so insignificant it was lost amidst specks of dust and hairs that over time had also photocopied. Nobody could doubt that Raúl always intended to take his party to this island, where Jim Gillespie had released the chimps forty years earlier, so why didn't he leave behind a map to that effect?

I believe the deception was deliberate. Started by Jim and picked up again by Raúl, it was designed to ensure the colony of chimps was left in peace. A ploy to prevent those students lucky enough to visit once from ever visiting again, taking family and friends and spreading the word. The chimps' survival was precarious enough without exposing them to the death knell of eco-tourism. But neither Jim nor Raúl would have been criminally stupid enough to leave behind such a misleading map without a proper map as well in case something went wrong. All I had to do was prove that such a map really had been left, and uncover why it had neither been made available to the rescue party nor produced for the coroner.

A week or so after the inquest, with 'Ysan's Story' finished as far as I could go, and galvanised anew by the unexpected publication of some of Clarabel's bark drawings, I kicked off a visit to Manchester by visiting the Orwellian University to track down and talk to Raúl's last secretary, the woman who handled all the paperwork for the trip.

She was nervous, defensive and in a hurry to be rid of me. Yes, she had photocopied the map produced at the inquest, she said. Yes, it was unclear. Yes, even the original looked ancient. She'd suggested to Raúl she produce a new one but he'd said there was no need.

'And what about the envelope he gave you to be opened if anything went wrong?'

'You know about that?'

'What happened to it?'

'I don't know. It just disappeared. But it wasn't my fault.'

After a deep nervy breath she told me that the university had been in such a hurry to install a replacement after Raúl handed in his notice that they'd immediately emptied his office for decorating, moving all his books and papers into the basement. When the field-course party failed to return she'd tried to find the envelope again as Raúl had instructed but it had disappeared. 'But we don't know it contained a proper map,' she said.

'Of course it did. So why didn't you go to the inquest and speak up for him?'

'What difference would it have made? Raúl was dead. He had no family. Besides it was put to me, quite forcefully by certain people, that it was best for everybody if we let Raúl take the blame. Otherwise ... well, people might have blamed me.'

CLARABEL'S BABY

Mid-February 2008

After the meeting with Raúl's secretary, I refocused on my main reason for visiting England in February 2008: to investigate the surprising content of one of Clarabel's published sketches. There were four drawings in all, spread centrefold in a colour supplement along with a short synopsis of the group's island adventure and an even shorter piece on Clarabel, about whom the magazine clearly knew little. Then some in-house pundit had anonymously written a short piece on the technique of drawing on bark and a fairly sniffy appraisal of her style.

Clarabel's drawings are remarkable, the figures hovering somewhere between cave painting and cartoon but with selective patches of intricate detail, all set against backgrounds that I can only describe as economical Impressionism. The meld is powerful with an undeniable eroticism in the stance and movement of the bodies, and all achieved with just a sharp stone and a sheet of bark, the medium imparting its own primitive aura to the scenes.

Three of the published bark drawings held no contextual surprise for me. One shows the whole group on the beach, searching for their lost clothes, while behind them a glow in the sky takes on the not very subtle shape of a nuclear explosion. The second shows three naked men and a bikini-clad woman gazing on at the burning base. And the harrowing third shows Raúl's screaming face pressed hard against the cabin window as he drowns, his boat slipping beneath the surface of a sea with towering waves. But the fourth . . .

Clarabel portrays herself with wild wavy hair, generous curves, huge breasts and rampant pubic hair covering most of her belly. By her side is Antonio (complete with gratuitous oversized erection). They are sitting on the mossy log at the waterfall and in Clarabel's arms, suckling, is a baby. A baby girl.

Why had I never heard mention of Clarabel having a baby? Why had Ysan kept it from me, even inventing a hysterectomy for her friend?

Until then I believed that Ysan had never told me an outright lie. Now I couldn't be so sure, but I had to know. So I resolved to look into Clarabel's medical history – and to get my hands on more of her drawings. I phoned Rose, who refused to comment on the baby. If I wanted to know its story, she said aggressively, I should ask Clarabel. She knew nothing about a hysterectomy.

During the week in England following my confrontation with Raúl's ex-secretary, I made two important contacts. The first, in Manchester, was Professor Herbert Holding, whose laboratory had carried out the medicals on the students and staff taking part in the expedition. I found my way to his office in the Orwellian's medical building. Although he was at first hesitant, once I'd introduced myself as a friend of Raúl's, Herbert gave me a warm welcome. 'A brilliant man,' he said, blue eyes twinkling beneath a shock of unruly white hair, 'and a dear friend. It's criminal the things being said about him.'

To begin with he was cagey about releasing Clarabel's medical notes. But when I told him my main interest was in clearing Raúl's name, he agreed to help, citing the loophole in the release forms that all the students had signed which allowed their data to be used for any research that he might consider appropriate.

But my excitement had barely begun before it was quashed. If Clarabel had ever had a Caesarean and hysterectomy, she would have a fairly identifiable scar above the pubis that was likely to be recorded under 'Other Observations', but there was nothing.

With my investigation stalling, I visited my second contact. I'd phoned the newspaper that published Clarabel's drawings to find out how they had come by them. That call led me to an arts agency in London and the third floor of an Edwardian terrace house in a back street just off Tottenham Court Road. There, I was curtly invited into an untidy overflowing office by a well-dressed, trim, thirty-something woman with bobbed brown hair and hazel eyes who introduced herself as 'Max'. There was a computer, an old leather settee, endless filing cabinets and in the corner a sink, a kettle, a jar of instant coffee, a half-empty bottle of cheap whisky and an assortment of dirty mugs and glasses.

Unsmiling, Max looked me up and down, as if judging my worth, and frostily asked my business. When I told her I desperately wanted to see Clarabel's drawings, she laughed scornfully. 'Did Sledge send you? Anyway, the answer's still no.'

I told her about the book and my conversations with Ysan. 'It could be tremendous publicity for the drawings.'

'What was your name again?'

I told her.

'Sounds vaguely familiar.'

I reeled off the titles of my previous books but saw not a flicker of recognition or interest. Only a frown. 'Wait a minute. Aren't you the guy the tabloids caught naked on a beach with the other girl?' I nodded my assent. Her manner changed immediately and she said that if I came back at seven o'clock with a Chinese takeaway and a decent bottle of whisky, she'd see what she could do for me.

As we settled down later to pore over Clarabel's drawings (which grew more erotic with every sip of expensive malt), Max told me how she had ended up as Clarabel's agent. In August 2007, after everybody else had flown back to the UK, Clarabel had contacted Max by phone from the mainland. Faxes of a few drawings had been sent, and soon after a contract had shuttled between them. 'The moment I saw those faxes, I knew. Pure gold dust.'

Not long after, all the bark originals arrived by FedEx, along with a contact address (a Post Office box number on the mainland) and Clarabel's bank details in Manchester. The last direct contact Max received from Clarabel was a crackly voicemail in September saying that she was going back to the island and wouldn't be picking up mail or be able to telephone for several months. 'Something about a baby, I think. And I haven't heard a peep since. It's so frustrating. I've got one of the national galleries interested in an exhibition of her work. But only if she attends to promote it. And I've got to wait months before I can even talk to her. We'll have to sort out something better than this, baby or no baby.'

When we left her office at eight the next morning to grab a quick breakfast before I left for the airport, I was clutching a folder containing several sheets of thumbnails of Clarabel's drawings. To my excitement – and dismay over what it told me about Ysan – amongst the bark sheets in Max's possession I discovered a sequence showing Clarabel giving birth, but my first real chance to examine it was on the plane back to Spain. This particular set of sketches was in the form of a comic strip (but without speech balloons). Each 'frame' was small even in the original so, knowing I'd see nothing in a thumbnail, Max let me have a full-sized photocopy of this sequence.

Clarabel is depicted lying in the mouth of a cave at night, near a fire, and the weather seems dire: palms bowed in the wind, rain drawn in sheets, lightning raking the sky. But the main thing to interest me was the date.

In a minor betrayal of her scientific training, Clarabel always writes the month below her initials in the bottom right corner of every drawing – and for this sequence the month shown is April. Conception, therefore, was soon after they arrived on the island back in July, which in turn means, from Ysan's accounts, that the father could have been Sledge, in his sleeping bag on the very first night. Maybe that was why Rose was so reluctant to talk to me on the phone. Maybe, also, it was why Sledge had been so tetchy with me at the party. Perhaps the tabloids had been right. The big man did have things in his cupboard he'd rather nobody knew about: a baby with a student.

I did consider another possible father, Antonio, and wondered whether Ysan had also lied to me about his fertility. But unlike Sledge, Antonio wasn't present at the birth. From first frame to last, the drawing seems to span about thirty-six hours: darkness, daylight, then darkness again. Yet in all that time only Sledge, Rose, Ysan and Clarabel appear to be present. Is that any sort of proof of paternity? Probably not, but it is strange. Where was everybody at this seminal moment in the group's time on the island to welcome the first baby?

The date told me something else as well. Until Ysan miscarried, the two friends would have been pregnant at the same time. Why Ysan hadn't told me this – or indeed anything about Clarabel's baby – I couldn't know for sure, but I suspected an element of jealousy. Clarabel's baby survived to be born, but Ysan's didn't.

As I drove home that night along the Spanish mountain road, I was beginning to wonder if Ysan's entire account was anything more than lies or, at best, half truths.

THE RAFT

C larabel uses the comic strip technique to tell many stories from the group's time on the island. One of those stories, over three strips, is the building of a raft.

The first strip, dated October to December, is both funny and sad. Sledge is in charge, but in fact receives little help from anybody. Antonio and the lads are absent from all the frames, and Henry from most of them. Where Henry is shown he is mainly staring lustfully at Jill who, in turn, stares continuously at Sledge's erection and cartoonishly huge balls. Sledge then works manically, trying to fell a single tree over and over again. His efforts are portrayed by multiple arms, and sweat flying off in all directions. Also flying in all directions are the heads of ineffectual stone axes as soon as they impact the trunk.

In a second strip, dated February to March, everything changes. No longer do the heads and handles of stone axes part company. Small trees are felled. In the background, at the water's edge, a raft is taking shape. Sledge still has multiple arms but now – a favourite device of Clarabel's, I was to discover – he also has multiple penises. And helpers too: Jill, Abi, Clarabel and Alexi. The final frame shows the beach at Orchard Bay and a finished raft, complete with rudder and oar, simply waiting to be pushed into the sea. Sledge stands proudly by, arms crossed, while Antonio is shown laughing and Henry is holding up his hands, gesturing 'No'.

Although the group always insisted to the news media that they democratically refused to let anybody risk their lives by trying to escape, Clarabel suggests otherwise. In the first frame of a third sequence (dated March), Henry appears to have stumbled across Jill having sex with Antonio. In the second, Antonio has lifted a struggling Henry off the ground by the throat and is about to throw a punch. In the third, Henry is pushing the raft out to sea with help from Abi, and in the next half dozen, Henry first heads across Orchard Bay towards a huge wave marking the position of the coral reef, then he loses his oar and the rudder, drifts clockwise round the bay, and finally jumps off and sits morosely on rocks while Sledge and Antonio rescue the raft. In the final frame, Henry is still on the rocks, the raft is back on the beach, and the onlookers are walking away, laughing.

This left me perplexed about a whole range of issues. Why did the group never admit they had once allowed Henry to sail away on the raft? What happened around January to strengthen the stone axes and revitalise the raft project? Why did Clarabel show Sledge with multiple penises? And what was Jill doing having sex with Antonio?

From the glimpses I'd had in Max's office, I suspected that Clarabel's other drawings would provide me with all the answers.

SLIPPERY SLOPE

Early March 2008

The fact that Clarabel's revealing bark sketches ended up in Max's hands implied that Clarabel was playing no part in any cover-up. Either she was defiantly putting her career first, or she didn't know what a threat her sketches were to the story the group had decided to tell. Whatever the reason, Sledge and the others must have been horrified when they saw Clarabel's first pictures in print. Not those four sketches specifically, but the thought that hundreds of others were waiting to spring into public view, which explains why Sledge had quickly tracked down Max and tried to bully her into not publishing or displaying any more.

On my return to Spain, events dictated that I had to travel and couldn't work on the book for a fortnight or so. When I did finally return to my villa at the beginning of March, eager to get started again, there was a parcel waiting for me. It was from Max and there was a note inside:

22 February 2008
Not heard from you. Hope you haven't lost interest. If you have, these should get you going again. I've printed

out a selection of full-pagers for you in super-crisp detail so you don't miss a thing. They show our friends on a very slippery slope. Why not write it as a narrative like the bits of Ysan's story you sent me? If you need any help on the female perspective, just ask.

Make Clarabel famous and us both rich. We're relying on you.

Enjoy!

Ma(x)

Even before really looking at them, I e-mailed back.

2 March 2008

Thanks for the pics – and sorry I haven't been in touch. A proposition: how about actually including some of these in the book? They'd be fantastic.

x

3 March 2008

Sorry, no chance. You describe them, make them notorious, whet everybody's appetite. Then I'll sell them to the highest bidder.

Love and war, baby!

x

Having full-sized pictures let me see just how much detail Clarabel always put into her work. But my initial satisfaction at having more than thumbnails slowly soured as I flicked through the collection. Max had clearly selected the set to lead me along a particular path and I felt I was being manipulated into both what to describe and how to describe it.

The series starts quietly, supporting Ysan's assertion that the group had a period of voluntary sexual abstinence – driven mainly, I'm sure, by a fear of pregnancy in such a place. From July through early September 2006, nobody is shown having sex except Clarabel with Antonio and Rose with Sledge. Even Henry and Jill are abstaining as Ysan also described. There is one hilarious cartoon in which Jill is shown in the foreground wearing a horrendously spiked chastity belt and a smile. Henry is sitting on a rock, fiddling with himself, and looking frustrated, thunderous and morose all at the same time.

All of this reassuringly corroborates Ysan's account of those months. Clarabel's portrayal of the groin-slicing argument between Alexi and Dingo on the beach is also in accord, as is an angry drawing of Ysan having sex with Antonio, both portrayed as half-human, half-dog, while Clarabel and Danny approach between rocks in the background. Two of the September drawings though don't tally with Ysan's descriptions.

Ysan mentioned nothing of homosexual activity to me, yet Clarabel has drawings of both women and men indulging. There is a sketch of Alexi with either one or two unidentifiable other women playing sexual games while two owls sit on a rock nearby. One *or* two because in Clarabel's hands the event is shown via an almost Picasso-style contortion of hands, mouths, tongues, breasts, vulvas and protruding clitorises. There is also a more detailed and identifiable close-up of the groins of two men, with Pete's grasping hand completely hiding Ian's tiny erection while Ian's hand is dwarfed by Pete's monster.

Whereas Ysan barely even began to describe the group's sexual odyssey for me, Clarabel takes me all the way. Her explicit drawings as selected by Max show that from September onwards the group really did career down a slippery slope to spend a few months in an Elysium (or abyss depending on attitude) of openness and liberation. Raúl would have loved to see the lads indulging in public contests over who could ejaculate furthest, a sport that he'd once told me the earliest anthropologists had often observed in previously uncontacted tribes from North America to Australia. He would have enjoyed too seeing Sledge working his way through most of the women, and Jill, once 'broken' of resistance by an unexpectedly neanderthal act by Henry, working her way through all of the men. Finally, Clarabel portrays group sex on several occasions. Who with whom and how often? Clarabel shows us everything: brief stabs at monogamy giving way to increasing promiscuity and openness until, one by one, each of the women conceive. Pregnancy doesn't seem to end the women's promiscuity immediately, in fact briefly it seems to increase it, but then slowly either the women lose interest in sex, or the men lose interest in the women, or both. In the later months, sex ceases to be the main focus.

Conjugal harmony? Not a sign of it beyond the first four months.

At this point, I could have constructed sexual histories from Clarabel's sketches for each person on the island, then dramatised them as Max had urged. But I decided not to, for reasons I shall soon reveal. But one history, I did need to unravel and with care: Ysan's. Her story as depicted by Clarabel never quite made sense, and it was in trying to find meaning where little existed that I eventually discovered what everybody was hiding, Ysan included.

GETTING PREGNANT

April 2008

Conceiving isn't a precise science, we all know that. Some women need only to get within spitting distance of semen and they conceive immediately. Others have rampant unprotected sex lives, week after week, year after year, even with different men, yet still don't conceive until one day, curiously, it just happens. Nothing should really surprise us. Yet back in December 2007, watching Ysan displaying her wonderful body on that Spanish nudist beach, it somehow seemed unbelievable that having miscarried as early as September or October, and surrounded by so many virile and eager men, she didn't conceive again until the very end of her time on the island. So I had put it to her bluntly. Why hadn't she?

'Simple. I didn't have sex. Antonio was the last.'

'There was Danny.'

'Danny?'

'You know, conjugal harmony and all that,' which made her laugh.

'Once, right at the end, that's all. We weren't that much of a couple, you know.'

Months later and abandoned by her, I returned to the same question, because her answer had been undermined by one of the super-crisp prints Max had sent me. According to Clarabel's sketches, Ysan and Abi had once taken part in an orgy at the waterfall with the four lads and Henry.

My musings were interrupted by the arrival of an e-mail from Max:

4 April 2008
Guess what? A parcel arrived from Clarabel that might interest you. If you fly over to look at it I'll let you take me to an expensive hotel for the weekend.
Ma(x)

My hopes that the package meant Clarabel had returned to the contactable world were soon dashed. The parcel, containing multiple sheets of bark, had been posted seven months earlier in September 2007, just a couple of weeks after she'd dispatched her drawings. But this one had been sent by surface mail, not FedEx, and from the stamps plastered over its outside it had visited at least the Philippines and Thailand and spent some time en route in more than one customs office. It's a wonder that it arrived in one piece at all. Or maybe it didn't. Maybe parts of it had been lost on the way.

I didn't get much chance to study the parcel's contents that weekend. Just enough of a browse to decide that I was looking at a set, complete or otherwise, of Ysan's field notes on the chimps together with sheets of prose and diagrams, the rough draft of a manuscript or manuscripts. Whether this was Ysan's original set of bark sheets or the backup she'd made as insurance against Abi, I couldn't then tell. All I knew, because Ysan had told me, was that Ysan herself had already received a set way back in August 2007. Clarabel had FedExed that one to the university and Ysan had received it by courier while she was still recuperating in hospital. But on a note inside the new parcel, Clarabel asked Max to find out Ysan's home address and to forward the parcel by registered mail.

'And I guess I'd better do it,' said Max. 'But I couldn't see any harm in letting you have a look first.'

Clarabel also said that Max would be interested in the contents and suggested she photocopy them all before sending them to Ysan.

'And I will,' said Max. 'But they look desperately tedious. All M1s, F3s and squiggly drawings. Why Clarabel thought they'd interest me, I can't imagine. But if you're interested I'll get Annie to photocopy an extra set for you while she's at it. But you might not want them.'

Of course I wanted them. But that mid-April weekend, their usefulness, if any, was eclipsed by a completely different realisation. Relaxing on the hotel bed with Max, and searching for something complimentary to say, I remarked that she was still 'tight as a teenager'.

'Another bonus of never giving birth,' she purred proudly. 'Can't think why so many women do it.'

At this a memory of Ysan clicked into place. Ysan had walked into my life just a few months after the mother of three of my children had walked out, swapping me for a consultant paediatrician from one of the larger London hospitals, and freeing me to move full time to my holiday home-cum-writing retreat in Spain as I'd been wanting to do for years.

In one particular detail, Ysan proved to be more similar to my parous ex-partner than she was to nulliparous Max. Why I didn't register the fact immediately when Ysan was in my arms I've no idea. Probably I was too enraptured by her. Or maybe I needed reminding of the havoc giving birth can wreak on a woman's body. But with Max's words, I realised something important. At some stage in her life, Ysan had given birth – and the chances were it was on the island.

So by mid-April my view of Ysan's history was this: miscarrying Raúl's baby in September, she must have conceived again very quickly, presumably during one of the orgies that she hid from me. Any other way she wouldn't have had time to give birth to a baby large enough to leave its telltale signature on her body, yet still have time to conceive again, to Danny, just before they escaped from the island. Something must have happened to that second baby at birth, or soon after. Maybe it was even stillborn, because Clarabel never draws any live baby but her own on the island.

Inspired, I scoured the drawings all over again, looking for anything to hint that Ysan was pregnant in the summer of 2007. A few seemed to show what I was looking for – a tall blonde with a clearly swollen belly – marked for May, June and July. The problem was, the blonde could equally well have been Abi who, like Rose, gave birth at the end of July, just before they were rescued. In fact, every sketch of a pregnant blonde from the front shows her with nippleless breasts and dark pubic hair. And in every one for the same months that shows a blonde with nipples she isn't noticeably pregnant.

The search was disappointing but not conclusive. I also failed to find any sketches of Clarabel herself pregnant. Plenty of Rose and Abi and a few in the later months of Jill, but none of Ysan or Clarabel. This anomaly seemed very strange, but for a while slipped into the background of my thoughts, supplanted and pushed there by something altogether more sinister.

Poring over the details in each drawing, I began seeing things that produced a quantum shift in my attitude. Bit by bit, aspects of Clarabel's pictures grew inconsistent with liberated sex between consenting adults. Things seemed to have taken place that would do more than embarrass some of the men and might even send them to jail.

PAIN AND PLEASURE

April/May 2008

I cannot really understand why Clarabel portrays her males, human and chimp, with erections. Perhaps the explanation is as simple as she gave Ysan. But whatever artistic merit her symbolism possesses, for me it was a hindrance, charging almost every scene with lustful tension. Even an image of people sitting round the fire for an evening meal possesses an air of imminent sexual irruption. The danger of misinterpreting scenes was ever present.

Despite knowing the risk, I convinced myself that in three cases my suspicions were valid. For the record, as the following e-mail correspondence shows, Max disagreed from the beginning, though at first I couldn't understand why.

28 April 2008
Hi Max – I think I've discovered something. That picture dated January that you like so much. The one with the five women showing their bums and the lads moving along the line. I've just taken a magnifying glass to it (don't say a word!). Can you have a look at the original for me? If you look closely at the woman on

the end – it has to be Rose – I'm sure she's got her wrists tied together. And those squiggly things on the sand behind each one that we thought were symbolic snakes, I think they're some sort of rope or vine. I think the lads tied the women up, then cut the cord from their ankles to make life easier. I think it's rape. And it's not the only case. What about that one from November? The woman at South Bay – I think it's Abi – being humped by Henry with the four lads crowding round. Look at that marbling effect on Abi's body. I think that's supposed to be bruising. And look at the expression on the men's faces, not to mention the ♂s.
R
x

28 April 2008
Come on . . . You're just clutching at sensationalist straws. You'll be trying to tell me the orgy at the waterfall was rape next. Settle for what you've got. Just think sex. The November one is just a gang bang. Abi's probably having the time of her life. As for that scene in the cove in January. Even if you're right about the cord (and it's not that clear), have you never heard of bondage? They're all just having fun. A game. Why not call it musical c*nts? That'll work. Just sex, OK? Sex is safe.
Ma(x)

Max had read my mind. It *was* the waterfall event I'd been most convinced was rape, and she was shrewdly forcing me to come clean. The scene in question is the series showing Ysan, Abi, Clarabel, the four lads and Henry. I'd never really been comfortable imagining Ysan voluntarily taking part in an orgy with those men, and Max must have known it.

The waterfall episode is illustrated over a sequence of five sheets, the amount of drawing involved showing how significant the occasion was for Clarabel. Two of the five sheets are 'comic strips' and three are full-sized, powerful and disturbing. The very first 'frame' in the sequence shows Yoan and Abi meeting at the waterfall. Wild-eyed, they appear to be shouting at each other while the four lads lounge on the moss. Nobody else is around.

The next frame is strangely chilling. Not just because Ysan has fear etched into her face and posture, yet is still laughing. Nor because the lads, also laughing, are now standing confronting her from behind Abi, who looks explosively angry. But because, out of all the images I've seen, this is the only one in which Clarabel has portrayed men without erections, the lack of arousal exaggerated to such an extent that it must have significance, making them look more nervous than lustful. Then everything changes.

In a single large drawing, Clarabel sketches the view from the ground, as if someone – it must be a woman or women – is lying on the moss looking up. Surrounding her (or them) are four standing males, bending forwards, looking down. Their heads would be touching but because Clarabel has used virtually a fisheye-lens perspective, everything is distorted. All we can see are four pairs of legs stretching up like tree trunks, four pairs of arms hanging down like branches, and obscuring each face because of the perspective we also have four oversized phalluses reaching for the sky, and almost touching each other. It is a threatening forest of male limbs and genitals. Max had interpreted this picture as showing that both Ysan and Abi had lain on the ground in sexual invitation and the lads had responded as lads would.

In the next frame, only Ysan is having sex. She and Abi are both on all fours, facing each other. Abi's face is contorted in a scream (of encouragement, according to Max) while Ian and Pete seem to be restraining Ysan by the shoulders, and Dingo is penetrating her from behind. The next is an almost exact repeat, except that this time it is Danny doing the penetrating. Max claims we can't be sure both pictures show Ysan, one could be Abi, suggesting that Dingo has sex with one and Danny with the other.

According to Max we're witnessing a frantic orgy driven by two sexually frenzied women. I told her she didn't know Ysan. She said she didn't need to.

In the next sequence, Clarabel appears on the scene like a voluptuous Boadicea wading into battle. And from then on, she is the only one 'entertaining' the men. Abi is leaving the clearing. Ysan is in the waterfall, washing herself. Clarabel is now on all fours on the moss. Ian (of all people) is having sex with her, and Pete, Dingo, Danny – and Henry who has appeared from nowhere – are queuing behind.

The episode ends with two individual drawings. One is clearly symbolic, Clarabel being penetrated by all five men at once, each of them with two very long penises (which I assume is Clarabel's way of showing that she had sex with all five of them twice). But it is the last drawing that really sets me thinking and upsets me the most. Clarabel and Ysan are lying side by side on the moss. Both are looking up at us looking down on them, both have their legs slightly apart, and both have liquid flowing from them and spreading over the moss. The flow from Ysan is darker than that from Clarabel.

'Blood and semen,' according to Max. 'Clarabel is symbolising the pain and the pleasure of sex. The guilt and satisfaction of total abandonment. Look at their faces.'

I have looked, again and again, agonising over the expression of total despair on Ysan's crumpled face and pondering the unmistakeable hint of satisfaction on Clarabel's. In the end, I just had to tell Max what I thought.

3 May 2008

You knew, didn't you? Yes I do think the waterfall scene is a rape. Abi and Ysan have argued (again) and Abi has egged the lads into exacting revenge for her. Ysan has been gang-raped and Clarabel has rescued her, offering herself to make them leave Ysan alone. And it worked.

R

x

3 May 2008
Oh, sure! Now why the hell would Clarabel do something
like that?

I got on the phone.

'She was protecting Ysan. To save her from having a miscarriage. But it didn't work. Her baby with Raúl was killed by rape.'

'But you reckon Clarabel was pregnant too. Three months by then. What about her worrying about miscarriage?'

'Oh, a gang bang would be nothing to Clarabel, any more than to you,' I said carelessly. 'To Ysan it would be traumatic. Rape happens. It happened on the island.'

'Not in Clarabel's drawings it doesn't,' she said, then slammed down the phone.

She refused to answer when I called straight back, so I e-mailed instead.

3 May 2008
Sorry, Max. That was unkind of me. But why are you so set
against it being rape? There's something else I've got
to tell you. In the very first drawing at the waterfall,
Ysan is carrying a pile of bark. I think the waterfall
business happened the day that Ysan met Maisie on the
racetrack. It was the last thing Ysan told me about
before she broke down. I saw her face on that nudist
beach; I saw her pain. You didn't. She'd just reached
the point in her story where she was about to be
waylaid, raped and miscarry. And lose Raúl's baby.
Maybe she even conceived her next baby at the same time.
It's not impossible. Or maybe she was attacked again,
later. That's why she didn't want to tell me. Because
that next baby, the one that was born or stillborn in
June, was conceived through rape. No wonder she
stopped talking to me.
x

3 May 2008

Apology vaguely accepted. But I am getting fed up with your obsession with Ysan, trying to make her out to be so squeaky clean after the way she let you down. If you're so concerned about her reputation, just leave her out of the juicy bits. There's plenty else you can describe. Just stop pleading her case with me, OK? I really don't care. Clarabel's my client, not Ysan. Mainly though I'm worried about the legal aspect of this rape business. Are you really so naïve you can't see what a huge mistake it would be to even hint that things took place that might be construed as criminal? Are you really so desperate to be sued for libel? And you know what would happen. Clarabel's drawings would be made sub judice. I wouldn't be able to sell them. Not for years. Maybe never if magazines thought they might be sued too. No, I'm sorry. If you're determined to go down the rape line, I withdraw my permission for you to so much as mention Clarabel's drawings. You'll have to get your evidence somewhere else. Her drawings are crap evidence anyway. She uses symbolism. Allegory. Five men with two penises! And look at that drawing of a Christmas pudding with a ring through it for Christ's sake. Have you spotted it? What the hell is that about? Anyway. Think about it. I don't want to cross you off my hotel list, but I will if I have to. Get back to me when you've seen sense.

3 May 2008

OK! OK! I'll think about it. (By the way, it's not a Christmas pudding, it's a blackberry. I thought that was obvious.)

IN MEMORIAM

Early May 2008

While I was pondering Max's ultimatum, I turned my attention to something quite different. On the January sheet of thumbnails is a depiction of what looks like a funeral. Antonio is on one knee, head bowed and maybe crossing himself. By his side is a structure that looks a bit like the skeleton of a wigwam, with something dangling from its apex. Henry and Sledge are standing around looking dejected and five women are doing something unidentifiable. The drawing stands out from the others from January in a variety of ways, but because it was only a thumbnail I couldn't pick out the details I wanted.

The fact that the picture was on a sheet labelled January was no surprise. At the inquest, just about the only date on which the whole group agreed was that on which Dingo and Maisie died: 24 January 2007. But two things about the picture did surprise me. Given that neither body was ever found, why did the ceremony look like a burial rather than a token memorial? Secondly, and even more curious, was the nature of the vegetation. The first could easily be Clarabel reinterpreting the occasion or my misreading her intention. The vegetation though, that's different. Something's amiss.

Rain first appears in Clarabel's sketches in November and disappears in May. Ground vegetation is sparse from July through October, seems to be growing quickly by December and by January is luxuriant. The glade during the January memorial service is bereft of almost all ground cover, whereas in a meeting of the women there in February it is overgrown except for an area around the wigwam that the women are shown clearing. Swallowing my pride, I e-mailed Max:

10 May 2008
Max, I know our agreement over the drawings is still on shaky ground, but please could you do me one huge favour? Could you check the date for me on the memorial service sketch? (it's on the January thumbnail sheet.)
x

11 May 2008
No.

Convinced the vegetation looked more like July than January, I double checked whether there were other drawings of the glade from other months. There weren't – not definitively – but it was during this check that I noticed something I hadn't really registered before. Clarabel produced fewer sketches in some months than in others. Two months in particular stood out as under-represented: October and January. Had she been ill? Depressed? Maybe, but September, the month according to Ysan that Clarabel was really feeling down, appears to have been her most productive. Maybe it was simply that fewer things happened to inspire her in October and January.

I noticed something else, as well. The group had always claimed that Dingo and Maisie paired up quite early and often went off to do things together. Their swimming out to the coral in January was just the last tragic example from a long history of adventures. What I noticed though was that

Clarabel never actually shows Dingo and Maisie together. She doesn't even sketch their death. In fact, after September, Clarabel simply never draws Maisie.

My first thought was Clarabel had become jealous of Maisie's friendship with Ysan. But then another possibility occurred to me: of all the characters on the island, Dingo and Maisie were perhaps the two most adventurous. Maybe they went off exploring the island together at the end of September, so Clarabel simply never saw them to draw. That seemed closer to the truth.

CHIMP WARS

W ithout Clarabel's drawings, I knew I didn't have the book I wanted. But convinced the group was hiding serious misdemeanours, I also knew I wouldn't be able to let the matter drop. It was an impasse I was still thinking about when an A4 envelope arrived in my Post Office box from Manchester.

11 May 2008
Hi,
I told Ysan she should be writing this letter, if only to thank you for abandoning your book and for not bothering her further when she asked. But 'Better not' was all she would say. She is very busy, coping with the new baby (17 April, 3.5kg, a boy, named 'AR' – see if you can guess what it stands for) and studying for finals, just around the corner. Actually, I'm doing most of the baby-minding, the proud grandmother bit, though she's insisting on breast-feeding. Anyway, I'm sending the enclosed to you instead. It's a copy of Ysan's scientific paper on the chimps, just published. I'm so proud of her. She also asked me to tell you that

thanks to this paper – and as long as she gets a good degree – Professor Sarah Balfour in Canada has offered her a PhD position to carry out research on bonobos in DR Congo, starting September. She thought you'd like to know. Scary, eh? My little girl in a place like that with all the trouble that's going on. It really should be her telling you this.

I'm sorry things didn't work out. Maybe when everything's sorted and most things forgotten the three of us can meet up again.

Sincerely

Molly

PS. I'm her mother and I'm 42. And you are what? 48?

Actually, I was 45 at the time but I couldn't see the relevance now that Ysan wanted nothing more to do with me. I did write back to Molly to thank her, to ask her to congratulate Ysan, and to say that I too really hoped we would all meet again. Then, more out of curiosity than because I thought it would help with my book, I sat down to read Ysan's paper, which had been published in the *International Journal of Island Primatology*.

Entitled 'Rabbit-hunting behaviour and strategy in feral chimps (*Pan troglodytes*) on a Pacific island' the paper was a fairly dry presentation and analysis of the data she'd collected from up her tree. There was nothing scientifically earth-shattering about it as far as I could see, but knowing the story behind it all I couldn't help but feel tiny surges of admiration as I read. And at the very end, Ysan described something that I really could use, something terrifying.

I already knew that this nightmare had happened because Clarabel had devoted four full-sized sketches to the denoue-ment, but because of Max's embargo I wasn't sure I'd ever be able to describe it. Ysan now provided the means as well as some useful background. It had nothing to do with rabbits, but Ysan justified its inclusion on the grounds that it was a unique observation on chimp behaviour: a coordinated attack on people.

ADDENDUM

Fighting between neighbouring groups of chimps has been reported before; so have attacks on humans. Goodall (1986) and López-Turner (1995) both report troops of males systematically murdering others from a neighbouring group and the Guardian *(25 April 2006) reports a case of twenty-seven chimpanzees that escaped from a Sierra Leone preserve and attacked the occupants of a taxi, killing the driver. Late on in my year of observation, the island chimps also showed murderous intent.*

Early in the dry season of 2007, chimp numbers in and around the orchard increased from the dozen or so that were permanent residents to a population of around thirty. The influx from other parts of the island triggered what can only be described as gang warfare. The result: noisy bedlam. Several times a day, the sound of screeching, squabbling chimps would fill the air. It was loud even from down on the beach; on the racetrack it was sometimes blood-curdling.

Among the residents, M2 either died or fled during the conflicts. M1 not only survived but also stayed more or less in charge. In the process, he acquired three new females, several nasty wounds and an even darker side to his personality.

With the chimp wars in abeyance or over, people returned to spending leisure time at the orchard, but on one such day the unexpected occurred . . .

Ysan then goes on to describe a vicious attack on the people, but because of the literary protocol of a scientific paper her account continues in the same dry vein. Clarabel's sketches (the thumbnails are on a sheet labelled July) give far more sense of the fear and bedlam than does Ysan's description. The following is my interpretation of what is happening at four key moments in the attack. If necessary, I would claim it was an embellishment of Ysan's words, not Clarabel's drawings.

At first the people are surrounded by onrushing chimps. Ysan doesn't name names, but I could guess that the men are Sledge, Antonio and Henry, the women are Clarabel, Ysan and Jill and the baby is Clarabel's daughter.[2] Gangs appear from all directions, not least M1 and his females crashing out of the orchard as if they've been lying in ambush. A female chimp, ahead of the rest, scoops the human baby from its leafy seat on the ground but is pursued by another female chimp, followed in turn by Ysan and Clarabel, screaming.

A pile of writhing bodies develops on the ground. The two female chimps, in wrestling for the baby, have dropped their prize, giving Ysan the chance to dive onto her, clutch her, and fold protectively into the foetal position. In his turn, Antonio throws himself over Ysan, shielding both her and the baby with his body. On top of him, mauling, trying to pull him away to get at the woman or baby, is M1. All around them with teeth bared and arms flailing, chimps are wrestling, slapping, scratching, jumping, stamping. Mainly they target each other, but they also attack people. Clarabel and Jill are bowled over. Sledge is on the ground, a broken bow in his hand and a chimp biting at his arm. And Henry runs into the distance pursued by a couple of smallish chimps. I can just imagine the air resonating with the sounds of apes and humans: sounds of aggression, sounds of fear, sounds of panic. The smell too as the chimps freely defecate.

Next comes rescue. Danny, Ian, Pete and Alexi arrive. Pete, as if multi-armed with multiple bows, fires arrows in

---

[2] The baby is old enough to sit, therefore too old to be either Ysan's second or Rose's or Abi's first, even if any of these had been born by then.

all directions at fleeing chimps; Alexi and Ian chase other chimps with spears. Picture the pile of bodies – Clarabel's baby, Ysan, Antonio, and M1 – in the foreground. Imagine looking straight at M1's backside as if it's an archery target and Danny has just scored a bull's-eye with his spear, pushing hard, impaling the huge ape who glances backwards in angry pain, poised to spin round and attack. Nearby, Sledge, spurting blood from his arm, is staggering to his feet and reaching for a large rock.

Finally, we can focus on M1 and Antonio, both crumpled on the ground. M1, with Danny's spear still protruding from its anus, has its head squashed beyond recognition, the bloodied rock nearby. A pitiful but I suppose fitting end for a chimp with the genius to work out how to ambush rabbits and eventually humans. Antonio lies nearby, apparently lifeless, with gashes and hanging flesh and skin everywhere. It really is a wonder he survived long enough to reach hospital.

As for the baby, neither Ysan in her paper nor Clarabel in her drawings gives us any clue as to her fate. All I knew was that when Clarabel was rescued, she had no baby.

HIDDEN TREASURE

Mid-May 2008

The fate of her baby wasn't the only thing to concern me about Clarabel. I was also bemused by her actions while Antonio was in hospital in the weeks following rescue. For a start, where and how did she live? Did she, as is usual in many countries, stay and sleep by Antonio's bedside, acting as an extra, dedicated nurse? And for money, did she draw from her own account in England? Or did Antonio give her access to his bank accounts, or maybe shadier sources of finance, on the mainland? Either way, she did have money. Not only did she maintain herself but also she found, phoned and faxed Max, then dispatched three parcels of bark. It was those that confused me most.

The first two parcels, Clarabel sent in the first half of August 2007: one was her own collection of drawings which she sent to Max; the other was a complete set of Ysan's data sheets plus a rough draft of the scientific paper just published, which Clarabel sent to Ysan via the university. Both of these parcels were sent at great expense via FedEx and both arrived within days. They were mailed so soon after rescue that Clarabel must have had both sets of bark with her on the rescue boat. But what about the third?

This third parcel, the only one that I saw and for which I had a full set of photocopies, was very different. It was sent cheaply by surface mail to Ysan *via Max*, took months to arrive after a long detour, and probably arrived incomplete. Most intriguing of all, it was posted in September – around the time Clarabel left her crackly voicemail about a baby on Max's answering machine – a full fortnight *after* Antonio had left hospital. What had Clarabel been doing in between? Because she hadn't once contacted Max. Had she been back to the island to collect the third set of bark sheets and promptly returned to the mainland again to post them? If so, why, because those bark sheets weren't that important? They shouldn't have contained anything that Ysan didn't already possess from the previous parcel. They were just a backup.

The questions kept going round in my mind – and there were more. Why did Clarabel say that Max might be interested in the contents of parcel number three? What could Ysan's data sheets and draft manuscript on the chimps possibly have to do with Clarabel's sketches?

When Clarabel's third parcel arrived, both Max and I had cursorily flicked through the contents and seen nothing of particular value to either of us. But a month on, with my investigation at an impasse and inspired by Ysan's published paper, I had a second and closer look.

Each sheet of field data had dates written on it but the collection as a whole was far from ordered. It was as if Clarabel (or the world's customs officers) had simply thrown them together into the parcel. So I set about putting them in order, from July 2006 to July 2007. And I had date-sorted and already glanced over a variety of these sheets before I finally realised what I'd been missing.

Suddenly, a sequence of words amongst the coded data caught my eye: *Saw more today. C still not drawing me p. Why?* I rummaged at random, and found further entries: *15.8.06 So scared. But R says R-*; *2.11.06 WC r. Serves her right ...* And fragment by fragment, Ysan's journal emerged. But even that wasn't the end of the treasures hidden in those sheets.

I had recognised at the beginning that this third parcel contained not only data in shorthand about the apes, but also the rough draft of Ysan's manuscript. So whenever I came across a sheet covered with prose or diagrams, I simply put them to one side in a box I'd labelled 'manuscripts'. But not until I tried putting these other sheets in order did I realise that some of them weren't part of Ysan's manuscript. They weren't even Ysan's. To judge from the handwriting, different sheets had been written by at least five different people.

How did these bark sheets, bearing the testimony of others from the year on the island, end up in the parcel? The answer mattered little to me; I could mull on that later. Far more important was the realisation that these writings would not only allow me to verify or otherwise the contents of Clarabel's drawings, they could if necessary stand in their stead.

KEEPING QUIET

Late May 2008

When Max first withdrew permission for me to use Clarabel's drawings as evidence for violence or rape, I'd worried that I wouldn't have enough material to produce a book. As May 2008 drew to its close, I began to feel I had the opposite problem: too much information, and much of it contradictory. Clarabel's much-travelled third parcel had provided me with a set, complete or otherwise, of Ysan's journal; a series of medical records from Rose; a few diagrams that I thought were from Ian and Danny; a sheet of obscenities from somebody left-handed; and fragments of a narrative written by Abi. They were all more or less legible on the remarkable bark.

As I started piecing these different sources together, I began to understand what had driven the group to concoct their story of morality and camaraderie. And the reason they could rely on each other to foster and protect the lie wasn't friendship, trust or loyalty, but something stronger: self-preservation. Among them, the chief motivation for lying was a joint fear of either prosecution or persecution.

Admittedly some had more to fear than others. As far as I was concerned, Danny, Ian and Pete had all committed rape on at least three separate occasions. Maybe a drawing of Clarabel's showing the same trio in a three-orifice intercourse with Alexi in May also shows rape. But this I doubted. From what Ysan told me, no man would put his cock near Alexi's mouth and teeth without her clear prior consent.

To my list of rapists we could add Henry. He raped Abi and was, at least, present at the waterfall. Jill might even argue that his caveman tactics when he finally broke down her resistance also represented unjustifiable force. Which left, among the men involved in the cover-up, only Sledge – but although I'd seen no evidence of anything criminal by him in Clarabel's drawings, he still had something to hide. Uninhibited promiscuity with students might not be viewed too favourably by his university employers, if it was ever made public. Nor might his failure to prevent the male students in his care from behaving so reprehensibly.

More difficult to fathom was the evidence the women were hiding. Only Abi, through her part in provoking Ysan's rape, seemed to have behaved criminally. But Rose, who with her son Regis had been living with Sledge since their return, might not want the truth about Sledge's behaviour to be made public; and Jill might not wish it known that she'd had sex with all seven of the men on the island. That left Alexi and Ysan. Would Alexi really care what others thought of her sex life? She was self-assured and seemed almost to enjoy provoking a strong reaction in others. So what was she worried about? As for Ysan, what could she possibly have done to make her afraid of alienating the rest of the group?

Little did I know as I sat down to unravel Ysan's journal and read Rose's medical notes for the first time that I was about to find out. And when I did find out, I was devastated.

MURDER?

End May 2008

With photocopies of all the sheets of bark in envelopes, sorted and indexed by author and date, I settled down to answer some stubborn questions. Mealtimes slipped past unnoticed and it was a wrench even to go to bed. My only companions were swallows feeding their noisy young in a nest above my office window. I consumed cup after cup of coffee by day and glass after glass of wine by night. Disciplining myself – otherwise the multi-subject ants' nests of coded, abbreviated scrawls would have driven me mad – I worked through the sheets afresh for each new topic.

I began with the fate of Ysan's and Raúl's baby. Had miscarriage really been triggered by the rape at the waterfall? With an uncomfortable mixture of sadness and excitement, I opened the two September envelopes, Rose's and Ysan's, to work my way through the sheets, waiting for the event to be noted. Not surprisingly, Rose records the episode first. Ysan did not manage to write about it until a few days later.

Sep 25 (R):[3] *Ysan bleeding after being kicked, hit, and then raped by Dingo & Danny. Clarabel fetched Sledge who carried Ysan back to orchard. I made her comfortable. Told her to relax. She hasn't lost it yet . . .*

Sep 26 (R): Hallelujah! Ysan's bleeding has stopped – and baby seems OK.

Sep 30 (Y): Wonderful! Wonderful! Wonderful! Such a relief. Baby must be so tough (and Clarabel such a hero.) Sledge has banished the whining cow[4] *and four bastards to South Bay. Henry, too. They deserve their fate. On their own together until Raúl lets us go. Perfect purgatory.*

I'd been wrong but didn't mind, having hated the idea that Raúl's and Ysan's baby had been killed by rape. So when and why did Ysan miscarry? This reprieve could only be temporary; her first trimester had only another week or so to go.

There was nothing further in the September envelopes, so I opened the two for October. Alert for anything that might signify a miscarriage, I grew increasingly mystified. All I could find from then on were entries like:

Oct 15 (Y): We don't care what they think, do we Baby?

Dec 5 (R): Ysan about 5 months. Baby lively. Me and Abi both sick as dogs.

---

[3] It is usually fairly obvious whose journal entry is whose but I've included an (R) for Rose and (Y) for Ysan anyway. In their originals, both journals make for difficult reading. Clipped and full of codes and abbreviations they require intense focus and even then are sometimes ambiguous without checking forwards and back to other entries for clarification. So to make life easier for the reader I have cheated a little and not only spelled everything out but also turned the entries into reasonably grammatical sentences. This loses their flavour a little but really was necessary.

[4] Ysan's name for Abi.

Feb 28 (R): Ysan almost 8 months. Keep telling her not to worry. Jill now pregnant too. It will be his, I know it.

Ysan had lied to me. She didn't miscarry in the first trimester or even soon after. So when did she lose it, and why? And why didn't she want to tell me? The temptation to rush through the sheets was tempered by the need for care in case I missed something important. Ysan describes feeling like a beached and bloated whale; how it will be such a relief to return to normal; how terrified she is of the whole process and worried that she, the baby, or both will die in childbirth; how she wishes her mother was there. Her final entry about her pregnancy seems sadly ironic:

Mar 13 (Y): Silly, I know, but I keep making Rose promise she won't let me or Baby die.

I turned to Rose's late-March notes. She makes occasional reference to Ysan needing reassurance, but even by the end of the month, there is no resolution. So whatever happened, it had to have been in the month of April. I opened the envelope and there, second sheet down, was the denouement:

Apr 4 (R): Our first baby! Smooth, despite Sledge's fumbling, the insects, and the storm. Clarabel a great support. A girl. Gorgeous. Ysan's called her Maisie.[5]

Maisie had to be the baby that left its signature on Ysan's body. A healthy 'gorgeous' girl, but destined never to leave the island. No wonder Ysan had lied to me. Whatever the baby's ultimate fate, how much easier to say 'miscarried, first trimester', when I asked.

---

[5] In honour of student Maisie, who, according to the date of death – 24 January – given for her at the inquest, had been dead for over two months at the time of baby Maisie's birth.

Having a baby to look after marked the end of Ysan's chimp watching. I at first surmised and could later prove that Ysan turned from collecting data to drafting her manuscript, an occupation much more suited to the demands of being a new mother. With Maisie asleep by her side, I can imagine Ysan laboriously scratching away on bark, fantasising about the luxury of a word processor or even just a typewriter.

I only had notes from Rose on what happened next and on Ysan's performance as a mother, and it seems the ex-nurse wasn't terribly impressed. The following is a tiny sample of her growing concern:

Apr 30 (R): Ysan just lays Maisie on the sand while she writes, then ignores her, even when she cries.

May 5 (R): Clarabel found Maisie face down on the sand. Ysan hadn't even noticed – too busy writing.

Jul 1 (R): Ysan impatient with the baby. I asked if she was feeling hostile. Told me to mind my own fucking business. Postnatal depression?

Jul 19 (R): Clarabel found Maisie abandoned on the beach at Safe Harbour yesterday. Ysan nowhere to be seen. Not sure Ysan can be trusted with Maisie any more.

But Rose may not have had a chance to confront Ysan, because on the evening of 20 July, she gave birth herself. The next day, she wrote:

Jul 21 (R): Who said you can't deliver your own baby? A boy: Regis. Born as the sun went down yesterday. Beautiful moment, but only after a long, tiring day. Just Abi with me now while the others gather food for a party. Abi moaning she's in labour (tenth time this week). Regis quiet at last.

This must have been the day that the group on the racetrack was attacked by chimps, because, in her next entry, Rose wrote:

Jul 22 (R): Antonio serious. Many injuries. Much loss of blood. Sledge just one bite, on his arm. Nasty, though. Ysan ran off with baby Maisie straight after the attack. She told Clarabel she was just going 'somewhere' and we haven't seen her since. Looked everywhere.

And that was the last mention of Ysan on the island, though Rose does also record:

Jul 28[6] (R): Now Danny has disappeared. He was still looking for Ysan + baby. We all fear the worst.

Seeing Danny's name mentioned as if he were part of the group again was a surprise. All I'd known before that was that it was he, Pete, Ian and Alexi turning up like the cavalry during the chimp attack on 21 July that probably saved lives. Maybe it was his heroic role – the spearing of M1 – in that terrifying episode that led to the whole group being reunited, all past behaviour excused.

July 28, just a week later, must have been around the date that Ysan and Danny discovered the tiny yacht at the bay near Safe Harbour because a week after that, on 4 August, the two of them – without baby Maisie – were picked up by the passenger ship sailing about 100 km from the mainland. So what did happen to baby Maisie?

---

[6]A small point, but the fact that Rose was still writing her notes after both Ysan's disappearance and Antonio's mauling by chimps meant that neither of those two could have been the ones to find Rose's sheets of bark. My guess is that Rose was so stretched when the rescue boat arrived – attending to her three-week-old baby, Regis, and also making sure that a still seriously injured Antonio was handled carefully, that intentionally or otherwise, she left her notes behind. Then, when Clarabel returned to the island with Antonio at the end of August, she found the sheets and put them along with all the others in the third parcel – to Ysan via Max – during her brief visit to the mainland in September.

Rose clearly suspected that Ysan, already in the grips of postnatal depression and traumatised by the chimp attack, simply left her baby somewhere to die, or even killed her. So, for Ysan's sake, to avoid an inquest into the baby's death, the group at some point agreed not to reveal to anybody that she had given birth on the island. Ysan's going along with this deceit suggests that she had something to hide. And possibly infanticide.

At last I knew why Ysan hadn't broken ranks from the rest of the group, and why Sledge had trusted her, and her above all the others, to tell me the group's story for our book. Ysan had as much to lose as anybody on the island, if not more. If her colleagues thought her guilty of murdering her own baby, so might a coroner or jury.

SACRIFICE

Early June 2008

When I first discovered the fate of Ysan's baby, I was stunned. Ysan was unpredictable and prone to attacks of introversion and anxiety, but I would never have thought her capable of harming her baby. Rose clearly thought differently, but mainly because of incidents Clarabel told her about. So could a deterioration in Ysan's friendship with Clarabel play some part in what happened?

I had been wrong about Clarabel. Rose's journal makes it clear that Clarabel never became pregnant or gave birth on the island. So the birth sequence, dated April, that Clarabel drew portraying otherwise had to be a fiction. For reasons best known to herself, Clarabel had swapped identities with Ysan in her drawing; it was her friend giving birth on that wet and windy night in April, not Clarabel herself, and so it was Ysan's baby at the centre of the chimp attack, not hers. I'd been right about the jealousy, just wrong about the person.

That Ysan and Clarabel arrived on the island the best of friends is beyond doubt. Ysan's journal and the occasional note from Rose make that clear. They also make clear that Clarabel really was infertile. So when Clarabel intervened in

Ysan's rape at the waterfall, she wasn't risking miscarriage herself. But neither, I began to assume, was her act one of pure altruism. Max's less flattering view of the incident wasn't totally wrong. Five days after the event, Ysan wrote:

Sep 30 (Y): Clarabel refuses to let me thank her. Acts as though she hates me – and I told her I know why. She'd sacrificed herself for my baby, not for me, but I didn't care, it was still heroic. It was true, she admitted, but not why she was suffering. So I apologised for the pain and humiliation she'd endured for me and Baby, but that wasn't it, either. She'd humiliated the lads, not them her, she insisted. Lining up for a free fuck. How pathetic was that? How pathetic and desperate. Then she told me about the source of her agony ... she enjoyed it! 'Five men, ten fucks in an hour. What sort of woman enjoys that?' she screamed. She came three times and when it was over she wanted more. She'd gone to find Antonio for number four. 'What does that make me?' she cried. Calmly, I told her: somebody a lot like my mother – who I also love. 'At least your mother got pregnant. Ended up with you. Will I? No chance!' We hugged. I stroked her hair.

The waterfall event seems a cathartic moment in their relationship. Not least because of the acknowledgment by them both that Clarabel felt more protective of the life inside Ysan than of Ysan herself. From that time, the impression we gain is that Clarabel is constantly protective of the baby. Her anxiety for it to be born safely becomes obsessive:

Nov 4 (Y): Clarabel sat with her arm round my shoulder. Shielding me and Baby. Protecting us. I think she'd have fought for us, if Sledge and Antonio had lost.

Jan 20 (Y): To save us, Clarabel offered herself, but Dingo punched her in the face. Called her a whore. He didn't need charity, he said.

Whatever happened on 20 January caused a change in Ysan. From that day, her data sheets and journal entries rapidly dwindle, ending completely in mid-March. Or so I first thought.

I'd never bothered reading the rough draft of Ysan's manuscript on the rabbit-hunting chimps, which had arrived at Max's in Clarabel's third parcel word for word, once I knew what it was. But fired by a new idea, I scoured each sentence, and sure enough I found hidden amongst the prose the occasional dated aside, a continuation of her journal. It was suddenly obvious: Ysan made her journal notes on whatever sheet of bark she was holding at the time.

The dates show that she really did begin the first draft of her rabbit-hunting paper at the end of January, productively filling her days in the safe company of others, particularly Clarabel. But she worked slowly, waiting for the moment she was dreading – giving birth. Then, only a week after Maisie was born, she returns to writing, and completes the draft by the end of May. It was an amazing feat of perseverance, and still not the end. Through June and July she even makes a back-up copy, though it was still incomplete when the chimps attacked on the twenty-first.

Over that period, she gives a disturbing picture of a growing anxiety over Clarabel. Here is just a sample, starting from her first comment on the birth:

Apr 11 (Y): I'm alive. We're alive. Rose was great, though I still hurt like hell. Maisie 1 week old. So beautiful. Can't describe how fantastic it feels to look down at her on my breast. See her gorgeous lips, wide blue eyes, fair, downy hair. My baby. So perfect, so precious. Petrified I'll drop her. Never held a baby before. Clarabel follows me around the whole time, asking to hold her.

May 10 (Y): Clarabel and Antonio keep taking Maisie on walks. Anybody would think they were her parents, not me. I only saw Maisie today when she was hungry. Feel like a dairy cow. Clarabel actually put Maisie on her nipple, using it as a dummy to calm her. I said never do it again.

Jun 10 (Y): Caught Clarabel nursing Maisie again. Another argument.

Jun 30 (Y): Clarabel was feeding Maisie chewed banana. Far too soon for weaning. I think she's desperate to make me redundant. Then what? Must be alert.

Jul 10 (Y): Dreamed Clarabel killed me to have Maisie for herself.

Jul 17(Y):Feeling so randy. Antonio? Clarabel can go to hell.

Jul 19 (Y): Clarabel accused me of trying to kill Maisie. Said Rose was convinced I'm depressed. Don't think I can stand living with them all much longer.

And that was Ysan's last ever journal entry. Two days later she ran away to be alone with her baby immediately after the chimp attack. But where? And at what point afterwards did motherhood become too much for her?

How much Ysan's journal reflects an obsessive imagination and how much Clarabel really did act suspiciously is unclear. Clarabel did, after all, once tell Ysan 'Just have it. I'll look after it.' And Clarabel did save the baby through her sacrifice at the waterfall. So she could easily have felt entitled to a share of the day-to-day mothering. And her drawings from the time could easily hint at something sinister as Ysan feared. But that might just be artistic exploration of her feelings. Just as she never drew Ysan pregnant, she never once draws her unequivocally as a mother. She shows Ysan with a baby by her side – usually in some sort of difficulty, face down in the sand or crying and ignored. But all the Madonna-like 'woman and child' drawings are of Clarabel herself, usually with the baby on her breast and sometimes with Antonio beside her. If I'd been Ysan, I too would have worried.

Initially, I was quite happy to believe that Clarabel had returned to the island because of – in Max's words – 'something to do with a baby'. But once I'd decided Clarabel never had a baby, I needed to question the whole scenario. Was the baby she mentioned to Max in fact Ysan's? Had Clarabel found some way to wrest baby Maisie from her friend before the rescue without anybody else knowing, then returned with her to the island to avoid giving her up?

The facts are these. Ysan ran away from the orchard with Maisie in her arms on 21 July 2007 and nobody from the island reported seeing Maisie again. By 28 July, Danny found where Ysan was living, but has never mentioned finding the baby. All we know is that baby Maisie wasn't on the tiny yacht when Danny and Ysan were picked up. Equally, when Clarabel and the others were finally rescued from the island on 8 August, the only babies on their boat were Regis (Rose's son) and Orchard (Abi's daughter). Antonio discharged himself from hospital on 24 August, the same date as Clarabel's last fax to Max, so the very earliest the pair of them could have arrived back on the island was 28 August. No four-month-old baby could survive being abandoned in such a place for so long.

So whose was the baby Clarabel mentioned to Max in her crackly voicemail a fortnight or so later? My new belief was that there was no baby. Max either misheard or misconstrued; Clarabel did after all occasionally address Antonio as 'babes'. Why Clarabel chose to return to the island nobody knew, but all members of the group found returning to civilisation difficult. Maybe Clarabel simply couldn't face it. Or maybe she didn't want to leave Antonio. Or maybe, having found herself an agent at the hub of things, she simply preferred to stay in the region to work. And who can blame her?

THE GARDENER?

Mid June 2008

E ven before I began to read through Ysan's journal and
Rose's medical notes looking for every mention of
Antonio, I knew the man had been an important figure to
Ysan. Their early friendship transcended language. It was a
sexual attraction, constantly simmering, even though Ysan
claims it boiled over only once. Ultimately, by shielding
Ysan with his body during the chimp attack, Antonio
probably saved her life. Her baby's too, albeit briefly. What
else, I wondered, had passed between them?

One thing I hadn't expected, and perhaps the most
touching, was that Antonio may have hoped he was the
father of Ysan's baby. Ysan has two journal entries that hint
at this, the first written in the aftermath of her rape by
Danny and Dingo at the waterfall, the second a couple of
months later:

> *Oct 1 (Y): Antonio shocked me the day I was raped. I
> was lying on the sand alone where Rose had placed me,
> trying to stay calm and halt the miscarriage, when he
> ran up the beach to my side. Kneeling and with such
> gentle words, he placed first his hand then his lips on*

my stomach. For a few moments, he was pure concern, moving hair blowing over my eyes, stroking my cheek, caressing the mound of my belly. Suddenly, he exploded, jumping to his feet, shouting and gesticulating in the direction of South Bay. Rose and Clarabel rushed over to calm him.

Dec 2 (Y): Antonio and I were standing at the tunnel. He was angry with me for what I'd done. Called me 'Tonta', and 'Loca', and kept saying 'Bebé'. He knelt down. Grabbed me by the hips. Kissed my tummy. Then buried his face in my bump and spoke to Baby inside.

From what we know, it isn't possible for Antonio to have been Maisie's father. Aside from his mooted infertility, Ysan's first signs of pregnancy had appeared well before their sex on the beach. Of course, something may have happened between the pair of them earlier, on one of their jaunts to the castle, that Ysan decided not to tell me about. But Ysan's journal entries always point to Raúl, not Antonio, as the father. In Antonio's hopes, though, might lie his throwing himself between M1 and Maisie on the day of the chimp attack. It was a brave act by any standards, and whatever the circumstances perhaps no less than what we would expect from the man, but it would be particularly understandable if he thought that Maisie might be his daughter.

Picking up on this element was a bonus. My main reason for investigating Antonio was quite different. It had always seemed implausible that Ysan and Danny simply stumbled across the yacht on which they escaped. There were so many bays, so many caves, and each so dark, but I thought they must have had some idea of the most likely place. So how did they get that idea? My guess was from Antonio.

Of all the people on the island, Antonio was the most independent. The others needed him, he didn't need them.

Not only did he absent himself from the group daily for his runs, but on four occasions he left the group for much longer. Ysan had already described one such absence (11–23 September) to me, but he also disappeared for four days in October (14–18), a fortnight in January (4–18), and another fortnight in April (2–16), the last explaining why he wasn't present at the birth of Ysan's baby on 4 April. Where he went on these occasions and why is unclear.

According to Rose:

> Oct 15 (R): Antonio away looking for (student)[7] Maisie. Sledge couldn't stop him.

> Jan 4 (R): Sledge furious. Antonio's gone in search of the lads. They've disappeared from South Bay.

> Apr 2 (R): Have the lads kidnapped Alexi? Antonio gone to find out.

According to Ysan:

> Oct 15 (Y): We've looked everywhere for (student) Maisie already. Why has Antonio decided to leave us now? What's he really up to?

> Jan 4 (Y): Missed Antonio taking the boat. MUST see him bring it back. Last chance.

> Apr 2 (Y): Antonio won't find Alexi. He never finds anybody – because he's not really looking.

As Ysan told me during her outburst against Raúl at my villa and as I described in 'Ysan's Story', she'd always believed there was a boat hidden somewhere in one of the

---

[7] Ysan's wonderful gesture in naming her baby Maisie in honour of her dead friend could cause confusion here, despite there being no overlap in time between the two Maisies on the island. At the inquest, the date of student Maisie's death was given as 24 January. But baby Maisie wasn't born until 4 April. Even so, I have chosen to identify which Maisie is being mentioned in the journal entries whenever there is the possibility of confusion.

caves in one of the bays. And of course, she was proved to be right. Or was she?

There was a boat – the tiny yacht on which Ysan and Danny eventually escaped. Everybody seems to believe it was one that Jim Gillespie had taken to the island and left there to amuse himself (by all accounts each year with a different female companion) on his annual visits in the summers leading up to his fatal heart attack in January 2000. But this wasn't the boat Ysan had told me or the others she was looking for.

Rose's medical notes suggest that from the beginning she thought Ysan's claims about Antonio's fishing boat that they arrived on were obsessive and an indication of her fragility of mind:

Sep 8 (R): Ysan won't let Raúl go. Can't properly grieve for him. And all this talk of a boat.

Oct 8 (R): (Student) Maisie's absence affecting us all, particularly Ysan and Alexi who were already on edge. Ysan blaming herself, and still obsessing about Raúl and a boat.

Obsessive or not, from early November onwards, Ysan's journal turns to records of positive action.

Nov 7 (Y): Told Sledge I had to be allowed to go off on my own despite the chimps and the lads. I needed more data, I said. He said no, then tried to kiss me. Rose nearly caught him. I promised I wouldn't tell her what he'd done if he let me do what I wanted.

Nov 8 (Y): I hate getting up in the dark, but it is necessary. Nobody must know where I go each day. They must all think that I'm watching chimps every day. Today I trekked to Safe Harbour and watched the castle instead – and I was right. Antonio came by the direct route, loping over the hot rocks and through the spiny scrub like he was running across a meadow. If only I could do that instead of toiling through the forest. When he reached the foot of the castle he went straight into a cave. An hour or so later, he reappeared and retraced his steps towards Orchard Bay. Where did that cave lead? Raúl or the boat? I'm going to find out.

She made several attempts. For example:

Nov 9 (Y): I waited inside the cave Antonio entered yesterday. Disgusting. Pitch black. Damp. Stinks. Bat shit all over floor. Very slippery. Antonio came again. Walked within a metre of me in the blackness. But no way could I go after him.

Nov 12 (Y): Waited behind rocks on the beach at Safe Harbour, watching sea-level caves, but Antonio didn't appear.

Thereafter, about once a week until early January, Ysan went to Safe Harbour to wait for Antonio to enter or leave one of the sea-level caves, but he never did. It was an incredible feat of determination and endurance for a pregnant woman. She records the rains setting in on 13 November and, all the time she was trekking to and from the area to spy on him, she was growing less and less agile. But it wasn't until she was about six months pregnant that she called an end to this covert surveillance. On 2 January, a 'dismal' day, she was nearly swept away while crossing one of the rivers that had once been dried-up beds. Two days later Antonio disappeared for a fortnight and despite her recorded irritation and determination to watch him return, she makes no mention of having tried.

After January, Ysan seems to lose interest in the boat, her journal entries slowly focusing more on the prospect of giving birth 'under a bush'. Then, after she has given birth, her main preoccupation with Antonio regards the way he and Clarabel begin to act as surrogate parents to baby Maisie. That and beginning to lust after him. But nine days before the chimp attack and her disappearance with her baby, she hatched the following:

Jul 12 (Y): New plan! Excursion to Safe Harbour, near where the boat must be hidden. Stay a few days. 'Relax' Antonio with female company. Bore him with too much time on his hands. He's bound to slip away to check up on it. All I'll have to do is follow. Shame Clarabel will have to come with us, but I'll need her to have (baby) Maisie while I follow him.

Jul 13 (Y): Just the 3 of us plus baby here at Safe Harbour. Any day now!

Jul 14 (Y): Antonio took us for a walk to cliffs 2 bays north of Safe Harbour. Just sight seeing but . . . Maybe Safe Harbour never was Safe Harbour after all!

Jul 18 (Y): Breakthrough! Antonio went for a run. I followed. He went to that bay again, 2 bays north, but this time all the way down to the beach, where he visited a tall cave. Couldn't follow him down or for longer because I'd left Maisie on the beach near where Clarabel was swimming. But I could find that cave again.

And evidently she did, because it must have been from that bay and cave that she and Danny made their final escape. So Antonio did eventually – inadvertently – show her the means of escaping the island. Which begs the question. If Antonio knew that Jim's yacht was in that cave, why hadn't he told the others?

The final mystery over Antonio, and in some ways the most intriguing, is where he went on his daily jogs. In part, maybe they really were simple exercise. Antonio wouldn't be the first man (or woman) to feel the need to run at least once a day. But if so, why – as Ysan discovered – did he then visit the dank, dark caves during his runs and spend a couple of hours inside?

Ysan also told me that, perhaps surprisingly, Antonio showed no withdrawal symptoms when the group first adjusted to life without cigarettes and alcohol. Then we also had:

Sep 9 (Y): Antonio seems obsessive about his breath. Always chewing some peppermint-flavoured twig to keep it sweet.

Oct 15 (Y): Antonio's fingers are still yellow. How come? Even Clarabel's have gone back to pink.

Jan 19 (Y): Kissed Antonio after he rescued us. We all did. I'm sure I smelt rum on his breath and beard.

And we also knew that occasionally he became uncharacteristically irritable for no apparent reason.

Putting all this together, suppose that the caves gave access through something of a labyrinth to the Pacific face of the castle. Nobody else ever made their way through that labyrinth, so we have no description of what the Pacific side might be like. Probably, like the other cliffs, it is a mixture of bare rock faces and vegetated ledges ranging from large to small. What if Antonio had discovered some sort of garden there – perhaps first planted by Jim – in which tobacco and cannabis still grew? Perhaps he also had the means for fermenting a crude form of alcohol. It's not uncommon in the region for all sorts of vegetable material to be used to satisfy a widely felt need, and Antonio would surely have known how to do it. Maybe he needed to visit his 'garden' often, almost daily, to tend his 'crop' and indulge himself in the fruits of his labour – and became grumpy when supplies temporarily ran out.

So why didn't he share his produce with at least Clarabel? Maybe he could only produce a little, or was worried about word getting out. I could understand that. I liked the idea as an explanation for his absences.

THE FUGITIVE

Late June 2008

A lmost on a whim, as a break from scrutinizing Ysan and Rose's hieroglyphics, and certainly more in hope than expectation, I typed 'Navarro-Diáz' into my Internet search engine. After a page of mainly Facebook entries and trivia such as 'Navarro-Diáz is the 2516th most common *apellido* in Spain', I found an entry that was concerned with Antonio, or more particularly his ageing father, José Luis.

The entry was in Spanish and was from a Madrid newspaper that specialises in news items involving Spanish ex-pats from around the world. Roughly translated and dated 5 September 2005, only ten months before Antonio sailed Raúl's group to the island, it said:

> *Fijian police are investigating the possibility that the death of a retired local fisherman on one of the outermost islands was a case of murder based on mistaken identity. Señor Don José Luis Navarro-Diáz, 91, born in Ronda, Andalucia, but living in the Pacific since escaping the Civil War in 1939, died when the car he had just unlocked, exploded. The car belonged to his only son, Antonio, who only the week previously had*

been acquitted of the rape and murder of the daughter
of a man reputed to be one of the region's premier drug
barons.

The item sent my mind scrambling. Was Antonio a fugitive? Had he come to the island with Raúl for sanctuary? Might he always have planned to return to the island after Raúl's field trip was over, even alone if necessary? How much better to be living on a remote, uninhabited island than forever looking over his shoulder on the mainland, especially once he had Clarabel for company.

And . . . Might Antonio, the saver of lives, even have been guilty of the crimes of rape and murder of which he'd been acquitted?

BETTER THAN PORN

End of June 2008

Although I tried to stay neutral, it was difficult not to take Ysan's side in her conflict with Abi. I knew that 'Ysan's Story' was just that, based on her version of events, not Abi's, and that maybe actions or words had passed between them that Ysan had kept from me and that could put a different slant on the matter. So my mind wasn't closed when I began to read through the few sheets Abi had written, wondering if I might find something image changing. But the following extracts had no such effect:

> *... Her screams were better than music .... Watching Dingo and Danny rodding the filth from that bitch's golden hole ... (was) ... better than porn ...*

and a later event, probably January:

> *... I was hoping they'd kill her ... but ... the pathetic bastards couldn't even manage that.*

Abi's 'journal', in its original form,[8] is a continuous, undated, virtually unpunctuated outpouring of words.

---

[8] For reasons of clarity I have tidied up the grammar of the excerpts that follow.

Perhaps written in one go, retrospectively, maybe even as late as March 2007, it was more a therapeutic unloading of how badly life, people and everything had treated her; how she deserved better; how one day she would 'dance on graves'. It gives me no pleasure to say so, but Abi really does come across as the spiteful, egotistical, egocentric, devious bitch that Ysan always portrayed her to be in our conversations. I'm sure she will go far in her chosen career.

Having said all that, some of her scrawl makes it difficult not to feel a little sorry for her:

I begged them not my face. They could fuck me, I told them. They were going to anyway, but don't hurt my face. I was crying, but they didn't care ... Henry started it, the cruel bastard. All I did was tell him to get out of my way but he just turned on me and started pushing and slapping me. Then Dingo joined in, punching me, pushing me on the ground, kicking me, laughing, enjoying it ... I screamed for the other three to stop them but they just laughed. Didn't hit me just laughed waiting their turn ... I stank of them. So sore I bled. An hour in hell. Rose says my nose is broken so it's over I may as well forget it ...

Sledge let Henry stay!!! Made me live with him after what he did to me and after what he did to Jill. He didn't make Golden Hole live with her rapists did he? I told him it wasn't fair, but he just said I was lucky to be there at all, that I deserved to be back with the lads and that if I didn't shut up that's where I would be ... Blatant favouritism ... Stank ... When all this is over I'll make fucking sure Henry pays for everything he did to me, the bastard. Both bastards. They're all bastards ...

Predictably, Rose shows Abi sympathy for what she has been through:

Nov 2 (R): Abi returned last night. She'd been beaten and raped. Idiot Sledge wanted to send her away. I think her nose was broken. Did my best. Ysan + Alexi told her about (student) Maisie.

But Ysan certainly doesn't show sympathy:

Nov 2 (Y): So the WC[9] was raped? Serves her right. Staggered down the hill, a real drama queen. Waited until we could see her, then collapsed. Sledge carried her down to the sea. She had a black eye, a swollen face, and was cut and bruised all over. Sat hunched at the water's edge. 'Come to gloat?' she said. I had. 'Look at my face,' she sobbed. I was. The moonlight made her look ugly, made her eye sockets seem black and empty. She kept moaning. Then she had the gall to blame me. 'See what you've done? Happy now?' I told her it was justice. She'd reaped what she'd sown. If she hadn't turned them all into rapists, they wouldn't have raped her now. Then she said they were coming. Tomorrow or the next day. They were wound up, excited – determined. We couldn't stop them. And this time Dingo was planning something really special for me. That frightened me.

Four weeks later, Rose was recording:

Nov 30 (R): Abi being sick. Probably pregnant. Join the club!

which almost certainly means that Orchard's father is one of Abi's five attackers.

Once again, Ysan shows not the slightest sympathy:

---

[9] WC was Ysan's abbreviation for Abi. Whether it only meant Whining Cow or also toilet I never discovered.

Dec 5 (Y): We'd all guessed anyway, but WC admitted today she was pregnant. We were in (student) Maisie's glade. WC was all tearful. Milking it as usual. 'So that's it,' she said. 'It's all over. As if a broken nose wasn't bad enough.' Rose tried to tell her it had healed well, that you couldn't tell, but she snorted that she could tell, a camera could tell, and that it didn't matter any more anyway. Stretch marks, saggy tits, all the rest. That was the end of it. Alexi told her she could always model for Mother with Baby.[10] *We all laughed. Then . . . I had to do it. I told her that if she didn't want the baby, she only had to say. All she needed was to be raped again. To be kicked and beaten. Maybe she should wander off and find the lads. Or better still, I'd arrange something, get the three men to gang bang the body divine, and that I'd goad them on. I could pull her hair and spit in her face while they were raping her, like she did me. Make absolutely sure that it hurt, and that she cried. I enjoyed saying that. Bitch, aren't I?*

It seemed strange to me that Ysan could even tolerate being in Abi's company after Abi's role in Ysan's rape, let alone be part of a chatting group in a glade. But maybe she had little choice. The Orchard Bay group was such a confined community, Ysan and Abi could scarcely avoid each other and neither could safely leave Orchard Bay to live alone. Perhaps the bitchiness shown in this conversation was Ysan's way of coping.

Ysan still felt hatred for Abi until at least a fortnight after giving birth:

Apr 17 (Y): Pregnancy is being really unkind to Abi. It's obliterated her figure, ruined her gait and for some reason thinned and dulled her hair. What a shame!

---

[10] Ironically enough, Abi's first modelling success *was* for this magazine, appearing with Orchard, both coyly naked, on the cover.

But that entry was the last with such a tone, her animosity becoming submerged beneath the growing worries that Clarabel was taking Maisie from her. Did that mean that the enmity really lessened or that it merely mattered less? It seemed unlikely that two people who had once hated with such passion and done such things to each other could ever truly forgive and forget, but when I saw them together at the reunion party the following autumn, although I saw no warmth between them, they didn't behave as bitter enemies. So what happened? Did they declare a truce? If so, why and where? On the island? Back at university?

It was Rose who told me.

STATURE

End of June–beginning of July 2008

In my previous scans of the journals, looking for other key words, Sledge's name came up often, but I hadn't read any further. Now it was time to discover how much of his philandering, shown in Clarabel's drawings, Rose had actually known about. And from that, I wanted to piece together her reaction. How did their relationship change over their time on the island? And what, if anything, could her notes tell me about the interplay between the Orchard Bay group and the lads that Sledge had driven out?

First and foremost, Rose's journal was medical – a detailed account of just about every cut, bruise, strain, sting and bite people suffered and the treatment she offered. Among the roster of woes, she even hints at a case of piles:

Sep 22 (R): Ian bleeding from his anus again – and in a right state after what he says was a fall. Most people who lose their glasses don't end up in the state he does. Bruised arm and torso, probable broken rib. Told him to be careful but he shrugged and asked what could he do?

In most instances, Antonio would provide herbal remedies, which Rose asked him to name or describe. I haven't presented any of this but her notes really are a fantastic record of natural medicine under field conditions.

Amongst all of this, she often writes about Sledge. Nothing sentimental though. Nothing about their early days except for medical information regarding his injured feet. Nor are there any details from the period when their relationship was going smoothly. But later ... once I'd teased everything out, the story made fascinating reading. And it seems that Rose never guessed at Sledge's earliest infidelities with Clarabel. Her first suspicions, in fact, were directed at Ysan:

Sep 15 (R): They were on the beach sitting shoulder to shoulder, watching the fantastic sunrise. I was too far away to be certain but I'm sure I saw Sledge put his hand between Ysan's legs.

Nov 7 (R): Ysan again. I'm sure they were about to kiss – and from the way Sledge hid his front when he walked away I reckon he had a hard-on. Ysan gave me the old 'fly in the eye' story when I arrived. I'm not that stupid.

Rose soon became distracted by her own state. Two days later, she recorded that her period was late. A week after that came the first nausea, and she gave Sledge the news.

Nov 16 (R): He wasn't exactly thrilled. His first words were 'How come it took you so long?' God, I'm feeling so sick.

Then she gained the first concrete evidence of his promiscuity, but it wasn't with Ysan:

Nov 25 (R): Not even 10 days since I told him I was pregnant! All I could see were legs wrapped round him and blonde hair. I thought it was Ysan but it wasn't. The bastard was fucking Abi. I told him he was never touching me again.

Abi wrote an undated description of what I suspect was the same event and implies that there was more to this intercourse than mutual attraction:

I thought Rose was going to hit me she was so wild. I told her he'd made me – that if I didn't have sex with him he'd send me back to South Bay so that the lads could do what the hell they wanted. What was I supposed to do?

So amongst all the other things in his cupboard, headmaster Sledge has been hiding some coercive sex after all. His name completed the list. At some time on that island, every single man – except perhaps Antonio – forced a woman into sex.

Bit by bit, Rose realised how little Sledge cared for her now she was pregnant. By December she was writing:

Dec 15 (R): Caught him today with Clarabel AND Jill. Their faces! Is there anybody he isn't shagging? Ysan told me he's been with Alexi too – and she doesn't even like men. What blackmail did he use on her, I wonder?

And by February:

Feb 20 (R): Now he doesn't even have the decency to stop or apologise. I found him fucking Jill and he didn't even falter. In fact I think having me watching excited them both. So sod him.

And after that, she really doesn't seem to care and stops mentioning Sledge's sexual exploits. But his promiscuity wasn't the only cause of conflict between them. The pair appear to have a fundamentally different philosophy about how to handle people. Rose emerges as a liberal humanitarian, Sledge a traditional disciplinarian. These differences seem first to have appeared when Sledge banished Abi, the lads and Henry from the Orchard, but grew deeper and more acrimonious as time went on.

Sep 27 (R): What is the point, Sledge? They're not going to stay at South Bay – four spunky lads like that. It will only cause more trouble. You should have talked more and shouted less.

Nov 5 (R): So Sledge and Antonio beat them up last night. Drove them away. Big fists. Big deal. Pompous fool said the lads were rapists and deserved to be banished until they could be given the legal punishment of jail. It'll just make things worse. Danny said they'd take us, one by one. Dingo said he'd kill Sledge, and probably meant it. Men!

Jan 1 (R): I told him it's a new year. What better time to invite them back? The whole group is arguing about it all the time. Alexi says all men are rapists just waiting for the chance. Abi says she doesn't care what happens to the four of them. They've ruined her life, she'll happily ruin theirs. I say they're basically decent lads just pushed too far. Sledge shouldn't have banished them or humiliated them. By now, they'll genuinely hate him. Hold him responsible for their day-to-day misery. And they'll probably hate us women too for complicity. Time for the olive branch.

Jan 20 (R): He tried to justify himself. What was he supposed to do? he said. He was actually crying. The things he did to you, he said. But I'm here, I told him. So are you. Never heard of talk or reason? Now he's in big trouble.

Mar 28 (R): The man's a fool. We've got four pregnant women here. We can't be having arrows flying around. I told him to swallow his pride, invite them back. But calling them vermin and himself a leader, he decided fighting was the answer. I told him he'd just signed somebody's death warrant. I just hope it was his and nobody else's.

Who was really in charge on the island in the later stages of their time there? Of course, I am guided by Rose's own notes, but my impression is that, bit by bit, Rose grows in stature, her voice of reason resonating with kindness and common sense, while Sledge's stature seems to shrink and become brittle. One of the best examples of Rose's humanity comes not from anything she says about Sledge, but in the way she tried to put an end to the war between Ysan and Abi. This is what I found in her notes:

Apr 27 (R): I'd had enough. Abi was desperate to hold the baby, but Ysan always refused and said Abi would harm her. When I caught them at it today, I read the riot act (Clarabel called it a sermon!). They weren't men, I told them. So why behave like men? The men were all idiots. They'd betrayed, fought, kidnapped, hurt, raped – and worse. They'd caused tension, stress and bad feeling; turned a paradise into hell. But at least they had an excuse – they were men and couldn't help themselves, not while they had balls. Abi and Ysan had no such excuse. They were women – the only hope of peace and sanity. What did it matter now which of them was the prettier, or cleverer, or had the prospect of a more glittering career? One had a baby. The other would soon. New precious lives whose health, happiness and survival might depend on their unity. Let the men carry on with their testosterone games, I said. It was up to us women to show what being human was really about. I didn't expect them to forgive each other.

I knew they'd never be best friends. But I begged them, just don't be enemies. A truce. Be nice! Trust each other. Help each other. Then, without asking, I took Maisie from a panic-stricken Ysan and lowered her into Abi's arms. Maybe I shouldn't have done, but I did, and it may even have done the trick. Ysan allowed Abi to hold Maisie for a while, let her gaze down, finger her tiny hand. And for her part Abi, in tears when eventually she passed the baby back, said, 'She is beautiful, Ysan. I hope mine is as pretty and healthy.' Even if their truce doesn't last, I felt quite proud of myself.

To me it was clear that Rose held the group together through their most difficult months, whereas Sledge nearly rent it apart. Just one more entry makes the point:

May 3 (R): He couldn't even see the courage Alexi had shown. Living with the three of them in exchange for their no longer trying to kill him and Antonio. Voluntarily, I told him. Sacrificing herself to save people from being killed. Not that he would understand. And he didn't. Just kept ranting about what they'd done to us. How Alexi must like being humiliated. I told him he was an idiot, that if he had half the sense and courage Alexi had, we wouldn't be in the mess we are. But he wouldn't have it. All he'd say was that she'd prostituted herself. That it wouldn't solve anything. In the end they'd turn on her. She'd end up dead and, arrows flying again, we'd be right back where we started, but with one more person killed.

Maybe it was because all my main informants were women, but when I'd read Rose's notes for the last time I really thought I had a feel for what had happened on the female side of the sexual divide. It fell a long way short of the story of friendship and camaraderie that they peddled for the press and the inquest, but even so, despite the stress and strife over men and babies, there was still some sense of empathy that just wasn't there for the men. But maybe, I told myself again, that was simply the result of my lack of information. There were so many hints, but also so many frustrating little details missing. I seemed a million miles away from understanding what had happened between the men, particularly between the lads and the rest of the group, and how both sides reacted to Sledge trying to call the shots.

TAKING OVER

Nothing even approaching a diary by a man had landed in my hands. Maybe none wrote one or maybe they were more careful where they left their sheets of bark. But there is little doubt who scrawled the sheet of expletives that I found in the treasure trove that was Clarabel's third parcel. The slope of the writing suggests a left-hander. None of my sources mention who was right- and who was left-handed, but Clarabel's drawing of men in a row masturbating in the ejaculation contest shows only one using his left hand – Dingo. And I can't imagine Sledge, Henry or even any of the other lads filling a page with minimalist drawings of female genitals and penetration or finding gratification in writing the words 'fuck' and 'cunt' several dozen times. Scrawled at all angles, phrases crossing each other, it was the stuff of men's toilet walls – and less eloquent even than most of those. There was another reason to think it was Dingo's work – his father's occupation:

Take no shit from anybody.

Watch out for scheming whores – offering themselves then screaming 'rape'.

Never trust an open cunt.

Take, don't accept.

I'm the man. Beat up scum. Clear the shit. Take control. A one-man police force. Dad would be so fucking proud of me here.

Dingo may have despised authority and women even before he arrived on the island. Yet Rose called him a decent lad pushed too far and we'd been told that student Maisie became his partner. So perhaps it was the island that fuelled a build-up of unspent aggression: the sexual frustration of being naked surrounded by nakedness; the jealousy early on of seeing other men gaining sexual gratification when he – with the highest sex drive of them all, according to Ysan – wasn't; the humiliation of being banished. Whatever the explanation, one of his more complete scribbles tells of a blistering resentment for Sledge:

Jail? What does he know about jail, stupid old bastard. One day I'll fuck his whore and put an arrow straight through his oversized bollocks.

The other sheets I found from men in Clarabel's third parcel are quite different. One, I think, is from Ian and gives instructions for rope-making. Ysan had described how frustrating the brittleness of the vines had been for them all, how they were useless as bowstring and as snares for rabbits. And presumably it was the lack of good binding material that caused Sledge so many problems with his stone axes when he first set about building a raft. Evidently it was Ian who revolutionised the raft-building enterprise. From somewhere, he seems to have remembered that strong cord can be made by twining fibres stripped from certain plants. The sketch in my possession shows a palm leaf and how it should be done. Why do I think that this was Ian's brainwave? Because 'asshole' was written across the sheet in Dingo's left-handed script and the sheet's producer had crossed out the offending word and replaced it with 'pervert'; it was their kind of banter, according to Ysan. Besides, Ian seems the most likely among the gang to have absorbed such a not-so-trivial piece of information.

Another of the sheets was produced, I think, by Danny because one of his diagrams shows the positions of 'Ian', 'Pete', 'Dingo' and 'me'. The whole sheet depicts a plan of attack. The various crossings-out and general crudeness of the scribbling make me think it was produced while the four of them were living at South Bay and talking about how to get back into the orchard.

1. Get a female hostage, preferably Ysan because she looks pregnant.
2. Tie wrists and ankles.

A diagram shows the wrists tied behind the back and manacles round the ankles, leaving just enough length for the captive to walk, or at least shuffle.

3. Surprise group. Aim bows at men (Pete on Sledge, Ian on Henry, Dingo on Antonio). If it gets edgy, Pete to shoot at Sledge to show we mean business. Just keep them at bay while we tie Ysan (or other hostage) to tree. Threaten to hit her belly with club if the men don't cooperate.

Danny shows where the four should stand to avoid getting in each other's line of fire.

4. Tie men to trees.
5. Tie women's wrists and ankles.
6. Take to cove.
7. Shag, shag, shag.
Then what?

And underneath that question the writing changes and Dingo has written:

Get rid of Sledge and Bear.
Take charge.

They never did take charge. The question is, did they ever really try? I was convinced they did and felt fairly sure I knew when they made their main effort. Not in November when Abi warned that the lads were coming and Rose records just a fist fight, which Sledge and Antonio won easily, but later. From all the hints I'd seen in Ysan's and Rose's notes, I thought the attack occurred around 18–19 January.

The only time Clarabel shows the lads with people from the Orchard Bay group is in what Max called the 'musical cunts' picture, dated January. The drawing suggests that the lads did get their shags, but later journal entries show that they didn't succeed in their main objective: taking over the orchard. But I knew few real facts about the actual events of that night. Abi was disappointed Ysan hadn't been killed and Rose was appalled by Sledge's behaviour. I also knew from the date given at the inquest that only a few days after the surmised takeover attempt, Dingo and Maisie went on their ill-fated swim.

After ploughing through everybody's journals, the story of this failed takeover seemed to me the one great remaining mystery. It was something nobody wrote about and Clarabel had not recorded the events in her drawings. I could go no further with the resources I possessed. My only chance of enlightenment was to start asking some direct and uncomfortable questions. It was time to start meeting the people whose lives I had been teasing apart for the past nine months from pieces of tree bark and cartoons.

MEETING PEOPLE

Early July 2008

8 July 2008

Hi All

You may remember me. We met at your reunion party last September. I'm the guy who you asked to write, with Ysan, the 'official' version of your stay on the island, but then changed your mind. So now I'm going it alone with a different publisher. The interviews with Ysan until last December told me a lot and since then I've been researching a number of other sources, such as copies of Clarabel's sketches which her agent loaned me. My book is now 99% written and naturally contains a lot of information about each of you.

Before I send it to my publishers, I thought it only fair to show you all, individually, what I'm intending to say and to talk a few things over. I know Graduation Day is next Monday, 14th, and most of you will be busy, but perhaps you could each suggest a few days, times and places around then so I can work out a schedule. I'm flying into Gatwick, so will be seeing Henry in London and Pete near Reading at the end of my trip. If you can't see me, I suppose I'll just have to publish what I have.

I look forward to seeing you.
RB

As I hit the send button, I didn't expect anybody would dare turn me down, and they didn't. I didn't send the e-mail to Ysan. For her, I had other plans.

Boarding the plane for England I was excited. Regardless of whether the group would confide in me, or deny my suggestions, I already had enough material for a book that would tell a dramatically different story from the group's version. Even without Clarabel's drawings, if Max's embargo was final, the audience that had followed their stories so eagerly when they first returned would be astonished. And if I could get just one of the group to describe the big event that I was convinced occurred, the publication of my book would be only the beginning of a chain of events that would keep the group (and my book) in the public eye for months to come, if not years.

My strategy was simple, but powerful. I was going to use the bits and pieces of evidence I'd collected against each to trick or goad him or her into telling me more about the others. Where I didn't have evidence, I was prepared to lie a little because I was sufficiently confident my hunches were right. Best of all, I was seeing the two most vulnerable people at the very end. Hopefully, by the time I saw those two, I would have enough leverage to make them tell me everything.

I was long past questioning my own motivation in all of this. Of course I was interested in producing a book that created a stir, but only if it also told the truth. And quite naturally, as I'd unravelled events, I had come to admire some of the people on the island and dislike others. The latter I wanted to be publicly confronted with their crimes. But if I am honest, I was also being driven by a wish to have some good come out of Raúl's untimely death.

In a TV interview, Raúl famously once said, 'If you really want to know what humans are made of, just try returning them to the wild. Make them live naked amongst apes. You won't like what you see, but maybe then you'll understand. Modern society is just a way of hiding us from our true selves. That's how fragile it is.' And he then went on to catalogue the range of ways in which he would expect 'liberated' people to behave. Among many other details he predicted a stage of coercive sex while some people tried to cling onto their abstinent or monogamous pasts. But the phase would be brief. Women would quickly revert to their 'natural state' of being openly promiscuous and from then on all sexually motivated aggression would be between males. 'Just like chimps,' he'd said with a smile to the camera.

That interview was just one instance of many illustrating the pleasure that Raúl gained from shocking students and the public alike into thinking about human nature. Ysan had seen and recorded the programme and confessed as much during the last three traumatic days of our time together in Spain. But unlike those of us who really knew Raúl, she took his words seriously. Which was why she had so quickly accused him of marooning them deliberately in an attempt to test his predictions. I had never believed her, even for a moment, any more than had Sledge or the others who knew him well. But it was uncanny the way the group's behaviour while on the island had mirrored his prophecy. Somebody needed to point that out, and I saw myself as the person to do it. It was just such a pity that his life's view had only been vindicated as a direct result of his dying.

My only real sadness in regard to the book was for Ysan and the fate of baby Maisie. But my new hope was that if I confronted Ysan with what I had discovered she would change her mind and collaborate with me again. She would either endorse what I had deduced, and fill in the gaps in my story, or refute it all with good reason. Now she had finished her studies and was about to graduate, I hoped she would feel free of Sledge and the university's inhibiting influence. Quite probably, she would also prefer to tell her own heart-rending story through me than have me guess at the remaining blanks. And as a would-be research student, she might even enjoy helping me vindicate Raúl's theories to make amends for her earlier suspicions about him. It was worth a try, so the moment I was ensconced in my hotel room I phoned Ysan's home. With graduation only two days away I was certain she would be around. I was nervous. And terribly excited too at the prospect of being able to pick up our fledgling relationship from where we'd left it. More than I wished to acknowledge, she had made quite an impact on me, as she had on Raúl. And foolishly, perhaps, I felt protective after seeing how vulnerable she had been at Christmas, now knowing just what had caused it.

Molly answered, and when I asked if there was any chance of speaking to Ysan she immediately said 'No'. Not because I was still *persona non grata*, though I probably was, but because Ysan was no longer in the country. As soon as she had received her degree results and sorted out the paperwork for her doctorate, Ysan had opted out of the graduation ceremony and taken her now three-month-old baby son, AR, on the first plane to Fiji on her way back to the island. I'd missed her by just a few days.

'The island! Why?'

'Well ... Let's just say to sort out some unfinished business.'

I asked when she expected her back in England. Molly laughed and said probably not for years. 'She's going straight to Canada to register and such like, and from there to the Congo.'

Cursing my luck, wondering if I would ever get the chance to see Ysan again, I tried to focus on the week ahead. Suddenly I was nervous, even slightly scared. It was the thought of meeting Sledge again.

SLEDGE AND ROSE

14 July 2008, midday

Considering what Rose had written in her journal, to my surprise, if not horror, Sledge and Rose were still an item. I had met them, of course, since their return from the island (just the once, at the reunion party way back in September) but even so the sight of them now was a shock. In my mind's eye, as in the pages of 'Ysan's Story', Sledge still had a magnificent Viking beard, long blond hair, and bulging muscles, a true alpha male. But now, clean shaven, short-haired and wearing a suit and tie – on his way to a party for graduands and their families that afternoon, he said – he seemed ordinary but still very large. And Rose – in my mind always magnificently naked with glistening skin and flashing eyes, tending the injured while spreading words of peace and harmony – now in her scruffy blouse and jeans she simply merged unremarkably into the bustle of the university bar where we had arranged to meet.

Nervous though I was, it calmed me a little to see that they were too. Sledge was florid-faced, making the long white scar near his right eye even more conspicuous. He was forever licking his lips, as if they were dry, and when at last we sat at a table, he attacked his pint of beer as if it were going to be the first of many. Rose kept glancing at him, seemingly worried about what he might say or do. My plan was to anger Sledge by using Rose, and hope that in the heat of conflict they would both be less than careful about what they said.

I wasted no time on pleasantries, getting straight down to business and telling them what I would be saying about them in my book: what giants they had been in keeping the group together; how at first their relationship had been an example to everybody; how around the time that student Maisie ran off with Dingo, and Rose conceived Regis, their relationship began to crumble; about Sledge's harem; their disagreement over how to handle the lads . . . but I didn't get any further. While Sledge fumed into his beer, Rose began laughing awkwardly, and told me I had 'the wrong end of the stick'. Especially about Maisie and Dingo. Wherever did I get the idea?

'Ysan, for one.'

Rose smiled patronisingly and told me quietly that I should be careful about believing anything Ysan had told me. They had quickly realised it had been a mistake electing her to be my co-author. She had lived in something of a fantasy world during much of her time on the island and had done ever since.

'I know that was your opinion. You thought that mentally Ysan coped badly with pregnancy and motherhood. And maybe she did.'

I could see them slowly realising that I knew a lot more than they'd expected.

'But she wasn't the only one to tell me about Maisie going missing. You did too, Rose.'

I let Rose bluster out her denials of ever having told me anything, then I broke it to them about her medical notes. 'I thought it only fair to tell you. But it's not really student Maisie's disappearance I want to ask you about. What I really want to know is what happened when the lads tried to take over the orchard in January. Evidently Sledge did something you didn't like, Rose. What was it?'

It was the last thing I said to them. Sledge reached across the table, grabbed me by my collar, and pulled me to my feet. 'I warned you,' he growled. 'Right at the beginning.'

Then he marched me to the bar door and pushed me out, something that hadn't happened to me since I was a student out on the town with Raúl, who had a knack for upsetting people much larger than ourselves.

Sledge had the parting shot. 'Just leave it. All of it. You publish any of this and there'll be only two losers: you and Ysan. Did you know that infanticide is still classed as murder, depression or no depression?'

I watched him go back into the bar, even stared after him for a while as I harnessed my anger. He hadn't told me anything I didn't already know and what he had just done made my plans for him so much easier to justify.

ALEXI

14 July 2008, evening

After everything I'd learned about Alexi, I'd been looking forward to meeting her again, this time properly, and I had high hopes of confirming things that were so far no more than hunches. From what I knew, Alexi was unpredictable, maybe even unstable, and I was seeking to exploit those traits. She was also, as far as I could see, the person with least to hide. Least to lose too from breaking ranks. Not only that but also, just like Ysan but unlike all of the others, she hadn't given evidence *under oath* at the inquest.

Alexi had invited me to her flat. It was the evening of the same day I met Sledge and I was still bristling with anger, resolve and a desire for revenge. I didn't recognise the address, but knowing Alexi did not come from an affluent background, I expected to find her living in small and dingy accommodation not far from Moss Side where the city's students find somewhere cheap to live. But she confounded my assumption and lived, instead, on the fourth floor of a modern block not far from the city centre, with a magnificent view over the city and The Quays. Maybe she did have something to lose after all.

She looked strained when she opened the door, her loose-fitting black tracksuit disguising her thin frame and making even her Middle-Eastern complexion look pale. I offered my hand in greeting, but she didn't respond. Just said, 'Please be quiet. I've only just got her to sleep.' She looked me up and down. 'I remember you now. From the party . . . and from those pictures of you and Ysan on the beach. So you're going it alone with the book, are you? Don't expect a warm welcome.'

'I don't. Not at all. But the book is going well. I can't give up now. Can I come in?'

I followed her into the lounge, an untidy place with women's clothes strewn about the floor. A glimpse into the adjoining kitchen revealed such a stack of dirty dishes I wondered if there were any plates left in the cupboards. Her four-month-old daughter, Ellie, slept on the settee, covered with a quilt, pillows on the floor beneath in case she fell. As I sat down, a slim young woman strutted into the room wearing just a bra and knickers. Without even acknowledging me, she threw a few garments around, and quietly asked Alexi if she'd seen a particular top. Then she sauntered out of the room.

'The wife,' said Alexi brightly. 'Ellie's other mum. We're both doing teacher training next year.'

'Nice place.'

'Present from Grandpa.'

'Yours?'

'Christ, no! Ellie's grandpa. Danny's dad.'

'Danny? Does he live here too?'

She laughed quietly, looking nervously at Ellie, still sleeping, then shook her head. She didn't even try to disguise the sarcasm in her voice – or was it derision? – when she told me Danny was way too busy with his new TV career. The deal was that each weekend she trekked off with Ellie to his parents' house in Cheshire, let them see their granddaughter for a day and Danny would turn up if he could. They understood though that she and Danny were never going to be soul mates. They could handle that.

'I presume they understand about your wife?'

She nodded.

'So this wouldn't surprise them, either?' I showed her Clarabel's Picasso-style sketch.

'Is that me and Maisie? My God! Anyway, no! Why should it? It was just fun. Scratching itches. Nothing heavy. Not like now. Maisie liked men too much.'

'And neither you nor Danny's parents have any doubt that Ellie is Danny's daughter?'

I showed her a sketch of her and Sledge, then the triple-orifice sketch, then the musical cunts.

Her coal-black eyes widened with fear and then anger. 'Is this blackmail?'

'No.' But maybe it was. What kind of reaction did I expect from any of them when I revealed copies of Clarabel's illustrations?

I kept my tone of voice neutral and explained how all I wanted any of them to do was tell the truth about that year. To come clean. To say what they had done and how they had behaved. To stop defending what was fast becoming an indefensible position. To drop the public relations exercise that would crash down once Clarabel's exhibition – her illustrated narrative history of their year as survivors – was unveiled. I was offering them the opportunity to explain themselves before the accusations and investigations began.

'I owe it to Raúl to make a record as truthfully and non-judgmentally as I can. I'm not deliberately trying to blackmail anybody and I'd appreciate the same in return. But I'm not afraid and I won't be stopped. If it's not me, it will be someone else when those pictures are seen. So I suggest you all take advantage of someone sympathetic while you have the chance. Someone who knew Raúl.'

And I wasn't bluffing. Whatever any of them said, or whatever Sledge threatened, I was going to publish every single event I had discovered as objectively and accurately as possible. But if I had an opinion of any of them, my impression of Alexi had always been favourable. I told her that she above all should be proud of how she'd behaved.

Frowning, she asked me why. So I told her what I knew of her 'sacrifice' in living with Danny, Pete and Ian.

She sat down, and stared at me in silence. Slowly, her aquiline face broke into a mischievous smile. She laughed, still quietly. 'I'm no martyr. You think it was only altruism? Well, it wasn't. Maybe at the beginning. To stop them trying to kill Sledge and Antonio, but not later. I actually got a thrill out of having three men lusting after me. I'd have preferred three of the girls, but beggars and choosers, you know.'

She went on to tell me that it made her feel powerful, and really dirty. Really risqué. She liked that. In fact, if Ian and Pete had been a bit more . . .

'Attractive?'

'I was going to say dynamic.' She laughed again. 'Actually Ian was kind of cute once you got to know him. And Pete . . . well, Pete was certainly different.'

I thanked her for her candour. Even admired her for it, despite my shock. And I tried not to allow my relief that she wasn't holding back from becoming too obvious. I couldn't have wished for more than this, especially as after my confrontation with Sledge I had begun to expect a lot less from the rest of them. I asked her if Pete had shown any signs of instability by the time she had joined their breakaway group on the island.

She shook her head and said he'd seemed completely happy living that life. 'He was amazing with his bow and killed so many birds for us to eat when we were on the move.' Did I know, she asked, that the four of them had explored the whole island during those three months, end to end, side to side? 'It was an adventure. You know, real adventure. Total freedom. None of us, not one of us, had ever experienced anything like that before. And Pete lived for it. He was born to it.' Then Alexi sighed and looked at her feet. 'But on the way back. On the boat and on the plane, we could all see him getting wound up. I mean really tight. Because of his dad. At having to see his own dad again. It was coming back home that screwed Pete up, not life on the island.'

'Do you know what Pete and his dad argued about? What made Pete take a knife to him?'

Alexi shook her head.

Feeling uneasy, I walked over to the window and looked out across the city skyline. 'Will my book mess everything up for you? Will Danny's parents be able to cope with knowing how you behaved?' There were some people from the island whose lives I had no problem with unsettling, but the thought of hurting Alexi scored a direct hit on my resolve.

'Will it make any difference if I said it would?'

'Probably not.'

At which she shrugged and said she didn't care anyway. 'Unless you were on that island, and saw what it did to people. What it made them do, you can't understand. Anyway, I've never been too bothered about what people think.'

'Danny's parents?'

She laughed. 'They only care about Ellie. Their grand-daughter.' She looked up at me. 'And yes. There's been a paternity test.

'Did any of the others have paternity tests?'

'Everyone did.'

'The results?'

She looked right into my eyes. 'It's not for me to say.'

I nodded and said I understood, but felt irritated. It wasn't vital for me to know who fathered who but it would be interesting. Yet I couldn't see any way of forcing people to tell me.

Accidentally, I trod on a dinner plate concealed by the strewn clothes. The clatter woke Ellie who immediately began screaming. Alexi glared at me, then hung her head in her hands.

'You may as well go. She can scream like this for hours.'

I apologised, but hadn't finished. 'But I wanted to ask you about Ysan's baby.'

She shook her head. 'You're seeing Danny tomorrow morning, aren't you? At Sale Water Park? I'll be there.'

DANNY AND ALEXI

15 July 2008, morning

When I arrived at Sale Water Park, Danny was putting an expensive-looking dinghy through its paces for a TV clip to be filmed that afternoon. I stood and watched just a moment too long. An eager young man from the TV crew joined me. 'Beautiful, isn't she?'

'I don't know anything about boats, I'm afraid.'

'She's a skiff. A twenty-niner. A young man's boat. You need athleticism. Danny's good. Look at the trapeze and the spinnaker billow. Look at her go.'

'The red sails look good.'

Not far away, Alexi was holding Ellie and watching from the bank. Making my excuses, I joined her and while we waited for Danny to join us, I managed to fit in the vital unasked question from the night before. What did Alexi think had happened immediately after the chimp attack when Ysan ran away with baby Maisie?

Shrugging, Alexi said, 'It was an accident. What else? Even Ysan nearly died. Hitting her head like that, breaking her ankle. It must have been some fall. They were disgusting, those caves. Thick with shit, crawling with rats and cockroaches. Nobody knows how long Ysan was out cold.

It could have been days. Poor little Maisie didn't stand a chance.'

I suddenly found myself struggling to stave off the image of Ysan lying unconscious in the gloom of a dank cave, her baby screaming in the darkness by her side. A scenario which offered no consolation for the alternative featuring Ysan deliberately abandoning Raúl's daughter in such a place.

'So you don't believe Rose's theory. That Ysan was suffering from postnatal depression? That motherhood suddenly became too much for her? Maybe triggered by the trauma of the chimp attack? That she deliberately took her baby to the caves? And left her there to die?'

I thought Alexi was going to cry. She looked away from me and kissed Ellie. Then asked me if I really needed to mention that Ysan had given birth on the island. Did it really make that much difference to my book? Or if I felt I had to, because it was Raúl's baby too, couldn't I just say the baby had died from the injuries she suffered during the chimp attack? They would all back me up, she said. She was sure they would. Was there really any need to mention the caves? Or depression? Then she squeezed my arm. 'Please. And you never know, it might even be true. None of us actually knows that Maisie was still alive when Ysan ran off with her. Nobody heard her crying. Ysan might have reached the caves then discovered her baby was dead.'

'What does Ysan say?'

'Ysan? Oh, it's obvious she doesn't really know. It was that knock on the head. She tells all sorts of stories. None of them make sense. They're not worth repeating.'

'Try me.'

But she wouldn't and the harder I pressed the more vehemently she refused. She was hiding something, that was obvious. Something to protect Ysan, but nothing I could say would make her yield.

As Danny approached us, his cocky smile was the only thing I needed to see to remind me why I was there. I reached out to shake his hand. 'Ah, the hero. We meet again. The man who sailed to safety.'

He beamed.

'And who killed M1.'

His smile faded a little, as if unsure it was a compliment.

'And who raped Ysan. And Abi. And maybe five females in the cove.'

'Is that what you're going to say?'

'Unless you can convince me it's not true.'

I had expected a flat denial but he was too clever. He'd anticipated my move. He said he'd no idea whether he'd raped Ysan and Abi. It was rough, it was exciting, but to this day he didn't know whether they really felt he'd raped them. 'Ask them, and publish their replies.' He went on to say he would abide by whatever they said and face any consequences. Clearly I hadn't caught him off guard.

As for the lads' behaviour with the five women at the cove, Alexi added in his defence that it certainly hadn't been rape. She'd been one of those five. It had been a game. The women had goaded the men, saying that none of them could come five times, once in each of them. And they'd been right, none of them managed it.

'Pathetic,' she said with a smile.

'But they tied you up.'

'That doesn't make it rape.'

I turned to Danny. 'You planned it.' I told him about having his plan of attack in my possession.

'Just a game.'

'So where were Sledge, Henry, Antonio, Ysan and Maisie? Student Maisie, I mean. Tied to trees?'

They laughed and asked if I really thought Sledge would let himself be tied to a tree. 'They just didn't want to join in, that's all. Ysan was too pregnant, Sledge was too moralistic, Henry wasn't invited, and Antonio was off on one of his walkabouts.'

'And Maisie?'

They hesitated and exchanged glances. 'Maisie,' Alexi eventually said, 'was too ill.'

Feeling heavy with defeat, I managed a smile and said I didn't believe them. They asked me to prove otherwise.

I watched them exchange triumphant, if not mocking, glances. And then something occurred to me. I looked at Danny. 'When you found Ysan at the caves, before you went to the boat, she'd already broken her ankle, and hurt her head. It didn't happen on the boat. So how did you get to the boat? It was a long way, two bays north. Did you carry her?'

'More or less.'

'But surely she wanted you to help her look for her baby first?'

'Her baby was dead. I took one look in those caves and knew it. No way could a baby survive in there, not for five minutes, never mind five days.'

'Five days? Surely even Ysan couldn't survive there for five days.'

'Well she did, didn't she. That's how long she was missing. She's obviously tougher than you think.'

I backed down. 'You could at least have tried looking for the baby.'

'No I couldn't. I hate caves. They panic me. Look, I don't want to talk about it, OK? None of us do. I didn't believe her about the boat, but I agreed to take her there. Anything rather than the caves. And that's how we ended up saving everybody. Anything else?'

I could see I would be wasting my time persevering. I did my best to smile and tried to relax him a little. 'Alexi said I should ask everyone about the results of the paternity tests. So I'm asking. How many children did you father while you were on the island?'

Alexi answered for him. 'Only Ellie.'

'I think two: Ellie, and Ysan's second child, AR. Who else could be his father?'

'Ask Ysan, and ask her what AR stands for while you're at it.'

* * *

But on the tram journey back to the city centre I worked it out. Remembering Ysan's intense sexual frustration when she was at Safe Harbour alone with Clarabel and Antonio, a day or two before the chimp attack, it all became clear. There was no other possibility. Antonio was the only other man she could have had sex with, so he had to be AR's father. Which in turn meant he couldn't have been infertile as Ysan had claimed.

ABI

'So what lies are you going to write about me?'

Abi was being photographed on the viewing terrace at Manchester Airport when I arrived. She kept me waiting nearly thirty minutes and when she did eventually flounce across to me in what looked like a pale-blue, full-length ballroom dress, I could tell from her expression that somebody had warned her about how much I knew and the sort of things I was likely to say. Close up, I could see she was plastered with make-up: heavy foundation, blusher, glossy red lipstick, and thick mascara.

'No lies. But I'll describe how you were beaten and raped by Henry and the lads, and that Sledge blackmailed you into having sex with him. How do you feel about those events now? Will you press charges against them? Or sue me for libel?'

'I'll leave the libel decisions to Sledge and the university. So . . . is that it? Nothing else?'

'Only that you tried to burn all Ysan's data.'

'A mistake.'

'And you urged the lads to rape her while you watched.'

'Prove it!'

'"Better than porn" is the phrase I recall from your scribbles.'

She blanched with anger but calmed down sufficiently to complain about a breach of privacy. She hadn't meant anybody to see them. Hadn't meant what she wrote. She and Ysan had even become friends.

'Not by January. You wrote then that you hoped they'd kill her. What were they doing to her? What happened that night? Was Ysan tied to a tree? Did one of the lads hit her in the stomach with a club? Why will nobody talk about it?'

Abi glanced around herself. The anger had gone; now she was just nervous. The photographer beckoned to her, tapping his watch. Abi nodded, said she was coming. I was running out of time. 'I'm going to say Maisie was killed by the chimps. How do you feel about that?'

Now Abi looked both alarmed and confused.

'It was Alexi's suggestion. To make life easier for Ysan. Instead of saying Maisie died in the caves. It doesn't really make a difference for the book.'

She sneered at me. 'I see. You fell for Ysan too. You'll lie for Ysan but not the rest of us. Why should *Ysan* come out of the whole thing smelling of roses? I don't see why we all had to cover up what really happened in the first place. Ysan should have been held to account over killing her baby . . . but what the hell. If you've found out what happened and are happy with the chimp story as a cover-up, that's up to you. And if the others are happy with the deception, that's up to them. I'll go along with it. Why should I care anyway? I've got my career to think about.'

I watched her stride away, her dress backless to below her waist. She hadn't even been at the racetrack when the chimps attacked, never mind the caves, so her certainty over Ysan's guilt was just a vicious mask for a continuing animosity, nothing more. I wanted to ask her which of the men had turned out to be Orchard's father, but decided I'd be wasting my time.

IAN

17 July 2008, midday

I talked with Ian in the student bar while he was waiting to play chess for the Orwellian against a team from Victoria University. With thick glasses and a chess club tie, he was looking geeky again. I suggested that we should sit at a corner table where we were less likely to be overheard. Then I asked if he'd really won the ejaculation competition or whether that was just Clarabel being kind. I showed him the sketch. He went bright red but then seemed to remember a new persona he was capable of, collected himself, and began to talk openly, even proudly. Yes, he had won it, he said. And more than once. Small he might be but he could shoot better than any of them.

'Pete was so big all he could do was dribble. And Dingo was really pissed off that I beat him. It was his idea. He wanted to humiliate me, but it didn't quite work out that way.'

'I guess you knew all about what Pete could do,' I said, showing him the mutual masturbation sketch of the pair of them.

I swear he shivered, but then he collected himself. 'So what. We all grew frustrated as hell, watching the women, seeing Raúl with Ysan, then Sledge and Antonio with Rose and Clarabel. It was worse than prison. Of course we did stuff. Better than nothing. Do you have a problem with that?'

Holding up my hands I said of course not. I just wanted to tell him what to expect in my book, that was all. And in fact, of all the men he didn't come out of things too badly. There were times when he was stoic and informed. A lot of readers would really sympathise, especially over details like having to cope with piles.

'Piles? I never had piles.'

I told him about Rose's medical note.

'This is going to be some book, if that's the level of care you've taken over getting your facts right. I had an accident, that's all. No glasses, you see. I fell. Sat on something sharp.'

'Are you sure? Is that really what happened?'

'Of course I'm bloody sure.'

'OK, I get the message. You don't want people to know. I'm not surprised. But what about the cord? You must be proud of that. Your discovery changed everything, didn't it? Bows. The raft. And its other uses. Care to tell me about those?'

'What do you mean?'

'How about tying people to trees? Did your cord really manage to hold Sledge?'

'He couldn't move.'

Realising what he'd just admitted, he added, 'It was a challenge. I told him it would hold him. He said it wouldn't. But I won. It was just fun. You get bored. Play games.'

'Nothing to do with trying to take over the orchard then?'

He laughed nervously then looked at his watch.

'One last thing. I've got you down as the only man on the island who didn't father a baby while you were there. That's what the others said. They even laughed at the suggestion. Presumably it's true.'

'No, it bloody isn't true. I'm just as capable as any of them. One of Jill's twins is mine. The girl. We all shot and I scored. Put that in your book and publish it.'

JILL

19 July 2008

It was Saturday morning at eleven when the taxi dropped me outside Jill's semidetached house in south Manchester. 'Just outside the dodgy bit, not quite into the posh bit,' she'd told me on the phone. The place had been her marital home with Henry. Now, there was a FOR SALE sign outside. 'The divorce settlement. That's why it's so untidy, inside and out. I'm in no hurry to sell.'

Her nine-month-old twins were fractious, making conversation difficult. Without preliminary, I asked if Henry was their father. 'Could be anybody,' she said, which was my cue to tell her that I knew she knew who the father was.

'My business, don't you think?'

Jill was nowhere near as round as the last time I'd seen her when she was eight months pregnant, but I would still have called her plump rather than voluptuous. And she was becoming increasingly stressed as the children stepped up the volume.

'As far as I can see, you're the only one who left the island with nothing to hide.'

'If you don't count infidelity and promiscuity. The moment Sledge banished Henry to South Bay I threw myself at him. And over three days in January I had sex with all seven of the men. But you knew that, didn't you?'

'Just assume I know nearly everything.'

'Ah . . . that's the word, isn't it. *Nearly*.'

'OK. So did Henry rape you that evening in November? The time he dragged you across the sand? Or was it just a game?'

'We were married. We had sex. He left a few marks.'

'I don't see what being married has to do with it.'

'Well I'm not accusing him of rape, whatever you say in your book. Henry's suffered enough.'

She had a crying child on each arm, so I reached out and took her son from her and began walking up and down, trying to calm him. Grateful, Jill asked if I had children.

'Four. But they live with their mothers, now.'

'So you know how to change a nappy, then. They're only wet . . .'

Jill began changing her daughter and with an amused expression dared me to help her by changing her son. Unperturbed, I unbuttoned his pale-blue babygrow, asking as I did so why she had gone along with the group's cover-up, which I knew to be lies from beginning to end.

'What cover-up? You can be as devious as you like, but you won't trick me into saying anything about Sledge.'

Removing her son's nappy, I smiled. 'I know it happens, but never thought I'd come across an example: twins with different fathers.'[11]

Apart from my own two sons, I hadn't seen that many nine-month-old boys without their nappies. But even I could tell that this one was unusually endowed for his age.

'I knew your daughter was Ian's, but I didn't know your son was Pete's, not until now. Does he know?'

---

[11]Fraternal (non-identical) twins come from two eggs and two sperm. Usually those two sperm are from the same man – but not always.

PETE

20 July 2008, midday

I caught a train from Manchester, stayed at Reading overnight, and arrived at Radmoor Psychiatric Hospital by taxi, Sunday lunchtime. It hadn't been easy to arrange and I could only hope it would be worth the effort. I was working on the assumption that if I gave Pete just a hint of what I was going to reveal about the rapes by him and the others in my book, he would realise there was no going back and that here was a chance to settle a few scores.

We met in a bare room, sitting either side of a table, plastic mugs of coffee in our hands while a couple of wardens lounged at a table in the corner. I'd been warned that Pete had become unpredictable and that I was to be careful not to provoke him, a challenge I less than relished. But I began by complimenting him on his beard which was quite as magnificent as Ysan had once described to me.

'Is it better than Sledge's yet? My father tried to make me shave it off, you know.'

I told him that Sledge no longer had a beard, so yes it was, which pleased him. I congratulated him too on his son. I'd seen him just a couple of days earlier, I said, and thought how beautiful he was. From his expression, that pleased him too, but he passed no comment. Just sipped coffee and stared at me.

'A rabbit,' he said suddenly, 'ten metres. A pigeon in midair. Has anybody told you? You should put that in your book. I was fantastic. Used to be captain of the archery club you know?' Then he paused and stared at me again for a while in silence. 'How much *do* you know?'

I gave him the 'nearly everything' line. Glancing at the wardens, I added that I did have a couple of things I wanted to check with him. He nodded.

'The others have all agreed that I should say Maisie was killed by the chimps. And I'm sure you can understand why,' I said quietly. 'Is that OK with you?'

At first, he looked surprised by the question but then gave a disinterested shrug. 'Sure. What do I care? It's what happened after all. So I was told.'

'Thank you. And I want you to think about a night in January. The night you and the other three tried to take over the orchard. The night you tied up the five women and raped them. I want to hear your version of what happened. The others all said it was your idea. Was it?'

A leer spread over Pete's face. His dull steel-grey eyes brightened. 'That night! Amazing! Just imagine it! My cock dipped in five women and coming in two of them. They came too, you know? Two of them, Rose and Jill. Came with me. Not with the others, just me.'

He then fell quiet, and looked at the table, smiling to himself. Catching a glimpse of his crooked grey-black teeth, I can't say the smile was pleasant either. 'I wonder if I'll ever have sex with a woman again?'

Wanting more than reminiscences about the sex, I began to feel tense. If Pete, more than anyone else, let me down about the orchard raid, I wasn't sure I would ever find out what happened. Ian and Danny were sticking to the authorised story and Dingo was dead. I cleared my throat. 'What about Sledge? Where was he during the sex? Surely he didn't just let all this happen around him?'

'He had no choice. He was tied to a tree. So was Henry. And Ysan. And Sledge was injured. My arrow had sliced his quad. Blood everywhere. And Dingo had damn near put one through his eye. Brilliant. We all thought he was dead. And if Antonio hadn't come back that night, he probably would be and we'd all still be there now. Just us and the women. And Dingo would still be alive.'

He leaned across the table. 'Do you want to see it?' he whispered. It wasn't obvious what he meant but I could guess.

'Later. So Antonio came back. What happened then?'

'How should I know. I was in the cove having a go with Clarabel. Dingo had gone back to Ysan. He reckoned he liked it with pregnant women. By the time we wandered back, Antonio had untied Sledge and Henry, and Dingo had gone.'

'Gone where?'

'Swimming. That's what Sledge said. Made out that he and Antonio had swum out to stop him but Dingo had insisted and then kept bumping into the coral. Mind not on the job, according to Sledge. "Messy. Very messy," he kept saying, and grinning while he said it. If you follow.'

Excited though I was at this revelation, I was also confused. 'But what about Maisie? Where was she? How did she die?'

Pete didn't answer.

'I know,' I said, a novel thought hitting me. 'Maisie died trying to save Dingo, not the other way round? She swam out with Sledge and Antonio and when they attacked Dingo, she tried to save him. Sledge and Antonio killed Maisie too. Maybe by accident. Is that it? Pete! Is that what happened?'

'You're trying to trick me, aren't you? Seeing if I've remembered? You already said it. Maisie was killed by the chimps.'

I took a sip of coffee, hoping he'd follow suit and calm down a little. 'No. I meant the other Maisie. Dingo's girlfriend.'

'Dingo's girlfriend? Dingo didn't have a girlfriend. Why are you trying to confuse me? You know what? I don't think you know anything about anything.' Pushing angrily at the table between us, he stood suddenly. The wardens also stood, poised as if to intervene. 'Is this in your book? Because if it's not, it bloody well ought to be.' He dropped his trousers.

The wardens rushed to his side to restrain him, but the monster was already on display.

HENRY

As we sat on a bench in a warm Green Park on a Sunday evening, eating ice cream while a handful of hopeful pigeons looked on, I tried to imagine the slight and round-shouldered man by my side as a harbourer of intense and rapacious lust. It was difficult. There weren't many things I wanted to ask Henry, or really know about him as an individual, and this may have been a common reaction and lifelong source of torment for the man. A terrible and corrosive angst that found a sluice on that island. But those few questions I harboured were vital to the investigation. And with the small talk over, I opened by telling him I would write that it was he who began the rape of Abi.

'It wasn't rape, it was justice. After what she'd done to Ysan, after the way she'd taunted, teased and goaded the five of us while we were living at South Bay, she deserved everything we did to her.'

'She could press charges. Once it's made public.'

'No she won't. Not against me. She couldn't. I'd be no use to her in jail. She needs me working, paying the maintenance money for Orchard, my daughter.'

There was genuine pride in his eyes, as if whatever else people said about him, nobody could take away the fact that he'd fathered a child with a beautiful and soon to be famous model, regardless of how it had happened.

I let him have his moment before asking about his abortive attempt to escape on the raft, which seemed to have made him a laughing stock. I knew he'd just caught Jill having sex with Antonio. Is that what drove him to be so foolhardy?

'The final humiliation. The last straw. For weeks they'd all been saying I was the one that should try to escape. Nobody used the word "dispensable", but it was pretty obvious that's what they all thought. It was bad enough when I caught Jill with Antonio in the first place. Then she tells me – in front of everybody – how much she'd been enjoying herself with him, and Sledge too, and for weeks on end; she even added that being gang-raped by the lads was better than consensual sex with me. I couldn't take any more. I just had to get away. I'd have gone, too, if the stupid little raft that that bastard Sledge built had been up to the job.'

I nodded and with some apprehension broached my final question. Surely he owed none of them anything, least of all Sledge, after the way they'd all treated him. Now he'd moved away from all of them, why not tell me straight about Dingo and Maisie's fates?

Pete's final revelation that Sledge and Antonio had killed Dingo and my wild guess about Maisie had both troubled and excited me. But how did they do it? The group seemed so comfortable with the idea of them drowning that perhaps the ocean really was a participant in their deaths. I remembered Alexi's words about Ysan's baby being mortally injured by the apes – 'It could be true'. And this was the level of logic they had so long rehearsed in order to become comfortable with the enormity of what they had done, or at least become complicit in by not acting. So maybe Dingo had been knocked out, and taken to the coral reef – the official site of his death – to let the waves and razor rocks do the rest. And maybe Maisie had died, or been killed, trying to save him.

'Henry, were Dingo and Maisie's deaths really accidents? I've been told by another in your group that they weren't. The others won't confide in me, but it's obvious they are hiding something, so I only have one testimony to rely upon. And my instinct is to believe it. So if I was to say, in my book, that Dingo was drowned by Sledge and Antonio and Maisie died or was killed trying to stop them, would you support me?'

Henry stared at me for a long time, then looked away. Melted ice cream dripped from his hand and onto his shoe. Distractedly he licked his hand clean. A pigeon took to the air and flapped noisily around us. I held my breath as I waited for an answer, terrified even the faintest exhalation would disrupt his recall or make him decide to lie.

'It was Pete, wasn't it?' he said at last. 'Pete told you. But he's crazy. Dingo died out on the coral trying to save Maisie, exactly as we all said under oath at the inquest.'

MAX

M y attempt to link Dingo's and now student Maisie's deaths with Sledge had been thwarted, but my visit to England wasn't over yet. It was all but three months since Max had given me her ultimatum over the use of Clarabel's sketches, but at last I felt I was ready to negotiate with her again. An hour or so after leaving Henry, I went back to my London hotel and e-mailed from my laptop.

```
20 July 2008
Hi Max
Remember me? I've been busy since we last met and can
now prove everything - rape, violence, maybe even
murder - without using Clarabel's drawings. My
feeling, though, is that when you hear the story, you
would rather the drawings were a part of it. I'm here in
London now. When can we meet? (Soon, please. I want to
get back to Spain and move on with writing this thing.)
x
```

I hadn't really expected a reply until Max went into her office the next morning but an answer came back within minutes.

20 July 2008
OK, tomorrow. See if you can convince me. But I can only
give you from 2-3. I have this cute young artist for the
rest of the afternoon and it might run on – I haven't
decided yet. And don't you dare 'x' me after ignoring me
all this time.

Max's reaction to me at the door was one of studied
indifference. But the moment I finished a quick summary of
my findings she transformed into the tactile, flirtatious
woman I'd known before. 'Of course you can refer to
Clarabel's drawings,' she said. 'As many as you like.' But on
the condition, she added, that I made sure the art was not
the *only* evidence upon which anything contentious and
potentially litigious was based. And it was difficult to define
which of us grew more excited as we worked out the best
strategy for our mutual interests. A strategy, we quickly
agreed, that should see a simultaneous publication of the
book and exhibition of the sketches.

'We should celebrate,' she said. 'Which hotel are you
staying at?'

I told her.

'That'll do. See you there at eight.'

'What about your artist?'

'He can wait. He visits my office a lot more often than
you do, and probably won't make me half as much money.'
As if summoned, a lanky, unkempt, but not unattractive
young man, who reminded me of a young Raúl, appeared
in the doorway of her office. I wasn't quite ready to leave
as I had one vital favour to ask: I needed a full-sized,
super-crisp of the funeral-cum-memorial scene dated January, the picture featuring the wrong vegetation. The
drawing she'd denied me back in May.

'Ask Annie on your way out. And don't forget our next
appointment.'

As if I could. Getting in the mood for celebration with an
afternoon coffee and brandy, I took the funeral sketch from

its envelope and studied a full-sized version in detail for the first time.

Five women were scattering flower petals picked from two distinct trees. Some had landed on Antonio's head and shoulders as he knelt crossing himself over a tiny mound of soil. The object suspended from the apex of a wigwam made from spears was a nose ring or similar and beneath Clarabel's signature was 'Oct'. The ring surely belonged to student Maisie. In which case she must have died in October – a whole three months before Dingo. Whatever else had happened, they didn't die saving each other from drowning near the reef as per the official story. So how had Maisie died? They'd clearly found the body in order to extract the ring and bury her remains. And why had the group been so desperate to cover up what happened? Maybe, contrary to all my suspicions, it was Maisie's death that threatened them all, and not Dingo's. And maybe that threat did still centre on Sledge, even if not for the reasons I'd first guessed.

'Why was that sketch put with the January section?' I asked Max later. Unwound and softened by our recent exertions, refreshed by a shower and pleasantly drunk, we sat at a table in the hotel restaurant.

Max shrugged, frowning. 'Annie assumed it was January because that was the month they all said Maisie and Dingo died. Why, what's wrong?'

'Clarabel signed it October as the date of composition. And the plants, Max. They're right for October but not for January. Maisie was buried in October, I'm sure of it. She died before Dingo. And the group are all lying. Because they have something terrible to hide. Something else.'

THE MESSENGER

As I drove away from Málaga Airport the next day I received a call on my mobile. It was Molly. 'Alexi has just phoned me and told me what you've been doing. I need to speak to you. In person. It's urgent.'

'Sorry, Molly. I'm driving. On the motorway. I'm on my way home. Phone me there in a couple of hours and we'll arrange something.'

After all the excitement with Max, during my first day back at home I began to suffer a letdown. While waiting for Molly's call, which never came, I began drawing out on paper the various threads to my book, and I could see just how many gaps still remained. But where and how could I possibly find the evidence I needed about the fate of Ysan's baby, Dingo and Maisie's deaths, and Sledge's culpability? I was mulling everything over as I floated naked on a lilo in my swimming pool when I heard a voice that nearly stopped my heart.

'And I thought a writer's life was all hardship and hovels.' The voice came from the side of the pool, making me turn so quickly I slipped into the water. Silhouetted above me against the evening sun, I saw a figure I failed to recognise straight away.

'Mind if I join you?' she asked, and she was naked and in the water almost before I had the chance to work out what was happening.

'Don't get excited,' Molly warned as she trod water by my side. 'I'm here on business. I caught the very next plane.'

We were dressed in my cotton bathrobes and sharing a bottle of wine on the patio. But the alcohol and setting failed to relax her. Despite her entrance, she was agitated. Unable to meet my eye, I could sense her building up to something. Her unease was making her drink quickly, short sips but every few seconds.

'This isn't easy, Robin. Not for me. But it's not the sort of conversation we can have any other way.'

I nodded. 'What's on your mind, Molly?'

She stared up at the darkening sky, her long fair hair hanging behind her, still dripping water. Then with a sigh she looked me in the eyes. 'Alexi tells me you're still going ahead with your book, and that you found out about Ysan and her baby.'

'Yes. I have heard a few things. Shall I tell you what I'm going to write?'

'Don't bother. Whatever it is, it's wrong.'

I laughed. 'How do you know?'

'It just is. Ysan phoned from the mainland and when I told her that you were still writing your book, she asked me to talk to you. She wants you to go to the island. I've got to persuade you.'

It was my turn to drink. 'That's absurd. Why should I do that? How could she phone you, anyway? I thought she was on the island.'

'She was. Now she's back on the mainland. With Clarabel. Clarabel's on her way to Fiji and Ysan needed to tell me things. She was desperate. She needed my help. And when she heard about you, she said you could help too. In fact, she said that you were just the person. But you need to go to the island.'

'Why me? Why can't you go?'

'Because I'm not a friend of Raúl's. Nor am I writing a book.'

'Stop playing games, Molly.'

She drained her glass. 'Baby Maisie is still alive. She's on the island. Clarabel has been looking after her this past year.'

I already knew that couldn't be true. 'How could a four-month-old baby survive on its own for the month or more until Clarabel returned? Especially in those filthy caves. There is no baby, Molly. You know there isn't. Ysan ... Well ... She's had a difficult year. And it sounds as though she still isn't over everything.'

Molly poured herself a fresh glass of wine, emptying the bottle, and took a long swig. 'Maisie survived because somebody was looking after her during that month.'

'Who? And don't tell me Raúl.' As soon as Molly had told me that Ysan had sent her, I had a feeling that before long Ysan's old fantasy would be mentioned.

'Of course Raúl! Who else? He really is still alive, you know. But Ysan knows you won't believe it unless you see him for yourself.'

I couldn't stay seated. I paced back and forth, doubtless cutting a ridiculous figure in my bathrobe. 'Do you really think I'm going to go halfway round the world on the word of some demented girl? Raúl is dead. He has to be. And so is baby Maisie. This is all one big cover for something. And it's probably infanticide.'

Molly's face soured and she began rummaging inside her overnight bag. Her robe was falling apart but she was too angry to care. Finding what she wanted, she got to her feet. 'Open another bottle of wine. Switch on the veranda and pool lights, and while I have another swim to try to forget what you just said, take a long hard look at those.'

She slammed pieces of paper onto the table, then strode to the side of the pool. Letting her robe fall to the floor, she jumped in, splashing water everywhere.

* * *

'Sorry, I don't understand,' I said once Molly had finished her swim and pulled her robe back on. 'These may as well be in Chinese.'

'And I thought you were a scientist. That,' she said, pushing one piece of paper towards me, 'is the medical certificate for Ysan's new baby: AR. Look at his blood group. He's rhesus negative. And those are paternity tests for him against all the men on the island.'

'How?'

'Herbert – you've met him, haven't you – has in his deep freeze a semen sample from Antonio that Raúl once brought back, and blood samples from everybody else, including Raúl, taken before they left. He gave us a little of each for paternity tests – for all the babies conceived on the island, not just for AR.'

'But why test AR against all the men? How many did Ysan have sex with?'

'Only with Antonio and Danny for certain . . .'

'Antonio doesn't surprise me. But Danny? After everything she told me he'd done to her?'

Molly almost snarled. 'I know. Bastard, isn't he. And there's more. When he met Ysan at the caves, he refused to go in to look for Maisie and said he'd only help Ysan look for the boat if . . . Well, you can guess. She could scarcely put her foot to the ground for Christ's sake. But she was so convinced there was a boat there and so desperate to get to it that same day – but needed to be virtually carried – that she gave in. It was all she had to bargain with.'

My opinion of Danny, which I had thought couldn't get any lower, reached a new depth. And I could see Molly felt the same.

She drank again, shivering as if the wine were sour. 'But Ysan always had this vague memory of sex with somebody else. And she thought it was Raúl; that he rescued her and Maisie from the caves, nursed her – and had sex with her. But the doctors warned her that the position of the blood clot meant she couldn't trust any of her memories between going into the caves and coming round from her operation.

And when Rose and Sledge visited her in the hospital, they tried to convince her that the memories of Raúl were just her subconscious trying to protect her from what really happened to Maisie. Imagine how she was feeling all the time you were pressing her for information. Because at the time even she half-believed that her baby had died and that it was her fault. That she might even have killed her. She had nightmares every night. Nine months of sheer hell. She was going crazy. It was awful for me to watch. And it lasted right up until April when AR was born. Then everything changed. Look at the papers.'

I tried again, but it didn't help. The sheets were a quagmire of symbols. A list of DNA sequences found in the tissue samples from Ysan, AR, and eight men.

'You'll need to help me out, Molly. I can't follow . . .'

Emptying her glass of wine with a long gulp, Molly stood, a little unsteadily, leaned on the table and rearranged the sheets of paper. Her robe was falling apart again, but now neither of us cared.

'Let me make it easy for you,' she said. 'Raúl is AR's father. Thirty billion to one chance that he's not, or something silly like that.'

'I still don't . . .'

'God, you're slow. AR was conceived in July 2007. A year after Raúl was supposed to have died. Do you understand now?'

She tottered a little, supporting herself on the table. 'Do you have any food? I think this wine is going to my head.'

Molly stayed the night in one of my guest rooms and slept soundly. In contrast, I scarcely closed my eyes. Partly, I was hoping that Molly would suddenly appear at my bedroom door and slip seductively into my bed. Sadly, she didn't. I was also wrestling with thoughts about Raúl which were far from clear cut. I had no idea whether the sheets of paper Molly had shown me proved what she claimed. But even if she had convinced me that Raúl was still alive, I'm not sure which way my emotions would have swung. I didn't know what to think.

But there was a further reason I couldn't sleep. A fear was growing that I was being manipulated into something that was definitely not to my advantage. Why was I suddenly being summoned to the island? If AR's paternity tests really did prove that Raúl had survived the night of the fire, there was no need for me to travel all that way to see for myself. And as for Ysan being innocent of infanticide ... Why couldn't she simply come home with her baby daughter, have another DNA test to prove that she was the mother, and free herself of all suspicion that way? For the first time since my investigation began, I wondered if I was in danger. Maybe the group, Ysan included, had decided that I couldn't be allowed to get any closer to the truth, and sending me to the island was the way to silence me.

The next morning, Molly and I breakfasted and swam until it was time for me to take her to Málaga Airport. Irritatingly, she refused to give me any details about how Raúl was supposed to have survived the night of the fire, how he came to be looking after baby Maisie at the time Ysan and Danny escaped, or the real reason Ysan wanted me to visit the island.

'Ysan wants to tell you everything herself. You will go, won't you?'

But Molly did tell me one thing that interested me. As we drove along the *Autovía Mediterráneo* towards the Málaga mountain, I asked, 'Does Herbert know that Raúl was AR's father?'

'No! He didn't actually do the tests. He just gave us the material.'

'So why haven't you told him? He was a friend of Raúl's. In fact, why haven't you told the university, the press, the police, everybody, that Raúl's still alive?'

'Ysan doesn't want anybody to know. Only you.'

I immediately felt uneasy again. 'Why? Why only me?'

'Ask Ysan!'

NERVES

23 July 2008

While delivering Molly to the airport, I'd received an e-mail from Max.

23 July 2008
Tried phoning but you were out and your mobile was off
as usual. Guess who made a collect call this morning?
None other than the elusive Clarabel. She's on her way
from the mainland to Fiji. Something about visas.
Ysan's subbing her the money. And Ysan has told her
about your book and her drawings being published.
Clarabel wanted to know how much she's being paid!
Maybe the simple life is beginning to pall. So I told
her about the gallery and the exhibition. And warned
her that Sledge is trying to bully me into not showing
any more of her work, but that she mustn't worry.
Anyway, the main thing is, they want you to go over
there. Clarabel's going to be on Fiji for a while. She
can meet you and take you to the island. Isn't that
brilliant? You lucky bastard. Think how much better
you can write about the place if you've actually been
there.

```
So . . . Drop everything. Phone me. I'll even get Annie
to book your flights.
Ma(xxx)
```

Gripped by the feeling that things were spiralling out of my control, I phoned immediately and told Max about my meeting with Molly. 'That's the second invitation to the island I've had in two days. Something is going on.'

'Then get out there and find out what it is. What's stopping you?'

'To be honest, I'm worried. What if somebody is trying to get me out of the way, to stop me writing my book?'

'Not Ysan, surely? And certainly not Clarabel. After everything I've told her, she wants your book published, to promote her drawings. The people here maybe, Sledge and the others. But that's even more reason to go, not stay. And there's something else. Because of what your book can do for her, I've a hunch that face to face Clarabel will tell you everything you still need to know. No more loose ends.'

I hesitated, knowing it made sense, but still uneasy.

'Come on! You can't turn this down. And you've got to go *now*. How else will you find your way to the island without somebody like Clarabel to show you?'

And only a couple of hours after I'd given in, Max e-mailed.

```
23 July 2008
Flight details attached. You leave from Málaga for
Heathrow on the 30th, then on to Fiji via Tokyo.
Everything you need will be at the British Airways desk
at Heathrow. Clarabel said she'll meet you in the foyer
of the Holiday Inn Hotel, Suva on Fiji at 11 a.m. local
time on 4 August.
I've had a great thought. If you're worried about
Sledge or some hired help suddenly visiting your villa
and trying to 'dissuade' you from writing your book,
```

why not stay on in Fiji to finish it off. Once the
manuscript is with your agent and publisher what can
Sledge do? You can stay on Fiji for four months without
a visa. Longer if you bother to get one. And I'll come
and visit you for a week or so! It's time I had a
holiday.

Phone whenever you can.

Take care

Ma (x)

PS. Some sad news. You know that only a few months after
student Maisie was officially pronounced dead the first
time round, her dad caved in to his alcoholism and died
of liver failure? Well . . . I've just heard that her mum
has died too. It was in yesterday's evening paper.
Overdose it seems. Just coming up to the first
anniversary of learning that the group had been found -
but that her daughter was dead after all. There's
nobody left. What a tragic family!

X-RATED

4 August 2008

'So you're Robin,' she said as we first shook hands. 'Ysan's told me about you. So has Max. That was really careless, getting caught on the nudist beach with Ysan like that.'

Clarabel and I met at the Holiday Inn, Suva as arranged, and from then on I was completely in her hands as she took me from the hotel to the airport and eventually a plane. She was just as I imagined: beautiful, voluptuous and an incorrigible flirt. Her body language – the way she smiled, laughed and kept touching me on my arms and shoulders – could easily have fooled me into thinking she was attracted to me. Except that her manner was exactly the same with the concierge, the taxi driver, the guy on the check-in desk and the stern and beefy Fijians who ushered us through baggage security.

Clearly bra-less, she was wearing a loose white blouse and a full, light, ankle-length, pale-green skirt. Her wonderful auburn hair tumbled about her shoulders and swayed as she walked.

'The Moll Flanders look,' I murmured.

'Pardon?'

'Nothing. I thought you'd be more tanned.'

'It doesn't happen. Dirty pink with freckles. That's as good as it gets.'

And that was just about the limit of our conversation until we were in the air, the only two passengers on the small, twenty-seater plane that took us on the first stage of the island-hopping flight north from Fiji. The solitary bored-looking air hostess was all ours. Generously, Clarabel let me have the window seat so I could be as 'entranced' as she had been by the sparkling blue Pacific and the gems of islands that passed beneath us. On the horizon, there was a procession of towering cumulonimbus clouds, their tops spread out like anvils. But around us there was nothing but clear blue sky and sea.

'So why am I here?' I asked as we settled down after ordering a couple of sandwiches and a bottle of water each.

'Wait until we're with Ysan. This was all her idea. Let her tell you. She and Antonio are waiting for us on the mainland.'

'Ysan's mum hinted it was about Raúl and baby Maisie.'

'Just . . . Wait.'

I had a surge of irritation at the way these two young women were manipulating me without telling me why, so I retaliated. 'But maybe there *is* something you're prepared to tell me about baby Maisie . . . In Ysan's journal, she said you were trying to steal her during those last few months on the island. Were you?'

Clarabel smiled wickedly. Her teeth looked perfect. 'I was doing worse than that. I was dreaming up ways to get rid of Ysan completely.'

Unable to speak for a while, I searched her face for clues of whether this was a joke. Clarabel just smiled. 'Are you just trying to shock me?' I asked. 'Does Ysan know?'

'She knows. We threshed it all out this last week or so. But I've come to my senses and so has she. We're friends again. As strong as ever, I'd say. I'm sure I'd never really have done anything nasty to her, but who knows? The island did horrendous things to us all, not just to the men. There was something driving me, from deep inside. I wanted that baby so badly. I was devastated when Danny told us all about the caves and how the baby must be dead. I hated Ysan for what we all thought she'd done. Two Maisies dead, we said. The name must be jinxed.'

'Like student Maisie's family. Have you heard what's happened?' And when Clarabel said no, I told her.

Clarabel fell quiet, and looked past me out of the window, her eyes glistening.

'Will you tell me what happened to *student* Maisie?' I asked. 'It's still a mystery to me. I do know she died in October, not January, and that you all buried her in the glade. But you didn't draw anything to show what happened, and neither Rose nor Ysan wrote about her death in their journals. Of course, there were big chunks missing from that parcel you sent Max.' I explained about the parcel's itinerary through the Philippines and Thailand and about pages being lost. 'Will you tell me now?'

She looked uncomfortable and seemed to avoid answering. 'Is Sledge really trying to stop Max from publishing any more of my drawings?'

'Don't worry. Max has everything under control. I think Sledge is worried she'll sell the drawings of him with all the women.'

Clarabel gave an almost strangled laugh. 'He'll be worried about more than that. What are you going to say in your book about Dingo's death?'

'I'm not sure yet. My suspicion is that Sledge and Antonio killed him. But nobody will back me up, so I'll have to choose my words carefully. And I still wonder if Sledge and Antonio weren't involved in student Maisie's death too.'

She looked me in the eyes, her emerald irises shimmering as her pupils contracted. 'That's what I was afraid of.' Then she looked away. 'Antonio had nothing to do with Dingo's death,' she said at last. 'Or Maisie's.'

'Really?'

'No!' She stood and opened the overhead locker, shouting to the air hostess in the rear as she did so. 'He's going to need a brandy. Better make it two.'

When she sat again, she was holding three fat A4-sized Manila envelopes. 'I hadn't the nerve to send these to Max a year ago. On this visit, I really meant to. That's why I took them with me to the mainland and Fiji. But I still couldn't.'

'So why show them to me?'

'You'll understand. Look at October first, then January.'

The brandies arrived, and Clarabel gave me the envelope labelled 'October (2006)'. It contained half a dozen or so of her bark drawings. Originals! Almost the first I'd seen.

The sequence began with a couple of scenes, both actually dated September: student Maisie creeping along the orchard edge, spear raised, stalking rabbits while in the distance an audience of chimps watched her intently; then another of her checking a snare against the same backdrop. The first sketch dated October was a montage of people searching: Antonio statuesque on a rocky outcrop, others peering into bushes, and so on.

'Maisie just suddenly disappeared. We were worried sick.'

Another montage of four pictures followed. In all four, the central character is student Maisie. In one she is being raped and strangled by the lads, in another she is falling from a cliff, in another she is drowning in the sea, and finally she is on the beach and being bitten by what looks like a snake.

'Just theories,' said Clarabel. 'Maisie went missing as the sea snakes arrived. They come on land to lay their eggs, you know, just like the sea turtles. Several of us nearly got bitten, and according to Antonio they can kill you. By the time Maisie had been missing a fortnight, that's what we thought might have happened, but couldn't understand why we couldn't find her body. We were so wrong.'

The next full-sized picture is on the racetrack. Overhead, an eagle is flying with a snake in its talons. Antonio is holding something between his thumb and forefinger, which an inset shows to be the blackberry and ring that in a separate, indecipherable drawing Max and I had commented on before. Others from the Orchard Bay group are clustered around, all holding spears. Alexi is looking away and being sick.

'It was the first thing we found. Ysan and I saw the sunlight glinting from the ring. It still makes me feel like throwing up when I think about it.'

I wasn't prepared for what came next. I gasped deeply, involuntarily, as I turned the page.

The sketch showed a rock, half-hidden by grass. And by its side a human skull, broken in two halves. No brain, no eyes, just traces of gore. And a ring, dangling loosely from a crescent of thick black hair on skin. I stared in disbelief.

'Horrendous, eh? Sometimes I can't believe I made myself draw it all.'

On the next sheet, arrayed on a large leaf were the two halves of the skull, an arm bone, part of a leg bone, a complete hand, all stripped of flesh – and the blackberry, now minus its ring. Only then did I realise what it really was. I looked at Clarabel in horror. She looked away, clearly struggling with the memory.

Worse was to follow: a close-up of Maisie's face, eyes wide open but staring lifelessly, mouth fixed for a scream. Her wrenched-off head is in M1's hands, about to be smashed against a rock. In the background, other chimps are having tugs of war with detached legs and arms while two more have their heads buried in Maisie's disembowelled belly. Having wondered what had happened to this caring and determined young woman for so long, the drawing made me feel physically sick.

'Did this happen soon after Ysan had her last meeting with Maisie on the racetrack? The same day Ysan was raped, and you . . .'

Clarabel was crying silently into her glass of brandy. I took a very long swig of my own, understanding with greater force than ever exactly why Ysan had broken down at that point when recounting her story to me.

'Why show them to me now?'

'We all agreed that we would never let Maisie's mum and dad know what had really happened to her. But you've just told me that they're both dead. So there's nobody to protect any more. People may as well know what she really suffered. You tell them, I'll show them.'

I looked out of the window for an age, trying hard to shut out the terror and pain Maisie must have felt during her last moments as M1 began yanking at her head. I failed. 'I hope it was quick,' I muttered.

'So do we all.'

I took a deep breath. 'What about the January drawings? They can't be worse?'

Clarabel handed me the envelope. 'Depends how you look at it. They're all X-rated.'

In the first drawing, Clarabel shows herself at the moment Dingo's fist strikes her on the cheekbone. They are near the tunnel. The other three lads are carrying bows and quivers full of arrows which even have flights made of feathers. Ian has lengths of cord draped over his shoulder and Danny is in the process of tying a pregnant Ysan's hands behind her back.

The next sketch is set under the palms at Orchard Bay. Now both Ysan and Clarabel have their hands and ankles bound exactly as in Danny's plan of attack. Danny is holding Ysan by the wrists and pointing aggressively – or is it nervously? – at a menacing and advancing Sledge. Henry and the women seem to be skulking, frightened, in the background. Ian, Pete and Dingo have their bows trained on Sledge, and Pete has fired an arrow that is about to slice through Sledge's quad muscle on his right thigh.

Next we see Sledge, Henry and Ysan each tied to a tree and the other women – Clarabel, Alexi, Rose, Jill and Abi – all now manacled. Inset is a close-up of Sledge with a snarling Dingo only a metre or so in front of him holding a bow he has just fired. The arrow seems to have gone straight through Sledge's right eye and embedded itself in the tree trunk.

'I don't understand.'

'It was an illusion. That's what we all thought had happened. In fact the arrow had sliced his cheek. Pretty close, though.'

Dingo had clearly lost control. The next sketch shows Rose, still hog-tied, lying on her back in a cove with Dingo standing astride her, bow drawn, and with the stone arrow tip only centimetres from her belly. Rose looks defiant.

'You've seen my drawing of what happened after we all calmed Dingo down, I suppose.'

I nodded. 'We've called it musical cunts.'

Clarabel chuckled quietly. 'That's close.'

Next comes a scene set back at the palm trees. It is in moonlight. Sledge and Henry are still tied to trees but Ysan is on her hands and knees, head bowed as if about to be beheaded, while Dingo is about to penetrate her from behind. In the shadows, only recognisable by the whites of his eyes, a shadow lurks holding a club. It must be Antonio.

My hands shook as I turned the sheet to look at the next picture, wondering if at last I would discover Dingo's true fate.

Antonio is slumped on the ground with Ysan tending to him, while to their right, we have four cameos of Sledge with Dingo, each one further down the beach. Sledge, multi-armed, punching a sagging Dingo. Sledge, multi-legged, kicking a prostrate Dingo. Sledge dragging Dingo's lifeless body down the beach. And finally, Sledge with Dingo out at sea, near the coral.

'Antonio tried to stop him but Sledge was too strong. Then Sledge killed Dingo. Simple as that. He even bragged about it, until Rose tore into him. Only then did he seem to realise what he'd done. He broke down, started crying.'

'Didn't anybody go and look for Dingo? He might not have been dead.'

'Antonio did swim out to look, both that night in the moonlight and first thing next day, but there was nothing. Besides, Dingo was probably dead long before he got sliced to pieces on the coral. Sledge said he'd dragged him through the water face-down. He never even spluttered.'

My mind was reeling. 'Sorry, I've got to ask. Did Sledge really kill Dingo on his own or did you just draw it this way to make people believe that he did? To protect Antonio?'

Clarabel handed me the third envelope. 'Read these. They're sheets from Rose's notes and Ysan's data sheets from October and January. You'll recognise the writing. They'll say the same thing. The sheets didn't go missing in the Philippines or Thailand. I just never sent them.'

I downed one brandy and poured the next. I didn't need to ask Clarabel why she had revealed all this now. She was abandoning Sledge in order to protect Antonio, that much was obvious. But I didn't care. I was too busy savouring the pleasure of knowing that I could nail Sledge at last.

But on the heels of pleasure came unease. Suddenly Max's advice seemed sound. The thought of being alone in my Spanish villa for a few months, finishing off a book while the people my book could send to jail for rape and murder were only a short plane flight away no longer appealed. I was very glad to be on the opposite side of the world, sitting next to Clarabel, drinking brandy, on a plane, on my way to a desert island. And a writing retreat on Fiji seemed an excellent place to finish my book. But first, I had to meet Ysan, and Antonio – and maybe even Raúl.

INFAMY

4–5 August 2008

Clarabel and I were together for about eighteen hours on our way to the mainland, and four of those were spent trying to sleep on benches in a stiflingly hot wooden barn that passed as a terminal building on one of the tiny islands. At intervals, large moths and grasshoppers flapped into our faces, smaller whining insects tried to crawl up our noses and into our mouths and ears, and once an hour a uniformed guard with a gun and a large mongrel of a drooling black dog would wake us up and tell us that we had to sit, not lie.

On the plane on the second leg of our island-hopping flight we tried to catch up on our sleep. But we also found time to continue our conversations from the day before. I told Clarabel everything I had gleaned from her drawings and we discussed them in fine and intimate detail; she did enjoy talking about body parts and sex. And more than once she wanted to talk about Max's plan to coincide an exhibition of her drawings with the publication of my book.

She was excited, hardly able to keep still in her seat. 'It hasn't really sunk in. It never once occurred to me when I was drawing them, that one day somebody would examine them so closely. Or that they'd be published. Exhibited. Sold for money. Used in a book. It's all amazing.'

I asked her where she went from here. Had she been drawing more over the past year? Was she going to carry on using bark or switch back to paper?

She wrinkled her pretty snub nose. 'Paper, probably. But I haven't done much on either. It's not been the same since everybody left. No real inspiration. Just me, Antonio . . .'

I waited for the 'and', but it didn't come.

'The plan is that if all goes well, me and Antonio will go with Ysan to the DR Congo. Help her out, you know? With her bonobo research. With babysitting. Everything. It's so exciting. I can't wait.'

'Babysitting? Who? AR? *And* baby Maisie?'

Clarabel gave me a cheeky smile. 'Should be plenty of inspiration for me in a place like the Congo and plenty of challenges for Antonio. Wait till you meet him. He really is a wonderful man.'

At the airstrip and tiny terminal that passed as the mainland airport, we phoned for a cab, then waited thirty minutes for it to arrive. Clarabel showed the driver a piece of paper, a map that Antonio had drawn to indicate where he and Ysan would be waiting.

'What happened to Antonio's rickety bus? The one that he used to drive you all from this airport to the cove when you first arrived back in 2006?'

'No idea. He drove it off somewhere before we sailed, and came back on foot. We were waiting ages. All he says now is that he had to get rid of it.'

When Clarabel told me we were nearing the end of our journey, my heart raced at the thought of meeting Ysan again. I still had no real idea why she had invited me, but the fantasist inside hoped it might include continuing where we had left off. Memories of her and myself on the beach in Spain had never been far from my mind. And at home I still had the published newspaper photos.

The taxi stopped at the top of a cliff, leaving us to walk and sometimes scrabble down a narrow rocky serpentine path to the beach. Clarabel had warned me in Fiji to travel light. All I had was a rucksack. A fishing boat was moored offshore and we had been seen, because the lifeboat began lowering from its gantry and somebody eventually began rowing for shore. We all three arrived at the water's edge together. The rower was Ysan.

Ysan was as desirable as I remembered, just larger breasted. Her hair had grown since our last meeting and was now about shoulder length but untidy and uncombed, her lack of interest in her appearance still evident. Her shirt was too big for her and torn at the shoulder and her baggy shorts were anything but flattering. She was barefooted.

She smiled at me warmly, her wonderful eyes shining, then gave me a platonic kiss of greeting on both cheeks. 'Thank you for coming. I guess we've got a lot to talk about.'

I tried to look calm, not to betray my excitement at seeing her again. 'Why I'm here would be a good start.'

'Soon! But Antonio wants to get under way. It's the tides. We have to go now.'

On board the fishing boat, Clarabel introduced me, in surprisingly good Spanish, to Antonio. He and I then exchanged a few comments about my journey, also in Spanish. He was just as I had pictured: broad-shouldered and Mediterranean-skinned with tangled dark hair and a full black beard and moustache. Shirtless, he was muscular, though not as heavyweight as Sledge, and when we shook hands, his palms were sweating profusely from the effort of manhandling the lifeboat into position. His manner was warm but determined, maybe even threatening.

'*We're relying on you,*' he said in Spanish. '*If you can't persuade him, I may have to kill somebody.*' At which he laughed coarsely.

I also met Ysan's son, AR, four months old, with short dark hair, beautiful lightly tanned skin, a toothless grin, and a propensity for smacking whoever was holding him in the eye whenever he became excited.

It was suggested I might like to rest for a while on one of the four beds below deck and, much as I wanted to begin asking questions, my brain was sluggish through jet lag and lack of sleep, so I gratefully accepted. Bed was an exaggeration – just a doubled-over blanket on a wooden base – but more than I would get on the island. Despite the discomfort and the swaying of the boat, I slept for a full three hours.

When I emerged above deck, the sun was nearing the western horizon. An atoll about a kilometre to starboard showed no signs of habitation, and there were no other boats to be seen on the sea. Only then did I fully appreciate that for the first time in my life I was about to enter one of those rare parts of the world that was uninhabited, except for us.

My three companions – and AR – were now all naked.

Ysan smiled at me, a twinkle in her eye. 'This is what the island does to you. Are you staying like that or joining in?'

No stranger to being naked amongst nudists – Raúl's influence from our younger days – I joined in. Soon after, I was handed a plate of food, a risotto of sorts with bits of vegetables and flakes of fish, and a full bottle of water and a half-empty bottle of rum.

Ysan sat by my side on the deck. We were under the swinging creaking lifeboat, our bare backs resting uncomfortably against the hull. Loud and fairly drunken laughter from Clarabel and Antonio drifted from the forward cabin.

'Clarabel's well ahead of you,' said Ysan as she began to breast-feed AR. 'But I'm not drinking alcohol for a few more months.'

AR was rooting, having trouble finding the nipple.

'What does AR stand for? Nobody seems to know.'

She laughed. 'And I thought it was so obvious. "A", the person who saved my life and "R", the father, bastard though he is. Antonio Raúl, of course. Seemed a good idea at the time.'

I waited until AR latched on. 'OK, Ysan. Tell me now. Why am I here?'

She gave a look of apprehension, as if she were worried how I would respond.

'First, I want you to know something. This is Antonio's original fishing boat. The same one that brought us to the island when we first arrived. It never did sink, just as I always told you. Raúl never even sailed it on the night of the fire. By then, it was already safely tucked away in a nice big cave on the next island. That was what Raúl and Antonio had been doing all the day that Antonio pretended he had a bad stomach. They'd taken this boat there and then come back. Of course, they were hidden from our side of the island.'

I laughed in disbelief. 'The next island? How could they get back? Or even go there next time they needed the fishing boat?'

'Easy. They'd planned all that. The other island was near enough for Antonio to swim if he really had to – but it was never necessary. That was what the tiny yacht was for, to go backwards and forwards to check on the fishing boat, spend some time maintaining it occasionally. The yacht wasn't Jim's. Raúl and Antonio had towed it there the October before our trip. That's when they set everything up. The yacht was a lot easier than the fishing boat to hide from us – and quieter.'

'Now why should I believe any of that? This could be any fishing boat.'

'Look up there, on the underside of that beam. Do you remember my describing it to you? See the lichen growing over it. Danny carved that two years ago, on the journey over.'

I could see it and I did remember. The graffiti was a carved picture of a heart with an arrow through it, *Barbie* written on one side, *apes* on the other. I gave a sharp intake of breath. It was impressive evidence about the boat, but not *proof* of anything about Raúl. 'If Raúl's alive when we reach the island I will humbly apologise for ever doubting you. I might even be prepared to believe that he planned the whole thing – but never as a ten-year breeding experiment. He just wouldn't. For a few weeks, perhaps, just to see how you coped. But then – I would guess – everything went wrong. Maybe this boat's engine wouldn't start and the radio died. Something like that. And Raúl couldn't face any of you until Antonio got it working again. That's why Antonio had those fortnights away. He was working on the boat. But on your island, not some other island.'

She laughed. 'Man, are you in for some shocks! We weren't meant to be there for only ten years. Raúl has told us everything. He's actually proud of what he tried to do, that's how deranged he is. We were meant to be a founding colony, like the chimps. A colony for somebody to stumble across years or decades in the future, maybe even after we were dead and our children had inherited the island. Can you see what he really wanted? Lasting, posthumous, scientific infamy; the man who dared to set up a breeding colony of humans alongside his mentor's breeding colony of apes. That – and to live the rest of his years naked in the sun, studying apes and humans side by side.'

I shook my head, hardly able to take it all in. It seemed so unbelievably crazy, so unlike the Raúl I'd always known. But what did Ysan have to gain from lying to me now? Bit by bit, I was reluctantly beginning to believe that everything she was saying might be true. And bit by bit I was even beginning to hope that it was all true. Because if it wasn't – if Raúl wasn't still alive and waiting for me on the island – why was I being taken there? Briefly, my stomach lurched. Did it no longer matter to them what I thought or how much I knew, because they were taking me to the island to leave me there to protect Sledge and Antonio from being accused of murder in my book?

She laughed again. 'Guess what Raúl told me? The reason he wouldn't have sex with me right at the beginning was nothing to do with a vow to his dead daughter and partner.

It was because he couldn't risk getting me pregnant. Scientifically, he couldn't be part of his own experiment. It would spoil his data. Back then, he valued me more as a data point than a lover. What do you think of that? Of course, after a year of celibacy and watching everybody screwing, he'd changed his mind and wanted me to live with him. What a hope!'

Not for the first time since arriving in Fiji, my mind was reeling. 'It's too much, Ysan. It's all too weird. Just tell me why I'm here. I'll think about Raúl seriously once I've seen him and know that what you're saying is true.'

She took a deep breath. 'Right. Well . . . Here it is. I . . . We . . . That's me, Clarabel *and* Antonio. We want you to persuade Raúl to let us take my Maisie off the island.'

I nearly choked on my food. It was the last thing I'd expected. 'Why me?'

'We've all tried to persuade him, but he won't budge. "Maisie's as much mine as yours," he says to me, "and she's staying right here." Now we're losing patience. Clarabel and I want to get on with our lives, our careers. To go to the Congo. And Antonio wants to come with us. But none of us will go without Maisie.'

If this was all a pretence, Ysan was acting it well. I looked at her sternly. 'I think you should give me the whole story. Then try to tell me why I can change his mind if you three can't.'

PERSPECTIVES

8 August 2008, dawn

I can't deny the excitement I felt as we sailed past Saddle Island. And with the sun rising astern, Ysan pointed out our destination to me, the place that had assumed such a mythical, magical and even evil status in my mind. I felt trepidation too. If Raúl really was there, how could I face him, knowing what he had tried to do? He had to be a changed man. And could I really persuade him to give up his daughter? And if he wasn't there . . . I didn't even want to think about it. It was too late. I had no escape. Was that why they had refused to tell me anything until I was on the boat?

'Why can't we just grab Maisie, take her to the boat, and all of us just sail away?' I asked Ysan.

'Because unless Antonio cooperates, it's impossible. We need him to do the sailing.'

'And he won't?'

'"Raúl has to agree," he says. "He loves that child, as we all do. I cannot take her from him, my friend, by force." Antonio's very strong on loyalty.'

'Is he? What about his loyalty to you? And Clarabel? You both want to go to the Congo. Would he deliberately separate a child from its mother?'

'Of course not. And he's fed up with his loyalties being pulled both ways. Because he wants to go to the Congo just as much as Clarabel and I do. He likes the thought of us all being a family together in the jungle. It excites him.'

'A family? Surely Antonio doesn't still believe he's Maisie's father.'

'Emotionally, he does. Maisie calls him *papá*, just as she does Raúl. And she calls Clarabel *mamá*, which is more than she calls me. I can't even speak to her properly yet. She understands more Spanish than English. Guess how that makes me feel.'

She glanced at me, her bewitching eyes transporting me back to the beach in Spain where everything began. 'But logically . . . No, Antonio doesn't really believe he's Maisie's father. Not any more. Not since Raúl told him a couple of weeks ago during an argument that he was infertile. It was a horrible moment. Antonio refused to believe it at first, but once Raúl convinced him . . . Antonio actually cried. He was so upset, he wouldn't speak for a whole day. And at last I think that maybe their friendship is growing thin. Because suddenly there's jealousy. Raúl has fathered two children with me. Antonio hasn't fathered any, and never can. I think Antonio is pinning a lot of hope on your visit to give him an honourable way out of his dilemma.'

The island's coastline began to resolve into bays and promontories.

'South Bay,' said Ysan, pointing. 'That's where we'll dock.'

'Not Orchard Bay?'

'This boat's too big to cross the reef there.'

I gazed forwards, wondering whether Raúl – if he existed – had seen the boat approaching and would be at South Bay to greet us. And wondering how he would react when he saw me. As Clarabel joined us, I had a puzzling thought. 'Ysan, how did you get here last month when you first arrived with AR?'

She shrugged. 'How else? I hired somebody to bring me though I needed to do a lot of the navigating.'

'Wasn't he curious about why somebody like you would want to visit a deserted island with a young baby?'

'Actually, it was a she. A widow. An amazing woman. And she spoke a bit of French. I told her my husband was there, studying the wildlife. And luckily, Antonio met me on the shore, but I still told her that if I wasn't back on the mainland by 1 August to come to fetch us. It would mean something had gone wrong. Of course, she didn't need to. Antonio had his boat – this boat – here.'

Clarabel followed on. 'Antonio and I had to hire somebody too, once Antonio had discharged himself from hospital. We went to the island where Raúl and Antonio had hidden this boat, before sailing across to where it all began. Can you imagine how I felt when we finally arrived here and I found baby Maisie alive and being looked after by Raúl?'

Perhaps on Ysan's behalf, I bridled a little. 'Triumphant, maybe? Why didn't you let Ysan know that her baby was still alive?'

Clarabel looked offended. 'I didn't know Ysan thought her baby was dead. How could I? But I did make Antonio take me straight back to the mainland on his boat so that I could phone Ysan and tell her what was happening. And I thought I may as well mail the last of the bark sheets at the same time. But I didn't have Ysan's number or address and her mum turned out to be ex-directory. So I had a big problem, because I didn't want anybody but Ysan to know that Raúl was still alive.'

'Why not?'

'I think I'll let you work that one out. In the end, I left a cryptic voicemail with Max – "Until Ysan comes, I have to stay on the island because of a baby" – and asked her to pass it on to Ysan, assuming that Ysan would understand but Max wouldn't.'

Ysan was staring ahead towards South Bay, her expression impassive, as if our conversation meant nothing to her.

'Sounds fairly half-hearted to me,' I said. 'And it certainly didn't work, because all Max heard was "baby". Nothing about Ysan or passing the message on.'

Clarabel shrugged. 'I did as much as I could. Neither Antonio nor I wanted to hang around on the mainland for a second longer than necessary. I've told Ysan I'm sorry the message never got through. But I'm not going to pretend that what happened didn't suit me. I've had a fantastic year, pretending I'm Maisie's mother. Two men fucking me too. In a way I'm sad it's all over, but in another I'm not. Raúl's getting weirder by the day. And the Congo should be brilliant – as long as *you* can persuade Raúl to let Maisie go.'

We began to hear waves crashing on the reef that guarded South Bay and I thought I could pick out a speck on the far distant shore. I pointed the speck out to Ysan and Clarabel. I was becoming tense, wondering what I was going to say to Raúl if he really was there.

'Before I challenge Raúl about all the things he's responsible for,' I said to the pair, 'maybe you two can explain something to me. The men were raping you women left, right and centre. Yet none of you are pressing charges. Why not?'

'I'm hardly the person to ask,' said Clarabel, amused by something.

Ysan chuckled, too. 'You should have heard her, that day she found me being raped at the waterfall. She was wonderful. "You want sex?" she shouted. "Is that all you want, you pathetic bastards? I'll give you sex. Come on. Screw me, not her. For free. On a plate. No rape. No guilt. Line up. The brothel's open. Who's first?"'

They were both laughing. I shook my head. 'Is that really something to laugh about?'

'Oh, don't be so stuffy,' snorted Clarabel.

'Dingo had been raping Ian, too,' said Ysan. 'From my tree, I saw him do it once. Really vicious. Ian was forever covered with bruises.'

'And the poor sod's bum used to bleed,' added Clarabel.

I groaned. 'And I thought he had piles.'

Clarabel thought this hilarious, but Ysan didn't. 'It doesn't surprise me that you don't understand why nobody's pressing charges. And I guarantee that your readers won't understand either. It was a different world. Different standards. Different rules. Whatever Dingo and Pete did on the island, one's dead and the other's lost his mind. I'd say those are heavy prices, wouldn't you? And in another life, Ian wouldn't have hurt a fly. I doubt that Henry would have done either.' She was looking flushed, angry. And Clarabel was no longer laughing.

I wasn't buying this. 'But what about Danny?'

'Ah, Danny? What about Danny? He raped me, no doubt about that, and he raped Abi.'

'So shouldn't he pay for both? You nearly miscarried as a result. And Abi got pregnant.'

'She did, didn't she. Have you seen Orchard? Isn't she beautiful? Abi adores her. I know Danny isn't Orchard's father, but he could have been. They all raped her. Paternity was a lottery. And scarcely a week before Danny and Dingo raped me, I'd been trying to find the courage to goad one of the men, maybe even Danny, to do just that to get rid of my baby for me. Think about it. Then what? Danny – with Ian, Pete and Alexi – risked his life to save us from the chimps. M1 would have killed me and Baby if he hadn't. And even that's not the end. Danny nearly died sailing that pathetic little yacht near enough to the mainland to get me to hospital and get everybody else rescued. What he did was incredible. Try putting all that into a balance sheet of right and wrong and see what you come up with. All I know is that if somebody like you can't even see that the only decent thing is to wipe the slate clean, what chance do you think Danny would have against a hawkish lawyer with twelve tabloid readers for a jury?'

'Calm down!' said Clarabel. 'You'll curdle your milk.'

Ysan didn't laugh. 'The only real villain in all of this is your friend Raúl. And I hope you're going to tell him so. There he is, look. On the shore. That "speck" is him.'

GHOSTS

The speck *was* a figure on the shore. In fact there were
two, one large and sitting, watching us approach, the
other smaller and running about amusing itself, the way all
small children do on a beach. I could see them clearly once
we'd begun to sail smoothly across the bay after pitching,
yawing and rolling over the coral, our sweaty naked bodies
washed by blissfully cool spray. Antonio weighed anchor
about fifty metres from shore, and he, Ysan, AR, Clarabel
and I completed the journey in the rowing boat. Little
Maisie, a mini-Ysan with her sun-bleached blonde hair and
honey-brown skin, scampered into the shallow water shouting *'mamá'* and made straight for Clarabel, not Ysan. My
gaze though was riveted to Raúl.

Over the years, Raúl had managed to endow 'bohemian'
with nuances that few others could or would want to
manage. It was all part of his charisma and undoubted sex
appeal for certain types of women. But as he stood,
nervously I thought on seeing me, to welcome us ashore,
even I thought he'd taken wildness of appearance to a new
level. His black hair was well past shoulder length and
tangled beyond repair, and his equally black beard now

reached his breastbone. He was so tanned, his skin was mahogany, but still not dark enough to prevent his vast carpet of black pubic hair from being his most noticeable feature. Nervous myself, I walked up to him to stand face to face.

'What are you doing here?' he asked stonily.

My emotions were so confused, I felt numb. 'I was invited. I thought you were dead. And still worthy of loyalty.'

Neither of us knew how to react and we just stared into each other's eyes. Then – as if by reflex – we did as we always did when we hadn't seen each other for a while: we embraced and slapped each other's backs, but it was the first time, as far as I could remember, that we'd ever done so naked. But our actions were tentative and mechanical, without warmth or enthusiasm. Then we separated and my anger surfaced. 'You've been such a stupid crazy bastard, Raúl. Ysan's told me everything. A founding colony! How the hell could you do it?'

He stared at me with a strange expression – contempt, I think – then laughed. 'There are two sides to every story.' Then he turned his back on me and embraced Antonio.

'Are you sure you can manage the whole thing barefoot?' Raúl asked me. From South Bay, we had all trekked to the orchard for breakfast, then Raúl had offered to take me on a tour of the island. So we could talk properly.

'Quite sure.' I wanted to experience everything just as everybody else had done. Besides, I thought I could cope. My feet were fairly tough and my skin tanned from barefoot, naked summers at my villa.

Just as we were about to set off for the tunnel, Raúl turned to Antonio and asked him in Spanish whether he, Raúl, could still trust Antonio not to kidnap baby Maisie while we were gone. Antonio replied that nothing had yet changed. Unless Raúl agreed to Maisie leaving, he wouldn't take her. And as Raúl knew, Antonio Navarro-Diáz was a man of his word. But, Antonio added, he wanted Raúl to think very carefully about what I had to say.

The exchange was a relief to me, unless it was for my benefit, because the new thought had been gnawing at me that perhaps I was a sacrifice. Maybe Ysan, Clarabel and Antonio had struck a deal with Raúl. They would trade me for Maisie. When Raúl and I returned from our tour, the rest of them would be gone – and I'd be stranded on the island. It was a stupid thought: Raúl would at least have demanded a woman.

Raúl took me first to Maisie's glade, then through the tunnel to the waterfall before leading me on the long route to Safe Harbour and the castle. It was a curious, if not bewildering experience. Ghosts were everywhere. I'd already pictured Sledge tied to a tree at Orchard Bay, Dingo firing the arrow that sliced his cheek. And Dingo, pummelled and kicked to death then disposed of like waste on the razor rocks of the coral reef. Then as we crossed the racetrack to visit student Maisie's grave, I imagined the horror of her being ripped to pieces by chimps. Was her other nipple still mummified in the grass? At the waterfall, I heard Ysan screaming while being gang-raped on the moss with Abi spitting in her face. And as we crossed the now dried-up river bed I felt Ysan's panic as, six months pregnant, she was nearly swept away by the river. As each ghost sent shivers through my body, my loathing for the man by my side grew stronger. But as I needed to concentrate on where I was putting my feet, conversation was difficult. But I tried.

'How can you live with yourself, Raúl? All that suffering you caused and have continued to cause. Let alone what would have happened here had Ysan and Danny not been rescued.'

'Shit happens everywhere, Robin. Rape, murder, savaging. Who knows what would have happened – to any of them – if they'd been in Manchester for the year instead of here.'

'Is that it? Is that how you sleep at night?'

'It works for me.'

'Well not for me. Or a jury.'

'Is that a threat?'

'I'm not sure yet.'

We walked on in a grim and tense silence. I eventually broke it, still smarting from his callous self-justification. He was a man of science, rational, and a warm and compassionate human being. Or at least he had been. But I began to wonder if I'd ever truly known him, or just been taken in by a façade – a mask that concealed a fanatic. 'A founding colony, Raúl. That is so sick.'

'I was liberating them. Like Jim did the chimps. Giving them a proper life. They should be grateful. I wasn't just going to watch them, you know. After a couple of years, I was going to join them. Tell them the storm had taken me to Saddle Island and that I'd only just got the boat working again, but that as I crossed the coral here it really had sunk.'

'Join them! Why?'

'For the excitement. A new beginning. Unspoilt. And for the sex. To be part of it all. One day, when we were eventually found, we'd all have been infamous. Founders of a stone-age colony in the modern world, breeding alongside chimps. It was a fantastic idea.'

'It was perverted. Sadistic. Cruel. Not to mention criminal.'

'Don't be so bloody unimaginative.'

We arrived at the foot of the castle and I followed him through the entrance to a cave. Inside, Raúl reached up to a ledge and retrieved a torch.

'Don't you have two?' I asked.

'Not here, but don't worry. I can find my way through in the dark if necessary. So can Antonio. But concentrate. Watch your feet, it's slippery. And always keep your left hand on the wall. Or you can hold my hand if you want.'

I used the wall. He shone the torch forwards and down and I edged along. The caves were everything people had described. The air was dank and fetid, the walls wet, and the floor covered with gooey stinking bat guano. Once away from the portal, Raúl switched off the torch for a moment. We were in total blackness, a cavernous void. 'Listen,' he said.

Holding my breath, I heard bats shuffling about above my head and a nearby dripping of water.

'Imagine you'd just stumbled in here without a torch and had no idea of the layout. What would you do?' Raúl asked me.

'Panic.'

'Exactly. Just like Ysan.'

He switched the torch on again and we walked forwards a few metres. 'This is where she fell.' With his light, he traced out the edge of a hole in the floor, about three metres across. It was the entrance to what was effectively a funnel, the steeply sloping floor of which was uneven.

'She tumbled down there. Hit her head. Dropped baby Maisie.'

'And broke her ankle?'

'No, she did that on the way out nearly a week later, just before she met Danny.'

'But why did she come here with her baby in the first place and take such a stupid risk?'

'Isn't that obvious? Antonio had been mangled by the chimps and Ysan thought he would die if he didn't go to hospital. She was convinced I was on the other side of the caves, which I was. And that I still had his fishing boat, which I did. So she came to call me out and to beg me to use the boat to take Antonio to the mainland and hospital. I'd seen the chimp attack, I'd seen her coming and I heard her shout from inside the caves. Then she went quiet and her baby started screaming. So I came to investigate. Ysan was unconscious at the bottom of the funnel, and Maisie was in the guano making a God-awful noise.'

'And you didn't think to try to save Antonio?'

'I knew it would take more than a mad chimp to kill him. But I couldn't leave Ysan and the baby, so when Ysan regained consciousness, I took them both to where I was living.'

'Which is?

'Follow me. Careful going through and down the funnel. It's dangerous. Ysan and Maisie were very lucky to survive that fall. But after the funnel it's fairly straightforward.'

It was far from straightforward. I had no idea where we went. There were so many options, so many turns; so many slopes, mainly down. At times we seemed to be going back on ourselves, at others round in circles.

'How can you possibly find your way through here? Even with a torch.'

'There's a formula. It's not as difficult as it looks. Antonio's dad and Jim found their way through first, then they taught Antonio and me.'

'What's the formula?'

'Just follow me. We'll come out at my cave.'

Raúl's home cave was on the side of the castle looking out to sea, not visible from anywhere on land. From the tennis-court-sized ledge outside the cave entrance a gently sloping path led down to a much larger area the size of a football stadium. It was covered with trees; Raúl called it Jim's orchard. A mini-version of its namesake at Orchard Bay, it also boasted the occasional rabbit, several freshwater trickles and pools, and fenced-off patches of cannabis and tobacco plants.

I chuckled, scarcely believing that my wild guess about Antonio's 'garden' had proved so accurate. 'So when did you set up this self-contained little paradise to live in while you watched everybody?'

'Needs a woman to be a true paradise, but we set it up for Jim at the same time as the main orchard. It was meant to be somewhere he could live while watching the chimps from a distance, without disturbing them.'

From the mini-orchard, Raúl took me on a long and zigzagging path down to just above sea level. Standing finally on an overhang, twenty metres or more above ocean and rocks, I could see a person would need to be a mountaineer, with equipment, to go the rest of the way down to the beach.

'The only safe way to the beach is through the caves,' said Raúl. 'Which is what I do whenever I want to fish or get coconuts. But the tunnels are complicated.'

There was no remorse in his voice or manner, not the slightest hint of awareness that I might hate him for the casual, sometimes even proud way he was narrating his mad genius to me on this tour. But I had stopped berating him, having seen already that there was little point. He was convinced everything he'd done was perfectly reasonable. Now I just wanted to know how he pulled it off.

'So where did Jim watch the chimps from? Same place you watched the people? You couldn't see anything from this side of the castle.'

'And they couldn't see me. Not even the smoke from my fire, as long as I lit it far enough inside my cave. Do you want to see the telescope? It's a bit of a climb.'

We retraced our steps to the 'tennis court' and the home cave, then took another crooked path over rocks to near the summit of the castle.

'You can't actually get to the top from this side. It's too dangerous, even for a goat like Antonio. So . . . Follow me. Caves again.'

'Are you saying that the only way to get into and out of this place is through the caves?'

He didn't even bother to answer. Just grinned through his bushy beard as he led me through a narrow cave entrance and collected another torch. Within minutes, we were high up on the south side of the castle and looking out over Orchard Bay, the racetrack, South Bay and the waterfall. Set up in the cave entrance was an impressive-looking telescope, complete with heavy tripod and pilot finder with fine adjustments.

'The cave of the winking light,' I muttered.

'Sorry?'

'Nothing.'

'I use my binoculars a lot of the time, but if I want to get in close, I use the scope. I'll just find the others and show you.'

Scanning with his binoculars, he then pointed the telescope towards the waterfall, fiddled with the adjustments, then stepped away and with some pride offered for me to take a look.

I actually gasped. The scope was so powerful, the optics so clear, I could almost imagine I was at the waterfall with them. Then realising what was happening, I turned away.

'What's the matter?'

'Nothing.'

He chuckled. 'Not used to seeing people having sex, then?'

But it wasn't just seeing sex that had bothered me. Clarabel had been sitting on the fallen log, playing with the children, while on the moss only metres away and in plain view Antonio was openly fucking Ysan. I felt sick with disappointment and jealousy. What had Raúl turned these people into?

My jealousy turned to anger. 'Nor are most people, Raúl. Not in public.'

'Well they should be. Apes don't give a shit about screwing in front of everybody. Nor did the early humans. So why should we?'

'I don't know. Maybe it's progress. Ever thought of that?'

'And maybe it's not. Have *you* ever thought of that?'

I'd seen enough. I wanted to do what I'd come for and leave the island as soon as possible.

Back at the mouth of his home cave, Raúl told me to sit. He had something to show me. From somewhere inside his cave, he fetched a bow with arrows, and a huge gourd shell containing liquid of some sort. 'I can't believe how long it took them to work out how to make a decent bow,' he said, laying his on the ground.

'What's in the shell?'

He scooped some into half a coconut shell and offered it to me, also taking some for himself. 'Try it. Here's to the past, and the future. *Salud!*'

I didn't respond, just sniffed the bouquet – it smelled of rum – then gingerly sipped. 'Oh my God. That's horrendous. It's got an aftertaste of chimp shit.'

He chuckled. 'Antonio makes it out of some root or other. He chews it, spits it in a gourd with some water, lets it ferment a bit, then decants it. He says it's supposed to be chewed by virgins . . . But watch it. It's got a kick.'

'No thanks. I'll stick to water.'

Grinning, he downed his in one go. He gasped, and in his watering eyes I could see his mood had changed. 'Fun's over, Robin. Why are you here? Or shall I tell you?'

I shook my head and told him that first I wanted answers to two questions. How did he end up with baby Maisie when Ysan escaped the island? And how did he keep Maisie alive for that month after the others had been rescued? She hadn't been weaned. Did he grow breasts?

The look of pride returned that he'd been wearing so infuriatingly since we'd started our tour. Far from being dulled by madness, his green-blue eyes were sparkling. 'I improvised. Coconut milk. Ground-up grain – a sort of porridge. Chewed-up fruit. She loved banana. And occasionally I put rabbit's blood in the porridge, a sort of black pudding, to give her some iron. She just about got all the nutrients she needed. But it was hard work and not ideal. I was fairly relieved to see Antonio come back with Clarabel. But babies are tougher than they look, and she was nearly four months. Anyway, it worked. Look at her now. Isn't she beautiful? I can't imagine life without her.'

He took my drink and began swigging that as well. 'As for ending up with her . . .' He claimed that once the group had been on the island for a year, he'd seen what he most wanted: the shedding of civilised mores, revealing the creatures they really were. Phase one was just about over. And learning that he had a new daughter, being with Ysan again, the expectation of having sex again, of intimacy and affection, changed things.

'Did you rape Ysan? When she conceived AR? I can't believe she let you willingly.'

'She was just very, very drunk.' Grinning, he raised his coconut shell, took a swig. 'I wanted her to stay here. But she wouldn't cooperate. Pissed off though she was with the group, she still wanted to go back to them.' Irritation creased his face into a grimace. 'I didn't realise she'd found the yacht. Or that she was planning to escape. But she wasn't well. She was having terrible headaches and double-vision. There was confusion too. She wanted to go back to let Rose have a look at her.'

'And you were prepared to stop her? She might have died.'

'But I didn't know that. All I knew was that if she left me and took Maisie with her she wouldn't come back. So I tricked her. I pretended to relent and to show her the way through the caves. But once she'd clambered up through the funnel and reached back down for Maisie, I switched off the torch and took Maisie back to this side of the castle.'

'Weren't you worried she'd tell the others that you were still alive?'

It seemed not. He said he was confident they wouldn't believe her, any more than they had before. If anyone was curious, they'd never find him and probably disbelieve her ravings. And if Rose really thought Ysan was suffering post-natal depression, as Ysan had told him, when Ysan arrived without Maisie, Rose would assume the worst: that Ysan had either abandoned or even killed her baby. So as long as he had Maisie, it would only be a matter of time before Ysan came back to him. 'But the silly girl tried to follow me and that's how she broke her ankle. After hobbling and crawling back to the cave entrance she met Danny and they escaped.' He'd become angry at the memory of his plans being thwarted and Ysan's abandoning him. 'I'm fed up with answering questions. Now it's your turn. Why are you here?'

I took a deep breath. I'd come halfway round the world for this moment. 'You've probably guessed that I'm writing a book about what happened. But I had no idea it would turn out this way. It's just preposterous. A litany of criminal acts. No tale of nobility in the face of insurmountable odds, blah, blah, blah. Quite the opposite. Virtually all the men will have a lot of explaining to do when it's published. Abi too. But you don't have to be one of them. You're the biggest villain of the lot and deserve to go to jail more than anybody. But if you release Maisie, I promise I won't tell the world what you've done.'

He didn't even flinch. He chuckled. 'How disappointing. I was hoping you'd say something to surprise me. Watch this.'

As I gazed on, he selected one of the coconut shells, then walked over to a rock to balance the shell on top. When he came back, he picked up his bow and an arrow. The distance was only about five metres, but it was still impressive that he hit the shell so cleanly.

'Practice,' he said. 'That's the secret.'

He lodged another stone-tipped arrow on his bowstring and held the weapon loosely by his side.

I was growing tense and impatient. 'Well? Is it a deal? About Maisie? You haven't answered.'

'How far, do you think? Ten metres? More? For one of these arrows still to be lethal?'

I shook my head in a show of bravado. 'Stop it, Raúl. You wouldn't kill me. Any more than I would you.'

'You'd send me to jail. Clothed! No bloody sun! Nothing to study. I'd shrivel and die. What's that if not killing me?'

'But that would be justice not murder.'

'Anyway . . . I don't need to kill you. All I need to do is leave you here. There's no escape, except through the labyrinth.'

'Ysan and Clarabel would send Antonio. He'd come for me.'

'Would he? Are you sure?'

To which the short answer was no.

RESOLUTION

Raúl had been trying to scare me and, after he'd succeeded and laughed a lot, he began leading me back through the caves. But the fright had left its mark. My hands were clammy, my mouth dry and my guts churning. Remembering how he'd tricked Ysan, I wondered if he was simply taking me to the heart of the labyrinth, there to switch off his torch and leave me to die. And a few minutes in, once I was hopelessly lost, he did switch off his torch.

I was in total blackness, and all I could hear was his hand slapping the wet wall as he felt his way into the distance. I swore continuously, shouting the words in his direction, but refused to beg him to come back, knowing there was no point. Then I went quiet and tried to follow him. In a travesty of blind man's buff, I kept one hand on the wall and the other stretched out in front of me, my bare feet forever slipping and stubbing rocks. My breathing became laboured, tiny gasps between holding my breath and trying to listen for him. But he was silent. Had he gone?

Suddenly, he squawked as my hand found his beard in the darkness. Then he dissolved into uncontrollable laughter. He switched on the light.

'Bloody bastard!' I shouted. 'For Christ's sake don't do that again. You'll give me a heart attack.'

But he did do it again – twice, until even he found the joke wearing thin. So it was with great relief that I discovered we were at the funnel. Clambering up and through, we moved on out of the cave portal to the sanctuary of bright sunlight and fresh air. And I will never go into a cave, any cave, again.

Crossing the racetrack, we disturbed a troop of about a dozen chimps. From their midst a large male ran forwards, stopping only a few metres short of us as Raúl shouted at him. The chimp stared at us with a deadpan expression that on a human would have conveyed studied hatred.

'He's new,' said Raúl. 'From a troop on the north of the island. Antonio's seen him before. Already he's showing the same cunning and sadistic aggression as M1, and M1's father before that. I've told Clarabel and Ysan ... Never come here alone, or ever with the children unless either Antonio or me is with them.'

'You mean, this chimp scares even you?'

'A little. I must be getting old.'

I changed my position to place Raúl between me and the chimps as we walked.

The others weren't at Orchard Bay, triggering still further fears that I really was a sacrifice while the others made their getaway with Maisie. But it seemed Antonio genuinely was a man of his word: we found everybody at South Bay on the sand beneath the palm trees. While Clarabel sat with AR on her lap, Antonio and Ysan were playing a game of boules with coconuts. Every time either of them made a throw, Maisie would scamper off, struggle to pick the 'ball' up in her tiny hands, then bring it back to them. The coconuts were heavy for her. I couldn't look at Ysan. Not because of the news I had for her but because of my disappointment at having discovered that she and Antonio were still lovers.

All three adults looked at me expectantly as Raúl and I drew near. Glumly, I shook my head.

Ysan exploded with anger at Raúl. 'What! I don't believe it. How could you say no? Do you want him to denounce you in his book? Do you want the police to come and cart you away to jail?'

Raúl smirked. 'It would need a team of commandoes to winkle me out of those caves.'

Ysan couldn't contain her frustration and anger. 'You sadistic bastard,' she shouted at Raúl, and threw the coconut she was holding in his direction. 'Can't you see what you're doing to us?'

'Hey, careful! That nearly hit me.'

'Good!'

Clarabel turned to Antonio and in an angry voice told him that there was no longer any choice. He had to forget about being a man of his word and any loyalty he still felt for Raúl. He had to help them take Maisie off the island. '*Now!*'

Antonio didn't immediately say no, and began gesticulating and almost growling in Spanish at Raúl. '*If Robin exposes you in his book, he exposes me too. For helping you. What friend would let that happen?*'

Raúl waved a dismissive hand at Antonio. '*And what friend would take a man's children and his women and leave him in a place like this, alone. The answer's simple, Antonio, and you know what it is. Nobody leaves. We all stay here. Robin too. No book, no police. It's best for everybody. We can still be that founding colony. Sink the boat, Antonio. Like I've asked you to before. Then there's no escape. No more decisions. That's the only way. Think of the life we could all have here.*'

Clarabel, still holding AR, turned on Raúl. 'Stop it, Raúl. That's the craziest thing you've said yet. You didn't even sink the boat the first time round. And none of us would let you do it now. What about my career? What about Ysan's?'

Raúl sneered. 'Career? What career? Scratching pictures? Writing boring papers that nobody reads? I've been there and look where it's got me. You're better without it.

Nakedness! Freedom! Sex! Reproduction! They're the only realities.' He began to move down towards the open beach.

'*Where are you going?*' shouted Antonio.

'*For a swim,*' Raúl shouted back, and continued striding between the palm trees.

Antonio sprinted and caught Raúl just before the open beach. Grabbing Raúl's shoulders, Antonio twisted him round. '*Stay away from the boat.*'

'*I'm not going to the boat.*'

'*You are! I can see it in your eyes.*'

Ysan snatched up Maisie. 'Clarrie. Come on. Boat. I've had enough of this. Bring AR.'

As the two women with the children scurried past Raúl and Antonio, Clarabel shouted in Spanish, '*Time's up, Antonio. We'll give you ten minutes, and if you're not on board by then, we'll sail the bloody thing ourselves.*'

Antonio looked concerned, but Raúl laughed with derision. '*You'd never get across the coral.*'

'*Who cares! Anything's better than being stuck here with a madman like you and a coward like Antonio.*'

Antonio swore at Clarabel for insulting him; Raúl darted forwards and caught hold of Ysan's arm, then tried to pull a confused and screaming Maisie from her. In the struggle, Maisie nearly fell. Antonio intervened, pulling Raúl away and telling him to be careful. '*You want to hurt Maisie?*'

Struggling out of Antonio's hands, Raúl turned and pushed him in the chest. '*Get away from us, Antonio. She's my daughter, not yours. She's got nothing to do with you.*'

For a few moments, the two men glared at each other. Then, without warning, Antonio landed a single almighty punch on the side of Raúl's head. We all heard the cracking of bone. Raúl staggered backwards until stopped by the trunk of a palm tree.

The blood appeared instantly, even before his eyes glazed over. But he didn't fall immediately. For a few seconds – once his knees had buckled – he slipped slowly down the trunk, his bare back scraping against the bark. Then he keeled. And only then, no longer supported, did he fall, landing heavily on his back on the black sand and scattering the fiddler crabs that had ventured there.

We all stood and stared in silence, except for Maisie who began to scream and shout '*papá*'.

Raúl didn't stir. Blood was bubbling from the gash on his temple. The thin liquid, pouring over his deeply tanned skin, was filling his ear and disappearing into his hair, staining the tangled strands.

Exchanging glances, we all hesitated. There were broken coconut shells nearby. I grabbed one and ran down the beach to the sea to fill the shell with water. Then I ran back, spilling much of what I'd collected.

Washing Raúl's wound, Ysan tried to see how long and deep it was but the blood was still oozing too fast to tell. So she tried pressing the sides together, trying to stem the flow. Raúl's eyes were closed and he seemed not to be breathing. Ysan felt for a heartbeat, but was shaking so much she said she couldn't tell whether one was there or not. Antonio knelt too. Parting Raúl's lips, he breathed into his mouth, then pressed down hard on his chest. Again he returned to his mouth.

I'm not sure who made the decision; we were all panicking, jabbering to each other in Spanish and English. Maybe it was Antonio because it was he who picked up Raúl, placing him over his shoulder like a rolled-up carpet. We all hurried down the shore towards the rowing boat and once aboard we lay Raúl uncomfortably on the floor and Antonio began rowing with all his strength.

When we were halfway to the fishing boat, Raúl vomited violently, then suddenly sat bolt upright, his expression confused and frightened, his pallor grey except where blood ran freely again from his temple.

'Where are you taking me?'

'To the mainland. To hospital,' I said.

'Like hell you are. *Antonio, turn this fucking boat around.*'

Antonio glanced at Raúl, but didn't falter in his rowing.

Awkwardly, Raúl struggled to his feet, setting the boat rocking, then staggered towards Antonio, stepping over my feet, then Ysan's. Seeing Raúl coming, Antonio rested his oars, then looked at each one of us in turn, as if wanting to be told what to do.

'*Turn it round!*' Raúl shouted again.

'*No! You're going to hospital.*'

'*No I'm not. I'm not going anywhere. And neither's Maisie.*'

Raúl reached for his daughter. The vision of him jumping overboard with the child flashed into my mind as it must have done Ysan's because she lunged and pushed Raúl away. As he stumbled, the boat rolled wildly and Raúl struggled to keep his balance. Nearly capsizing us again, Clarabel lurched forwards and pushed him, using the flat of both hands on his chest. Quickly, Raúl went over the side. He never made a sound but rose almost immediately from the sea spitting with rage. He snatched out and gripped the side of the boat. But as he tried to either haul himself back on board or tip us over, Antonio struck Raúl's knuckles with an oar. The terrible noise of fingers slammed under wood was followed by Raúl's scream.

Traumatised with pain, he slipped back into the water. Antonio hurriedly replaced the oar and resumed rowing. Maisie and AR were both screaming and crying. Ysan and Clarabel were shouting, 'Go! Go!' and urging Antonio onwards.

Raúl grabbed for the boat once more; we heard the fingernails of one hand scratch the hull but as Antonio generated speed, Raúl drifted further and further behind while still trying to swim after us. But our advantage was short-lived. Once we'd reached the fishing boat and while Antonio was winching the lifeboat aboard, Raúl gained on us. He shouted and swore, ordering Antonio to wait. Antonio raced across the deck and began raising the anchor. Clarabel finished the job while Antonio swung inside the cabin and started the engine.

Raúl never reached us. And once the vessel chugged towards the coral, he faltered, exhausted and in pain. Clutching his injured fingers under an armpit, he screamed at us as he trod water, then slowly, disconsolately, began swimming back to the shore of South Bay.

Unable to rid my mind of the bleeding, ghost-like, wild-eyed, but terrified madman who had been pushed so unceremoniously overboard, my guts twisted and I sat alone and aghast. My reaction was complicated, confused. I knew I was angry that a man once admired and trusted by so many had become so contemptible; and I was sad that a lifelong valued friendship had ended in such a sordid way. But I was also distressed and horrified at how little chance Raúl stood once his friend, Antonio, turned against him. And what had we done? Kidnapped a treasured daughter from a loving father and torn her from the only home she had known. Yet we had also reunited that same child, who had endured so much, with her mother. My stomach was a knot, my throat closed by a lump.

Ysan sat by my side, holding Maisie. She began to cry. And so did I. Another moment and I would have put my arm around Ysan to comfort and be comforted, but Clarabel did so first. Feeling excluded, I simply watched through watering eyes as Raúl shrank from view until he was finally wiped from my sight.

LAST WORDS

I took Max's advice and stayed on in Fiji to finish the book. For a while I occasionally saw Ysan, Clarabel, Antonio and the two children. It took a fortnight for the British High Commission to sort out birth certificates and a passport for baby Maisie; 'father unknown', Ysan happily recorded, just as her mother had once done, though with more reason. Then another fortnight was needed for the five of them to obtain visas for their onward journey, first to Canada then to DR Congo.

Clarabel has already sent Max her first sketches, on paper, of Congolese village life. And, during a brief visit she made to the University of Kinshasa, Ysan sent me an e-mail. Attached were photographs of bonobos having sex – 'face to face, just like humans,' she wrote – plus a photograph of herself with the others in their new home.

The five of them are in a jungle setting, Antonio standing in the middle with an arm round the shoulders of Ysan on one side and Clarabel on the other. Ysan has AR perched on her hip and Antonio has Maisie, now over eighteen months old, on his shoulders, little legs round his neck, hands clinging to his shoulder-length untidy hair. All five are laughing and, it's hardly necessary to say, all five are naked, Ysan looking as beautiful as ever, Clarabel too. I felt a fresh surge of jealousy.

Max kept her word and came to holiday in Fiji, staying with me for a fortnight. We lodged in a hotel just a short walk from a palm-dotted tourist beach with all amenities. The path from hotel to beach was lined with man-high red and green poinsettias. We snorkelled, sailed over the coral in glass-bottomed boats, lazed on the beach and drank cocktails as the sun set. Humming-birds drank nectar from nearby flowers, flocks of fruit bats flew overhead from their daytime roosts and on one occasion a black-and-yellow sea snake slithered across the grass in the twilight, reminding me, as so many things do, of the tragic student Maisie whom I never met.

Apart from that luxurious and relaxing interlude, my writing retreat has been in a two-roomed wooden hut with a veranda, electricity and an Internet connection, just off a much more secluded beach. And that is where I am sitting as I write these final paragraphs.

I tried to heed Ysan's advice to make my balance sheet of each person's behaviour as fair as possible – and the reader is at last in a position to decide who deserves what. So is the Crown Prosecution Service. Sledge at the very least will need to defend himself against the charge of murder. Maybe the rapists will need to defend their actions too. And Abi. But who else?

Antonio? Ysan and Clarabel both begged me not to accuse him in my pages, but I cannot do as they asked. I have put too much effort into trying to unravel the truth of what happened on that island not to state what I believe now. Which is that Antonio conspired fully with Raúl to strip those people and strand them on the island; and that he is also a murderer. Though, to be fair, I still cannot prove either claim.

Ysan and Clarabel both insist that Antonio is innocent of murder; that if anything he tried to prevent Sledge from killing Dingo, not help him. And that is how Clarabel sketched the event, but despite her denial, I believe she was dissembling. Why do I believe this? Because the envelope of sheets she gave me from Rose and Ysan – the sheets that she had previously held back – do not support her drawing in the way she claimed. There is still no description of what happened on the day the lads tried to take over the orchard. Critically, a few sheets are still missing, which surely means that they were destroyed to hide the truth. So, confused though Pete is, I'm more prepared to believe his version – that Sledge and Antonio together beat up Dingo and dragged him to the coral – than I am to believe that it was only Sledge. And I have little doubt that when Sledge is in the dock and the other members of the group – those not in love with Antonio – are called to the stand, they will say the same thing. Or, in one final conspiratorial effort to protect Sledge, they may even blame Antonio alone.

Antonio's role in the planning and execution of the whole island episode is also clear in my mind. On the night of the beach party, he surely helped Raúl steal and get rid of the group's clothes, and to set fire to the base, exactly as the pair had been rehearsing during their 'naked pantomimes' ever since their arrival. Then, through the months that followed, Antonio protected both Raúl and the boat's whereabouts from Ysan's suspicions. To me, he is as guilty as Raúl over the whole 'founding colony' crime. And in some ways even more so. At least Raúl had some higher academic motive, inhuman though it was. In his demented mind, he may even have believed he was 'liberating' them all, like the chimps, into a better life. But Antonio – the hunted man – merely wanted sexual thrills and companionship during a self-imposed exile.

It took a while but I can see now why the trio of Ysan, Clarabel and Antonio invited me to the island. They had reached an impasse. Raúl couldn't leave the island without being arrested but knew that as long as he had Maisie he would be guaranteed companionship. Everybody *wanted*

Maisie, but Ysan also *needed* her as proof that she was innocent of infanticide. So why didn't she and Clarabel simply call in the authorities to rescue Maisie from Raúl? The answer was Antonio, the two women's lover, because if Raúl was ever arrested, then so too would Antonio. It was an impossible situation for which only two people could offer a solution. One was Antonio himself who could at any time have taken Maisie by force if he could only subjugate his loyalty to Raúl; maybe, in the end, I was the catalyst he needed. And the other was me, who potentially could have solved the situation to everybody's advantage. Because if Raúl had agreed to my offer of silence in exchange for baby Maisie, that silence would also have kept the secret of Antonio's complicity. It was such a perfect solution it was worth the trio's trying, but it failed. And in failing, it placed Antonio's fate in my hands. The three must have known that this was always a risk, but I believe they knew that time would be on his side.

To Antonio's credit, he never once tried to convince me to lie on his behalf, nor did he ever threaten me. Maybe his confidence came from knowing that by the time my book was published, he would be ensconced in the Congo and safe from extradition, having exchanged one life of exile – on the island – for another. And maybe for a while he will be happy with that life, at least while Ysan, Clarabel and the children are with him. But surely he cannot stay safely in the Congo forever, with so much mayhem, even genocide, in the country? And besides, how long can such an arrangement as theirs last before stress, jealousy, ambition and circumstance combine to rip it apart?

Even if Ysan and Clarabel manage to share Antonio sexually, without jealousy, one day Clarabel will have to give way to Ysan over being Maisie's mother. And inevitably, the two women's separate ambitions will push them towards leaving Africa for Europe or North America. But once my book is published, Antonio will be unable to use his passport without being arrested. So what then? Will

Clarabel really sacrifice everything to stay with him? Will Ysan? I don't think so; their unusual 'family' cannot survive forever.

And finally, what of Raúl? Shall I end my book by saying that he is dead? That is, after all, what the world already believes. And he could be dead. None of us saw him reach the shore of South Bay. His head injury could have made him lose consciousness again, causing him to drown. Is he a skeleton on the sea floor picked clean by fish? Or shall I portray him alive and alone, a broken man with broken dreams, and nothing but hooting, promiscuous and dangerous chimps for company? Continual reminders of the men and women he once decreed should live out their lives, naked and breeding, alongside them. He will be forever wondering whether a boatload of men were on their way to arrest him for his crimes. Wondering ... and one day maybe even hoping.

Read more dark fiction from Virgin Books

The Grin of the Dark

by Ramsey Campbell

Tubby Thackeray's stage routines were so deranged that members of his audience were said to have died or lost their minds. When Simon Lester is commissioned to write a book about the forgotten music hall clown and his riotous silent comedies, his research plunges him into a nightmarish realm where genius, buffoonery and madness converge. In a search that leads him from a twilight circus in a London park to a hardcore movie studio in Los Angeles, Simon Lester uncovers a terrifying secret about Tubby Thackeray and must finally confront the unspeakable thing he represents.

9780753513811

Teatro Grottesco

by Thomas Ligotti

In this peerless collection of dark fictions, Thomas Ligotti follows the literary tradition that began with Edgar Allan Poe: portraying characters that are outside of anything that might be called normal life, depicting strange locales far off the beaten track, and rendering a grim vision of human existence as a perpetual nightmare. Just by entering his unique world where odd little towns and dark sectors are peopled with clowns, manikins and hideous puppets, and where tormented individuals and blackly comical eccentrics play out their doom, is to risk your own vision of the world.

9780753513743

My Work Is Not Yet Done

by Thomas Ligotti

When junior manager Frank Dominio is suddenly demoted and then sacked, it seems there was more than a grain of truth to his persecution fantasies. But as he prepares to even the score with those responsible for his demise, he unwittingly finds an ally in a dark and malevolent force that grants him supernatural powers. Frank takes his revenge in the most ghastly ways imaginable – but there will be a terrible price to pay once his work is done. Destined to be a cult classic, this tale of corporate horror and demonic retribution will strike a chord with anyone who has ever been disgruntled at work.

9780753516881

The Unblemished

by Conrad Williams

Enter the mind of a serial killer who believes he is the rightful son and heir to an ancient dynasty of flesh-eaters.

Follow the frantic journey of a mother whose daughter is infected with the stuff of nightmare.

Look through the eyes of Bo Mulvey, who possesses the ancient wisdom a bloodthirsty evil needs to achieve its full and horrifying potential. A man upon whom the fate of the human race depends.

One of the most powerful horror novels of our time, *The Unblemished* is an epic tale of history and destiny, desperation and desire, atrocity and atonement. It is a savagely beautiful tale of a mother's determination to rescue her daughter, which plunges you into the monstrous world of serial killers and a cannibalistic apocalypse that rips through modern Britain.

9780753513514

One

by Conrad Williams

This is the United Kingdom but it's not a country you know or ever want to see, not even in the howling, shuttered madness of your worst dreams. You survived. One man.

You walk because you must. You have no choice. At the end of this molten road, running along the spine of a burned, battered country, your little boy is either alive or dead. You have to know. One hope.

The sky crawls with thick, venomous cloud and burning red rain. The land is a scorched sprawl of rubble and corpses. Rats have risen from the depths to gorge on the carrion. A strange, glittering dust coats everything. The dust hides a terrible secret. New horrors are taking root. You walk on. One chance.

9780753518106

Banquet for the Damned

by Adam G Nevill

Few believed Professor Coldwell was in touch with an unseen world – that he could commune with spirits. But in Scotland's oldest university town something has passed from darkness into light. And now the young are being haunted by night terrors. And those who are visited disappear. This is not a place for outsiders, especially at night. So what chance do a rootless musician and burnt-out explorer have of surviving their entanglement with an ageless supernatural evil and the ruthless cult that worships it?

9780753513583

The Perils and Dangers of this Night

by Stephen Gregory

A bleak mid-winter. An icy wind blows through the corridors of Foxwood Manor, a boys' prep-school deep in the woodlands of Dorset. It is the end of the Christmas term and the old house is empty save for the headmaster, Dr Kemp, his wife, and the one boy who has been left behind. Alan Scott, 12, abandoned by his feckless mother, faces the grim prospect of Christmas alone with the Kemps. Until, at dusk the following afternoon, a vision from the outside world arrives at the school: Martin Pryce, a suave, arrogant ex-pupil, and his bewildered girlfriend Sophie. And, as the snow falls heavily on the house and the surrounding woods, a story of revenge and retribution unfolds: a web of half-truths and innuendoes woven into a bizarre game of hide-and-seek through the corridors and dormitories of the school . . . and a series of shocking revelations which lead inexorably, horrifically, to a bloody climax on a crisp, lovely Christmas morning.

9780753513798